Broken Evolution

by

Brendan Cody

First published October 2010 by Solitrix Books.

2nd Edition - September 2013.

ISBN: 978-0-9565811-2-9

"The problem that I set here is not what shall replace mankind in the order of living creatures (–man is an end–): but what type of man must be *bred,* must be *willed,* as being the most valuable, the most worthy of life, the most secure guarantee of the future."

Friedrich Nietzsche, 1895

ONE

CIA Headquarters, Washington DC
16th September – 3:08pm

Paranoia is healthy. It had become Joshua Harker's mantra since joining the CIA. He analyzed intel with extreme prejudice, unraveling threads of foreign malevolence. Screens of text wound past his bulging eyes. He rubbed his eyelids across to their crow's feet. In his work cubicle, this dark felted womb, he was detached from the world outside Langley except for the bit-pipe pumping data into his PC. It was the umbilical cord feeding his professional paranoia. Josh tapped page-down, over and over. The droning click of it made him sleepy. He sipped vending machine coffee.

Silberman thumped closer. Josh singled her out by sound alone. Her wide cowboy gait on stocky pumps approached like a drill sergeant's. He never did figure out what wrong turns in life led him here to work for a spectacled boss ten years younger than him. Her short-sightedness wasn't limited to her eyes either. No imagination. No real instinct. Rita was a paper pusher, playing the political game. She treated the CIA as a ladder to be climbed, like the corporate world she'd been hired from. In Harker's mind, she was the wrong person in the wrong job.

Josh swivelled his back to her at the cubicle entrance. He exchanged coffee beaker for a sculpture on his desk and fingered it absently. It was a fragment of DNA made from bent paper clips; he'd made it himself. One of the guanine molecules was squashed, so he twisted back the clips of the hexagonal bond. Josh held it at arm's length to admire his work.

She loomed behind him. Breaths billowed onto his neck. Josh felt her rage at his frivolous use of agency time. He pretended not to notice. It surprised him how much he enjoyed such a childish thing and he resolved to do it more often.

"Could I have a word with you, in my office?" she asked, looking at the sculpture in his hand. "That is, if you're not too busy."

Harker lolloped into her office after her.

Rita shoved a manila folder across her desk. It was the report he'd finally submitted three days ago. The scribbled feedback on the cover sheet was damning:

1

Too speculative. Insufficient evidence to warrant tasking or submission to the Bioweapons Intelligence Unit review panel.

And that was it. Six months work. Gone. In a few pen strokes.

It wouldn't make the President's Daily Brief. No: it wouldn't make it past the bulldog defiance of his nearest boss, Analysis Supervisor Rita Silberman.

"Maybe next time you'll take a task that's assigned to you," she said.

It always surprised Harker that, small though she was, her words boomed like a foghorn.

"I don't get it," he said. "You were so enthusiastic when I suggested this. You gave me the go-ahead," Josh insisted.

"Yes I did," she replied flatly.

Josh's heart sank. It dawned on him he'd been out-manoeuvred.

This had been his baby. It wasn't raised by a finding, like most CIA reports. Joshua suggested the idea himself and thought it odd at the time when Silberman approved his request. Back then he suspected she'd use the results of the report to enhance her standing. Climb the next rung. Now it was painfully obvious why she'd sanctioned the work. She'd waited patiently – he was sure – before playing this card. Rejecting the report would stop it in its tracks. A slap in Harker's face, intended as a warning not to defy her authority again. The report's content was irrelevant.

"Did you even read it?" Joshua asked.

She stabbed with her eyes.

"Of course I did! You think I would reject a report unread?"

Josh flapped to a middle page, pointed, and recited. "... A directed and concerted effort by the eminent Japanese biotechnology company, Shimura Biotech, to harvest all data from genetic databases via the internet ... the end purpose of which can only be to gain competitive advantage over American research companies in the field of biotechnology ..."

Rita blew through closed lips. "Oh, come on Harker. A biotech company searching through public access genetic databases is hardly corporate espionage. It's just shrewd business practice. This isn't the 80s, Harker. The Japanese aren't the economic enemy anymore. Their economy is in worse shape than ours! Why don't you try this decade's threats for a change? There's hundreds of terrorist cells out there who could be planning a bioweapon attack at this minute. Why can't you track them down instead of wasting agency time with this rubbish?"

"Rubbish? The CIA's mandate is to protect from all foreign aggressors, even those engaged in industrial espionage. Especially now our economy needs all the protection it can get."

"There's no industrial espionage in this. It's just a load of half-baked scaremongering with no real evidence."

Joshua's fingers scurried to page forty-three. " ... Shimura Biotech has also engaged in detailed searches regarding American scientists involved in genetic research at the most advanced level. The searches and evidence of cyber-infiltration detailed in Appendix B prove the capture of details about our elite scientists' lines of research, the organizations they worked for, and personal information extending as far as contact details, lifestyle, medical records and family histories. Such details could be used to influence, bribe, coerce, recruit, or spy on the work of these scientists. Within months or years of these suspect searches, a few of America's most valuable biotech assets – some of those targeted in the searches – had moved on from their jobs. Two had died, four had changed address, and three of those did not re-register address within the United States. Two had booked one-way tickets ... to Japan."

Josh closed the report, his case made.

Silberman appeared unmoved. "Let it go Harker."

"I know the Japanese," Josh explained. "I've lived there."

"Well, bully for you. And what did the Japanese ever do to you? It must have been pretty bad if you feel the need to set the dogs of American Intelligence on them again."

"Actually, it was the best year of my life," Josh replied, gazing away. "And I learned their ethics – business is war."

"You didn't get a little too close to them, did you?"

Harker glowered. "Are you besmirching my loyalty to this country?"

"Oh I don't doubt your devotion Harker. It's your patience – the lack of it – I have problems with. Did you know the Director of the DST lodged a complaint about how much time your research took up on their server clusters? And then there's the bandwidth bottleneck from your data mining processes to the NSA."

"I didn't know they complained," he replied coyly.

"Of course not. You don't bother with the politics, do you? Just leave the mess for me to clean up. I don't like the wrong kind of focus on my department. You need to learn to work within due process."

"The 'due process' for investigation is that you dig until you find. That's the only way it gets results. If you had more experience, you'd know that."

"Ah, now we get to the heart of it! You resent me as a boss, don't you? Am I not able enough for you Harker? Or is it because I was hired after you? Or ... do you have some problem with female authority? If you do, get it out in the open now. In the long run, I'm sure the CIA would be grateful to know."

"Not at all, Ms. Silberman." Josh laced "Ms. Silberman" with sarcasm. "I'm all about equality of the sexes. I can dislike an incompetent woman just as equally as an incompetent man."

She shook her head. "I don't know why you joined the CIA."

"Well, maybe I wanted to work somewhere that suited my cynical nature," he joked.

She rattled her head again.

"Two years you've worked here as an analyst and you just won't gel. Joshua — I don't think life in the CIA is going to be easy for you. Think about it."

Harker took the signal that the conversation was over and retreated to his cubicle.

Rita Silberman had quenched the fire Harker had lit for his new career in the CIA. He knew she'd trap him now in a depressing daily routine — answering e-mail queries, phone calls, reading screens of text and writing the pointless mundane reports she wanted written. The routine had a name: constructive dismissal. She wanted him out; he sensed it. She'd always been wary of him, from the start. He could solve the standoff by requesting a transfer, but it would please her too much. Joshua was adamant. He would give Rita no such satisfaction.

The CIA was supposed to be his career reboot, but perhaps Rita was right. Perhaps *he* was the wrong person in the wrong job. With age pursuing him in his thirty-ninth year, he refused to fail and have to restart again because of another incompetent boss, this one ten years his junior.

Josh sat in his cubicle and stared at Silberman's scribbles on the cover of his aborted report, then looked up at the clock slipping onto another minute. 15:27. Two hours before knocking off. Harker thought he might leave work early, but didn't. No one waited at home for him anymore. Just an empty house.

TWO

Columbus, Ohio
16th September – 10:08pm

Senator Mark Olsen sat alone by the fireplace, embraced by armchair leather as warm and cracked as his own aged skin. He dreamed of playtime with his grandchildren. He dreamed of overdue retirement, unaware he wouldn't live to reach it.

A rattling noise outside stirred him. Of the many challenges of getting old, poor hearing was not one of his, but rising from his armchair was. Shuffling his aching joints towards the window, he peered out across the grounds. The old oak next to the house creaked like him in the chilly autumn breeze. Its branches spilled moonbeams across the lawn. The occasional leaf hurled itself to the ground: the natural world was falling into decay.

Craning upwards, Mark saw nothing but shadows.

Just the wind.

Shrugging it off, he poured himself some Jack Daniels. Slapping down the tumbler onto the coffee table next to his briefcase, he collapsed back into the chair and let loose a deep sigh. That briefcase was hard to open lately, not because of sticky hinges, but because of the growing gravity of its contents – a heavy burden to bear. Above him, his wife, two daughters, and three grandchildren looked down warmly from their picture frames on the mantel. Liz was with them in Vermont. Business had kept Mark from tagging along this time. Only eight months away now – retirement. Then he could at last unshackle himself from burdensome briefcases. He could start to enjoy the world again, if only, he thought, he could forget all he learned about its dark mechanisms and his part in building them.

The case still loomed unopened.

Mark took a sip of bourbon and licked his moustache before ticking out the combination on the case's dials. He lifted out some papers branded with a red *classified* watermark and started reading, scribbling notes as he went. Concentrating on his work, Olsen quickly forgot the noise outside, until … a loud, urgent creak erupted from the stairs behind him.

He froze. His wife had pestered him for weeks to get a hammer and fix the damned thing. His laxness became a chance now, to save his life. Mark turned to face the stairwell and saw a silhouette standing there. Only the firelight chasing across the loose black clothing revealed the intruder's presence at all. It wore dark gloves, and black two-toed *tabi* socks. Intense blue-grey eyes were all that was visible through the face scarf. Fire reflected from the intruder's eyes. It sped down the last steps while reaching into its pocket, striking at Mark like a lightning bolt.

The Senator had never wanted to greet death sitting in an armchair. He had done time in military service, but death waited until here and now, late in his life, to rush at him with what looked like a knife in its hand. Mark dropped his pen and his bourbon and shot to his feet faster than in many recent years. It wasn't enough. He had taken just three steps towards his attacker when it reached him. Mark made a vain attempt to swing his fist, only to have it snatched from the air, used to pivot him around, and folded up neatly between his own shoulder blades. Facing the fire now, Mark struggled and writhed, trapped. He was larger, but less skilled. Each attempt Mark made to release himself caused painful resistance from shortened old tendons around his arthritic shoulder.

On his back, he felt a small cold object press against his shirt. With his free hand, he clawed with fat fingers at the head behind his own, mauling like a cornered animal. The face scarf around his assailant's head came free in the struggle and fell to the ground.

Mark heard a click from behind. He stopped. Waited. Fearing the worst.

Faintness came. His struggle stopped and his limbs fell limp, their effort now pointless. Another click. The hand that held his arm let go and the intruder took two steps back. Mark looked down on himself as if checking his body was still there. He rubbed the back of his hand over the base of his spine, expecting to feel warm damp blood. Nothing. No pain. No knife wound. He turned slowly to face his enemy.

"What have you done?" he asked.

No answer came.

The newly revealed fresh-faced man blinked back. The oddly generic features of his face made it hard for Mark to place him at first. The piercing eyes of a Scandinavian tore right through Mark as if he didn't exist. They were wrapped in slightly narrowed eyelids – hinting of some Eastern ancestry. The skin was sallow bronze, the nose classically Roman, hair blonde. It was a youthful, handsome face, oddly missing an attractive quality, the whole being less than the sum of the parts. It was a concoction that seemed not to belong, that would make any observer react instinctively, yet reluctantly, with repulsion. There was something intangibly distant and alien about it – a face that God himself should have shunned, Mark thought.

Mark's face fell. The flabby folds of his skin melted as recognition finally struck.

"Oh my God ... you!" he exclaimed. "No. No, don't do this – "

His final word cut abruptly as blinding pain crystallized in his chest, becoming solid. From the blazing reservoir of pain swelling within his breast, a trickle leaked out and darted down his arm, then another, up the side of his neck – and another, and another. Wave after wave of explosive pain, each one stronger than the last, beat down upon him like hammers until he could take no more. He let a stifled yelp and doubled over onto the floor. Gasping, he flipped himself over like a beached trout, and shuffled through deep-pile carpet, willing himself back towards his briefcase.

It took all his effort to lift his right arm, deadened from lack of blood pressure, to reach up for a bottle of pills in the case. Unable to move his left arm at all, he held the bottle down at his left hand and began slowly twisting the cap off with his right. A terminal surge pulsed through his chest. With a strangled rattle from deflated lungs, his head wrenched back, his convulsing body twisted, and his spirit finally cracked. In the last motion of Senator Mark Olsen on this world, his cadaver fell with its back to the floor, and sent pills scattering across the room. His last memory was of his assassin slinking around him, replacing the fallen pen into a pouch in the briefcase, taking papers out of it, and padding away sprightly up the creaking stair.

By the fire, Mark's lifeless gaze looked up to the pictures of his wife, his children, and his grandchildren. He dreamt of retiring no more.

THREE

CIA Headquarters, Washington DC
17th September – 9.12am

Another day, another summons into Silberman's office.

Well, here we go again, thought Josh. *So what's it to be this time Rita?*

The air in her office was tainted with tobacco that he'd never smelt there before. Joshua wondered if the pressure of the job was getting to her, driving her to secret smoking. He thought better of it though. She wasn't one to break the rules, even in her own office.

Pinning him with her stare, Silberman sighed, and after a pregnant pause said, "Harker, I have a case for you."

She handed him an envelope, which he skeptically peeped into before removing the contents: a plane ticket and a hand-written address. The departure time on the ticket was three hours away, the destination: Columbus, Ohio. He looked at her. Confusion was inscribed on his ruffled brow.

"Senator Olsen was found dead in his home this morning," she explained.

Joshua's face couldn't hide the surprise.

"It hasn't been announced in public yet," she said. "You're to go up there on the next flight and conduct an investigation into his death."

Harker shifted in his seat and spoke up with a Kansas drawl that savored every vowel.

"Isn't that a job for the local feds?"

"The local crime scene examiners have been called in, but you're needed there too."

"Why?" he droned.

Silberman sighed deeply and threw up her hands.

"Do you always question your superiors, Joshua? Can't you just take a chance for career progression and run with it?"

"Career progress? Is that what this is? I didn't know you cared Rita," he said with a wry smirk.

"I don't," she replied, stone faced. "But the powers on the seventh floor seem to think you are the man for the job. Why? Your experience in homicide before joining the CIA, I suppose. Honestly, I don't know, and I don't care, but if it gets you out from under my feet ... I'll support it."

Ain't that the truth Rita. I should have guessed the opportunity didn't come from you.

"How has this become the agency's concern?" Josh quizzed.

"Look – a Senator doesn't just die, for whatever reason, without getting a lot of attention. Maybe he just choked on a fish bone. Maybe CIA involvement is only political, to show due diligence, who knows? Just do the job Joshua."

Josh found the sudden first name terms with Silberman disturbing.

"Do it well," she said, "get noticed and you might be on your way up. Do yourself a favour, and me too. Do not screw it up, or we're both in trouble, but you before me, I'll guarantee that."

A blasé Harker closed up the envelope and slipped it into his pocket. "Well, I wouldn't want to let you down so, Ms. Silberman."

He clicked closed the door behind him, snatched his Hilfiger crombie off the rack and left without delay.

Harker drove out of Langley and onto Dolley Madison Boulevard that day troubled. His past life in forensics had taught Harker to ask questions, and to suspect motives. His mind erupted with questions now. In his world a dead body had been a common thing, a dead senator perhaps less so, but to send the CIA to investigate was highly unusual. Why do it, if Olsen died of natural causes? This led to Harker's first suspicion that it might not be natural causes. The big question was – why him? Sure he had the skills, but then the CIA was packed with ex-cops, ex-feds, and ex-military investigator types who could do this sort of thing. And then there was the problem of the CIA investigating at all: CIA don't do US internal. This was the FBI's bailiwick. The incursion into another agency's jurisdiction would ruffle feathers.

There was an odor off this he didn't like. Too many questions.

Harker stopped home for his overnight bag and took flight to Columbus, anticipating answers. It would be good to get a taste of his old career again anyway, he thought. The CIA certainly didn't seem to be working out well. He could only hope the pain surrounding his flight from forensics had abated enough now to allow him to enjoy once again the work he had loved, if only for a while.

At least it gets me out of the cubicle.

FOUR

Columbus, Ohio
17th September – 8:23pm

Word had reached the newshounds. Harker's rented Chevy snaked through the news vans encamped along Zollinger Road. Turning into the gate, he found it blocked by a black-and-white. A cop approached, motioning him to crank down the window. Harker flashed his blue CIA staffer badge, and got a nod in return. He didn't need to be shy of his identity as a CIA analyst, just discrete. The reporters swarmed closer, noticing a new actor in the drama. Harker quickly hid the badge before an explosion of flashlights and clash of questions reached him. Speeding quickly beyond the opened cordon, Josh became protected by the closing electric gates.

Looking back at the caged pack of newshounds in his rear view, he asked the officer, "did someone call in a Code 20 here or what?"

The guy laughed, shrugged, and flapped his big padded arms like a rag doll.

"They snooped the police band, as always. These guys crash every party."

Harker chuckled. "Have a good one," he said and drove on up.

The Chevy bit the gravel as he hit the brakes. The Senator had a nice pad – a three story colonial-style mansion of cut stone and stucco. Mature oak and maple trees on the grounds shrouded the house from all sides. A clump of vehicles lay abandoned at all angles as if some giant kid had been playing with them. Muddy black-and-white police cars, a white and red coroner's ambulance, and one anonymous black sedan caught Harker's eye. Its waxed skin glistened. Must belong to the Feds. It was the usual collection of life that huddled around a death – a notorious death.

Visions of a hundred crime scenes flooded back, triggered by the cackling of police radios and the aroma of coffee imbibing weary officials. His banter at the gate reminded him what he missed about this work: fellowship. They were all in it together, with a job to get done, a crime to solve.

Cops huddled on the veranda, hanging around for something to happen. Harker singled one out. The officer's right hand was stuffed far into his black parka for warmth; the other hand gripped a steaming plastic cup.

"Who's the OIC here?" Josh asked.

"Feds are in charge, until the CIA gets here. Agent McAlister's the one you want –" He gestured inside with only his head; all his arms were occupied. "And who the hell are you?" asked officer armless.

"CIA," he said, trying to sound important.

"So you're here at last. Better report in so we can get our frozen butts out of here."

Harker walked on past the laughter, out of view, and stopped short of the threshold of the house. It had been a while since he'd last walked in on a crime scene – a lifetime. He felt his pulse rise and his palms sweat, made worse by some vague and visceral fear.

"Damn," he muttered, just below hearing.

Get yourself under control man.

He ducked in under police tape. Harker's presence was noticed immediately; he was the only one on the move. All eyes looked to him.

"Agent McAlister?" Harker bellowed.

"That's me," replied a man dressed in fine dark suit and knee-length wool coat.

"Joshua Harker" he said with an out-stretched hand. McAlister grabbed it and shook it all the way to the shoulder.

"Care to tell me what all this is about Mr. Harker? We've had people sitting on their hands for the last few hours waiting for you."

Avoiding the question, Harker asked: "Where's the deceased?"

"He's in the study out back, " McAlister replied, jamming his hands into his pockets.

Harker took in the ground floor. His eye caught a slender old woman sitting on the sofa next to a police counsellor who held her hand. The old woman didn't seem to need counselling, but looked as if she was entertaining the support out of courtesy. She was "a real piece of class", as his ex-colleague Sheridan used to say. Classy or not, no matter how she tried to disguise it Joshua could see she was hurting. Her eyes looked into a different world. He asked McAlister if she was Olsen's wife, which he confirmed.

"She came back this morning from a visit to the grandkids and found him dead on the floor. Looks like a heart attack," said McAlister.

The widow's eyes connected with Harker's. They shared a look only possible between two people who had lost a spouse.

"So he was alone when he died?" Harker asked, still looking at the widow Olsen.

"Yeah. Poor old codger. He's just come back from a work trip and stayed at home to finish up some work, apparently. You'd think he'd take it easy at his age."

McAlister let a respectful silence fall before switching on the accusing tone.

"You ask a lot of questions Harker, but don't give away too many answers. Why the hell are we all sitting around?"

"You don't need to come down heavy on me – I didn't give you the order to wait."

"Well when my boss gets a desist request from the Office of the Director of National Intelligence, I have to obey it. But when the examiner comes complaining to me that her stiff is growing cold while we're all here twiddling our thumbs waiting for you, I'm hoping that you're going to have some answers."

Harker was surprised. "You mean the body hasn't been examined yet?"

"No – we've taken photos of the scene, but that's about all. We were instructed to touch nothing until you arrived. What the hell brings the CIA to a natural causes anyway?"

"So you've no confirmed COD? You don't know for sure this was natural causes."

McAlister started to raise his voice. "Now look, it's simple: wife says he's got a history of heart problems. We're not expecting any surprises. The investigation team is only a formality. It's just PR, to show those press clowns outside and the brass that Uncle Sam is covering all the bases. Hell, if this guy wasn't such a big shot at home and abroad he wouldn't even be getting this treatment. He'd be zipped up in his body bag and out of here hours ago," he shouted.

Harker noticed Mrs. Olsen flinch. Her composure broke. McAlister seemed unaware. Like a hound on a blood trail, he chased. "I think that's why you're here Harker. You're just a suit from one more agency and you're wasting time. My time. FBI had jurisdiction here, and as far as I'm concerned you're just a freeloader here on a PR meal ticket."

Harker dipped his head, sighed, then mustered enough defiance to stab a look into the whites of the federal agent's eyes.

"You make a lot of assumptions Agent McAlister," he said. "Maybe that's why I'm here – to get the answers you're so willing to take for granted. Since you've already used your authority to declare this a natural causes without an investigation, then you won't mind if someone else has a look, now will you?"

Joshua whipped off his crombie and threw it on the hat-stand, signalling he was here to stay.

"I'm here to get answers. So – don't worry – you won't have to sit on your cold ass any longer," he told McAlister with deadpan sarcasm.

He looked over at the Senator's wife, caught her glance again, then lowered his voice and continued in little more than a whisper.

"First, you're going to get Mrs. Olsen out of here. I don't want her sitting down here when the ME is doing a rectal core temperature reading on her dead husband, and I don't want him wheeled past her on a gurney either. Get her upstairs."

McAlister opened his mouth to speak, but was cut short by Harker's flowing invective.

"Oh, and have the decency to shutter off the study before you walk her past it, okay?" Joshua didn't wait for the reply, just walked off to the study. That felt good. Harker was more important at this scene than any he'd attended. Now, despite McAlister's bluster, Josh held the authority.

Harker froze at the threshold of the study. His own body became as rigid as the corpse lying in front of him. The Senator's contorted shape lay by a coffee table, surrounded by pink pills splayed across a tawny carpet. The eyes were stuck, frozen open. Shocked blotches of color on the pale parchment of his lifeless face. Lividity had set in at the back of the neck where the blood set.

It was the moment Joshua had feared, the moment that set his pulse racing: this reminder of the last dead body he had seen – his wife. The scene surrounding her death had not been as neat and clean as this one. He strained to clamp down a torrent of emotion. Working on slow deliberate breaths, he focused on the task at hand, letting Silberman's words echo through his mind.

Just do the job Joshua.

It was the first time he found any of her words so helpful.

Two forensic investigators and the medical examiner were staring at him. Joshua realised he must have been still for a long time. He dragged himself out of the catharsis and prowled around the body.

These deathly puzzles were moments frozen in time – the only chance to study a man's death and extrapolate what preceded it – before hordes descended and changed it forever. On the face of it, the Senator had a heart attack, dropped his bourbon and had a last futile scramble for his pills; but something didn't fit.

In time, Joshua broke his solitude and spoke.

13

"Is the photographer finished in here?" he asked of no one special.

"Charlie, are you finished cataloguing in here?" one of them shouted out.

"Sure," a disembodied voice called back. "Used up the disk thirty minutes ago."

"Has someone got a glove?" Joshua asked.

The ME – a harsh looking woman – threw him a set of plastic gloves and a chilling glance.

Great. More attitude – just what I need right now.

In the opened briefcase, a blue-edged manila folder caught Joshua's eye. He snapped on a latex glove and slipped out the folder. It was Blue Stripe material alright; the colored band meant contents were under CIA compartmented security. Harker read the cover.

Project GENAFORM*
CLASSIFIED
ORCON PROPIN US ONLY

(* pronounced 'jen-a-form')

So the Senator was dealing with CIA classified material. Joshua began to see why he was on the scene. It surprised him to see such a file vulnerably exposed in the Senator's house. It was empty. There were no other documents in the case except for one single sheet of paper, hand-written, jammed down the deepest pouch.

Harker read the only line written on it:

We must take responsibility for what then becomes possible: broken evolution.

FIVE

Columbus, Ohio
17th September – 8:51pm

After some hands-on-hips musing, Joshua lifted a fountain pen from the Senator's brief case. He put it to his nose and sniffed it in front of amazed on-lookers. Still holding the pen, he joined the forensics crew. Two of them, wearing white boiler suits: a young woman and a greying middle-aged black man packing a few extra pounds. Josh held up the pen. "There's a residue coating this pen. I'd like it tested. And I need the results within a day."

"Oh yeah?" the older man replied. "You got cash to cover lab overtime?" His teasing wink stole away the harm.

"If needed, yes," replied Josh with a wry smile.

"You heard the man, Jill. Bag it and tag it."

The junior donned her gloves, dropped the pen into a Ziploc bag, and wrote on the label.

"We need a trace sweep done," Josh said, "between the stairs and the body."

"You kidding? It's long contaminated by now. Do you know how many people must have been walking over that patch since morning?" the older man demanded.

"Yes I do," Josh replied. "If you've a problem with it, take it to McAlister. He's the one who assumed natural causes, and let the mob loose over the scene."

The old guy puffed and shook his head. Joshua peeked at the badge clipped to his pocket – Lieutenant Robert Mitchell.

"Look Robert," Harker said casually, "I know this is a big ask and I'm sorry for busting your britches on it, but it's important. There's more to this than appears."

"Such as?"

Harker took him by the upper arm, and steered him to face the scene. "You see where he's lying?"

"Yeah – on the floor."

"But where on the floor?"

"Next to the coffee table. Are you messing with me?"

Harker shook his head. "No. Look again. You see the bourbon stain on the carpet? He probably dropped it when he started to have the heart attack, right?"

15

"Ok – so what?"

"But the body didn't fall near the dropped bourbon. The glass fell on the far side of the chair, so he was sitting on the chair when he dropped it."

"Yeah, and then he got up to get the pills in his briefcase. I don't see the problem here."

Harker smiled. "Look where the body is lying."

Robert Mitchell's eyes widened with childlike joy.

"His head is near the chair," Mitchell exclaimed, "but his feet are pointing away from the chair. Crazy thing – it looks like he got up, walked away from the briefcase, then came back to it."

"Exactly. Now you don't do that if you're in the middle of a heart attack and your pills are right in front of you, do you?" Joshua asked.

Mitchell replied, clearly enjoying the postulation. "Maybe he just forgot where his pills were. He made for the meds cabinet in the john, then remembered where they were, and didn't make it back in time."

A throaty female voice cut in. "No. He wouldn't forget where his pills were." It was the caustic Medical Examiner who spoke. "According to his wife, he was diagnosed with a heart defect years ago. He'd keep pills near at all times, and he wouldn't forget where they were."

"Sounds reasonable," Harker agreed.

The ME asked, "and is it reasonable to assume a heart attack before a medical examiner can ascertain the cause of death?"

Joshua replied, "One thing at a time, Doctor –?"

"Harris," she replied.

"Once the trace sweep is done, you can start."

Mitchell nodded his assent. "You're looking for evidence of someone else on the scene," he noted. "But there's no marks on the body – it doesn't look like homicide."

"He could have been killed without leaving a mark; pressure on the carotid artery?"

"That's unlikely." ME Harris pitched in her oar. "Pressure would have to be maintained until the end, yet he seems to have been free to move before he died."

Josh hummed in agreement. "It's hard to know while we're flying blind without evidence. So you better get sweeping Robert."

"Sure, whatever," the Lieutenant replied, joining his junior colleague. Over his shoulder he shared a parting comment with Josh. "It's Rob, by the way. Only my mother and ex-wife called me Robert."

Joshua's face melted into a smile that faded quickly as he took another look around the scene. The pill bottle, lying next to the Senator, caught his eye. He picked it up and had to suppress a chuckle at the irony of the manufacturer's label: Shimura Pharmaceutical. The brief reminder of his previous failed research project only quickened the need for a successful outcome here. He began to resent the ubiquity of that Shimura name in his life.

Ducking out under the plastic curtain, Harker joined the action in the hallway. Mrs. Olsen was being escorted upstairs, flanked by her support counsellor and Agent McAllister. As she climbed the stairs, Joshua noticed one step wobbled under their feet.

"Mind that step dear," Mrs. Olsen said to her escort. "Its quite tricky, you know. I asked Mark to fix it so many times, but I could never get him to do anything around the house lately. He was always so busy. 'When I retire –' he would say." Her words choked as tears took over, threatening her classy composure once more. The sound of sobbing followed her upstairs.

Loss and sorrow level us all.

With a keen frown, Joshua pondered that step. Could it have been what disturbed Olsen? His experience, his instincts, were kicking in, magnifying the little details that others trod over, and making new connections.

Going upstairs, he scanned the layout quickly before locating McAlister and asking him, "was there any sign of forced entry into the house?"

"No. Everything was locked from the inside, and no broken windows," replied McAlister before vanishing to busy himself elsewhere in the house. Josh didn't care what the FBI agent did; this CIA man was too busy conducting his own investigation. No indicators of forced entry closed off some possibilities but opened several others.

"Hey Rob," he shouted across, "have you got a glass strain viewer in your kit bag?"

The two forensic investigators were getting down on their knees in the study, one brushing the carpet with an electrostatic mitt, the other about to lay sheets of latent trace transfer film.

"Think so. Haven't needed one in a while, but there should still be one in the truck."

"Can I borrow it?"

"Sure. I'll bring it in."

Mitchell soon followed Harker upstairs, carrying an aluminium flight case.

"Where do you want it set up?" Mitchell asked.

"Let's start with this floor. Back bedroom."

17

"Why here?" Mitchell asked.

"It's closest to the trees. It would be the easiest window to get to."

Josh closed the door behind him, sat on the bed, and waited for Rob to find some evidence to vindicate him.

Mitchell assembled a tripod on the floor, talking as he worked.

"Don't mind McAlister. He's been giving grief since he got here. That's the real reason we're all so keen to get done here – to get shot of him. He's got his own troubles. Hell, who hasn't got their own troubles, right? There's only two kinds of people in the world: there's the kind who make life easier for other people, and the kind that make it harder. Could you hand me that mounting plate –?"

Joshua plucked a square of milled metal from the molded foam in the case.

"Thanks. Where was I? Oh yeah – we've all got our troubles. Thing is, the way I see it, you get so focused on your own troubles you start adding to other people's, before you know you're doing it. Now my problem is whether I'll be home in time to read my kids their bedtime story. But I guess as troubles go, that's not such a bad one. You got kids Joshua?"

Harker shook his head and was glad Rob took the sign he didn't want to discuss it. Implacable Rob just carried on with his verbal musing.

"No kids. That's a shame. That's not all that bad though, is it? I mean, some kids are more trouble than they are worth."

He took a camera shaped device from the foam casing and confided with a whisper. "You know, I shouldn't really be telling you this, but the examiner downstairs – Harris." He gave a long low whistle. "She's had a world of trouble with her kids. Single mom, been that way for years. You married Harker?"

Joshua flicked his head aside. Another no-go area. To avoid seeming rude, Joshua decided to say something. "Used to be."

"Oh, tough break. Divorce I suppose?" Rob waggled his head in dismay. "Society's own cancer that. I hate to see young couples splitting up. Breaks my heart."

Harker said nothing. His gaze was on the floor, but his mind wasn't in that room anymore. Mitchell's tales lured him back.

"Anyway, Doc Harris, she's got a teen in and out of juvvie all the time, and the other one – her son – is only eight and the poor mite has cystic fibrosis. When she's not working to pay bills, she's pounding that kid's chest to stop him drowning in mucous. We see each other on crime scenes regular and each time I see her, another piece of her has gone."

The story dragged Joshua away from his own concerns, and instead he pondered on how one random flip of a base pair, one adenine molecule instead of thymine, could cause a disease that has such a profound effect. Since he'd first learned about the workings of DNA in med school, the profound caprice of heredity always beguiled him; how one simple allele, a random mutation on chromosome seven, shared and copied by both parents, could be responsible for the early destruction of a child's life ... and a mother's personality.

"You just never know, do you?" Rob commented. "You never know what someone has to deal with in their life."

Joshua concurred, silently.

"But people like the Doc down there don't need extra on their plate do they? So the way I like to live is always to assume someone needs a little help, a little ease – anything just to make their day a bit lighter. Because you never know, do you?"

For a second time that day, Rob made Joshua smile. The muscles were out of practice.

He knew Rob was saying something important, without saying it directly. Was Mitchell's philosophical doctrine hinting that Joshua was pushing too hard, no different than McAlister? Rob might also have been signalling empathy. Did he sense problems Joshua harbored? Josh wondered if they showed. Mitchell's speech was simple and friendly, but Josh could see he was a sharp, astute man and not at all guileful. He was trying to put Joshua at ease, a service for which Joshua found himself grateful. Though he'd known the guy for less than thirty minutes, he knew he liked him, just as much as he disliked McAlister.

Josh knew he was right to push. None of them in this house would have investigated for murder. The least the Senator was owed for a lifetime of service to his country was a proper investigation of reasonable doubt. If there were any doubts about the cause of death, Harker would delve for it, for the sake of the Senator - and the Senator's wife. She was owed the truth too. Without pushing, without adding to their problems, how would Joshua ever discover the truth? All he needed now was the proof that he was right, before everyone started to detest the man from CIA.

"So what next Joshua?" Rob asked.

"Check all the windows."

"For what?"

"The polarizer on the viewer will show up the strain pattern on the glass. It should tell us if there were any disturbances to any of the panes."

"What the hell has this got to do with a murder?"

Harker took a step back in his mind and explained his thinking to Mitchell.

"Look, without any sign of entry, it means that an intruder might have disguised the point of entry, or –"

"Or?"

"Or they had a key to get in."

"Think that's likely?" asked Rob.

"No, not really. The Senator was startled by someone coming downstairs."

"Hell, I don't know. I'm not even sure there was an intruder. What makes you so sure?"

"Two things," said Harker, "the Senator's body fell from the direction of the stairway, so that means he was alerted to someone coming from upstairs. It could have been the sound of glass breaking that did it."

"There is no broken glass."

"Unless the broken pane was replaced on the way out."

"Oh, come on!"

"Long shot, I know. In fact, that rickety step makes quite a noise – it was probably enough to alert Olsen, but too late. But the strain viewer will show us if any of the glass doesn't look original. We just need to eliminate the possibility. And then there's the second thing that bothers me – the pen."

"The pen? Oh yeah. Why did you want that tested?" Rob asked while aligning the strain viewer with one of the glass panes and turning the polarizer lens.

"The pen in the briefcase is still tacky, and it smells of bourbon. So it might have fallen at the same time as the hooch, proving that Olsen was writing something in his armchair while drinking. The noise startled him and then he dropped the pen and the bourbon on top of it."

"Could be – but still doesn't prove there was an intruder."

"Someone had to have moved that pen from the floor back to the briefcase. That's the only clue of an intruder at all. If this was murder, then everything here was done to fake natural causes. Only when the Senator was startled did the plan change. The intruder didn't know about the creaking step, so it wasn't someone who knew the house well – not someone with a key either. If I'm right, and he was murdered, then it was done with stealth and with some weapon or poison that isn't even obvious to us yet. We're not dealing with your average assassin here. This is way beyond the curve. And if they had the know-how to disguise the murder and make it look like natural causes, then they'd damn sure have the know-how to disguise the break-in."

"Hmm. Sounds pretty neat – but unconvincing."

"I know: it's all still speculation. His wife may have replaced the pen; I still need to check with her about that. We need stronger evidence."

Rob peeped through the transparent back plate and adjusted the lens.

"If it was an intruder," he asked, "why would they have moved the pen?"

"Good question. Moving the pen was the biggest single piece of evidence that Olsen's death was no accident. It gave away the whole secrecy of the murderer's presence. Why jeopardize that for the sake of a fallen pen? It must have needed to be done to protect some greater secret about the murder." Joshua snapped his fingers. "Of course! It was moved to mask the fact that the Senator had been writing something, that the file contents had been stolen."

Rob checked at every windowpane upstairs.

"Nothing."

"You sure?"

Joshua took a peek through the viewer at one of the windows. Each windowpane's stress pattern appeared in multicolored glory: a rainbow spectrum of contours flowed around the glass, evenly spaced, the same on each one. No sign of stress, cracks, a breakage, or a replacement of a broken pane.

"It was a bit of a long shot," Rob said.

Josh smiled. Rob seemed genuinely disappointed for the CIA man. Josh walked around on the spot, tapping his hand on his thigh.

"Hang on! There's another way." He looked up, then sprang out onto the landing. There was a small hatch leading to the loft.

"Rob, you got steps and a flash light?"

Rob fulfilled the new request and went up with the flash light. In moments his voice boomed down from the loft.

"Home run CIA man!"

Joshua's head popped into the loft to see what he'd found. A thin layer of shotcrete insulant had been sprayed around the roof. Joshua looked where Rob was pointing the light. There was a crack in the insulant, big enough for a small man to fit through.

"Someone could have removed a few slates, come in, and put them back afterwards," Rob said.

Joshua nodded. "... but wouldn't know until after they broke through that there would be cracked insulation that would leave a sign of entry."

"Hmm. Could still be an old repair?"

"We can find out soon enough from Mrs. Olsen. Wouldn't hurt to widen your trace sweep to cover the area around that entry point. I doubt fingerprints would be left, but dust it to be sure."

"Looks like you might get your proof after all. If so, McAlister's gonna love this," Rob said with a wicked smile, clearly happy for Joshua.

The pair of investigators returned downstairs and were met by Rob's young colleague, about to add to the triumphant mood.

"Luck is running your way Agent Harker," she said, lifting up a clear polythene evidence pouch in front of him. Inside it, Joshua could barely make out a hair in one corner.

"I found it gripped in the Senator's hand."

Josh took the pouch and held it up to the lightbulb. With something this small only one thing was obvious: its color.

"It's blonde," Joshua said.

"Exactly," she said eagerly, "and the deceased, or his wife, don't have blonde hair. No pets either."

Josh looked at Mitchell, in whom he detected pride at the discovery of his young trainee. Now the forensics duo impressed the CIA with their own investigative skill. Mitchell stayed quiet, happy to let youth have its moment of glory.

Jill continued: "Do you notice anything else about it?"

Josh knew what she was getting at.

"Yes," he nodded, squinting at the tell-tale hair. "Yes – it's still got its follicular tag attached. Which means –"

"Which means the hair was still in the catagen growth phase: it didn't fall out, it was pulled out. There must have been a struggle with someone. It corroborates your theory."

Josh beamed at the young woman.

"Better yet, it means live skin cells," he added. "You've got DNA we can trace. Rob, I'm going to need another favour."

"CODIS search?" Rob guessed.

"Got it in one," replied Harker. "Check the past offenders DNA database."

SIX

Columbus, Ohio
18th September – 10:24am

Bullets of rain broke Harker's sleep the next morning. His head thumped. Late to bed and bad sleep left him more tired than before. Last night he wanted reminding of life as an antidote to the reminders of death. He'd been prompted out into the night, alone. He woke alone too, but not for lack of any opportunities.

The more predatory women in the club had enough liquid courage to drift near him with expectant smiles and a flick of their manes. The demure ones had glanced from afar and looked away as soon as seen, hoping for him to approach. Harker knew he was still attractive. How else could he have ended up with someone as stunning as Megan? His handsome features and athletic physique had made it easy to get the girls. Though he had a few grey hairs now, he kept his shape and could still pass for a man in his early thirties. Megan had often said his eyes – verdant green, open and compelling – had first attracted her, but that his smile sealed the deal. That same compelling glance still worked its magic for sure in the clubs. But the smile didn't follow. It couldn't. How could he offer a smile to any of those women? It would be a lie. Beautiful, brief, anaesthesia: they offered no more than that. But they couldn't numb the pain any more than the other failed distractions Harker had sampled these past years – the women, the substances ... the behaviors. Another brief encounter this night would only remind him that the woman he was with was not the woman he wanted. It only made the pain worse.

He'd contented himself just to sip the watered-down beer into the early hours, and like some ageing lecherous vampire, he'd sucked on the life energy – the euphoria – of that young crowd who were yet untainted by life's pains as they ebbed in a sea of smoke and lasers under the like-affirming mantras pumped out by the MC. Joshua had sat at the bar above it all, just sipping.

And now his head hurt.

He twisted his watch on the bed-stand. 10:45.

Next to the watch, he took his pill box, and removed one small white pearl from it. Modafinil. Stimulant of the Gods. He'd picked up this habit during the many late nights of study back in med school. It didn't fry his system like the hard stuff had. It pepped his mind better than any caffeine, and – best of all – it fell below the radar of the CIA's five yearly staff drug screenings. Harker took one long grounding breath and let the sharp clarity ooze like a glacier through his mind, scouring away all distractions. The fog blew from his mind, and his thoughts ran clear again.

Pills. Everybody uses them.

He thought of the pills around the Senator's corpse.

What killed him?

An intruder so skilled in concealing evidence must have been equally ingenious in disguising how his victim died.

Toxins?

He needed to talk to the Medical Examiner.

After a hasty brunch in the diner next to the motel, he called up ME Harris closer to lunchtime. He pressed her for an autopsy update while picking bacon out of his teeth.

He was greeted with sarcasm.

"Already? You CIA guys need to learn the way we do things in the real world."

It was superb sarcasm, Josh thought. She must practice it a lot. But after what Mitchell had told him, Joshua cut her some slack.

"Well then, when will you have autopsy results?"

"Tox tests could take days to come back, even with you breathing down our necks."

It was an odd call to send blood samples for toxicology tests, particularly for a supposed heart attack.

He asked: "Then you found signs of toxins in his system?"

She sighed, vexed. Josh pictured her taking a seat, preparing for a longer chat than she planned.

"I got started on the autopsy first thing. It's nearly complete. I haven't put any of this on paper, so don't hold me to it yet, but the signs point to a massive pulmonary embolism."

Joshua knew the term and it surprised him.

"I would have expected myocardial infarction ... if he had a weak heart," he said.

A momentary silence on the other end of the line. Was Harris shocked, he wondered, that he had medical knowledge?

She continued with a new tone of respect. "Typically, that would be so. Pulmonary embolism is rare and there's usually a history of it in the subject. Olsen had no episodes of it in his life. In fact, his heart should have been the last thing to kill him."

"What do you mean?" asked Harker.

24

"You know those tablets he reached for?"

"The ones scattered around his body, yes."

"Well, they wouldn't have done him any good."

"Then why was he reaching for them? I guessed they were some kind of vasodilator."

"No," she said sternly. "Vasodilators are over-the-counter, usually branded, like Hydralazine or Minoxidil. These tablets had no brand."

They were the pills Harker had noted as a Shimura Pharmaceutical product; he remembered they had no name on the label, just Olsen's name.

"The Senator's wife says they were part of a custom therapeutic regime – a prophylaxis – prevention against congenitally faulty genes that cause a weak heart. But ... they wouldn't have any effect on a heart attack once started. Reaching for them was just a desperate impulse of a dying man, I think."

Joshua's curiosity piqued.

"If his meds were supposed to repair his heart, then he shouldn't have died of a heart ailment at all."

"Exactly my point," Harris said.

"Unless the pills didn't work?"

Harris let out another dismayed sigh over the phone. "Shimura wouldn't put their name to a drug that wouldn't work – that's why their services are so sought after, and so damned expensive. Only the high-and-mighty like Senator Olsen can afford them."

Joshua wondered if Harris resented not being rich enough to afford such treatments to cure her son of his disease. How many times must she have cursed that fateful divide in pay grade which allowed some of the cadavers she sliced open to live well beyond their natural expiry date, while she herself returned home to a child she could do nothing for. Josh began to know the woman a little better, and with it came a revelation they were similar: victims of their own lives' circumstances.

She resumed: "by the time he died, the Senator had a heart as strong as a horse. I know – I've seen it. Such an expensive heart too. I really should mount it I suppose, or something."

The morbid humor of a pathologist on top of sarcasm. Doctor Harris had more than her fair share of problems, but he stayed quiet, and let her vent.

"Anyway," she said, calming down a little, "there was no obvious physiological reason for infarction or embolism."

Joshua realised now why she ordered the toxicology tests.

"So something triggered the embolism?" he asked.

"That's my guess. A large tumbler of whisky and the shock of your mysterious intruder wouldn't have been enough to cause it."

Poison. Could that really be it? Josh theorized. It could have been put in his whisky, he supposed, but that would have left enough traces to confirm a murder. This killer had gone to great lengths not to leave any evidence, so poison in a drink would be too obvious and easy to discover.

He asked Harris if poison could have been administered directly into the blood stream.

"I checked for puncture wounds," she replied. "Head to toe. There was nothing."

"Maybe poison could have been administered on the tongue, or even into the eye," Joshua said, breaking the silence created by his own musings.

"No. It would take too long to act that way," Harris replied. "Olsen would have time to raise the alarm."

Harker had read of new technologies under research. He surmised that a nano-syringe could have been used. Such a device could enter the skin and be directed toward the heart without leaving any visible sign. Only a study of the tissue with an electron microscope could possibly confirm it – and no forensic investigator would do that. It would be like looking for a needle in a field of wheat. No, no sign left that way. No proof: the way it had been intended.

Josh was becoming impressed with Harris; she was keeping up with every mental step. Once past her embittered exterior, it turned out Doc Harris was pretty good at her job.

"So what do you think might have caused it?" he asked.

"Well, there was an unusual degree of DIC around the heart. To cause instant excessive coagulation like that, and the ensuing embolism, you'd need high levels of fibrinogen – it's the body's own natural coagulant. Thickens the blood. But that wouldn't be enough. Maybe it could work in combination with a coagulation accelerator too, like thrombin. A cocktail like that would have to be directly delivered into the heart to have such a quick effect. But this is all guesswork – tox and haemo tests will confirm."

Harris's suggestion tracked; excess levels of the body's own natural chemicals would be an ideal, inconclusive poison. There would be no sure proof of murderous intervention. It was another dead end – a pun Harker considered sharing with the morbid pathologist. It would have been nice to make her smile, just once before the paths of their lives diverged.

"Doctor Harris –," Joshua said, waiting for her to reply.

"Yes?"

"What's your first name?"

The pause told of her surprise at the change of direction.

"Julia."

Joshua smiled to himself; even though she couldn't see it, he hoped she would hear it.

"Thank you for your help, Julia. I really appreciate it."

"You're welcome," she replied softly, sounding a little stunned.

After final goodbyes, they hung up. It felt good to be kind again to a woman in need of it. The months of enmity with Rita left him needing to. He had taken Mitchell's advice to ease someone's day, and discovered the bonus hidden in that advice: it eased Joshua's own life a little too.

It was to Lieutenant Mitchell that Harker's mind now turned, spurred on by the autopsy findings and the continuing need for evidence, any evidence. If he filed a report like this to Silberman without evidence, she would have him for brunch. Rita would be the one picking her teeth afterwards. Rob Mitchell and his team were Harker's only hope now.

SEVEN

Columbus, Ohio
18th September – 3:15pm

Josh called up Mitchell early afternoon.

"I'm over in the London lab now," Rob told him, "leaning on the staff, since you're not here to do it." Josh knew there was no malice in the jibe. They exchanged a laugh. "Anyway, we found something for you. I can't really go into it on an open line, but you should get down here ASAP."

Why, Josh wondered, was a member of the PD so concerned about unsecured phones? Must be something pretty damn big. A tingle of anticipation shot down Harker's neck.

He packed up his things, ready to leave Ohio after meeting Mitchell. Silberman would be barking for a report. Josh stuffed clothes into the holdall with his fist. As he packed away his Modafinil pill box, a thought niggled him. He thought back to the call with Julia about pills and poison. The killer consciously chose to go after the Senator's heart. It was Olsen's most vulnerable point. It would be the least suspicious cause of a natural death, given his congenital defect.

The killer must have known about Olsen's heart history!

That kind of medical information would be known only to a few. There was something, some link, some clue, he was missing ...

His mind wouldn't make the next taunting leap. Thoughts ran like treacle again. Not enough sleep last night, he supposed. He popped another pill.

* * *

The sun was setting when Harker pulled up to the Bureau of Criminal Investigation forensics lab. Moments after he'd signed in at the desk, Mitchell came down to escort him up. In the elevator Rob made small talk about Harker's drive to London and his views of Ohio. The rotunda floor of laboratories was like a giant glass cake, with each lab segmented and visible from all the others. It was thinly staffed, as he'd expect that late in the day.

As they walked through it, old sights and smells assaulted Josh. The tangy pungent cocktail of residual chemicals bloomed in his nose: blood, cordite, superglue, formaldehyde and acetone. Unique to a crime lab. He saw all the bizarre array of paraphernalia he'd used: computers, test tubes, Bunsen burners, a centrifuge, a bullet tank, freezers, steam irons and a range of once expensive-looking electronic devices, now battered by the operational demands of many deaths. The memories were so vivid to him, it could have been yesterday. Josh had sat on one of those stools, looking down a microscope – and Megan sat beside him – in Kansas City crime lab where they first met and worked together.

The emotional demands of this case increased by the minute. Joshua sucked in lots of air, and with it too, he hoped, courage.

The two entered a meeting room and sat on stools around a high table under harsh fluorescent lights. They were joined by a woman wearing glasses, a white coat, and hair cinched into a bun.

Rob introduced her: "Joshua Harker, meet Dr. Miranda Porcho, Director of the BCI London Lab."

Harker said hello, but she didn't reply, leaving Josh to wonder whether she was shy, or just resentful of the CIA setting her lab's priorities and overtime.

"So what have you got for me?" Harker asked Mitchell.

"Well, first the good news," he replied. "The pen checked out for whisky residue."

Harker nodded. "So he did spill whisky on the pen, and the killer must have replaced the pen in the briefcase."

"That seems plausible now," Rob replied.

Josh smiled. A second person confirmed at the crime scene.

"And the bad news?"

"Apart from the hair strand, we couldn't find any direct evidence of an intruder: there were no latent shoeprints, or fibers, and no fingerprints."

Joshua butted in: "but you got DNA from the hair follicle –? Don't tell me it's a strand of his dog's hair Rob!"

Mitchell nodded. "No, it seems human alright. And it's the only certain proof we have of another presence in the room. But you're not going to believe this ..." He reached for a file that was in front of him on the desk and shoved it towards Harker.

Dr. Porcho – the expert – had kept silent during this whole exchange. Josh read her body language. She folded her arms. Not defensively, he reckoned, but tightly, as if to hug herself. He'd misjudged her silence. She wasn't shy or sore. She looked ... anxious. What the hell could make her so nervous? Josh peeled open the flap of the file and began to scan the test results.

Porcho explained as he read. "The usual search through the CODIS database of past suspect DNA turned up nothing. We even went international: the Asian databases, ENFSI in Europe. All report negative."

Harker reached. "So whoever owns this DNA was never involved in a crime before, or maybe just never suspected of one?"

Porcho looked sideways to Mitchell before saying, "I don't think we can even make that assumption. There are anomalies with the DNA."

Anomalies? Harker was taken aback.

She carried on: "since we didn't get a database match, we decided to perform some of the standard DNA phenotype tests for gender, race, skin color. That way, we figured, at least we'd get a physical profile of the suspect. Keyed to certain codons, we quickly identified the genetic characteristics we were looking for. But on one of the tests, the alleles were not as expected."

"What do you mean?"

"We repeated the test, double-checking for contamination, but the same results came back all the time. Every single gene allele encoding a physical characteristic was homozygous."

Harker's face fell. He knew it was impossible.

Porcho extended a conclusion. "The DNA isn't a natural form, it can't be. It looks as though it has been artificially tampered with."

A frustrated Mitchell asked, "What does all that mean?"

Josh explained to him. "Every gene in human DNA has components that come from both mother and father – blonde hair from mother, brown from father, with one hair color allele becoming dominant in the child. If Dr. Porcho is correct, then every physical characteristic in the suspect's DNA was homozygous – identical in mother and father. It's never been heard of. It couldn't happen naturally, so the DNA must have been altered."

"Why would someone do that?" Rob asked Porcho.

Porcho offered no answer. Josh knew facts were the currency of a scientist, but he traded in speculation and motivation. Josh offered the most logical conclusion he could.

"Someone's DNA has been altered to disguise themselves, to prevent exactly the kind of trace that we tried here."

Mitchell shook his head. "In all my years in the force I've never heard anything so daft."

"Why not?" Joshua said rationally. "The killer went to extraordinary lengths to disguise his or her presence, so why not disguise identity too, if the resources are available to do it? Criminals have always kept pace with police skills, disguising themselves from each new forensic method: simple face concealment from cameras, or gloves to avoid fingerprints. Now DNA fingerprinting is the hardest to foil, but someone would find a way around it sooner or later."

Josh shared Porcho's anxiety. If someone had found a way to disguise DNA, her job had suddenly become a lot harder.

"But who would be insane enough to alter their DNA just to commit a murder?" Mitchell asked. "Who would even able to do it? I can't believe I'm even asking this."

"I'm not sure I fully believe it myself yet," Josh said. "It's pretty sophisticated stuff. As for who could do it – well, only those with the most advanced techniques and knowledge of molecular genetics."

Fingers clicked inside Harker's mind, where a theory coalesced. He threw a curveball.

"Rob: McAlister said Olsen had just come back from a business trip abroad. I didn't think it important enough to ask at the time, but I was just wondering – did he happen to say where that trip was?"

"We had lots of time to chew the fat before you arrived ... let me see ... yeah, I remember. He said it was in Japan."

Harker smiled.

"Did he mention which company?"

"I don't think he knew. Is it important?"

"No, just curious."

That wasn't true, but Harker didn't wish to share his suspicions. Only a few institutions in the world could conceivably alter DNA like that. Fewer still would have the kind of advanced weapon used by the assassin. And it was all beginning to point to one place. The killer knew of Olsen's heart condition. Josh remembered his report of a company engaged in espionage, including the medical histories of certain high-level Americans. He thought of Olsen's pills. Those types of custom pills would require diagnostic trips to the makers – a Japanese company. The pills. Olsen had reached for them before dying. He knew they couldn't save him from dying. That wasn't why he reached for them. What if ... he was pointing the finger at his murderer? Did Olsen recognize the assassin ... from one of his business trips ... to Japan?

Harker stopped himself. He was getting carried away. Silberman would never stand for it. Josh shook it off and worked with what he had.

"Is there anything about the DNA that could help find the perpetrator, anything at all?" he asked Dr. Porcho.

"If the changes were meant to disguise the DNA we shouldn't rely on it much for profiling the perpetrator, but the gender and telomere length are very difficult to fake."

"So you can be sure of the assassin's sex and approximate age?" Harker asked.

She nodded. "A male, early twenties or late teens. Blonde hair is certain too, since the hair strand wasn't dyed – the pigmentation is uniform. Oh, and the hair shaft is oval, with a medium-sized cuticle, so that implies a Caucasian."

Harker spoke. "Well, that should help some. Thank you both for bringing this to my attention. I'll take it from here," Josh said officiously.

Dr. Porcho headed for the door, clearly glad the problem was off her plate. Mitchell stayed.

Joshua folded over the test results and sealed the clasp, staring into space until Rob brought him back.

"Hey," Rob said. "Me and a couple of the lab techs I don't see too often are going for a drink after. So how 'bout joining us for a cold one before you head home?"

"Won't you miss your kids' tuck-in time?"

"Ah, sure. But it's not everyday the CIA comes to town, is it? Let's chew the fat over a beer."

Harker's watch told him he had an hour to burn before leaving for the airport check-in, and he was about to agree when his phone blurted out for his attention. The number and the flashing green padlock on the display told him the call was from Langley. He took it outside the room. It was Silberman.

"What's your progress Harker?"

"I have all I need here. I was just about to head home and – "

Silberman cut across him: "I understand you requested some DNA tests up there."

Joshua was speechless. She'd been keeping a very close eye on this, more than was usual. It wasn't like her to be so thorough.

"Harker, you are not to leave any DNA evidence there. Sequester it, and any other evidence or test records. Bring them back here."

"Well, that's not –"

"Was I unclear in some way, Joshua?"

"There are others here who need this stuff," he insisted.

"The CIA has authority on this case, and I'm ordering you to bring back everything. Where's the problem?"

Joshua heaved a sigh. He felt drained and did not have the energy or inclination to fight with her this time. Besides, he agreed: if news of untraceable DNA became public ... perhaps the CIA had a responsibility to protect this knowledge until it could be explained.

"I'll do as requested," he said, with a sigh.

"Good. I'll look forward to your report tomorrow."

He retracted the phone's screen and gave Mitchell the news.

"I'm sorry about this Rob, but I'm going to have to take the hair sample and all the test records."

"What? Now come on! You know how hard this is gonna make my job. How am I to explain to the Captain, or the DA, that all the evidence I collected at the Senator's has gone? They'll rip me to shreds. Come on man! You know what due process is."

Joshua looked him in the eye, but offered no word of excuse.

"The evidence never existed Rob. That's just how it is. If you've a problem with it, take it to a higher power."

Rob looked at the phone that Joshua slipped back into his pocket and nodded.

"Oh I understand Agent Harker. Big people and little people; is that how it is? Guess you are one of the big people after all." Mitchell whipped his jacket from the chair and left. Drinks were off.

That night, Harker left Ohio feeling he had stabbed a friend and colleague in the back. Of all people, he wouldn't have wanted to do that to Rob Mitchell. Joshua made life harder for the man who believed in making it easier for others. While driving to the airport words came echoing back from the depths of his memory, words spoken just after his wife's funeral, the same week he abandoned forensics for intelligence. After the funeral, his own Captain of Police had said to him: "Police investigation and espionage are two very different beasts Joshua. Police look for the truth; intelligence agencies hide it."

Harker hadn't paid much attention to those words back then; after all, they were spoken by the man Harker held partly responsible for Megan's death. He'd no respect for the Captain's self-gratifying paperback philosophies. The words Josh ignored then came back to haunt him now.

Joshua's confused mash of emotions collapsed under the apprehension of another buried report and the failure of betraying his new friend. His thrill in getting this assignment was replaced by creeping despair that threatened to drag him back to the solitary daily grind that waited in his cubicle.

EIGHT

Otemachi, Tokyo
18th September – 11:09am

Kazuki stood with his back against the wall, and a sword draped over his shoulder. The youthful, rakish, non-Japanese *gaijin* with blond hair and a shark-skin suit guarded proceedings that he could never hope to participate in. Down below, and distant from him, three men sat on floor cushions around a black-lacquered table. Haruto - CEO of the Shimura Corporation - sat cross-legged at the head of the table. His sixty six years sat well on him. Kazuki liked the way he aged with dignity. His silver hair was still a dense plume. His skin was pallid, having lost its youthful firmness but not its smoothness. It was health fortified as much by Haruto's will as by the concoction of regular, free doses of vivifying treatments provided by the pharmaceutical arm of the corporation he founded.

To Haruto's left sat Takahiro Watanabe, President of the Sumitoro Bank, a man of Haruto Shimura's age and standing, with a manner Kazuki admired – refined and calm. Watanabe's mood today (shared by all at the table) was especially reserved: reverent, as demanded by the ceremony.

Haruto took a jar of *sake* and poured into Watanabe's porcelain cup. He also poured into the cup of the younger man to his right – Haruto's own son, Taro. The cup given to Taro had less liquid, as customary for the junior.

Taro took the tiny drinking vessel, raised the cup to his face, and gave a steely stare to Watanabe.

"The Shimura-Sumitoro alliance," Taro stated and smoothly tipped the *sake* into his throat. He replaced the cup on the table and waited for Watanabe to drink.

The expected action didn't happen.

Watanabe glowered at Taro. Kazuki noticed the artery in the old bank president's neck throb, foretelling the outburst that was to follow. A curse exploded from Watanabe's graven lips, tearing through his calm facade. With the back of a flattened palm, he struck his cup, sending it tumbling across the *tatami* flooring, and on to the highly-polished tips of Kazuki's shoes. He tapped it aside. Kazuki looked to Haruto Shimura, who had flinched at the outburst, but Taro showed no reaction at all.

"Watanabe-san, do you seek to offend?" asked old Haruto.

"Shimura-san," came the reply, "this alliance is no longer wise."

"You have favoured it all along; why do you object now? To have come so far, only to rebuke us! Be careful Watanabe-san, or I might think you planned this as an insult."

"Forgive me Shimura-san, but I mean no insult to you. It is true that I have defended this union. I have been your proponent on the Sumitoro board, against those members cautious of dealing with someone of your background. I have been, and remain, your ally. You know that – how could you suggest I would set out to insult you?"

Kazuki smiled inside, and knew Haruto was smiling inside too. Haruto had always confided in Kazuki. The old man was his greatest mentor. Kazuki had discovered that Haruto had grown an extra sense or two on his erratic path through life. Those senses told him that the President of the Sumitoro Bank would never ally himself with anyone in business unless there was something to be gained. Haruto once told him that the board of Sumitoro would ignore Haruto's own criminal past and would bear the stigma of having a member of the Shimura Corporation on their board, but only for self-interest. With the resources of Sumitoro and Shimura combined, it would be a true *keiretsu*, a cartel to rival the might of an economically flailing Mitsubishi or Sanwa. Dire times provide opportunities for the brave, Haruto had taught him. A combined entity of both Shimura and Sumitoro could leverage and control in Japan in a way neither organization had yet known. Haruto had confided that a healthy balance sheet, not friendship, was the reason behind any allegiance Watanabe offered.

Watanabe continued: "No. I do not aim to insult you Shimura-san. But I think it is you who attempts to insult me. After all our efforts to build this deal, why are you not to sit on the Sumitoro board yourself, but instead ask me to admit this – ?" he stopped, avoiding an insult to Haruto's son.

Taro remained calm, showing no reaction. His fitting restraint seemed to please his father.

"This is my son you speak of. Taro will one day inherit the corporation I have founded. He is to be CEO when I am gone, so it is right that he should represent our interests on your board now."

"So you say." Watanabe sighed, mellowing through confrontation with logic. "But this was not expected – you were to be the representative. I have grave doubts about this alternative." He spoke softly now, as if advising an old friend. "We have known each other a long time, have we not?"

"Indeed," Haruto replied.

"Then permit me to say that you trust this young *kohai* far more than I am prepared to."

"Young? Taro is twenty-nine – older than I when I founded this corporation. Do not confuse age with experience Watanabe-san. I have trained him as best I know how. His seat on your board will be to everyone's benefit; it will continue his education – we learn by doing after all. That's how I achieved all that I have. Were it not for that experience in the harsh crucible of enterprise, I doubt the Shimura Corporation would be so attractive to you now."

"It brings me great joy to see the success you have made of your life, and your business. It gave me greater joy to know that you would be accepted into the Sumitoro family of commerce. But –" Watanabe shot a glance towards Taro. His voice sank. "– who you associate with now! It puts it all at risk. Certain ... rumors ... have recently come to the board's attention."

"What rumors?" Haruto demanded.

"Nothing confirmed, I hasten to add. And nothing I can give voice to here, but they are enough to frighten off our board."

"Pah! Our competitors' crude efforts to scupper our alliance, no doubt," Shimura proposed. "You know better than to let shrewd lies affect your decisions."

Watanabe shook his head. "You have no competitors here. In biotechnology you have monopolized many speciality markets. That's why this acquisition is so attractive to our *keiretsu*." Shimura permitted himself the conceit of a smile at Watanabe's flattering candour. "No: the rumors I speak of, Shimura-san, relate to activities outside of Japan; more than that, I cannot say. At Sumitoro we cannot allow fraught associations to endanger our high reputation. I'm sorry, old friend."

Watanabe stood to leave, bowing. Haruto stood and bowed. Kazuki bowed too. Taro remained seated; an insult of the worst kind.

"This ceremony –" Watanabe said, thrusting his hand over the table," comes from our warrior past. Duty!" he yelled. "It is all based on trust." Watanabe looked Taro in the eye and gave his parting remark: "I see no trust here."

With that, the President of Sumitoro Bank took his aides and left.

Haruto looked to the ceiling and released a long breath. Noting the distress, Taro sought to assure his father. "It is a ploy, father. You know banks always seek to place their own chairman on the boards of their *keiretsu* companies. Watanabe is playing a game. He just doesn't want to see a second generation of Shimura at the helm. They want to control the corporation outright."

Haruto strolled slowly, clasping his hands behind his back, stopping by an open *shoji* screen door that overlooked a little stone garden built onto the rooftop.

"Oh yes, and you understand games very well, don't you my son? What a pity you do not understand honor as well. You heard him: duty. This is not a game. He fears you will bring him shame in his dealings. He would not have been so emotional if he was simply playing some game – no, he meant it. Sumitoro will not back down and give us that opportunity again, so the corporation will now have to go forward without an alliance."

"Unfortunate," Taro commented.

"Is that all you can say? *Unfortunate?* I grow tired of your actions jeopardising all I've worked for."

"What actions? Watanabe was bluffing. He may never have intended to go through with this at all; it's pathetic of him to use some vague accusation to wriggle out of his promise. I thought him capable of more. Perhaps we are better off without such a man of low capability."

"He is a man of honor, and he respects me. He would have accepted you to the board, at my request, except that ... he fears you, and your methods."

Kazuki listened on, fearing that Haruto's last words were secretly directed at him.

Silence fell for a time in the room. Haruto clearly had no intention of breaking it. Taro, fidgeting, did.

"Watanabe makes accusations without proof. Is my father to do the same?"

"I have no proof either Taro, but if I find out that you had anything to do with Olsen-san's death ... " Haruto said, before stopping himself to reconsider, " ... perhaps enough has been said."

Another silence briefly laced the air between the two men before Haruto calmly said, "you draw unwelcome notice on us."

"My ambition is not fitting? My hopes and dreams for your business and its success in the next generation?"

Shaking his head, Haruto replied, "Not at any cost Taro. Your acquired ambition is to be commended, but in other matters I have failed you: honor, patience, obedience – perhaps even morality. All these you have yet to master. Perhaps you are still too young."

Haruto drew himself away from the jasmine scented air by the roof garden and returned to take up his place standing behind his seated charge. He placed his hands on Taro's shoulders and said, "I have given you life, my name, and my vision – all that I have to give. What more can any father do? The rest is up to you. I do not think you set out to dishonor me, but Watanabe-san was right in what he said: trust is the basis of loyalty and the source of all honor. I think you find trust hardest of all."

Taro stood up after a long thought, and held a low submissive bow in front of his father.

"I meant no disrespect," said Taro.

Haruto bowed also, with a warm smile.

"Go now," he said softly. "Leave me for a while."

Taro bowed once more before leaving. Once he was gone, Haruto spoke immediately to his youthful armed sentinel.

"Walk with me Kazuki."

The ageing magnate stepped out into the stone garden built on top of his corporate headquarters – an oasis of natural beauty sprouting from the Tokyo sprawl. Kazuki noticed how Haruto looked along the gravel pathway, now empty, where Haruto walked and talked with Senator Olsen just days before.

"Be very careful Kazuki," he said to his young walking companion. "Do not become embroiled in Taro's ways."

"*Sensei?*" Kazuki quizzed.

Haruto stopped to look his adopted charge in his blue-grey eyes. "Were you involved Kazuki? Are the same rumors reaching Watanabe's ears also offending mine? Tell me it isn't so."

Kazuki looked down before saying. "Does it matter who was involved? Was his death not to our benefit? His actions impeded your company's growth – I'm surprised that wouldn't please you."

Haruto shook his heavy head.

"This day grows dark indeed. My son – and now my adopted son too – both involved in this. Oh Kazuki, how you have been misdirected! I feel something about the collapse of the Sumitoro alliance that I never thought I would – I feel relief. I proposed Taro for it, and might have lived to regret that in my own lifetime."

Haruto sighed deep and long, then looked Kazuki deeply in the eyes. Kazuki saw a desperate hope in those old eyes that had seen so much of the wrong side of life.

Haruto continued. "Even though you are not Japanese in aspect, you have become Japanese in spirit, just as I raised you to be, perhaps more successfully than I have with Taro. All the training you received for combat, all that mastery, was ultimately for your own self-mastery Kazuki. Now, I look into your eyes and I see a soul fighting with itself. I see what you can not say, for fear of dishonoring me – that you killed Mark Olsen."

Kazuki said nothing, but bowed.

"Such is your admirable loyalty I know of you Kazuki – that you would do all you could to protect the Shimura family, even from itself. But that loyalty has been used to manipulate you. The disease in Taro's heart has become contagious." Haruto stopped to grab the young man's shoulders and turn them towards him. "You don't realize how much we owe to Mark Olsen ... and how much you owed him."

It seemed to Kazuki that Haruto burned inside, as if some secret he wanted to let loose was consuming him. Kazuki's heart raced. Instantly, the old tycoon stood back, taking on a new face, less fatherly, more stern. "But now is not the time for this. You have a special role in my family Kazuki – you are our protector. However, I must insist that from now on you only take orders from me – your *sensei* – and from me alone. No more orders from Taro.

Kazuki bowed to his master. "Yes, *sensei.*"

"Be aware it is not too late, Kazuki. We must always believe it is never too late."

"Too late for what?"

"For change."

* * *

Taro burst into his office, ignoring the waiting Kazuki. From the way Taro fidgeted, rubbed and sniffed his nose, Kazuki guessed that while taking a bathroom break, he'd also taken a little nasal refreshment again. The heir to the Shimura empire marched past him and flopped into the leather chair behind the desk like a child told to go to his room. Taro gazed through the floor-length windows at the glowing Tokyo afternoon. Kazuki always suspected Taro loved this backdrop to his activities. It suited Taro's ambitious views of himself, as a conjurer of commerce perched in this high tower, casting his spells over the city's enterprise. Kazuki sat with one leg on the black glass desktop in front of Taro, demanding his attention.

"You lied," said Kazuki.

Taro twitched a look up at the ceiling and changed the topic completely.

"Our father teaches us well, does he not Kazuki? He almost had me believing I was closer to running the entire corporation. I believed it! Believed he had proposed me to Watanabe in good faith, but Watanabe was having none of it. And now my father wins; he can use this incident today as an excuse to curtail my influence in the corporation, and at the same time use Watanabe's shameful outburst against him, to negotiate a better deal when Watanabe does return to make amends. Oh, he's lost none of his guile with age!"

"You lied," Kazuki repeated, calmly and insistently.

"Did I?"

"You said having Olsen out of the way would please Haruto."

"Oh, that's not what I said Kazuki. I said it would be in Haruto's *best interests* to have Olsen out of the way. How you interpreted that is your own problem." Taro's mouth gaped open, struck with some deep truth. "You *wanted* to please him, didn't you? That's why you agreed to do it."

"And you knew that, didn't you? You knew I'd do it."

"Oh Kazuki! You don't need to keep seeking Haruto's praise. He made you protector of the family, leader of the *yonkuichi* – his own personal guard – a position he wouldn't even trust me with. Surely that makes you his favourite?"

"That bothers you, doesn't it Taro? Yet you are the one he trusts to control his business empire."

Taro laughed. Kazuki didn't get the joke.

"What I control Kazuki is just a small fraction of the 'empire'. Shipping, Finance, Mining, Insurance, Chemicals, Electronics! He is just testing me, to see if I am worthy to inherit it all. And what do I have? The biotech arm of the corporation – the hardest in which to make a profit – the easiest to mess up, and the least financial damage to the whole corporation if I do. Now, tell me who he trusts."

"Right now, I don't think he trusts either of us, not after your stunt with Olsen."

"My stunt? Oh, you were the man on the ground Kazuki. Putting all those skills to use, and all the best technology Shimura Corp could muster to disguise it. And you still managed to foul up."

"I didn't foul up. Watanabe knows nothing. He's just nervous, collapsing the merger to protect Sumitoro's reputation, that's all. He knows Shimura has connections with Olsen going a long way back, but nothing more. There's no hard evidence linking it back to us, just as you requested."

"Isn't there?"

Kazuki gave his best poker face.

Taro elaborated: "then perhaps you'll explain to me why the CIA is investigating, why they have a man on the scene there?"

This time, Kazuki's eyes narrowed a little at his brother's revelation. Taro had means of his own – Kazuki knew that – so Taro's knowledge of CIA activities wasn't enough to surprise Kazuki.

"We even have a name, a pretty familiar one: Joshua Harker. Recognize it?"

Kazuki's stoicism shattered. His eyes widened and his jaw dropped on hearing the name.

NINE

CIA Headquarters, Washington DC
19th September – 8:49am

Harker completed his report on-board the red-eye flight back to Dulles airport. A CIA staff car waited to shuttle him to Langley. Someone sure was eager for the crime scene intel, he thought. Silberman? It still didn't fit. He dropped a copy on her desk. She summoned him back in ten minutes.

Josh stared into space while she smacked pages of his latest report. Harker noticed that alien odor of cigarette smoke again, stronger than before. Rita closed the report, with its tales of suspected embolisms and glass strain patterns, then scowled.

"This report tells me nothing," she said.

"It tells plenty. It just doesn't prove anything," Joshua replied.

"Murder." She heaved. "The report specifically mentions the possibility of murder. You should know by now the consequence of submitting something so tenuous."

"This isn't a court of law Rita. If there is reasonable suspicion, it should be reported," Harker insisted.

"Reasonable suspicion?" she scoffed, flapping to a page before reciting. "Concentrations of the chemicals thrombin and fibrinogen *slightly* above the normal levels present in the human body, *possibly* giving rise to the pulmonary embolism." She flicked another page. "A hair strand of unknown source, with anachronistic and unidentifiable DNA." She didn't even bother to locate the reference for the third: "and something about an unexplained cracked roof. Please! If I pass this, we'll both be a laughing stock in the NCS."

This report is under the Directorate of Intelligence. Why would she mention the Clandestine Service?

Josh found it hard to understand her indignation about this new report. Her rage, as ever, seemed driven by more than just the content.

"That FBI agent you brushed with – McAlister – he lodged a formal complaint through the office of the DNI, did you know that?"

Harker shook his head from side to side, slowly, defiantly. Was that it? Was Rita running scared because she looked bad to the intelligence mavens? No promotion for her this year.

"There's even talk from the General Counsel's Office about legal proceedings for interfering with a federal investigation."

Joshua listened, almost. He knew where this was going. Self-preservation is the first priority of a cornered animal, even a corporate animal like Silberman. Harker had gone into this blind, but his conscience was clear. Rita however, to protect herself from the wrath of CIA's seventh floor, would scapegoat him.

Josh was having none of it.

"You assigned me to this case Rita and I carried out my orders. Remember it was your order to remove crime scene evidence, and I followed it. If I find myself pursued by a disciplinary prosecution then in my defence I will be obliged to tell it from my point of view, and that won't reflect well on you, now will it?"

A dangerous remark, he knew, but it would provoke her. Josh didn't care, not today. Today, he felt like a fight.

"Are you *threatening* me Harker?"

"I'm simply giving you perspective Rita."

Rage festered in Silberman's eyes. Her entire body tensed like a panther before pouncing. She reached for a pen, about to scribble something inside the cover of his report. Another strike-out. Silberman's ever-present stamp of rejection was about to plunge.

Rita's phone rang.

Harker listened to the half conversation.

"Yes. I know, but –"

And it was over. Little room for protest; none for negotiation. She replaced the handset.

To his surprise, Rita put the pen down, closed the report and pushed it back over to him.

"You are to take this matter to the office of the DD/NCS immediately."

There was no emotion in her voice; all fight gone. The matter, it seemed, had been taken right out of her hands. Harker didn't know whether to feel relieved or worried, but just left the unsettling silence of Silberman's office and headed to a place he'd never been.

* * *

Leaving the pristine green glass block of the new building, Josh crossed the garden courtyard. He walked past staffers smoking and drinking coffee at plastic picnic tables by the Kryptos statue and entered the old headquarters building. It had a different vibe to the subdued campus atmosphere of his building. Here, in this concrete block pocked with narrow windows, the air seemed more musty, laden with tensions, in corridors where the Cold War had been held paralysed. Bounding up the stairwell, he passed floor signs translated into many languages. Josh climbed, until he could go no higher. Seventh floor. Executive Offices.

He passed through three checks, with guards stationed behind thick glass walls. At the third he collected his own escort who brought him to the secretary for the DD/NCS, who buzzed Josh through. Harker caught his breath before pushing open a heavy door, made heavier, he suspected, by the weight of conversations it held secret on a daily basis.

Harker knew about the role of the DD/NCS. The Deputy Director of the National Clandestine Service. The organiser behind all covert CIA black ops. It was a job unlike any other, not earned but entrusted. Few knew what the DD/NCS looked like. It was widely known he was a man, but his identity beyond that was a closely guarded secret, even within CIA itself. He was known only as Stanford. Such anonymity combined with his legendary espionage and counter-espionage duties had earned him the unofficial nickname "Standoff".

Now analyst Joshua Harker looked at him.

Stanford sat half invisible behind file stacks on the desk. Even seated, Harker could see he was tall. He stood to shake Joshua's hand. The shirt hanging limply from his hunched shoulders billowed across his thin torso from the force of his handshake.

"Stanford," he informed curtly. "You have a report for me Mr. Harker?"

Josh handed it over, adding another file to the burden of the DD/NCS, who gestured to take a seat.

Josh took in the surroundings while Stanford read the report. The oak panelled office was surprisingly small and subdued. It felt stale, its spirit worn out. Stanford rolled the pages with tar stained fingertips. The tobacco smoke memory of Silberman's office suddenly made sense. The pieces began to fit. Except ... Josh smelled no tobacco in this room. Surely a man brash enough to smoke in someone else's office would smoke in his own. Josh could see no ashtray either. In the trash can, next to the burn bag, no cigarette ends or empty packets. Another anomaly bothered him. Stanford wore suit pants, but no jacket. The only suit jacket hanging in the room, on a rack by the window, looked too short for a man of Stanford's height. It was an unreal situation for Harker – finding himself not only in the office of the DD/NCS, but also suspicious of him. Why would the DD/NCS, so protective of his identity, make himself known to a staffer like Josh, or Rita, anyway? Josh played along with Stanford's charade, for now.

The mystery man reached the last page and began flipping back through it.

"Is this report complete?" he asked.

"As well as I could, in the time."

Stanford looked over Harker with squinting eyes.

"So, what else have you got?"

Harker handed over the empty classified file he'd taken back from Olsen's briefcase.

"I think this belongs to the CIA," Josh said. "What was blue stripe material doing off-site? Isn't that a security breach?"

"Olsen was cleared for this compartmented information."

"Why?" Harker fished for more information, but failed.

"Before I answer that, I need more information from you Mr. Harker. This report is very informative, but not conclusive. It indicates the presence of an assassin, but says nothing about the assassin's possible identity or motive. Now, you're an intelligent man – you must have some suspicions about the murder, some ideas."

"Experience has taught me too much speculation in written intelligence reports is a bad thing."

Stanford broke into a smile.

"It can be damaging for careers," he agreed. "Wise, I'm sure, but what's discussed in this room stays in this room. Strictly off the record."

"I understand, but before I do that, I need more from you."

"Such as?"

"Assurance – that you are who you say."

Stanford reclined back. "Like it says on the door: The Deputy Director of the National Clandestine Service. Not a man to play games with. Now for the last time, who do you suspect of murdering Senator Olsen?"

Oh, what the hell!

Josh threw caution to the wind, and his career with it.

"I think the Shimura Corporation of Japan might be behind it." Josh delivered the blow. "You'll want to know why, of course, but it could be a long conversation. Why don't you light up? I won't mind."

The face of the ersatz DD/NCS froze. Josh saw unexpected questions going through the mind of the man claiming to be Stanford, who seemed unsure how to answer any of them.

A small laughing voice came from behind a stack of files on the desk. The speakerphone had been left on.

"It's okay Mike," the chuckling voice said through a tinny speaker. "We've been rumbled. I'm on my way."

The phone clicked off.

The two men continued a facial stand-off until the phone voice arrived. In the silence before that arrival, Harker could not resist a jibe at the impostor.

"What's discussed in this room stays in this room?"

It was met with a mischievous smile, the last expression before the thin man stood up to leave. The true Stanford walked in through a door to an adjoining office that was concealed behind a wooden panel. He held his hand out to Josh before taking up his rightful place in the vacated chair.

"Sorry about the deception Mr. Harker, you can take it from me I am the real DD/NCS. That man is Mike Kressler, my assistant. I hope you understand, but I rarely meet new people lower down in the organization, but when I do I prefer to deputize."

"To safeguard your identity," Josh continued for him.

"Yes, that's exactly right."

Harker was not so sure. The clues left in this office were an unlikely oversight. Josh had been tested.

"Please, sit," said the real Stanford. "You are an astute man; I can see I was correct to send you to Ohio."

"You sent me?" As soon as Josh asked it, he regretted such a stupid and obvious question.

Stanford picked up the empty blue-stripe folder left on his desk.

"There was nothing in it?" he asked Josh, who shook his head. "Then your assassin must have taken it," Stanford said.

"What is Project GENAFORM?" Josh asked boldly.

"Truthfully, I don't know, and now we might never know."

Stanford sighed, weighed down – Josh supposed – by the burdens of office. He walked over to the window and looked out over the trees to the Potomac river beyond. A flock of mallards scudded by. Stanford asked, with his back to Harker: "Tell me, why do you say the Shimura Corporation is behind Mark's death?"

Josh explained his theory that Olsen, in his last moments, used the pills to signal the connection to his murderer.

"They should've just spiked his pills if they wanted him dead," Stanford proposed.

Another test.

Josh shook his head. "No. Any link back to the perpetrator was avoided. Tainted pills would only have left traceable evidence. Besides, they would take time to prepare, ship, and have an effect. I suppose, the assassination might have been a last minute necessity."

"It's a tenuous proposition at best," said Stanford's back.

Josh felt his stomach churn. If Stanford shared Rita's hatred of speculation, then he could hand in his card right now.

Rita! Josh remembered the evidence she wanted sequestered. If all this was at Stanford's request, then he must know about the evidence. A chance for exoneration!

Josh made his case. "Don't forget, there is one piece of evidence: the assassin left DNA at the scene. There are anomalies in the DNA; it seems to have been altered. In-vivo alteration of a living person's DNA is very tricky stuff and there aren't many outfits that can manage it successfully."

"And you think Shimura Corporation can?"

"I know they can. They are known to be the best."

"Hmm. You did a good job on this ..." Stanford fingered open the cover of a file on the desk looking for a name, "... Joshua. Thank you."

Josh was speechless, unaccustomed to gratitude for his work.

"You are a capable man, I can see. To uncover all that you have on your own initiative is quite impressive. Most of what you say was already known to me of course, but that came from the efforts of resources I have at my disposal. Yet you deduced all this on your own, and in such a short space of time too. I can see that I was right about you."

"Right about me?" Harker shifted in his seat. "Was this investigation some kind of test too?"

"Another astute observation. While I did need my suspicions confirmed about Mark's death, and something to present to Director Panetta, there was more. I don't just pick unknowns out of the analysis pool for critical ops without some kind of verification of their abilities and character, and now, after your performance on the investigation, I'm satisfied you can handle it."

"Handle it? Operation? What operation?" Josh pushed questions out through a tightening throat.

"We identified you from a sweep through the 201s."

The CIA's personnel files. Stanford chose me. But why?

As if reading Harker's mind, Stanford answered. "I didn't just choose you because of your qualifications and investigative experience, but also because of your contacts."

Stanford delved into another file and presented from it a sheet of paper.

Harker stopped his jaw from dropping when he saw the crude scanned photo on it.

Oh hell!

Josh checked to ensure he didn't say that aloud. As he continued to digest the indigestible, the name below the photo confirmed this woman from the depths of Joshua's past, from a time long forgotten, eclipsed from memory by the previously impenetrable barrier of Megan's death. That barrier now shattered.

This was Tokiko Nakamura, now Shimura, wife to the President and CEO of the Shimura Corporation.

Josh looked up, his face like a drowning man searching for a life preserver. Only Stanford stood on the shore, intensely studying the reaction of a sinking soul.

"Perhaps I should explain," said Stanford.

"Yes. I think you should."

TEN

Gotanda, Tokyo
18th September – 10:43pm

In the darkening hours, a *yukata*-enrobed Tokiko Shimura drifted like a spirit through the Shimura home. Pools of lantern light beat back moon-cast shadows from vaulted pillars hewn of single tree-trunks. It made for an eerie house, she'd always felt, as if it were alive, enveloping her. The feeling was more intense this night; she had an inkling she was not walking alone. Shadows shifted like oil slicks behind her. When she looked back, all was still. Was that a wisp of moving air across the nape of her neck? Or was it her own unease? This was her home. Why, she wondered, had she never felt at home in it?

Pull yourself together Tokiko.

As she turned toward the bedrooms, Kazuki's intense gaze startled her. He stood sentry, still and solid, like one of the maple pillars. He always guarded the house wearing that sharp suit, those pristine shoes, and a *katana* draped over his shoulder. A captive tension shone out from vibrant eyes below his blonde fringe – Tokiko never saw such intensity in one so young. She was never sure whether it hinted at maturity of hidden years beyond his own, or whether Kazuki simply liked to appear intimidating as some sort of defense against the world.

Tokiko held a hand to her chest and breathed relief.

"You startled me Kazuki. I thought you were still away."

He bowed gently, then gave a reassuring smile.

"My apologies."

"No." Tokiko said, bowing in return. "The apologies are mine to give. It is to your credit that you perform your duty so well."

Kazuki looked a little perplexed.

Tokiko giggled to see that stern face puzzled like a child. To her, Kazuki seemed neither boy nor man, but trapped somewhere in-between.

Tokiko took his confusion away.

"Our family is indeed well protected from intruders," she said, "if the family itself can not detect the presence of our own sentry guards until we are almost upon them."

Kazuki understood and smiled again.

"Thank you. You are kind as always, but perhaps I am not so good at my duties if I frighten those I am sworn to protect?"

"Kazuki!" she said in shocked pity. "You don't frighten me."

She reached out to touch his arm in that moment, but thought better of rupturing his decorum and breaching etiquette. To her surprise, he reached out to meet her grasp first, but it was too late – she was hesitating already and Kazuki, in turn, retracted. From behind the barrier in Kazuki's eyes, Tokiko sensed his regret of a lost touch.

It was true – he didn't frighten her. There were many in Haruto's personal *yonkuichi* militia who regarded Kazuki with fear, if not respect. All of them were above Kazuki in age, but below him in rank. Their loyalty to Kazuki was not given by his status as Haruto's adopted son either, but by the youth's passion for the code of the samurai, and his hard-learned martial skills. It must have been hard for him as a foreigner, a *gaijin*, Tokiko always felt, to have earned that respect, and more – the solidarity – of those people.

Yet Tokiko knew he would never be one of them, always an outsider. His Caucasian looks must be a harsh reminder for Kazuki every time he looked in a mirror. She wondered: did he really feel Japanese, on the inside? Tokiko saw a different Kazuki. She saw the vestiges of vulnerability he could not hide and felt an affinity no one else could share with the young man.

When she joined the Shimura family – years after the death of Haruto's first wife – Kazuki was just three years old. As a stepmother, she never really bonded with Haruto's natural son Taro, but with Kazuki it was different. Two outsiders, latecomers to the Shimura dynasty. Tokiko was as happy to extend motherly affections to the little boy as he was happy to receive them. It seemed Kazuki had never experienced this new and wondrous thing called affection before. As much as Haruto instilled the stoicism of duty in Kazuki, so Tokiko tried to instil its balancing principle of compassion.

To break the awkward moment, simply, Tokiko said, "It's good to have you back Kazuki."

He bowed, precisely, and went surveilling the halls.

Tokiko sighed inside for Kazuki. He had no real childhood, as other Japanese did. Early in life, he had buried himself in studies of Japanese life and conduct to fit in and please his father. His schooling had been private. As a boy, he was self-reliant and would disappear for a stretch of days, never explaining where he had been or why. Kazuki would always be that self-appointed pariah.

Tokiko found the fire in the bedroom already blazing, lit by an attendant. Haruto could afford many, but they kept out of sight, for ostentation is not the Japanese way. It was quite enough for her husband to be able to afford servants, but indiscreet to show it.

She sat hugging her knees on the floor, up close to the flames. Her head lolled to one side, chin resting on forearm. The soft fluid warmth of the fire lapping at her bare forearms was comforting in this bedroom with angular decor. Pale blue moonlight spilt like silken milk onto her shoulders. The shadow lines cast by the frames of the *shoji* screens encaged her. Vacant eyes stared past the flames.

Her husband, fresh from his bedtime *onsen* bath, beat an imposing patter into the room. He thumped the cushions before slipping into bed, like he always did when things hadn't gone his way. These were the betraying indicators Tokiko had learned over the years; she'd had to. Haruto was from a generation that grew up just after the war, a group of Japanese men for whom discussing matters of business with women in general, and wives in particular, was unknown. For him, affairs of the heart are private. Even Tokiko struggled to gain trust from her husband on some days – days with family troubles. It could only have been Taro, she knew. Whatever he had done this day, Taro was always the source of Haruto's frustrations lately. She often wondered why he'd adopted Kazuki; was it to replace the son that so disappointed his father? But she'd thought better of that. Taro must feel Kazuki's presence threatening to his own position. Surely Haruto would have known that Taro would respond that way, when he adopted the young *gaijin*. It was with that thought, long ago, that Tokiko began to discover her husband's true nature. He did know Taro would feel challenged. Haruto did it to give a little healthy competition, to shake Taro's complacency, and up the ante for a complacent son who had grown up never knowing the harsh life that Haruto grew up in. Even at that, Haruto loved the public line that he'd adopted an orphan (as Haruto had been an orphan) to give something back to the world. Haruto, she knew, liked appearances and reality to be kept separate.

Tokiko spoke as her husband arranged the cushions.

"Kazuki's back," she said.

"Yes."

"He's been away for a while."

"Mmm."

Monosyllabic. Tokiko noticed Haruto never liked much to talk about his adopted son's doings, but she sensed something had changed between Haruto and Kazuki. Tokiko used her intuition one more time; she would at least make the pretence of being an attentive wife.

"Do you fear him?" she asked.

The sound of rearranging stopped.

"Who? Kazuki?"

"That's who I mean, yes. Do you fear what he has become – what the years of training made him?"

Haruto reached to turn off the lamp beside the futon.

"No. I fear what is becoming of my own son."

Tokiko was taken aback by Haruto's rare candour.

Another silence came, filled by lapping flames and katydid songs leaking in from the balcony.

"You're tired husband. You need sleep."

Haruto slipped in below the silk sheet, clicked off his lamp, and settled down. Even with her long back to him, Tokiko knew his eyes were closed already. She knew the nuances, unseen.

The fire cast long gruesome shadows on the wall, tousling over her husband.

"Come to bed," he muttered.

"In a while."

Tokiko took the signs for what they were. Haruto was beyond any healing effect of her words tonight, so amorous acts were substitute. It was a pattern they had fallen into. She would be expected to salve his woes, but without any of the reciprocal love of their first sexual encounters. She saw clearly now: to Haruto it was just a wife's duty. It was one of his more sordid traits that youthful naivety, or blind infatuation, had concealed from her until too late in their marriage. Tokiko learned the hard way: there is no bed so lonely as one shared with a familiar stranger.

She would wait until he was asleep, until any of his physical intentions were safely locked away with him in slumber. With the passing years, much to her own disgust and regret, she had become more and more repulsed by the thought of his cold hands snaking down to the base of her spine, clasping her closer to his lustful hips.

She loaded up the fire with a log and sighed, deeply. Forlorn, but for the friendship of some fickle flames.

To the world, Tokiko was the new model Japanese woman – beautiful, intelligent, a successful career, independent. Her private life, unseen by the world, was both boring and austere, where she was caught playing the role of dutiful Japanese wife for Haruto, a man of a tradition. A man who would manifest neither true love nor offspring to her. He'd adopted a sparring partner for Taro, but wouldn't even give her a child of their own. What manner of deceit had persuaded her to marry him? Had Haruto deceived her, she wondered, or was it worse than that, the most tragic deceit of all – self-deception? What drunken euphoric love-struck possibility had persuaded her he was not as he was?

She stopped herself. It was no use. This worn-down road always led the same place, a place where sadness waited, not solutions. She let it go again. It had been a terrible mistake; that was all.

ELEVEN

CIA Headquarters, Washington DC
19th September – 11:17am

Harker's eyes remained transfixed on the blocky scanned image of Tokiko while Stanford made for the coffee machine. He poured for himself then handed one to Josh. With a vacant look, Harker sipped caffeine comfort.

"You do know her, don't you?" asked Stanford. "Your 201 says you were in the same PhD program while on a student transfer year at Tokyo University."

Josh sipped. "Yes, I knew her."

"And she would know you if she saw you again?"

"For sure."

"Then you are the man for the job. Let's start with the file you recovered. I don't know what Project GENAFORM is, but Senator Olsen did. You see, the file was off-site because Mark was the author of the material."

It suddenly became clear to Harker. "Olsen was a CIA asset? I wouldn't have guessed."

"Good – we try to keep such things secret! But it seems we might have failed this time." Regret laced Stanford's words. He carried on, as if to justify: "the lifeblood of this trade is information. We take it from any source we can. Mark was our only reliable source of information about the Shimura Corporation. He had unique access to it at the highest level, and we had no choice but to approach him."

Stanford took his coffee to the window and looked out again. Harker got the feeling the DD/NCS would rather be out there.

"Mark's business interests almost outweighed his political ones. He was chairman of Genesys Technologies a while back – and still had a shareholding when he died. Have you heard of them?" asked Stanford.

"Of course. It's American – our closest competitor to Shimura Biotech. Was it commercial advantage, instead of patriotism, that made Olsen a willing spy for you?"

"Mark was more than a CIA asset," Stanford barked. "He was a good personal friend. His loyalty to his country was beyond reproach."

"Sorry." Josh demurred, sensing he'd touched a nerve.

Stanford let loose a sigh. He sat back down and spoke to Harker face-to-face. His voice lowered to more than a whisper.

"Mark had become very altruistic in his latter years, perhaps even idealistic – a far cry from any commercial greed he might have started out with. Back in better economic times, he fostered cooperation between American and Japanese companies. Both sides knew it was just a way to gain commercial advantage over the other. Mark played it. He used the opportunity to tap into the biotech experience of the Japanese – and more – to report back to us about any plans for Japanese economic aggression, or attempts at corporate infiltrations by the Japanese."

"Shimura must have known, surely."

"Of course! But it was never discussed. It's the game we all play. They worked with Mark to get information out of him too – whatever barium meal we chose to feed them. Disinformation. We slipped in the occasional truth, to copper-fasten Olsen's rep as a source of quality counter-intelligence for them. So long as they got something from him, they would be less likely to seek out other sources of commercial intelligence beyond our knowledge or control ... we determined what intel the Japs would get. Mark came to us, and became an excellent asset. The links he forged with Haruto Shimura from those early days turned into a friendship, and those links remained strong, at least, until he died. He had a way about him; he could amicably tease and feed information with Haruto, without causing any offense in their friendship."

Stanford pointed to the report he just read.

"Those pills you found – they show how intricately linked Olsen's life had become with Shimura's, and how technologically superior Shimura's Biotech division is – Shimura could provide DNA tailored medication to prolong Olsen's life, where Mark's own company couldn't."

"If they became such good friends, how could you trust Mark? I mean, you used him to feed false information – they could've been doing the same thing all along."

Stanford leaned back in his chair.

"It's not good CIA policy to 'trust'. All information is taken with suspicion, until verified, and even then we suspect it. But information, even misleading information, can tell a lot.

"Oh, there were those in Washington who were always suspicious of Olsen, perhaps because of that very dominance that Shimura always managed to maintain. Genesys cooperated on projects with Shimura Biotech. Some of those projects were funded by DARPA – military bioagent research programs. Well, when it came out that DARPA funds had been siphoned out of the American economy and into a Japanese company, Mark's reputation took a severe beating back on Capitol Hill, which I don't think it ever fully recovered from. But Mark was always willing to sacrifice anything – even his reputation – for the things he felt were right. Somehow, I always knew he had our best interests at heart, whatever the circumstances.

"He did change though. I felt he'd changed after that time, when he'd been snubbed for wasting DARPA funds. Something happened. His idealism exploded. It seemed to drive him to monitor Shimura Biotech even more closely. He even accepted a chair on the International Bioethics committee, which raised more than a few eyebrows around here. In the end, Mark might even have died for his ideals. But I'd like to think, if he had to die, it was at least to protect his country. Yes – I did trust him."

Stanford's sorrow was palpable.

"The point is this: Mark last hinted that he was onto something big, and I never found out what. That's the information he was assembling. If it was important enough to kill for, then it's something we need to know about, but with Mark gone his sources are closed to me."

"So you want me to open new sources for you in Japan, through Tokiko?"

"Yes, but only if you were the right man to do it. That's why I tested you, to see if you were capable enough. I'm convinced. So, with everything you know so far, everything not in the report, speculate for me."

This was it at last, Joshua thought. This was his moment to move beyond the constraints that working for Rita Silberman had placed upon him.

"The DNA was altered," Josh began, "to prevent us tracing the killer."

"Is that feasible?" Stanford asked.

"In theory, at least. The technique for in-vivo gene therapies has been used for decades. However, the knowledge of human proteomics necessary to make wide scale changes without affecting the developmental biology of the subject, without killing him – well, there are very few who could do it. I daresay Shimura Biotech is one. Heck, even my own researches last year indicated how they are amassing that kind of knowledge."

"Research? I don't remember anything about that on the BIU dailies. Did you file a report?" asked Stanford.

Josh fidgeted. "I submitted one, yes, but it was rejected and never archived; you wouldn't have been aware of it."

"Hmm." Stanford nodded absently. He curled his lip and scribbled some note on the back of a nearby page. "You certainly seem to know your field Mr. Harker. Yet your career seems to have been a little ... erratic."

"I couldn't pursue medicine, so I moved to forensics – it's no great secret. You've read the file."

Stanford nodded while continuing the analyst's bio: "and then moved to homicide, and then after leaving the force ... after your wife's death ... you decided to join the CIA."

Harker's throat tightened; he didn't reply.

"How are you liking work down there, in the DI?" Stanford asked.

"It's okay," Josh said vaguely.

"But?"

Harker delayed as long as he dared before admitting. "Well, my supervisor doesn't share your interest in my speculations."

Stanford nodded, still scribbling absently.

"Then perhaps this assignment is what you need too. We need you, Harker. Tokyo station has monitored that corporation for a decade and learned squat. It's surrounded by a protective shell. Haruto Shimura has his own private militia and perhaps even his own counter-intelligence resources – it's closed up tighter than a drum. Olsen was our only means of getting information out, and even he was finding it harder and harder to do lately. There's a new element."

"Which is?"

"Taro Shimura. Haruto's only son and heir to his corporation – the anointed one, you might say. He's immune from the persuasions of his father's friend. He always kept Olsen at arms length on his trips to Japan. Mark heard many rumors though, and suspected that new generation to be, in some ways, more ruthless than his father's. But now ... we don't have access to that second hand information anymore. We need your contact. "

That sinking feeling hit Josh's stomach again, sensing what was coming.

"That's why, after Olsen's death, I instigated the sweep for anyone who could open new links to Shimura Corp. Your name popped up top. We need your link to Shimura's wife. We need you to use her as a contact asset to infiltrate her husband's corporation. Confirm Shimura was behind Olsen's death, and – more importantly – discover why. What was it Olsen was on to?"

Harker scoffed. He was to be the 'raven' – to allure and seduce a female contact to gather illicit secrets.

"Unless ... is there any problem I should know of between you and Tokiko?" Stanford asked.

"You'd need to ask her. We didn't keep in contact. It was all a long time ago, and well, we lost touch. I didn't know she married so well ... I don't know what kind of welcome she'll give me now.'

"You are an employee of American Intelligence, and if you hope to succeed as one, you'll overcome whatever difficulties are required to protect our national interests."

"I work for the DI – I'm an analyst." Harker thumped his own chest with his fingers. "I'm not trained for this."

"Well, consider yourself transferred. I'll make arrangements for a quiet departure to the Clandestine Service immediately. They'll need to get you started on NOC training and build a legend ..."

Stanford stopped himself, and looked at his new charge.

"You're the most useful asset who can be deployed fastest into the field. Sure: you've got the contact we need, you've got the knowledge of the culture and the territory, and some technical stuff that I'm pretty sure no one else here would understand. But more than that, you've proven you have the curiosity and drive to push through and find the answers, no matter what the difficulties, no matter what anyone else thinks.

"On paper you had all the necessary skills, but I still needed proof you could handle it alone, and in Ohio, you've proved that. Okay, analysts and operatives have very different characteristics. Field work needs people skills more than analytical skills, but hey, the big secret is that field operatives are always learning, always have to improvise. I've been supervising asset recruitment for years, and for what it's worth, I know you've got what it takes. Look, bottom line – there's no way we send anyone out if they don't want to go. An unwilling person like that is no use to us. So, it's your call. But I need to know now if you're in, or out."

Joshua had received basic CAP training, but nothing had prepared him for NOC operations – non-official cover. NOC operatives were unlike the CIA officers who worked under the protection of State or Defense Department cover. NOC agents worked alone; if ever they were rumbled, CIA denied knowledge of their existence, and left them to the wolves. The dilemma played around in Harker's mind until, under his own counsel, he stated what filtered up.

"If all this speculation is true," Joshua said, "then Senator Olsen died getting the same information that you want me to chase."

"Yes." Stanford said sternly. "You need to accept it could cost your life too. Once you go in, you'll need to rely on your own resources; your training will have to be unusually brief and tough. If you do this, I need to know you are committed to it. Otherwise ... walk away now."

Stanford didn't paint a pretty picture, nor should he, and yet Harker thought: here it was – the brass ring.

He was never sure why he chose that way, that day. Was it mere selfishness, to ensure his life would burn with a purpose, rather than smolder away behind a desk under the watchful cosh of Rita Silberman? He was unsure why, didn't care why, but was sure of the decision.

"I'll do it," Josh heard himself say.

Stanford lifted the green handset of the internal line and stabbed five digits.

"Mike can you make arrangements for Joshua Harker please. Get him started ASAP."

Some unheard words came from the other end of the phone. When Stanford dropped the receiver he said, "go down to conference room 2 on the fourth floor and you'll begin briefing immediately. He'll have someone clear out your old desk and bring your belongings."

Josh was a little disappointed that he wouldn't get to see the look on Silberman's face.

"Will you tell my old boss?"

"No. Need-to-know basis only."

Perhaps the mystery of his departure would have to be sweet enough. Josh made to leave.

"Good Luck Josh," Stanford said.

Ex-analyst Harker tried to flick a smile before leaving, but knew it came out all wrong.

* * *

A wood panel creaked open into Stanford's office; his assistant crept in from the adjoining room.

"You were right then – he took the assignment," said Mike Kressler.

"Yes – I thought he would."

"How were you so sure?"

Kressler loomed over him with hunched shoulders like a big question mark.

"Instinct."

Before Mike could press it further, Stanford thrust out a piece of paper with notes scribbled on it.

"That report," he said, pointing to the handwriting. "I want you to find it and bring it to me. It won't be in the central registry because it never made review, so you'll have to hunt out soft copy."

"Is it important?"

Stanford dared not tell Kressler how important it could be, not yet.

"Locate it yourself Mike, don't get anyone else involved ... and keep it dark for now."

Kressler smirked. "What around here isn't?" He left on his covert errand.

Mike was a good guy. Stanford was grooming him to be a worthy replacement DD/NCS when he retired, but as for trusting him – that was a different matter. This job was a lone station. Secrets needed protecting. The greatest secret – the one he dared not reveal to his closest assistant – was the one Olsen had told him. The Shimura Corporation had recruited a mole within the CIA. He had told Stanford before leaving on that last fateful trip to Japan. Perhaps he had discovered the mole's identity too.

Was that why they had him killed?

Stanford stood and took point at the narrow window again. All was silent except for the slight hum of the vibration devices attached to the window panes, protecting him from any laser eavesdropping device outside the perimeter fence. The counter-measures technicians had checked them just this week, but to sense for himself the low random shifting hum was comforting.

A mole.

He was willing to believe Olsen's assertion about a mole. It might explain the famine of intel about Shimura from any source other than Olsen. That was why Stanford started mining the 201 files for any likely staffer with links back to the Shimura Corporation. It pointed right to Joshua Harker.

A corporation recruiting moles in the CIA was a worrying indicator. It was more than just counter industrial espionage, more than just a corporation protecting itself. Stanford didn't like the scale of ambition it hinted at. The arrogance of it. That alone made Olsen's work worth continuing. It had always been a problem getting reliable intel out of Japan. They close ranks, stay one step ahead. From the early days of the Japanese occupation under the OSS, through to the exposed

NOC debacle of the eighties, CIA success in Japan had been less than impressive.

They desperately needed new assets on the ground, just as much as they needed to rout out the mole.

Joshua Harker.

A loner, unhappy in his work, disgruntled with his superiors – the classic profile of a traitor. The CIA recruitment evaluators had dismissed the possible psychological disturbances in Harker since the incidents surrounding his wife's murder.

Harker.

A man with a dogged and strange fascination with the Shimura Corporation. A man who once had a close personal liaison with the wife of the corporation's CEO. Harker had suspicions about why Shimura Corp was behind Olsen's death, but never put them on paper, only voicing them off-the-record, when Stanford pressed him. Was he protecting them? Harker jumped at the chance to go to Japan. Was he jumping ship, back to his masters, before he was exposed as a mole and tried for treason?

There were other possible moles, of course. The unhappy nature of this game was that Stanford couldn't even share all this with Kressler, in case he was it.

Right now, Stanford didn't have enough information.

The world was changing. Terrorism a diminishing threat. They'd pursued it for so long, they'd taken their eye off the ball. The real threats had been ignored and worked away unchallenged. New ones emerged. An eternal game of whack-a-mole. While America had dissipated itself in the middle-east, attending to the scattered forces of terrorism, expending its own resources, finances, and personnel in the pursuit of a nebulous foe, Stanford believed they overlooked the older, more organized and better-funded threats that used the distraction to build in silence.

China. Korea. Japan – the old enemy, once trampled underfoot. The brooding Asian Tiger was rising from its slumber. The age of the pacific, as they called it, was coming. The east would do all it could to ensure its might, and one mole was no shock in that great scheme of things.

It was a necessary risk, sending an untried and possibly treacherous analyst out into the field. Sure, it might alert the Japanese too that they were under suspicion for Olsen's death, but he didn't care if they knew. Sometimes when you're working blind, Stanford knew that a little prod was necessary to see what lay in your path. It could be dangerous to prod a sleeping tiger though. If Harker was trustworthy after all, then it meant a mole still existed elsewhere in the organization. A mole that might know Harker had been sent out. They could be ready and waiting for him when he arrives.

I hope I haven't sent another worthy asset to his death.

Stanford felt the solitary weight of office.

Recruit. Infiltrate. Expose. Three purposes in sending Harker to Japan. It was the only way to perform this job successfully – never let an action have just one purpose, when it could have three.

Stanford exhaled deeply, cleared his mind of suspicions, possibilities, and strategies. He looked over the river, to the horizon. Somewhere on the other side of the planet, one middle-aged CIA agent, naïve or treacherous, would be making choices that would determine the outcome of all this.

All the pieces were now in their starting positions.

The game begins.

The DD/NCS spent a quiet moment watching the autumn morning sun ignite amber treetops along the banks of the Potomac.

TWELVE

Narita Airport, Tokyo
14th October – 7:21pm

The banking plane festooned the blackness beyond Harker's window with the warm lights of Narita airport. Highways and bullet trains sliced out to the horizon like blades of light, merging with the glare of Tokyo. In the distance, the lattice of glowing streets gave way to the occasional black empty space of a park or a shrine. There was some room still for natural spaces in the city where nature was permitted only under the terms of its residents, in sympathy with the frenzied economies of Tokyo city life. One of those black oases on the horizon was called Koganei Park. Over fifteen years ago he had last seen its lavish triumphant pink and white display of cherry blossom in full bloom; nature asserting its hold on the city. He shared it with a demure young Tokiko.

The plane made a long, slow swirl of an approach. Disoriented, Josh's thoughts spun with the runway lights below. It felt oddly like coming home.

Happy, carefree times, Josh mused. Any troubles he might have had in those days vanished now under the shadow of his life since. His purpose now was darker and the days ahead uncertain. He was falling out of the sky, baseless, suspended in time between past and future, and in space between east and west – the lands of promise and of strife.

Get a grip man.

Maybe it was just fatigue. The past weeks had been exhausting, his life thrown into turmoil since his meeting with Stanford. They were filled with dizzying hops from Langley, to the CIA's training camp – The Farm – and to Fort Bragg, and back. Each trip an intense bout of training, a condensing of normal NOC agent training. No wonder his head – and his heart – spun.

The training wasn't all physical; there had been theory of surveillance and infiltration, covert research tactics, combat and self-defence refresher courses, and his Japanese too had taken some refreshing. Cover was needed. They built a light legend around him. He would keep his own name and history, up to a point. First he was sheep-dipped; a term (which Josh found a little degrading) used to describe the process of erasing partial traces of his own identity. In fact, only his time in CIA needed to be covered. Josh would still maintain his name and his history up until his exit from Kansas PD. From then on his records would show that he returned to a career in research, and recently writing freelance for the scientific journal New Genetics. A backstop was provided in the offices of New Genetics so, if anyone rang to check, a voice would confirm Harker was contracted there.

It would work on many levels. Tokiko would not suspect, and as a journalist he would have excuse to seek interviews in the corporation. CIA Clandestine Service knew from bitter experience that using his own identity as much as safely possible decreased the chances of getting caught out by a simple slip of the tongue along the way – lies are easiest to keep when hidden in truth.

The suggestion to use journalistic cover had surprised Josh; it made a mockery of the CIA's publicly stated policy of not using that profession for cover. Journalists feared it would make them targets. Expediency laid waste to many of their policies.

And now, here he was: a new man, reinvented for surreption, stepping off a plane and into the future, but carrying old baggage. He wondered what Tokiko would make of him now, and what she would think of his life, or his pretence of one. Would she consider it, he wondered, worth his going back home for, to America, fifteen years ago?

Harker went through the rituals of travel, flashing his passport, collected his bag, and politely shaking his head when offered tourist information.

Long forgotten sights, sounds, and smells presented themselves. The alien incantations of the Japanese language bubbled in the air around him, from the PA system in the airport to the bullet train into Tokyo. It took him time to shuffle the words into meaning in his mind. When he spoke it, he had to consciously re-order his own thoughts to match Japanese grammar and etiquette. All personal pronouns had to be removed, or he risked offending. Such efforts reinforced his outsider status. That feeling of alienation grew as the distance to Tokyo shrunk.

The light zipping past the spearing train intensified. The task ahead entered his mind: to infiltrate the sixth largest corporation in this foreign land, identify a skilled assassin, and determine a motive. Weeks of training felt barely adequate now. Doubt gnawed his confidence. The Shimura Corporation was an intimidating nut to crack, for sure, but – he told himself – it was also inspiration, proof of what one man could achieve.

In preparation for the op, Josh had studied many files. He started with Haruto Shimura, eager to know what kind of man finally took

Tokiko's hand in marriage, and what kind of family she had joined. Shimura's file gave a tantalizing but patchy picture of the visionary behind the Shimura empire.

On paper, Haruto Shimura's early years could not have foretold the kind of position he was to take in Japanese society. Haruto grew up in the poor Sanya slum of Tokyo, orphaned at an early age, and adopted into Japan's mafia – *Yakuza* – in order to survive. For less capable young *yakuza* recruits, that would have been the beginning of the end of their story; their criminal career path usually led to death in gang clashes, but Haruto Shimura was different from the start. Reports of his early years stated he was clever, cunning, ambitious, and quickly climbed the ranks. The sordid details of how he achieved this were not listed in his CIA file, but Harker knew a ruthless nature was needed to advance within the *yakuza*. The true foundation of Shimura's character was built in those shrouded days guarding the sex parlors, running the gambling dens, and dishing out discipline down darkened alleys.

In time, Haruto's talent in corporate racketeering was recognized. He extorted blackmail ransoms from large companies, then moved into the *keizei yakuza* – the financial arm whose international political and commercial dealings were on a scale that far outstripped the kind of petty crimes on which Shimura had cut his criminal teeth. Such was Haruto's affinity for commerce, that he began to amass his own little business, starting with the purchase of a bankrupt chemical factory that initially fronted amphetamine production for the *yakuza*.

Ultimately, a new breed of younger *yakuza*, more vicious and ruthless, less honorable, challenged Haruto's ownership of certain assets. During a battle to resolve the ownership ambiguity, his wife was killed. It broke the cardinal unwritten *yakuza* code that gang members' families were never to be violated in any way, and it began a vicious open gang war that ultimately ended with the expulsion of Haruto Shimura from the *yakuza* entirely.

Cynical commentators claimed that Haruto had engineered his own expulsion, happy to be done with *yakuza* ways. Ostensibly free from *yakuza* entanglements and constraints, Haruto could focus on his own companies; his asset value began to swell. He invested in more acquisitions, trading criminality for legitimate business practices. It was a journey supported by those in Japan's corporate world who were in awe of Haruto's acumen, glad of his separation from the criminal underworld, but nonetheless happy to utilize Haruto's unique knowledge of that world. Dealing with *Yakuza* is just another cost of doing business in Japan.

Even more cynical commentators were doubtful. They believed it was a move to make Haruto more legitimate, a way of distancing himself from that "Black Mist" – the dirty world of corruption. Brave commentators in the newsweeklies would say the criminal paths leading to Haruto's success could not easily be closed off. They would say no one really leaves the *Yakuza*. They are unavoidable. But proof of the corporation's continuing links to criminal organizations was never offered, and remained a rumor until that very day that Josh travelled into the heart of the Shimura empire.

Harker traded train for taxi at Tokyo's Grand Central Station. The final part of his journey to the hotel brought him through those same streets in which Haruto Shimura was made. Most buildings were shorter than in the cities of America. The Japanese preferred low rise and urban sprawl in deference to the risk of earthquake. Sometimes, turning a corner, a more modern skyscraper would appear to erupt from the ground – a testament to Japan's modern quake-proof construction abilities, in defiance of nature's threats.

Harker craned his head up, looking beyond the mesmerizing array of neon lights adorning the street level façades, and further up to the pinnacle of one high-rise, decorated with a lonely pulsing air traffic beacon. It was the kind of building that Shimura now owned.

Josh recalled the CIA accounts of the days when his old flame Tokiko joined the Shimura Corporation, most of it sourced from many society magazine spreads.

Tokiko had joined Shimura Pharmaceutical straight from university as a valued acquisition, intelligent and bright. Within three years she was to become an even greater acquisition, married to the chairman of the board. She must have impressed many in the organization, rising quickly to lead commercial drug development. It made Josh smile to think of all the raised grey eyebrows among the male scientists who had been steadily doing the research, hunched behind racks of test tubes, hoping that if they could not climb the corporate ladder, it would gradually lower to meet them. But Tokiko must have met the challenge with that charming, seemingly playful indifference that carried her effortlessly through life, making light of her unintentional snub to any male dominance in the workplace.

Good for you, Tokiko!

It was during a presentation to the board that she first met him. Harker pictured her falling for Shimura's raw power, his dominant, commanding presence in those meetings, where he would ask nothing of her, but let the other board members compete to impress him by asking the most intelligent questions of her. She must have batted back each question designed to entrap her with agility and competency, and each time, causing Haruto Shimura to smile.

A dinner invitation would begin it, and a marriage invitation complete it. Another acquisition for Haruto Shimura.

As Harker looked upon the skyscrapers he wondered how easy it would be to get near such a powerful man, or his wife. *Yakuza* entanglements aside, a person with his history and present day interests would be protected and hard to reach. Josh had tried to contact Tokiko in the days before his departure, telling her he was due in Tokyo, claiming to want an interview with Haruto for an article on the driving visionary of the biotech industry. The invitation was met with ominous silence. Did the shroud surrounding her husband stifle Tokiko too? Or was it Tokiko herself who shrugged contact? It added to his fears about how Tokiko might receive him after all these years.

Realistically, Harker expected to settle for one of Shimura's appointed minions. Perhaps his first task the next day would be to force the issue, presenting himself at the headquarters of the Shimura Corporation.

But that was tomorrow.

As he finally drew up to the hotel, travel wearied, the *concierge* on his floor spoke to him in excellent English as he checked in.

"Harker-san, there are messages for you."

He handed two items to a surprised Josh Harker.

The first was a fine vellum envelope with Mr. Joshua Harker written on it in calligraphy. Slipping out the gold-edged card inside, he read the hand-scripted English text on it. It had been phrased specifically for him, an American:

Mr. & Mrs. Haruto Shimura
Request the pleasure of the company of
Mr. Joshua C. Harker
For a celebration after the Shimura Corporation AGM
15th October, 8pm
Shimura Building, Otemachi, Tokyo
Black Tie

A customarily elaborate map with directions was included in the envelope. The invitation was dated for the next night. Josh flipped the card around and asked the *concierge*, "can you arrange a tuxedo for me?"

His eyes widened upon recognising the location, and he injected more and more gentle bows in between his effusive words.

"Oh, yes. Will I reserve a taxi for you?"

"Please, and –"

"Sir?"

Josh's voice lowered a notch. "Do you know of a really good jewellery store nearby?"

The same discrete volume was used in reply. "I shall check with the female members of staff for the best and let you know."

"Thank you."

As the *concierge* began punching buttons on the desk handset, Josh split open the second package. In it was a pre-paid cell phone. He powered it on and entered the PIN security code that he'd agreed through the Office of Administration before his departure. After a few seconds, a cryptic text message emerged from the ether:

Commo 2. 23:00. Ronin.

Ronin: Josh recognised the codename of the local CIA officer. Commo: clandestine jargon for a pre-arranged meeting point. He looked at his watch – ten eighteen. That didn't give him much time. He powered off the phone immediately. The porter took his bag up to the room. Harker carried a second, smaller case that he asked the *concierge* to deposit in the hotel safe. It was a DNA scanner, only slightly expensive by CIA standards, but fragile, and he didn't want it damaged. That's why he'd brought it himself as hand luggage. It raised a few eyebrows in Stateside airport security, but his way had been cleared.

Josh grabbed his room keycard and left. Rubbing his eyes deep into their sockets in a futile attempt to stave off jetlag, he headed out again into the cold electric fire of a Tokyo night.

THIRTEEN

Shinjuku, Tokyo
14th October – 10:57pm

The shrine was walking distance from the hotel. It allowed Harker to practice his tradecraft, to do a little "dry cleaning" as the instructors called it – evasive routes and backtracking to shake off any tails. Besides, he needed to stretch his legs.

Josh pulled the battery from his cell phone; more advice from ops instructors. Standard procedure. Any phone is a potential listening device, with no visible sign except for a click on a hard line or battery drain on a mobile. They had done it before. Josh had read CIA history about the rumbling of the entire CIA NOC network in Tokyo during the eighties. All because they had been stupid enough to use the Japs' own phone network for covert communication. They listened in on every word. Harker didn't want to be the one to blow it here this decade, to enter CIA history for the wrong reasons.

He crossed the carriageways and meandered for a time through the thronging crowds in Shinjuku. The stimuli of the streets assaulted all senses: hyperactive neon strips and mesmerizing advertisement screens; the mechanical clatter and wail of arcade machines in the *pachinko* parlours; the murmuring backbeat of a thousand footsteps; the toxic odors of exhaust fumes mixed with the faint sweetness of confectionery shops and piquant cooking.

He took a long, indirect route to the shrine, making turns down side streets, stopping a while, then back-tracking. It was a popular area, the red-light district. Even at this time of night, the walkways were thick with people, which made it difficult to identify any possible pursuers. Harker, on the other hand, was very easily spotted, and he felt it. When satisfied he'd shaken off any potential shadows, he made for the shrine's entrance. At two minutes to eleven he powered on the phone just long enough to receive another brief electronic directive.

By the bronze guardian.

The market outside the shrine was at peak activity. The stalls glowed in amber electric lantern light, enticing tourist and local alike to examine the merchandise. Behind one stall, Josh passed by an unkempt *yakuza* with wild hair taking this weeks' protection payment from a trader.

Passing through the spot-lit red *torii* gates, marking entry to a spiritual oasis that nestled up against Shinjuku's red light district, Josh was reminded again of why he had loved this city so much. Simple things like the color of light could have such opposing meaning in such a confined context. Red for spirit. Red for passion. He loved how the Japanese paraded such contradictions overtly and with pride.

Here in this congested metropolis, commerce, criminality, spirituality, immorality, could all cohabit with harmonic ease.

The gates led up a walkway crushed between two grey office blocks. The shadow of bare trees cast by electric lanterns loomed like spectres at the gate. In the half-light, a bronze guardian statue of a dragon sat on a stone plinth, encased in a metal lattice cage.

Harker stood. Nearby, a short stout man in a long coat emerged from the shadow.

"Is this the only shrine in town?" he asked.

Harker gave the acceptable, pre-agreed response. "There are lots - but only one is open today."

Ronin did not shake hands, and no small talk either.

"Can I have your phone please?"

Harker gave back the phone he received less than one hour ago. The local CIA officer pulled out the SIM card and replaced it with a new one. As he fiddled with the phone's identification circuitry, Harker had a chance to study the man.

Under the dim light, just enough features were visible to determine that Ronin wasn't completely Japanese; some western blood coursed through those veins bulging out of powerful hands. It must have been difficult for this bulk of a man to adhere to the delicate mores of his society. From another file, Joshua knew Ronin's father to be American, so the mixed-race face was as expected. The face was round, almost cherubic, and perhaps friendly under normal circumstances. His eyes sat like small buttons sunken in the well-padded upholstery of his ample face. It was a face Harker could trust; it matched the picture in Ronin's file.

"Keep this phone with you at all times, but with battery removed. Only use it to signal a dead drop of information, texting Commo and time. I don't expect to see you again, unless necessary. Understood?"

Josh could only nod.

"By the base of the guardian is a case," Ronin continued without taking a breath. "When I leave, take it with you. It contains your firearm. You are aware that it is illegal to possess a firearm in Japan, yes?"

Josh nodded again.

"Good. Then keep it hidden. The serial number has been removed. If you are caught with it, you are on your own."

His abrupt colleague handed him back the phone. "I don't expect to see you again. This is our one and only face-to-face meeting. So, finally, is there anything more you need from me? Do you need help to access the organization?"

Taking him to mean the Shimura Corporation, Josh refused. "There's already an invitation waiting for me back at the hotel. I've contacted an asset on the inside, so I presume she arranged it. That's all I needed."

Ronin nodded his head brusquely and started to leave, but something seemed to draw him back. He assessed the novice spy through beady bovine eyes. "You haven't been at this work for long, have you?"

Panic tickled at Harker. "How can you tell?"

"Because if you had, you wouldn't make an assumption like that about the invitation. In this type of work assumptions get people killed."

Ronin walked away leaving his words hanging.

Why would he have said that, Josh wondered? Josh could only take it to be earnest advice. A man so reticent, focussed only on the task, made a point of offering him advice. How badly must Harker have appeared to need it? Once again he felt his confidence plummet. It brought him back to Stanford's sentiment – analysis and operations are two very different beasts, requiring different character. Assumptions, previously Harker's powerful allies in the area of intelligence analysis, could become a seductive menace in the field. Stanford was right on another thing too: Harker would have to continue to learn. Josh took the briefcase from its hidden location, and as he obfuscated his route back to the hotel, he could only wonder what other assumptions might be deceiving him. Assumptions might teach him some lessons this mission. He hoped he would survive these lessons.

* * *

Later that night Kazuki – without his *katana* sword– stepped into a private lounge above a club in the Ueno district. He scanned the joint until he spotted his target. There sat Taro, reclined in the burgundy velvet pit, cosseted by two skimpily clad hostesses with bare flesh writing all around him. Kazuki knew he'd find him here. If Taro's wife knew this was how he really spent those late nights at the office, it would be the end of that marriage! Sitting opposite Taro, with more girls, was a man Kazuki recognized as the leader of the local *yakuza* gang. This was one of their haunts. Here was Taro, consorting with them. Thick as thieves. Kazuki knew Taro kept resources and contacts of his own, but if Taro's father ever knew about his son's relations with the criminal elements that Haruto had long since shunned... it would be the end of so much more. Kazuki was the Shimura family's protector. Little did that family know his greatest burden was protecting it from itself.

The young man walked up to Taro while taking dagger looks from the *yakuza*. He shouted over the music.

"We need to talk – in private."

With a reluctant look, a half-drunken Taro shooed the two women away, slapping the backside of one, as if he were gauging the pedigree of a racehorse. The half dozen tattooed *yakuza* escorted the brothers Shimura to a private office out back to talk, and kept watch outside. The tiny office with unplastered walls was crammed full by two filing cabinets, some shelves, a desk, and two chairs.

Taro sat, bidding Kazuki to do the same. Kazuki sat with legs together, hands resting on his thighs, as if everything nearby was contaminated.

"I don't often see you in here lately. Come to unbutton that collar of yours? Unwind a little?" Taro teased.

"I thought you might like to know. Harker just arrived in town."

The corners of Taro's mouth wilted.

Kazuki allowed himself a smile. "What's the matter brother, didn't you know he was coming to Japan? Tut, tut. Perhaps your sources are becoming even more unreliable? She didn't warn you he was coming? Hmm. Well now, as I see it, there are two possibilities: either she didn't want to tell you, or she didn't know about his arrival. Either way, it doesn't bode very well for you, does it?"

Taro's temper began to unfurl.

"If it wasn't for you botching the job, Kazuki, he wouldn't be here at all! Don't have me to clean up your mess for you!"

"What, by using your *yakuza* gorillas out there? Oh, yes, you'll use me and my men for your dirty work when it suits you, but threaten us with *yakuza* when we don't."

"Right now, you should be thinking of your own skin," Taro said. "If Harker knows something from the crime scene, he could implicate you. And if Haruto finds out? Well – that's the end of your lauded position as protector of the family."

Kazuki's stomach churned. What a fool he'd been agreeing to take out Senator Olsen, to protect the reputation of the corporation – to protect Taro. It was too late to rip up that deal with this devil. Now this devil used it to manipulate Kazuki further. He felt nauseous. Then dizzy. Then faint. He left without another word, to get some air.

On the threshold of the club's entrance Kazuki looked back and saw his adoptive brother, unperturbed, rejoin the pleasure in the pit. Taro shared some words with the boss of the *yakuza* clan, and pointed over towards Kazuki. The boy-man, the *gaijin*, saw the two men laugh over in his direction before resuming their lurid enjoyment of feminine delights.

FOURTEEN

Shinjuku, Tokyo
15th October – 7:33pm

Dressed in a tuxedo, with bow tie undone around his neck, Harker rested his palms against the plate glass window of his suite. From here his arms enveloped the beating incandescent core of the Shinjuku district below. Car headlights pumped luminous blood through arterial roads into its neon enflamed heart.

His own heart troubled him. It wasn't fear; he had pushed aside Ronin's warnings and decided to attend the Shimura reception. The trouble was how easily he had laid aside those concerns and made that decision. In his mind, he rationalized away any danger, only to serve his increasing desire – he desperately wanted to see Tokiko again.

When he had known her, she was a sweet, demure, compassionate and energetic thing, belying a great strength beneath. Of his small circle of friends in Tokyo Medical who embraced this *gaijin*, she was the most supportive of his predicament as an American student in Tokyo with no knowledge of the people, the language, or the culture. She took him under her wing. It wasn't what he'd expected from a Japanese woman, him being a man, and years older than her – but such was the confidence and charm of that woman.

Her strength of character was evident, to the point of defying her conservative parents' wishes, when she began seeing Josh romantically. Her fire showed Josh the tremendous unobtrusive strength of a woman, in a subtle package. A rare combination of qualities he had only ever found matched once more, years later, in the woman he eventually married.

Mental comparisons between Tokiko and Megan lead him to distrust his own motivations. Josh reminded himself why he was here. The mission. The objective. One of his instructors at The Farm said recruiting an asset was a lot like seducing a woman. In this case, it was the same. He interrogated himself: why did he crave to see Tokiko again? Was she really just part of the mission, or was he making her the mission? If his desire for the reunion could so easily override his fears, was it blinding him to other real dangers he might face?

The open gun case lay on the bed, with a new Glock handgun pressed into the foam. In showroom condition, he thought. Never used. In his past, he'd been more used to pulling slugs out of cadavers than putting them in. Who, he wondered, would be the recipient of these virgin bullets? He intended not to find the answer.

Josh shook himself out of a reverie that sought to wither his attentions. He needed to be here, now, in the present – a present whose events were already conspiring to throw him off-balance.

He picked up the Glock and jammed it firmly into the concealed shoulder holster.

The phone chirped, heralding the arrival of his taxi. At the lobby, the rear door of the green cab opened itself as Harker approached. He sat into the lace covered seat and handed the map to the driver who examined with ponderous noises before driving off. The driver's pristine white-gloved hands steered the CIA man ever closer to his beckoning past ... and future.

* * *

Shimura corporate headquarters was more modest than Josh expected. Instead of an impressive skyscraper befitting Shimura's reputation, there was a simple ten-storey steel and glass building on one side of a shared plaza in front of a lit fountain. Just having a building in the Otemachi financial district was a supreme mark of achievement. All the top companies situated there, each one hoping to profit from fortune that they believed comes with proximity to the Emperor's residence.

Black limousines meandered along the street in front of Harker's cab; they carried the great, the good, the not so good, and the very wealthy. Each deposited its valuable human cargo in turn at the steps to the Shimura Building. Josh's taxi pulled up in turn and his driver walked up to the building himself to ensure that it was the right place for his own cargo. Tokyo taxi driver's had lost none of their professionalism over the years; to him, his cargo was no less important than those others in limousines ahead. When the driver returned to open his passenger's door, Josh offered a tip out of courtesy, already knowing the outcome. It was refused.

The two sentries at the entrance wore long coats, black gloves, and an earpiece each. Josh kept distant for now. Inside, just beyond the entrance, he could make out the upstanding paddles of a metal detector – secure but discrete, not to cause offence to guests. He would be frisked if he didn't ditch the gun now.

In all his time spent trawling the streets of Tokyo before, he never thought how difficult it would be to conceal a gun. Tonight he realised how insufferably neat it all was. Everything was minimal and functional, with no spare capacity to conceal something the size of a sidearm, and no litterbins to be found anywhere – the Japanese way of ensuring tidy streets. He turned the corner and eventually settled for a raised flowerbed in the plaza. When he was sure no one was looking, he quickly thrust his Glock and holster underneath a small bush. Satisfied that it wasn't visible, he crossed the plaza again and on into the domain of Haruto Shimura.

Harker was eye-balled by the two short mountainous men who took his invitation and waved him through. He passed through the detectors where a hostess took his coat in exchange for a glass of Dom Pérignon. The party took place in the atrium reception hall – a cathedral to the commerce which paid for it, and in whose lofty heights the echo of those same commercial conversations now hummed. The conversations weren't all in Japanese. As Josh walked through the crowd he heard English, some German, and languages he wasn't sure of – Mandarin or Korean. It was an international affair, with a suitably international ambience. Apart from the lilting *koto* music in the background to ease the digesting of canapés, there was little in this hard capsule of steel, glass and marble to indicate this was a Japanese celebration. Perhaps it was down to the host's desire to make all nationalities feel welcome, or perhaps, Josh considered, it was indicative of the host's own mixed nationality: Haruto was part Korean. Pretence of Japanese heritage might have offended those who genuinely laid claim to it.

As Josh sauntered, he shut out the incomprehensible trans-lingual hubbub around him; he might as well be listening to a chattering pack of penguins. It was a flippant thought, but it amused him. In reality he knew the conversations of these people dictated the fate of millions of people and billions of Yen. All the attendees wore anonymous black ... except one.

There, on the farthest side of the atrium, he spotted her.

Framed within his view by ice-sculpted cranes, a vision stood out from the crowd, not least because she was the only one wearing white. It was a silk brocade evening dress; looked expensive – maybe a Miyake creation (perhaps from next season's collection, given Tokiko's iconic status and her husband's connections). To look at her was to look into a dream, a vision of his past manifestly haunting his present.

It was – unmistakably – the woman he had fallen in love with decades before; it was Tokiko.

There she was: his own Madame Butterfly. Only this time, in their story, it appeared to have turned out better for Butterfly than Pinkerton. And how she had spread her wings! Flying high in the Japanese corporate world. Men constellated around her in restrained adoration; they were polite but awkward.

Her eyes rolled aside, as if sensing Josh's gaze on her, and she turned to embrace it. Two pairs of eyes looking at, through, and beyond each other across a crowded room, connecting in a place and time only they knew of. For a moment, the crowd dissolved and only two remained.

Then it happened ... she broke into a smile, as warm and welcoming as any he could have hoped for. By reflex, Josh smiled back. He had wondered if it would be an awkward reunion, but sensed only delighted warmth from her – a pleasant contagion that infected him without any resistance.

Tokiko's rose-colored lips mouthed an apology to her companions and she made for Josh, moving through the crowd with the grace of a swan and the rolling shoulders of a samba dancer. Three marble steps finally carried her down to his level, and were it not for the glimpse of her stilettos he would not have believed the ground carried her at all, but some ethereal force.

She stood in front of him in all her glory. Her jet black hair, kept in place by two lacquered hairpins, sparkled under halogen spotlights. Those hazel eyes he would gaze into for hours caressed his face again, feeling for new scars and wrinkles.

"Josh Harker," she stated, as if saying his name would make him more real. "Delighted to see you."

"Your favourite Kansas hick is back in town," Josh said disarmingly.

Tokiko laughed. "Of all the things you were Josh, a hick was never one of them. You look well – the years have been good to you."

It was a lie, Josh thought, but a charmingly agreeable one.

"They've been better for you," he replied, gesturing with his champagne flute to the regalia surrounding them, both human and material. "You've come a long way from the two-mat place in Ueno."

Her gaze drifted into reminiscence. "We had some fun there."

Josh caught his head lowering to gaze into champagne; he raised it immediately. They shared an awkward silence that was broken by Tokiko in up-beat tone.

"So, your letter said you're a journalist now?"

Josh allowed a wicked smile to play on his face. "Yes, and I'm after your husband."

Tokiko beamed. He liked that she still recognised when he was teasing her.

"Well then, I'd better introduce you two – follow me." She led him gingerly through the crowd, looking back at him frequently, like an enrapt teenager would.

At the back of the atrium, the crowd was sparse and the lighting subdued: it was where the important conversations were undertaken. By a cascading water-feature, a group of stolid men reacted to the arrival of Shimura's wife and the American. They peeled apart from each other like the black leaves of some budding orchid revealing the precious central calyx – Haruto Shimura.

All conversation stopped. A stranger had come among them.

Haruto was shorter than expected, but his diminutive height was the only attribute not fitting his reputation. He had elegant hair, flecked with just enough grey seniority to ensure authority. His face was healthy, with fewer wrinkles and liver spots than most men his age. The eyes were keen, and a relaxed expression conveyed confidence in the quantity and quality of his life's experience. To look at him was to see a face that divulged little of his inner mental workings, but could warmly convince you it was safe to divulge your own; to be observed – analysed – without feeling judged.

"Well Tokiko," Haruto said in a compellingly mellow, whisky-coarsened voice, "What have you brought for me?"

Harker was surprised by his good English, but on reflection thought it sensible Haruto would ensure every advantage in business, especially the international language of commerce.

"Haruto, meet Joshua Harker," Tokiko said.

Shimura bowed, and Josh reciprocated with a deeper bow – customary to the more senior man. Shimura then dispensed with his own cultural greetings and shook Josh's hand firmly.

The CIA analyst's instinct kicked in; as the hand was offered, Josh noticed all its digits in tact, but the tip of Haruto's little finger had younger skin than the rest. It was normal upon expulsion from the *Yakuza* to undergo the ritual severing of the little finger tip of the sword hand. Haruto must have used the facilities of Shimura Biotech to clone a new finger tip. No doubt it was a service offered for considerable profit to other *yakuza* evictees who sought to re-grow respectability for a legitimate business world.

"And may I introduce to you my son, Taro."

Josh exchanged bows with a younger man next to Haruto with tight black hair and small-rimmed gold glasses. Taro did not offer his hand. His thick-heeled shoes made him as tall as his father. Taro always looked slightly past, or around, but never at him. He reminded Harker of a small bird, ill at ease under constant vigilance for some swooping bird of prey.

Haruto continued the conversation. "So you are the journalist my wife holds in such high esteem. Were it not for her, you would not be here now," he said.

I'm not sure how I should take that Haruto.

"The regard is mutual," Josh replied diplomatically.

An awkward silence followed, far beyond the excuse of the Japanese tendency to reflect before responding. Shimura's face gave away nothing of the quiet considerations of his mind, but he studied Harker at great length that came across as neither rude nor threatening; it was simply relaxed and unhurried. When the magnate did speak, it was with a surprising economy of words: "Those she cares for are seldom worthy of such honor; and did we not know it, she would not care for us at all, I suspect."

He kissed the back of Tokiko's hand. Public displays of affection were generally frowned upon in polite company, so Josh took it for what it was – a marking of Haruto's territory.

An aide discretely intruded and whispered something into Taro's ear, who then excused himself from the company.

"Excuse me father, I have some party arrangements to attend to."

"Of course," replied his father. Abruptly, Haruto stated: "Tokiko tells me you would like an interview."

"Our readers would love to know more about the father of modern genetic research – if that's acceptable to you."

"I will ask my personal assistant to see if I have time available in my schedule. In the meantime, do enjoy the hospitality of our organization this night, Harker-san."

Haruto bowed once more and returned to an enveloping circle of corporate comrades. And that was it: their meeting was at an end. The only sense Josh could make of it was that Haruto had met, formed an impression, and acted upon it by inviting Josh further into his territory at this reception, where Shimura would have even more control, and Josh would have absolutely no safety net. With alarmingly adroit alacrity, Harker had been reeled in; such were Shimura's abilities, the kind that had built a commercial empire.

The interview, Josh knew, would never happen.

Tokiko gently ushered him away.

"Don't worry–," she said. Josh never could disguise his emotions from her. "He likes you."

"Only a wife could tell," he replied.

She laughed delicately. "Well, I for one am glad you accepted my invitation to come tonight."

It was clear to Josh now that Tokiko had been the cause of his invitation into Shimura's presence, intending to help out an old friend. But Josh wondered if she knew anything about the darker dealings of her husband's organization, of possible assassinations on foreign soil. He was loathe to voice those suspicions. Time had loved Tokiko with an affection that spared her the ravages of age. She looked as vibrant and beautiful as ever, so much so that Josh had trouble thinking of her as anyone other than that young woman, from years ago, who had needed his mature, considered protection against her own naive bravery. The roles had now reversed.

She led him to a quiet spot to be alone, out of sight behind a pillar near the racks of expensive coats. The erstwhile lovers nuzzled against the protective dark cloth parade of international acclaim: Lauren, Prada, Huntsman, Kawakubo, Miyake. Tokiko placed her right palm tenderly on Josh's cheek, something she would not have dared to do in the open.

"Troubled?" she asked

He relaxed his face, cleared his mind, and shook his head from side to side.

"Tell me you're not still running away, Josh. Are you?"

"I have little left to run from anymore." He looked around to ensure no one was watching them, took her hand in his, and kissed her palm briefly before letting go again. "It's good to see you again Tokiko. I really am glad things have worked out so well for you."

When he said it, something flinched behind her eyes. There was something there: something beyond the confidence she had grown because of her new-found societal position; something Josh could not quite place; an addition to her soul, placed there by the experiences of the intervening years. For a brief flash, it was like looking in a mirror – like she too was looking to unravel some unspoken regret.

She enquired tentatively, "did you meet someone new? Married?"

"Yes," he replied.

"Oh, I'm glad!" she exclaimed, with genuine relief. "I'd hoped it would work out for you ... after you left. But –" she hesitated while looking at his hand, "you're not wearing any ring."

"No, it's ... over now." Josh didn't have the heart to say any more.

They were disturbed by a shuffling in the coat rack caused by a latecomer or an early departer. Tokiko let her hand drift from his, like a boat slipping away from its moorings. A brief death touched him, just as it had when leaving her years before, just as he had died a little at the awesome sight of her again that night. The sight of what could have been – if he had just stayed in Japan. Suddenly, his true motive for taking the mission – the one he never admitted to himself – came clear to him.

The music softened and from the very back of the atrium a guttural cry rang out, startling them both.

"Oh, that's the demonstration starting," Tokiko explained.

"What demonstration?"

Tokiko gave a mischievous smile. "Oh, you'll like this," she said, guiding him towards the ruckus.

* * *

The security camera above, which had been watching their every move, tracked them. Taro stared at the monitor in the security booth. He flipped open his phone and dialled while walking out of the booth, out of earshot of the man operating the security console – a member of Haruto's private *yonkuichi* militia, loyal to Kazuki.

The other end, the phone picked up. "*Moshi-moshi?*"

"Doshida-san," said Taro. "I need to get some *yakuza* down to our offices."

"Why?"

"That photo I sent you, the CIA agent. He's here, now."

"Ah. We'll take care of it."

"Make sure they do it outside, when he is alone. Haruto is not to know of their involvement in this."

"Of course."

Taro thought he could almost hear the deceptive smile of the *Yakuza* boss across the airwaves.

"I mean it. Haruto can't know of our association, or it's off. I want Harker captured only, do you understand?"

"Why not kill him – take the problem out of circulation."

"Harker isn't the problem; his presence here means we've a bigger one," said Taro.

"Which is?"

"She didn't warn us he was coming." Taro breathed deeply.

"Ah, I see."

"We need to know what Harker knows. We need to know how much the CIA know about all this."

"Leave it to me." Doshida went off-line to make his dark arrangements.

FIFTEEN

Otemachi, Tokyo
15th October – 8:24pm

Simulated battle raged deep in the atrium. Clashing of steel emerged from a makeshift crucible of combat. The sounds echoed up the glass vault, all the way to the stars, as if calling on the Gods to spectate the spectacle.

Josh was taken by the hand toward the commotion, all the while taking note of a growing menace. More ear-pieced men stuffed into suits appeared and orbited closer like sharks around prey. He shrugged it off as paranoia; they were just gathering for the exhibition of combat. Then he remembered his mantra. Paranoia is healthy.

"Kazuki loves these company events for one reason only," said Tokiko, "– it gives him a chance to show off skills he's been practicing so long. You're still a fan of martial arts, aren't you?"

Distantly, Josh replied. "Well, I'm a bit out of practice since leaving the kendo club in Tokyo Uni, but sure, I can appreciate a good show."

"Then it's lucky for you he's back in time for the reception; you're in for quite a treat."

"Who's Kazuki?"

"Haruto's adopted son; he's also leader of the *yonkuichi.*"

"*Yonkuichi?*" he quizzed.

"It's the name Haruto gave his personal guard. Do you remember how the *Yakuza* got their name?"

"Sure. Ya-ku-za spells the three-digit point score of a losing hand in an old card game. It was a kind of joke – they regarded themselves as the 'bad hands' of society."

"Well, *yonkuichi* is Haruto's own little joke against them. When he disassociated from the *yakuza*, he needed to assemble his own private protection from them, and named it Yon-ku-ichi. It spells the point score of a winning hand in the same card game."

Josh smirked. "Cute."

The couple eased through the spectators gathered around a makeshift *dōjō* training ring. A raised wooden terrace encircled the *tatami* matting of the combat arena. A range of swords and other ancient instruments of harm rested on wooden racks.

Two men thrust *katana* swords at each other in the arena. The older one, obviously on the defensive, was dressed head to toe in full training armor. The other combatant, whom Harker took to be Kazuki, was more confident with a naked torso. Josh assumed Kazuki would be Asian, but recognised now that adoption knows no geographical limit. Kazuki was clearly a Western *gaijin*, with blonde hair and light ghosted blue eyes. He seemed on the cusp of manhood. Motionless, Kazuki could easily be mistaken for a boy, but equipped with such seasoned muscular weaponry pounding out masculine strike after strike upon his opponent, he clearly had the strength of a man. His bare torso revealed a tattoo stretched along his burgeoning left bicep: three Kanji characters that Josh recognised as Japanese numerals – *yon-ku-ichi*.

There was something else about him: an elusive, alien quality; as if he were a synthesis of characteristics; a kind of bland anonymity around his features that did not belong in this land or any other; it just seemed downright odd – like someone had been poking around in this kid's DNA.

Enlightenment struck Harker, hard.

That young man, so unfitting in these surroundings, fitted exactly a description given by Dr. Porcho in Ohio weeks before: a male in his late teens to early twenties, with blond hair and possibly blue-grey eyes. That was the description fitting the DNA of the hair strand. And if ever there was a person subjected to genetic alterations, then it was this man.

Josh verified with Tokiko. "You said Kazuki was away recently? Travel a lot does he?"

"More and more lately, although he never used to. He mainly stays close to Haruto and his family. He's our protector." A proud smile consumed her as she looked over her brawny young defender.

"I see."

In those eyes of Kazuki's, looking directly at him, Josh saw a stare he'd only seen once before. It was an intense look, stabbing out at all people, that set Kazuki apart from humanity. Harker saw it before, in a courtroom, in the eyes of the man who murdered his wife. It was the unmistakable look of a man who had taken a human life. A man who was himself separate from human life.

Josh wrestled disgust. This triumvirate of Shimura men governed Tokiko's life and affections now. The disgust was not only at them, but at himself, for leaving her. His leaving had made her situation.

"Tell me – was he away last month, about the sixteenth?"

"Oh, yes he was gone for a couple of days. Why?"

"No reason."

Kazuki was beaming back proudly at Tokiko while his opponent caught his breath. Tokiko smiled adoringly at him. There was a twinkling now in Kazuki's cold eyes. Visceral revulsion rose in the pit of Joshua's stomach to see it. The kind of affection hinted at by this young, fit, westerner's infatuated gaze at Tokiko crossed the bounds of mere duty. Josh hadn't the heart to tell her his suspicions, but he was convinced he looked at the last face Senator Olsen saw – his assassin.

Kazuki's last strike drove his opponent off-balance, into a corner, and into capitulation. The travelling assassin backed away and the crowds applauded him.

"Can nobody defeat me?" Kazuki roared, while backing out of the arena, starting to look tired.

The assembled audience laughed at his remark, some drifting back to refresh their drinks. Through the thinning crowd Harker noticed again the ear-pieced men of the *yonkuichi* closing near him. Several of them, standing by marble pillars just out of the light, seemed to be looking directly at him. Josh wrestled with the new information stimulating his synapses. A decision was called for, and quickly. If it was true, if Haruto had reeled him in, knew he was CIA, then he might never get out of this building alive. Even if he could manage it, he would never get near Kazuki again, never get the chance to prove his guilt. He knew what he had to do. He needed DNA ... and he needed to get it now.

Josh strutted over to the weapons rack, grabbed a *katana* by the scabbard and pointed its hilt at Kazuki, exclaiming loudly: "I will take that challenge."

Many of the retreating crowd gasped and turned around to see the fool. Josh saw the folded arms of *yonkuichi* nearby fall by their sides. Kazuki initially did not respond.

Harker continued to goad him. "Too tired?"

The man-boy motioned for Harker to take the arena center. Harker accepted.

As he slid off his tuxedo jacket and draped it over the weapons rack, Tokiko rushed up to him.

"Josh, what are you doing? Kazuki isn't one of those students in the college *kendo* club. He's made it his life's ambition to master *ninja* combat; he could take you to pieces."

Harker was still fit, but maybe not like his college days when his nimble power over the grid iron had the sorority girls – and even the guys – jumping in ecstatic expectation, testing the strength of the bleachers. He could do this. Winning it didn't matter.

"Why so concerned Tokiko?" he asked. "It's just a bit of fun, isn't it?"

Tokiko demurred, not looking like she agreed. Josh wondered if her concern was for him, or for Kazuki. Through the corner of his eye, he saw an equally concerned looking Haruto and Taro melting through to the front row of spectators.

It was now, or never, Josh thought, stepping into the arena.

"Kazuki, stop this." It was the voice of his older brother that insisted. Strange, Josh thought. Of all the voices to hear raised in protest, Taro's didn't occur to him.

"I will fight him," Kazuki said flatly.

"No," Taro repeated. "This is not wise." Kazuki ignored him, unsheathed his sword again and assumed the two-handed samurai grip in front of Harker.

Harker too paid no attention to Taro. He slid the *katana* out of its scabbard; its sharpened edge coruscated with spotlit brilliance. Even though he defied Taro, he agreed with his sentiment; this was not the wisest thing Joshua had ever done. Harker had seen proof of Kazuki's qualifications to lead the *yonkuichi* tonight. The right was secured through ability, not family connections. And if the same blond hair covering that scalp had fallen at the death of a Senator, then Kazuki was a young man capable of killing if he saw fit. And Josh? He himself had little to fight with but some college-level martial arts, and a rushed personal combat refresher course at the CIA's Farm training facility, and a hope – a hope that his older muscles would hold out until they got what he needed.

As the golden-haired swordsman hailed his weapon to point between Harker's eyes, the CIA man's first battle was against his own bubbling fear. His hands quivered as he held up his own sword. Like two dancers preparing for a very deadly waltz, they side-stepped in a circle.

A loud roar sounded, and it began.

Kazuki shuffled forward, and struck with calculated precision. The speed and power compressed into the blade were amazing and terrifying. The percussion point of the blade – one-third down, where maximum force occurred – careened toward Harker's neck. Josh reacted as fast as he could to block the blow. Only his readiness – balanced, with sword pointing out and up – allowed him to block the move in time enough to prevent Kazuki's sword from slicing deep into his jugular vein.

It was close. Millimeters. And it was only the most basic attack: Kazuki was testing him. Harker immediately pushed back with his blade, sending Kazuki's sword away to the left, hoping to force the man-boy back into a posture of readiness, balanced on both feet, giving Josh time to regain his own balance.

Kazuki did not cooperate.

In a dazzlingly acrobatic move, Kazuki pirouetted on one foot. The energy that Josh had put into pushing back the hostile sword was now converted, by Kazuki, into turning force. He used Harker's own energy against him. It was a move that would have left Kazuki vulnerable to a more capable opponent, but Josh didn't have the skill to take advantage of it, and presumed Kazuki knew that, or he wouldn't have made the move in the first place – it was a calculated insult. It was all Josh could do to thrust the hilt of his sword out to his right, just in time to meet the shattering eruption of steel on steel that sent shudders down into the hilt, weakening his grip still further.

Kazuki stood back and assumed the position for another more calculated strike, a posture more fitting of the Samurai way. Josh did not detect much of the old *bushido* discipline in this young man's technique; it was too brash. He was good, and could wipe Harker out any time, but seemed to prefer toying with him instead.

The next strike erupted, and the next, and still further strikes. Kazuki carved the air with scythe-like strokes. Josh did his best to counter each one, and succeeded each time, within a fine margin; the strikes were intended that way, he knew, to keep just within his ability to defend. His chest felt too small for his rampaging heart to beat in; the sweat clambered out of every pore, making it harder to maintain grip.

All his life shrank to one instant with each clash of blades. All his faculties focussed on primal moments of survival. All irrelevancies evaporated away in combat, all pain, all fear. And in those moments he found there was satisfaction to be had in the simplicity of purpose – keeping alive.

Exhilarated and surprised by his own ability to continue battle under such onslaught, Harker's strength remained. Kazuki continued to expend his, and – for a moment – Harker saw him wane. The boy's attack relented and Josh detected a small growing tremor in Kazuki's arms.

Something was wrong.

Kazuki lunged for the next attack. Harker took the opportune moment to let himself stumble back onto the ground. His opponent seemed to hesitate with a grimace somewhere between pity and disgust on his face.

"That's enough," the deep commanding voice of his father said from the sidelines.

Kazuki stood back and lowered his sword, apparently with exhaustion, not a desire to obey the instruction. He turned to go.

Harker saw his only chance and took it. He slashed out, catching Kazuki in the calf muscle with the tip of his sword. Kazuki yelped like a dog stepping on a tack. Instinctively, he held the wound. Blood oozed through his fingers wrapped around it. Lifting them away and looking at the blood, venom rose within him.

He struck at the CIA man on the deck. An enraged, bifurcating blade descended onto Harker.

Haruto bellowed, loudly and more uncontrollably than Harker ever did, or ever would, hear him. It rocked the glass vault to its very foundations and silenced all its inhabitants.

"KAZUKI!"

Josh saw the sword edge grow in his sight, until it was all he could see. There was only one part of his body he could move fast enough before being split in two: he closed his eyes.

Moments later the echo had subsided and silence reigned.

Harker felt a breath, then another ... faster now ... his chest pounded ... the pressure of his lungs gorging themselves on air.

I'm breathing ... that's something.

His mind sent the signals that normally opened his eyes, and to his surprise the lids rolled back. They revealed Kazuki still standing over him, frozen, sword extended into Harker's scalp. Was this the snapshot of death, Harker wondered, forever impressed on his soul? Was this the moment he became a star on the memorial wall in Langley's entrance hall?

His would-be killer stepped back, taking his implement of death with him.

Harker saw this was real; it was the continuing movie reel of his life. He reached up slowly and nervously to his forehead expecting all kinds of gruesome internal workings to meet his fingertips. All that he discovered was a sliver of blood from a break of skin – a tiny surgical incision.

Kazuki spoke to him with a soft tone, almost respectful: "Blood for blood." With that, he sheathed his sword and replaced it on the weapons rack.

He stretched his hand out to Harker, who took it. Kazuki lifted him from the ground with ease. Then the true intent of the kind gesture was revealed; Kazuki reached to take Harker's sword from him.

"I will clean and rack your sword," Kazuki said.

Harker let him do so, but ensured the blood-stained blade dragged across his tuxedo pants, hoping Kazuki did not notice.

"Too kind," Harker replied. He made no delay in taking advantage of a crowd stunned by his actions. He whipped his jacket on, pushed through them and made swiftly for the exit. It had been a calculated risk. He had risked his life. He might have lost all hope of learning anything from Haruto Shimura now – he would not trust Harker anymore. But, it had been worth it, he hoped. Only time would tell for sure, but Harker walked out of the atrium with the evidence he needed. Behind him, the patter of Tokiko's heels on marble pursued him. Josh made it to the door, where one of the *yonkuichi* watchmen was taking instructions in his ear and talking into his collar. Josh saw him move to grab him as he reached the revolving door. But the guard backed off when the wife of Haruto Shimura got to Josh first.

"Are you crazy?" she asked. "What did you do that for?"

He put his arm around her waist and gently steered her out the door with him.

"I'll explain outside."

To his shame, Harker found necessity dictate that he use Tokiko as a guarantee of his safety.

A black Lincoln lurched to a halt outside the Shimura Building, raising Josh's suspicions; it was the kind of American sedan that had cachet in the *Yakuza*. Four men rolled out, like facsimiles from a copier, with crew cuts and identical three-piece sharkskin suits. They each had a gold pin on the lapel. These were not understated like the *yonkuichi* inside. These were plainly *yakuza* gangsters. And they made for him.

Harker sped off as fast as polished leather soles would allow on smooth paving stones.

By the time he made it to the shrubbery and clipped the leather holster in around his shoulder, Tokiko caught up with him. She gasped, rooted to the spot, when she saw the gun. Josh couldn't look her in the eye.

"And what kind of a journalist carries a gun?" Tokiko asked.

He tried to start explaining, but a dozen feet clattered around the corner in pursuit.

"I'm sorry Tokiko. I can't explain here. I have to go."

"You're in trouble, aren't you? Is this something to do with Kazuki?"

"Maybe. I don't know yet, but I have to find out."

The front runner *yakuza* pointed in the direction of the couple and the pack accelerated.

Once again, Josh said, "I'm sorry." Saying it for the next twenty years would not be enough to express how sorry he truly felt.

In case he never got the opportunity again, he cradled Tokiko by the back of her slender neck and tenderly kissed her cheek goodbye. The American ran off toward Otemachi Station subway entrance. He ran as far as the platform before looking back, and saw the last thing he expected.

There, padding furiously after him in bare feet through the Station, was Tokiko, clutching her shoes in one hand, and elevating her dress hem with the other.

She always could surprise him.

* * *

Kazuki wrapped his leg in gauze. He figured the guests had been distressed enough that night, so escaped to the closeted security booth, where none of his father's guests would see more blood. It allowed him to hide too from the retribution of his father, who would be more distressed than his guests at the sight of a Shimura corporate function hijacked by violence.

A handheld two-way bleeped on the desk for Kazuki's attention. He flicked it on and shrugged it to his ear while he continued to self-repair. The entrance door *yonkuichi* spoke to him. "Harker fled. Tokiko went with him." Kazuki froze momentarily before continuing his repairs. "Should we track him down?" asked the *yonkuichi*.

"No, not yet. I don't want any *yonkuichi* in pursuit if she's there. If it got violent, well ... Haruto would not approve. Let them go for now; Tokiko must know what she's doing. If she doesn't come back soon, then we'll start a search."

"Maybe, but what of the *yakuza*? Some were chasing them down after they left."

Yakuza! Taro, you idiot!

He put down the radio. Kazuki had learned a lot about the appropriate projection of power, most of it very recently. Taro, it seemed, was not so wise in the use of his powers. And those powers were varied. Taro had a habit of bragging to Kazuki during drunken highs. It was then he would let slip the things he didn't really want Kazuki to know, but his pride demanded it. It was the only reason Kazuki had joined him in those drinking pits.

"Your high-and-mighty yonkuissshi," Taro had slurred into Kazuki's ear one night. "I have better. Me. I have. I know things your men could never find out. I know," Taro breathed closer, "that the CIA has been doing reports on my company's activities. Ha! I even know the name of the man doing it – Jossshua Harker. She told me."

It was true. Harker's presence here tonight was proof that Taro knew in advance. This was just one of the things Kazuki had gleaned about his brother's methods, but they were nothing his brother should brag about. It was only through the *Yakuza's* international links that Taro could have such connections. For that alone Haruto would despise Taro if he ever found out. What Haruto would do if he ever knew of Taro's other plans, Kazuki could only guess ... and fear. One day Taro's association with the *Yakuza* might come crashing down tragically around him – around all of them – just like it had for his father.

Taro slithered in next to Kazuki in the security booth.

"There you are brother."

"Here I am."

Tension crackled between them.

"How could you manage to let him injure you? I thought you were better than that. Not to mention the embarrassment for our father! His head-of-guard losing to an American cowboy!"

"You're not one to be giving lessons, Taro."

"Well, no major harm done, eh? Just a little bruised ego," he said with a gruesome smile.

"No Taro, no harm done." Kazuki stood up to leave. "Except this: that man – the CIA agent that your activities have attracted here – has just left with a sample of my DNA."

Kazuki had never seen Taro's face fall so fast. The boy wanted to take pleasure in his brother's shock, but Kazuki just couldn't mange it. He felt dizzy suddenly. To his relief, Haruto came to the booth to talk to his sons; it gave Kazuki the excuse to sit back down before falling down. Why was he dizzy? He hadn't lost much blood. A vulnerability overcame him and his head swam. It was no condition in which to spar further with his brother, or defend himself from his father.

Haruto asked, "can either of you explain to me why my wife is missing?"

Taro and Kazuki looked at each other like they did when they were young boys caught fighting each other. There are some things, Kazuki thought, that time and power can never change.

SIXTEEN

Shinjuku, Tokyo
15th October – 9:07pm

Josh's tirade cantered as fast as he did through Shinjuku station. He rebuked Tokiko.

"Go back Tokiko – now! You're in danger," he commanded.

"I'm in danger? Right now I'm the only thing between you and the *yonkuichi*, who won't be too pleased with what you did to Kazuki. They'll tear you apart Josh! And I'm not going anywhere until you tell me what you thought you were doing. I want an explanation."

They emerged at street level from the south exit, but were immediately forced back inside by what they saw – a black Lincoln came to a screeching halt on the road, to the haranguing honks of many horns. Men got out and made for the station, dodging recklessly through traffic to get there.

They ran.

Josh pointed back toward them and asked Tokiko, "did you recognise any of them?"

"No."

"Exactly! Did you see their lapel pins? *Yakuza.* Those aren't your *yonkuichi* protection. Like I said, you're in danger. Now quick, back inside," he shouted, taking Tokiko by the hand.

They scrambled to the east exit, weaving through the suffocating crowd of Friday night revellers. They paused under the glow of the light sculptures to breathe and assess the danger. No *yakuza* were waiting at this exit, none that could be identified.

"Why only the south exit?" Josh asked, rhetorically. "How did they know I'd be there, or even at this station?"

Harker looked down at the woman whose hand he clung to as if her life depended on it.

"Looks like your husband kept his old *yakuza* ties after all," Josh said.

Tokiko shook her head. "Not Haruto. He would never have anything to do with them again, if possible."

"Hmm. Well, the hows and whys aren't important right now. If we stay here, they'll catch up. We have to lose them."

Tokiko's erstwhile lover set aside thoughts of evasion for a moment and looked upon her with softened concern. She clutched her stilettos at her side and stood barefoot, not panicked, nor flustered, looking up at him, invigorated by the whole new situation. She had shed her societal dignity like an overcoat gone out of fashion, and had done it effortlessly, in a heartbeat. It reminded him why he'd always admired Tokiko; the way she could set aside the redundant paraphernalia of a past moment to become a new person, invigorated and reinvented, ready to receive the next.

But why? For what reason had she followed him? He hoped it was concern for him, but had to accept the harsher belief that she did it for the other men in her life – her family. She pursued him for answers, just as he pursued her for the same.

He stared at her feet; they must be killing her.

Shoes. Where to find shoes?

"Come on," he said. "Let's get out of here and see if we can find you something a bit less conspicuous."

Harker was acutely aware that keeping a low profile to evade *yakuza* all across the Tokyo night would be tricky for a six foot one Caucasian wearing a black tuxedo and a barefoot Tokyo socialite in a white limited edition Miyake cocktail dress. He removed his tie as they made for the crowds gathered at the meeting point outside a nearby mall. A group of *cosplay* teens dressed in gothic style – headed for Harajuku – fussed and giggled among themselves as they recognised Tokiko from her recent feature in *Biteki* magazine.

Her celebrity leverage came in handy. Tokiko borrowed items of clothing from some excited youths that surrendered them freely. Society fashionista Tokiko Shimura was asking *them* for *their* clothes! For Harker: a full length black leather coat, which stopped at his knees and cut across his shoulders when he leaned forward. For Tokiko: flat shoes in exchange for her expensive stilettos, and a silver-grey gothic lolita style cloak with deep purple frills. It looked good on her. She could make anything look good, Josh thought.

They had lingered too long. With the advantage of height, Josh saw their pursuers as Tokiko bantered with the teens.

"Time to go Tokiko," he commanded.

No stops for autographs tonight. He slipped the teens some Yen bills as Tokikio asked them to play dumb if anyone came asking.

The pair headed for the warren-like alleyways of the Golden Gai. Josh knew they could get lost in there for sure. They walked, more calmly now, through a multi-colored neon promenade of strip clubs and hostess bars. They manoeuvred through the punks handing out lascivious flyers for the joints, touting for the custom of jaded and drunken salarymen. Their raucous wails promised carnal delights, the details of which escaped Josh's dusty mastery of the Japanese language, but understood by that seductively cloaked figure propelling itself gracefully alongside him.

He caught a glimpse of her soft reserved smile peeping out from under the hood, which he duly returned. It was the first time he'd seen her free from the suffocating Shimura mechanism. The pressure of pursuit had eased now that they had their disguises. In new disguises, they could drop other masks they'd worn earlier in the night, and Josh began to sense an aura of liberation about Tokiko, one that she could not disguise.

The black and white frontage of an American-themed bar beckoned them into their old familiar haunt. It was set into a narrow alley, away from likely *yakuza* lookouts. Nesting there for a while seemed like a good strategy to Harker; let the heat subside, gather some thoughts, and decide what to do next. Good times were had here with fellow postgraduates. They'd brought Josh here that first week of study, thinking the themed bar would make him feel at home. He hadn't the heart to tell them how failed the theme was. However, the bar did succeed in breaking down those early cultural barriers with alcohol and the common embarrassment of caterwauling *karaoke* sessions, even when it wasn't *karaoke* night.

Different times.

The couple tucked themselves onto stools at the far end of the bar. It was a good choice: a cosy place, just enough of a crowd to mask them, and yet small enough to see who might overhear them.

Tokiko ordered *Maszake*. The barman arrived back with two wooden box cups containing premium *sake*, one of which Tokiko held within Josh's gaze and toasted: "to old times."

"The best times," he added, tipping down the warm tipple.

She had pulled back some of her fashionable street camouflage. The cloak draped off her bare shoulders revealed her pale features, flushed rose pink by *sake*. Even now, on the youthful end of her middle age, he still felt the need to catch a breath whenever he looked upon her. Without fear of her husband's reprisal now, he looked with a gentle affection and in the knowledge that such a look was absolutely appropriate, mostly because she appeared to need the comforting attention of warm friendly eyes.

They connected silently for a time, neither knowing what should be said, both wanting nothing to be said. Tokiko's smile melted a little, and she broke her gaze demurely, so charming in Japanese women. A precious moment that both knew could not last. Recent events needed to be addressed.

"We shouldn't stop here long," Harker said.

"Will you tell me now why you sliced Kazuki? What are you here for? I'm not a fool Joshua."

No, you never were at that.

Josh grabbed a deep breath and remembered the blood he hoped was still on his trousers. He reached down and scraped a few flakes of the caked substance into his pocket handkerchief, which he carefully re-pocketed.

"I needed a sample of Kazuki's DNA, and I wasn't sure I would get the chance again. I'm sorry I let you down in public, but it's too important."

"Why?"

"Not long ago, back in Ohio, one of our Senators died under suspicious circumstances. It looks like he was assassinated."

"Which Senator?" she asked, clearly fearing the answer.

"Mark Olsen."

He could feel her heart sinking.

"Did you know him?" Josh asked.

"Not well enough; he was just an acquaintance really. Haruto would invite him for a meal sometimes when he was in Tokyo. We'd have some interesting conversations about recent biotech research – he was in that line before, you know? Then he and Haruto would leave to talk business. It's a shame. I wish I'd known him better ... only now I never can."

Tokiko's eyes closed. Her elongated lashes were like the feathered wings of some rare and elegant black swan. They stayed closed longer than a blink. She stated, with eyes still shut: "you think Kazuki had something to do with it, don't you?"

"I don't think it's coincidental that it happened during the time you say Kazuki was away ... and I've other evidence that I believe links him to the crime."

Her head hung low as if some great weight had been placed on those slender shoulders. The passionate defence of Kazuki he'd expected to hear never came. It told Josh a lot. What she knew, obviously, was Kazuki's potential for murder.

Tokiko's head emerged from its laden grief, rising to display a desperate expression caught between laughter and tears.

"So what does that make you then? Do scientific journalists in America carry guns and investigate murders now?"

What it makes me ... is a liar.

He dissipated her question as best he could. "Nothing is certain until I get this DNA verified."

"I'm going with you," she said.

Josh couldn't allow it. He couldn't for a second time risk losing the life of the woman he cared for. He couldn't risk being responsible for that again. With a defiantly stern voice, he commanded, "No."

"If Kazuki is responsible for this ... I have to know, Josh."

"Listen, it's too dangerous – if you really want it, it means you'll have to come back to my hotel room with me."

Tokiko lolled her head to one side as if to say, "where have I heard that before?"

Josh nearly blushed when he realised what he'd said. "Not like that! The DNA trace from the scene for comparison is back in my hotel."

"So, let's get it and find out now," she said.

"You're forgetting the *yakuza.*"

"We've lost them."

Josh shook his head slowly. "They knew which station I was heading for. They even knew the exit I would take. That means ... they know which hotel I'm staying at. I don't want you there with me Tokiko – it's too dangerous for you."

"I can help. If it's you they're looking out for, then it's you that can't go there. You're the one in danger, not me. Please Josh, let me help."

Josh absently vocalised his runaway train of thought. "They were waiting for me outside the party. But by the time someone raised the alarm after I injured Kazuki ... the *yakuza* couldn't get there that quickly ... unless ..."

They already knew I was coming!

"What is it?" Tokiko demanded.

Josh completed, looking directly at her," they were on to me before the sword fight ... somebody knew I was coming to the party."

"I invited you. What are you saying, that *I* set *yakuza* on you?"

He retracted immediately, embarrassed by the suspicions of his new job.

"No, of course not. You must have told Haruto ... someone ... that I was coming?"

"No, I arranged the invitation myself. I was afraid he'd say no if I told him you were an old flame of mine."

95

Ronin's warning came back to him: assumptions get people killed. Harker worried he wasn't being careful enough. Did he brush away too easily the possibility that Tokiko was involved? Here he was, revealing his mission to her, taking her to the only precious proof he had. Was he blinding himself with resurgent feelings for her? It was naïve to think he, a college fling Tokiko had known for little more than a year, would receive more of her loyalty than her husband of nearly fifteen years. Stanford had sent him here as a "raven", to elicit secrets from her. What if she was the "swallow", the beautiful woman Shimura would use to elicit his secrets?

Josh didn't want to believe it, but had to admit the possibility. It would be wise to keep her close and under watch. He would give her the benefit of the doubt, remaining prudent and alert, living with the horrific ambiguity of this game. Josh put it to the back of his mind for now, but all the while the spectre of doubt haunted him.

If only he could know for sure: who betrayed him?

SEVENTEEN

New Jersey Avenue, Washington DC
15th October – 11:47am

The meet-up went as it had before. She'd texted his pre-paid mobile earlier in the day to request a rendezvous. When she arrived at the pay phone on Dupont Circle, he'd monitor her from afar before dialling. He knew her name, even though he didn't want to. She just blurted it out at their first meeting: Rita Silberman. Some goddamn analyst in the CIA with a penchant for danger and an inability to keep her trap shut when she should. She knew his name of course: Donald Cain. It was she who sought him out, probably from information in CIA files. She wanted a professional merc, with some special abilities. Silberman wasn't as professional. Cain hated amateurs in his business, just as much as he hated new, untried clients. Unfortunately, it was usually amateurs who most needed his services, and this new client would pay well for the job. It paid so well, in fact, that he was sure the money wasn't coming from her. She was just the cut-out. He didn't know who her paymasters were and didn't care.

Once she'd picked up the receiver on the short black phone kiosk, he gave her today's location then trailed her, making sure she was alone. Elaborate but necessary precautions taken to isolate and protect all parties. Today it was the Japanese American Memorial. He watched her uneasy pacing through the damp night mist underneath the bronze cranes perched at the heart of the monument. Cain heard somewhere that they chose cranes for this memorial because the Japanese regard the crane as a symbol of good fortune, longevity, and ... fidelity. He wondered if she knew their meaning. Was that why she looked so uneasy, knowing that her actions beneath those cranes mocked their symbolic fidelity, and insulted the sacrifice of those the memorial honored?

Cain, on the other hand, had long since grown out of such conscientious concerns.

When it was clear that no one else was watching them, he marched up to her, all the time casting investigative glances into the shadows. Donald Cain was not a tall man, but he had kept his Marine Corp physique, though it was well hidden under the padding of his woollen winter coat. His weight crunched the gravel under his shining black shoes.

Silberman took out an envelope and handed it over. He checked the contents quickly before slipping it into his own pocket.

She iterated the contents: "venue location, a pass, and pay-off merchandise for your contact, all as agreed."

"And my own pay-off?"

"Half has been deposited to the account already. The other half on completion, as we agreed. When you complete the job, the remainder will be wired."

"We agreed on cash payments," he said.

"No, you agreed. I told you last time – I won't handle large amounts of cash. It's one thing handling this stuff, but I won't get caught with suitcases of cash. They are too hard to explain away."

"But less traceable than a wire transfer. Well, what's done is done, but I don't want to hear you say I didn't warn you," said Cain.

"You won't. After this, we shouldn't have to meet ever again," said a resolved Rita.

"I hope not," Cain said, smiling gruesomely. "If we do, it means something's gone wrong. And those kind of mistakes are never mine."

He walked off into the shadows from which he came.

EIGHTEEN

Shinjuku, Tokyo
16th October – 12:41am

Tokiko strolled casually by Joshua's side on the way to the hotel. As they approached the lobby she noticed his total attention on their surroundings, not on her. She couldn't blame him; *Yakuza* entanglements were not to be taken lightly. Haruto had learned this lesson painfully. Tokiko knew her husband couldn't be pulling the strings of Josh's pursuers. It didn't fit that Kazuki would be behind the *yakuza* either – he had the entire *yonkuichi* at his disposal. At that, she wondered, why Kazuki might be behind Senator Olsen's murder, when he could send any member of his *yonkuichi* to do it. Tokiko directed her suspicions instead to the usual source of any difficulties in their family – Taro.

Could the American she walked with hold some of the answers? In the dark early morning gloom the man she once knew became eclipsed in shadow by this harsher, determined and somehow distant stranger. This was a different man than the carefree graduate she'd known.

All was quiet under the glass entrance canopy. The valet was off duty by this time. Harker's fleshy hand encircled Tokiko's wrist, bringing her stride to a halt. Josh took her on a roundabout route to the lobby entrance, stopping, making her stand for a moment out of sight behind a stone pillar while Josh glanced obliquely into the lobby.

"There's a small group of men sitting just inside the lobby. I don't like the look of them," he said.

Tokiko was led back to the other side of the street. Josh took a phone out of his inside pocket, and as he inserted the battery, he asked her, "are you sure you want to do this?"

Tokiko nodded. She smiled with it, trying to ease the strain written all over his face.

Josh dialled, and Tokiko listened to one side of the conversation that would determine the fate she had chosen for herself that night.

"This is Joshua Harker. I'm a guest, in room 426 ... I've had better nights, thank you ... has anyone been enquiring after me tonight ... I see ... thank you ... no, no I will be along shortly ... good night."

He snapped the device closed and examined the hotel as if it were a sample under a microscope. It was then that Tokiko realised why he had picked this spot; she could see straight into the lobby, to the reception desk, to the night clerk now replacing the handset. They, however, were masked from view by a blind spot in the street lighting. The clerk seemed to be calling over to someone, and at that point one of the men Josh had spotted in the lobby came over to the desk.

"Damn," said Harker. "The *concierge* just said no one asked about me. I don't like the look of this at all ... *yakuza*, I'll bet."

He looked at her; their gazes connected. "They could just be guests, I suppose," he said.

It was good of him, Tokiko thought, to try to reassure her like that. He left it to her to make the suggestion. If nothing else, Josh had always been a gentleman.

"No, Josh. It's too late at night for guests to be waiting around. They are *yakuza*, and they'd be on you as soon as you stepped in there."

"Maybe. Look, I'll try the *concierge* again; his loyalty has to be to his guests, after all."

Tokiko permitted herself a smile at his charming, but fake, naivety.

"He has to answer to the local *yakuza* long after the guests go home," Tokiko said. "They didn't look like the same group we saw outside the party, do they?"

"I don't think so," Josh replied.

"Good. Then they've probably only been given orders to look out for you. They won't think anything if I go in," she said.

Tokiko saw it: his darting eyes ransacking every corner of his mind, turning over its contents, frantically searching for a way, an alternative, so she would not have to go in. It was sweet, she thought. After all this time, he still cared for her.

"It's the only way, Josh. You know that."

His desperation stopped, replaced with calm resignation.

"Okay. Get in, get what we need, and get out fast."

Josh rang for a taxi.

"So, it'll be here in ten minutes."

In Tokyo ten minutes meant ten minutes; their prompt getaway was assured. Josh took out his keycard and handed it to Tokiko.

"The sample is in my room safe – the code is 0512." It was her birth date; Tokiko knew it couldn't have been coincidence. Josh chose that code when he arrived. Her birth date. He still remembered it. She must have been on his mind from the moment he arrived.

"There is something they are keeping for me in the main hotel safe – we'll need that too. I'll call and tell them you'll be collecting it, but not until the last possible second, in case they alert the *yakuza*. It should give you a chance to get out without them knowing. Stand by the elevator for a moment when you come down from the room, so that I can see you, and I'll make the call, and please ... be careful ... any trouble, just run out straight away."

"Of course. Don't worry Josh ... I'm a big girl now," she assured him, not at all feeling it.

Tokiko half-covered her cascading black hair with her hood and took off. Passing the *concierge* was easy. He simply acknowledged her drifting presence with a discreet bow. In his job, she was sure, he was used to overlooking the coming and going of lady callers in the early hours – provided they came and went discretely. Tokiko made a point of ignoring the seated *yakuza*, drawing as little attention as possible. It seemed to work. She heard low chatter among them, but no following footstep clattered on marble as the elevator door chimed shut behind her. Her chest was taut. She breathed out slowly, freely, releasing the tension. In between floors, her anxious mind tried to distract itself.

This new Josh, the one standing outside, seemed smothered under the pressure of the imminent events. But there was more to his suffocation, something suppressed, for so long, forever altering him. What had happened to him in her years absent?

In her attempt to divine Joshua's deeper soul, she knew it would be dishonest of her to ignore the state of her own, and so Tokiko allowed herself to ponder in that moment the dangerous source of her own desires. She tripped back to that instant leading here, when she had launched barefoot to chase an American into the Tokyo subway, placing herself squarely in harm's way.

What must she have been thinking?

Haruto had once said that you only really discover yourself when forced into an instantaneous decision. "Time to consider is the enemy of self-revelation. We procrastinate, rationalise, and fool ourselves into making the choices we desire, he would say, and all to justify our visceral reactions with reasons we can admire. When there is no time, the mind demurs, and the heart, unfettered by thought, must alone respond."

It was her heart that chased after Josh Harker in that second outside the party.

She had rationalised it both to herself and Josh – it was true – with the excuses of concern for Kazuki, for Haruto, and even her mooted search for truth that ostensibly drove her actions. They were all lies. It was not even an altruistic wish to see the old Josh, unburdened, free, and joyful once again. It was to see the Josh of old, indeed, but as a means to usher back those times before she had aligned her star to the stellar track of Haruto Shimura. To unwind, but not replay.

All her flimsy excuses wafted away in front of her own intense scrutiny. Just one harsh truth was left: no amount of excuses could forgive her infidelity this night. Tokiko Shimura, the feminine pinnacle of society, the dutiful Japanese wife. She had made it all a lie. Once given the slightest opportunity, Tokiko realised, she had replaced in her heart devotion and loyalty to her husband with retrospective infantile desire for the excitement of the past. And now, caught between both those worlds, she saw them both slip away. In that harsh moment of choice back at Otemachi, Tokiko understood, she might have destroyed forever the opportunity to live again in either world. She had created a third, new world, in which she must now live. An undiscovered land. It was exhilarating; it was frightening, and it was so long ago since she'd felt either of those things.

The elevator doors slid open to her future. An electronic door chime tolled for her, inviting choice again. She took a step out of the elevator, and another in the direction of room 426, and another, each step feeling more difficult than the last.

* * *

Within minutes, she was stepping from the elevator again, this time back on the ground floor, pausing briefly, as expected, by the elevator. She could overhear the *concierge* taking Joshua's phone call. When the call ended, she stepped up to the desk.

"I have an item to collect for one of your guests."

"Yes, of course. For Harker-san. How prompt." He disappeared for a moment through an open doorway and reappeared carrying a brushed aluminum case. Tokiko could afford no time for politeness. She took it by the handle and swung around to leave the lobby, fast, without appearing hurried.

Behind her trot, out of the corner of her eye, she noticed one of the seated goons rise and make for the *concierge*. Had they heard Harker's name?

Her pace quickened.

Glass door panels parted automatically and presented her with a sight of ... nothing. There was nothing and no one waiting under the canopy. No Taxi. No Josh. She stepped into the center of the entry plaza and looked across the street. Josh was no longer there. Did they get to him already? Her heart began to race. She dared to look behind. The *yakuza* hoodlum had rejoined his partners in crime and they were all on the move, towards her.

Her heart smashed up against its prison in her chest. Josh. Could he ... would he ... run out on her? A perfidious abandonment, both sobering and terminal.

An instant later, her heart leapt to see Josh seated in the back of a green cab pulling up in front of her. He must have been waiting out of view around the corner. Tokiko scolded herself for lack of faith in him.

Hopping out of the halting cab, he called to her, reaching to hold her arm, "quick, get in!"

Allowing her to chassé into the seat first, Josh plonked in after – her firewall against the approaching danger. The chasing pack now ran, and she saw one make a mobile call.

"Drive!" Josh instructed the cab driver. After a few sweaty moments addressing the driver's professional pride and unfamiliarity with such spontaneity and lack of destination, they were on the road. It gave Harker a chance to revisit the more colorful aspects of the Japanese language too. The Japanese keep the extreme curse words secret from foreigners, so the driver was shocked enough by the curses Tokiko had once taught Josh to spur his foot onto the accelerator.

"Did you get it – the sample?" Josh asked.

Tokiko held out a small, sealed plastic pouch containing a snip of hair in a tiny glass slide. She saw his face melt into a broad, beaming smile, as if he just won the lottery. She allowed herself to laugh a little at him, not in a rude way, but sharing his joy.

"You see – no need to be so worried Josh. And we're both still alive!" she teased.

With that, a black Lincoln appeared in their wing mirror and accelerated sharply, veering closer. At this time of the morning, there were few cars, leaving the Lincoln plenty of space to get close. Just as Tokiko noticed a looming silhouette leaning out of the chasing car's back window, Josh yelled at her: "get down!" He placed his hand on the back of Tokiko's neck and pushed her toward her knees while he lurched down and reached inside his jacket.

Bullets rained sideways through the windows sending explosive puffs of powdered glass into the car's interior. The speed with which he had reacted amazed her. Instinct taking control. She could not have responded that fast; they would be dead. It seemed more than instinctual. That rapidity could only be reached through training. Training ... as if this was his job.

Tokiko heard four tyres piercing in anguish as they bit into asphalt; the taxi driver had stomped on the brakes. It was the wrong thing to do, but then he wasn't trained for *yakuza* engagements. As their attacker's car shot past them, bullets pealed out again, and she could just make out the taxi driver's last flinch before he slumped dead onto the wheel.

Tokiko didn't scream; what would be the use of it?

The firing stopped, then tyre squeal from the attacking car. It was coming around for another run. Harker's rippling arm reached out above her, tensed just enough to steady the gun without constraining its aim. She saw Josh aim slowly through the windshield. His adrenalin must be pumping, aggravating his nervous system, and yet he concentrated his hand into perfect stillness. She could not resist the urge to look out. The Lincoln stretched its petroleum-fuelled muscle with an angry engine roar that drew the car nearer.

They were a sitting duck stopped like this, and once it drew up alongside again, that would be the end. The shadowy back-seat gunner was lining-up. Harker took his shot. Missed. Still too far away.

He fired again, this time taking out the front tyre. The *yakuza* transport surged wildly toward the concrete median. Tokiko found herself grateful for the splashy ride and poor steering of American built cars. The loss of driver control gave her fellow refugee time enough to move his arm ever so slightly up and take sure enough aim to pump a slug into the shoulder of the emerging gunner.

"Stay down!" Harker roared to her once he'd delivered the required bullets.

Some gaudy pink floral loafers donated to her by a teenager were the only view she had to accompany the thundering clash as the Lincoln smashed into the median at high speed and flipped itself over onto the road. Josh's fleshy paw, swelled with throbbing veins, pulled at the door release next to her, but it was jammed. He barged open his own door and pulled her out by her forearm, using gentle force that didn't hurt her in anyway. She caught the silver case with her free hand on the way out.

All fell quiet, except for the increasing murmur from drivers of impeded vehicles, who could not get past the carnage. One groaning hunched figure unfurled itself upside down out the back of the Lincoln. He rubbed his forehead, blinked, and shook his head vigorously.

"Let's get the hell out of here, before more arrive," Josh said.

They ran, once more, to lose themselves somewhere in the concrete labyrinth before the Tokyo dawn arrived.

NINETEEN

Shibuya, Tokyo
16th October – 1:34am

When they entered the sushi bar in Shibuya, they were met by an excessively friendly *mama-san*. Josh didn't doubt they looked in need of such hospitality. Josh and Tokiko took a booth, as invited. How they must have looked: sweat-stained formal dress under garish teenage garb, mussed hair, frazzled, hungry and tired. A pair of scrawny street strays direct from the night's territorial catfight.

Custom was brisk inside the open-all-hours bar. It was cramped, crushingly humid, and noisy (the customers were mostly drunk by this time). Harker's last ounce of energy was sapped. He sank into the darkest corner booth away from the bustle of the central island bar.

"I'm famished," a jaded Tokiko proclaimed from across the table, "and we need a drink." She checked the menu plaques on the wall and ordered from the passing waitress, "Set Menu 23 please."

Something cheap and cheerful, Josh thought, to match the mood of the bar, before adding, "I'll have the same."

"And two beers," Tokiko interjected, qualifying, "Asahi for me; he prefers Kirin."

The waitress made scribbles on the screen of her pad and walked back into the din surrounding the bar. She had to push her way past a customer blocking the bar who'd obviously had too much to drink; he was talking loudly at no one in particular and his limp arms flailed around erratically.

The two diners sat speechless until the beers arrived. Joshua filled Tokiko's glass and waited as Tokiko filled his in return. They sipped the muscle-relaxing honeydew brew and made moans of relieved pleasure.

"Your Japanese is still very good," Tokiko said to him.

"I've been practising," he replied, not wanting to get into an explanation of why.

The small case Tokiko had left to one side magnetically grabbed his stare. It looked at him like some pet with hangdog eyes anticipating a walk. Harker just hoped the contents hadn't been damaged in all the knocking about.

"What's in it?" Tokiko asked, as if reading his mind.

"It's a portable DNA analyser."

"Oh, is that all? You should have told me – I could have picked one up from the lab."

Harker justified for himself the course of action that put her within the clutches of the *yakuza*. "You wouldn't have one like this. It rivals all those bulky lab scanners; it's the latest thing."

Tokiko smiled mischievously at him. She unclasped the lid, opened the device, and without looking at it, she recited: "Designed primarily for use by forensic investigators in the field. Automated PCR amplification from samples as small as 0.015 gram. STR analysis within twenty five minutes. Electrophoresis and readout facility, and a comparator function that works within a 0.001% margin of error." She closed the lid, still looking at a speechless Josh.

Tokiko leaned in and whispered, as if telling a great secret.

"It's made here in Japan under license from Shimura Electronics. I was part of the team of consultants that designed it."

Josh laughed. He laughed at his own ridiculous staunch pride. "I'm sorry."

"That's ok," she chuckled, "you weren't to know."

It shamed him that he took her for granted, forgetting she was more than this attractive socialite, more than the adroit heroine that gambled her life at his side these last hours. So much more. She was to her scientific field what Mount Fuji was to its surroundings – a beacon, towering above while offering inspiration to the flat world below her. This Asian waif could continually astound him.

His finest moment since entering this perplexing country was when she presented the crime scene evidence bag to him. She could have run, taking it, concealing Kazuki's complicity in the murder. She could have shopped Josh in to the *yakuza*. This maddening mission had confused his mind. Just a short time ago, he suspected she was capable of betraying him. But by her actions, she saved him from that consuming madness. In that single, shining moment, she had shown he could trust her.

"Well, let's get started," Tokiko enthused.

"Excuse me?" said Josh, jolted from his thoughts.

"The scanner – let's get it going. It can work while we're eating. It's designed to be used anywhere."

"Oh, yes. Yes, of course." Josh glimmered.

He swivelled the clamshell case around toward him, popped the clasps and unfolded the lid. The interior was unremarkable, black, with a few lights, buttons, slots, and two plastic pipettes inlaid in a cavity. Josh would use the sample tray option. He depressed the power button and booted up the software, feverishly drumming his fingers on the table as the iconic hourglass spun on-screen. Like a child at Christmas, he could not wait. And why should he, after all he had gone through to get it? He'd had to take the sample from Kazuki directly, the only way he could be sure it belonged to him. Even a hair taken off his clothing was no guarantee that it belonged to Kazuki. A blood wound was certain.

Josh reached into his pocket, and unloaded its contents onto the tabletop. Out tumbled a handkerchief, the sachet containing the hair sample, and a small blue velvet box, tied up with simple silk ribbon.

"Oh, in all the panic, I forgot about that one," Josh said, pushing aside the little box.

"What is it?"

"That one's for later," he said to an intrigued woman.

First, the test.

He took the plastic slide from the Ziploc bag. The slide contained a DNA sample he'd taken from the crime scene hair follicle, before he'd handed it all over to Silberman. It glided smoothly into the scanner's sample slot and disappeared. Next, he ripped the sterile wrapper from a fresh sample slide, placed the sliver of plastic on the table, and tapped into it a fleck of Kazuki's dried blood from his handkerchief, then put it in the second sample slot. Josh stabbed buttons. The scanner began a low whirring to accompany it's on-screen words.

> *PROCESSING ... STR AMPLIFICATION IN PROGRESS ...*
> *5%*

The scanner was a remarkable piece of equipment; in twenty minutes it could do the work Harker would take hours to do with all the equipment of a forensics lab: DNA separation, microarray preparation, and the laborious task of comparing each and every gene by hand. All replaced by a machine. That's progress, he thought. Given that this device cost two year's salary of a forensic investigator, his old profession was safe for some time – long enough for the career to reinvent itself before machines did them all out of a job.

To anyone else eating nearby in the bar, the bizarre mechanical incantations and exotic sigils displayed by this little handheld mage must have made no sense, but it made perfect sense to these two operators who, dressed still in Goth apparel, looked somewhat like mages too.

Tokiko stood and shed her cloak. The beer, the company, and the automated forensic process that required no intervention, all seemed to combine to make her more relaxed.

Josh too shed his leather outer skin. He sipped beer, admiring her politeness not to ask again about the little box. He pushed the box of delight to her side of the table.

"I meant to give it to you at the party."

"For me?"

"A gift, for a friend not seen in a long time. Open it."

"You remember our customs!" she exclaimed, delighted, and bowed.

Josh also bowed lightly.

Tokiko slipped the ribbon aside and prised open the box. Inside sat a delicate chain necklace, at its centre a pendant bearing a symbol that she recognised as the double helix. The two strands of silver twisted over each other and supported a tiny, single diamond at their centre.

"Oh Josh, it's perfect ... thank you! Put it on for me?"

Tokiko pulled back her hair, exposing the nape of her neck. He looked around a little nervously, wondering if the inebriated Japanese would consider this a social taboo, but they were far too busy breaking social taboos themselves. Josh draped the delicate chain around her slender neck, and after he fastened the clasp he couldn't resist the urge to let his fingertips linger on her warm skin just a little longer than was necessary. He regretted it immediately, not because of any offence she took, but because the simple touch re-ignited in him the sensation of a lost love; a love that he would be unwise to pursue in these altered circumstances. She turned to smile at him, fingering the new little token of affection that adorned her.

Dishes were deposited in front of them. Josh sprinkled pickled ginger into his *ramen,* loaded up his chopsticks, and slurped into his mouth. He hadn't realised how hungry he was. The comforting taste welcomed him back to Japan.

"Hmm. Good noodles," he said, finding he had to raise his noodle-muffled voice to contend with the noise of a drunken barfly. Tokiko topped up his beer, and he reciprocated.

The warm food, the hum of the clientele, the softly lit smile of his dining companion. For the first time since landing he felt he'd truly arrived in Tokyo. He was enjoying a meal with a friend, a lover ... an ex-lover at best. He would have to be satisfied with that. The electronic chaperone that whirred between them certainly precluded any romantic mood.

Harker tried some polite chat to fill the gap in conversation.

"I don't suppose Haruto will be too happy that you are here."

"Perhaps, but I make my own choices. Haruto knows that."

There was indifference in her reply that he found curious.

"If it were me," Josh said, "I'd be tearing this city apart to find you."

She shook her head. "It's not his way."

"Oh, I remember. Saving face – the Japanese way. Setting his dogs off throughout the city, and alerting everyone that Haruto Shimura's wife is out of his control, that would never do."

"At the risk of using a cliché you've heard a thousand times: you're not in Kansas anymore Josh. There aren't any cowboys in this city."

"So who set the *yakuza* posse after me?"

Tokiko dissembled. Harker took it to mean she didn't know.

"Haruto knows where I stand," she said. "He will let me do my thing; he always has, and I respect him for that."

"Respect. Wow. That's some special thing you've got going on there. How does he feel about this relationship? I wonder does he 'respect' you too."

"Of course he does – I am his wife."

Josh mulled over a mouthful of noodles before swallowing, trying not to scoff at her words. "You make it sound like you're one of his business deals. Doesn't he *love* you?"

"Yes, yes I'm sure he does. Haruto isn't always so forward with his feelings, like you would have him be. We can be reserved, slow to display affection. Privacy – especially in matters of the heart – is to be honored."

"Even with those closest to you? Well, I don't recall that ever being your way."

She smiled.

"I'm an emancipated woman of the post-Olympic generation," she said as if reading rote from one of those many glib bios of her in the social columns. The way she laced it with charming irony was beautiful to hear. "I always opened up to those I trusted Josh ... but then I always was a very poor judge of character, wasn't I?" she teased.

"Not at all."

Now Josh smiled.

"No," she said more seriously, "its different for our generation, but for Haruto – for the generation that grew up after the war – things were held private, not to be talked about. But I know. I know some of his past, and I know when I look into his eyes what he feels."

Then she looked in Joshua's eyes. Eye to eye, across the table, there was no way for him to avoid that perilous probe. Eye contact was sacred and special, and right then Harker wished he could be elusive. Tokiko looked right into him. Josh feared what she might see, a fear heightened by what she asked him.

"And you? You're no longer married?"

"No ... it ended a few years ago."

"Oh, I'm sorry. Were there –?"

"Can we talk about something else?" Josh said abruptly.

"It's okay to talk about my marriage, but not yours?" replied a quizzical Tokiko.

Then it was Josh who dissembled. He hadn't quite thrown up a wall yet, but he gave her a look, letting her know that he was stacking the bricks.

"Fine," she said. "Then what else is there to talk about? How about that – oh, what's the phrase you had for it – the 'elephant in the room'? What is it that you are doing here Josh?"

The elephant in the room, sat between them, whirring.

PROCESSING ... STR AMPLIFICATION COMPLETE ...
... ELECTROPHORESIS IN PROGRESS (SAMPLE 1) ... 27%

The electronic oracle of truth would soon reveal the solution to Harker's predicament: if it confirmed Kazuki as a murderer, it would permit Harker to tell Tokiko the truth about his CIA assignment; if it exonerated the young man, Josh could kiss goodbye to yet another career, and all the risks he'd taken would make a fool of him in her eyes.

He just needed to bide a little more time. Except he did not have the words.

Tokiko soaked up the hiatus in the conversation this time.

"What's happened to you Josh? I feel like I just met an old friend, only to lose him again. You've changed."

"Oh, don't come over all psychoanalytical on me Tokiko, not now."

"That's the American way, not ours."

Ours.

There was that divide again. That hint of cultural disparity had always been the backbeat in their song. It had always been the simultaneous source of a delicate frisson and yet a delicious fascination. It drove him wild, every time. Flirtatious base instincts he believed abandoned to youth long ago flared up within him again.

"So what *is* your way Tokiko? Exactly what way is it that you would like to have with me?"

He tried a seductive smile. Tokiko was having none of it.

"Oh stop it Josh – you can't disguise it from me."

"What are you talking about?"

"You put up a barrier around yourself, and when you do start to bring it down, it's only to attempt some cheap chat-up line. Making passes at a married woman? Please! That was never you Josh. You're deceiving no one but yourself."

"That's rich! You accuse me of deceiving myself, but what about you? You spent practically the entire party at my side; you came running, barefoot, through the streets of Tokyo after me, putting yourself between the *yakuza* and a man you haven't met in years. Tell me why, Tokiko, tell me honestly why did you do all that – and then tell me you're not deceiving yourself."

They paused, their exposed souls stripped bare and lacerated, as only ex-lovers could.

The friction reminded Josh why they went their separate ways. Like any young Japanese woman at the time, the idea of an American man was appealing, but the realities of dealing with the cultural differences were difficult. The objections of her traditional parents to the relationship, combined with the end of the semester, became the excuses, rather than the reasons, for Josh's return to America and the end of their run.

Harker started to feel guilty. Was he really that gentleman she believed, when he'd known her before? Had he forgotten himself, he wondered. People's perceptions of us are non-negotiable. It was how she saw him. Changed. She was right, of course. Perhaps she was getting to the truth of it, a truth he'd hidden from himself. Perhaps secretly, Josh considered, he'd hoped that by coming here her intuition would reveal it to him. Tokiko could bring back the Josh of old, before pain had taken a hold in his life.

"Tokiko, I'm sorry. I'm really very, very sorry. I shouldn't have said those things."

She wasn't looking at him anymore, but beyond. His words began softly massaging her tender soul. They would take a little time to work, he knew. It didn't seem to matter, since the bar was getting extremely noisy to the point that they could hardly hear each other. There was belligerence in the air; perhaps their mood had been influenced by it, leading to the argument. But someone else's belligerence hit a much higher, more violent crescendo.

A bottle smashed against the bar and voices raised. The drunken barfly's body was now engaged in some tidal swaying as he lurched at the *sushi* master behind the bar, seemingly unaware that he pointed at him with a broken bottle. Fortunately, it was his non-lethal hand that he used to stab out points of his argument with a finger, more coherently than he could manage with his tongue. The culinary artisan tried to back away. Slurred words presented the greatest challenge yet to Harker's mastery of Japanese; he could make out something about having lost a job, and about his wife supporting him. In short: disgrace – the Achilles' heel of a Japanese soul. The *sushi* master seemed uninvolved, merely the outlet, but tried to take the unruly customer by the arm and escort him out. This only resulted in more aggression. Backing off, he shouted over the bar to a man in a silver-grey suit, someone Harker took to be the manager. The suited man flapped his hands and made a call on his cell phone. The heartfelt cries continued from the disgraced drunk. "My children –," he sobbed openly, beating weakly at the breast of the cook's white overall, "how do I explain their father can not provide for them?"

Belligerence was exchanged for morosity, and things calmed down again.

The DNA analyser was not distracted from its work.

PROCESSING ... STR AMPLIFICATION COMPLETE ...
... ELECTROPHORESIS (SAMPLE 1) COMPLETE ...
... ELECTROPHORESIS IN PROGRESS (SAMPLE 2) ... 87% ...
92% ...
... ELECTROPHORESIS (SAMPLE 2) COMPLETE ...
... COMPARING ...

The pixelated hourglass spun.

It was agony, but Josh was prepared to wait. Even with the limited processing power of the scanner, it could compare the 40,000 genes in just a few seconds.

The seconds sauntered by, giving his mind space to wonder about the outcome. So sure had he been that Kazuki was the assassin that he sliced a thousand year old sword into the son and bodyguard of the man who owned a portion of Japan. If Harker were wrong, he'd have to explain it back in Langley, to the DD/NCS himself. But worse ... how would he explain it to the woman so close to him now? What if the match was negative? There were no alternative leads. Where would he go then? Back on unemployment assistance perhaps.

Prepare to say goodbye to yet another career Josh.

The outcome became even more anticipated.

The hourglass vanished and a figure appeared. In large print, half the size of his palm, the career destroying device reported:

4.7% CODING ALLELE MISMATCH – COMPARISON NEGATIVE.

Harker's stomach churned, and it wasn't the noodles. Any court in the world would acquit a defendant based on a 4.7% difference in the genes. Even 0.2% would classify DNA as coming from a different person.

"Damn it," he blurted.

How could he have got it so wrong? Slumping back into the red faux-leather seat of the booth, he cast his head towards the ceiling. It hurt, and he didn't want to think any more.

As a small tray of jellied noodles was dropped off in front of Harker, he felt the pit of his stomach collapse, like the world around him. He rubbed his eyes with both hands and released a guttural sigh. He pushed the tray of jellied noodles away from him: he always detested that concoction. Tokiko, on the other hand, always loved them. She scooped them up to her narrow mouth, and folded them in, never once letting them touch her lips, like a butler meticulously packing a suitcase.

Tokiko looked at the results, then serenely continued to finish the noodles in silence. Josh was glad; her eating made a difficult conversation impossible to have.

When she was done, she arranged her chopsticks back on their stand and folded her arms.

Obligation dictated Josh be the first to speak. "Well, at least Kazuki is in the clear. You should be glad of that."

"And you were so sure. Why?" Tokiko said in a pliant, almost sympathetic way. Even now she sought to soothe his dejection. Harker doubted he would be so understanding in her situation. That made her better than him, and that made him want to be better for her. He wanted to be the old Josh, worthy of her again.

"His hair color matched, and his age fitted the DNA profile, but I didn't select him on a whim. I wouldn't want you to think that. We were looking for a culprit linked to the Shimura Corporation."

"We?"

He rebuked himself for the slip, and proceeded instead to tell Tokiko of a highly-trained assassin, matching Kazuki's skill, and tales of advanced devices such as nano-syringes and DNA camouflage used for dealing out death with stealth.

"You know, we do have devices like that under development."

Harker dared to let himself hope she might be coming to believe him. Tokiko turned the DNA scanner toward her and began conjuring up runes of biotech secrets on its screen. She spoke as she cast the runes.

"You said the DNA was camouflaged somehow, that the follicle cells' DNA didn't match the characteristics of the hair, right?"

"Sure," he replied.

"Well, one of the techniques we've been working on across two research departments is the use of nanospheres to penetrate a couple of centimeters down into the dermis. My department use it for cosmetic applications, but I've heard Taro's biotech division modified it as a delivery vector for somatic gene therapy. It injects recombinant DNA strands into existing epidermal skin and hair cells. One application of that could be .... to disguise DNA, as you described. But it would only alter trace material like hair and skin cells, and they would revert back after a time, so any trace material left at a crime would be out of synch with the donor's live DNA. The sample you took from Kazuki tonight was a live blood cell."

Harker groaned loudly and slapped his palms to his forehead, as if to knock the stupidity out of him.

"I'm an idiot. Not all of his DNA would have been altered."

Tokiko turned the scanner back to him to show the beauty of the electronic incantation she had uttered to the device through it's small keyboard.

"Look. Here's a list of the genes that are different between the samples. Notice anything?"

"Yeah ... they all cover physical characteristics." Typing in the chromosomal location code 15q11, he was brought to the EYCL3 gene, one of the genes encoding for eye color – green eyes, not Kazuki's striking blue eyes. Harker tried some more. "Look, the hair pigmentation genes: they encode for blonde hair in Kazuki's blood, but for brown hair in the altered hair follicle DNA, even though the hair itself is actually blond!"

"Someone slipped up," Tokiko replied. "If they'd left hair pigmentation out of the altered gene list, it wouldn't be obvious it was altered it at all."

Tokiko tapped a button, scrolling through the genes.

"And every gene that has been altered is homozygous – the same value on the X and Y chromosomes. That's very unusual, the X and Y chromosome DNA come from two different parents. It's rare to have so many genes with the same values coming from both parents. That's a give-away of altered DNA too." She looked sheepishly at Josh. "Sorry – look who I'm explaining it too."

He smiled. They'd studied this stuff together.

"That's odd," she said.

"What is?"

"Well, I've widened the search to include more genes, ones that weren't altered by the technique. Josh – they're *all* homozygous! Every gene in the live blood sample – Kazuki's own natural DNA – is the same on both parent chromosomes. How can that be? That goes far beyond mere camouflage. "

Josh remembered Porcho's allegation about the DNA. Every gene. Every single one. Even the non-coding so called junk DNA. The exact same base-pair values on both the X and Y chromosome. Josh knew that scenario could only happen if both parents were identical but that conclusion seemed too fantastic. He felt they were missing the point entirely. Something was certain – this DNA wasn't natural. And it surprised Tokiko just as much.

"Oh, Kazuki!" she exclaimed. Tokiko became lost in Joshua's eyes, waiting to be caught. "What have they done to him? Josh, what have they done to Kazuki?"

Kazuki could be an assassin, she seemed prepared for that much, but Josh could see this new revelation was too much for her.

"Who *are* you?" she asked Josh, no longer willing to defer. "How did you get involved in this?"

Oh, what the hell – she seems as surprised about this as me.

"Tokiko, I'm with the CIA," he whispered. It felt like a burden released, and now that he said it, it sounded a little ridiculous. But she didn't ridicule him. After this morning, would anything be unbelievable again? No. This morning the sun had not yet risen, and she was Alice in Wonderland, and would be asked to believe six impossible things before breakfast.

"I came here because I thought you could help me to figure all this out," Josh said. "And I'm sorry Tokiko. I'm really very sorry to have brought this on you."

She shook her head, looked at the scanner and mumbled, "this isn't your doing."

The restaurant had never been so quiet all the time they had been in it, as if a static storm were building. The drunkard at the bar made no noise and every diner or drinker had stopped talking. The cause of the lull soon became apparent; all eyes looked to a pair of men that came in and strode out a wide circuit of the bar, like vultures circling. Each was dressed in a suit and a long loose coat that came down almost to the floor. Rather absurdly, Josh thought, both wore sunglasses at night. Every customer looked away as the sunglasses scanned their way. Both wore identical gold lapel pins, the details of which he could not make out, but it told him enough to know they were of the local *yakuza*.

Instinctively, he made to stand up to leave.

Tokiko arrested his movement with a swift pat to his forearm.

"*Yakuza* called in to deal with the trouble-maker at the bar," she said. "Don't draw attention."

The pair stopped either side of the drunkard and barked questions at him. By this time, he was long past coherent conversation.

"Why not the police?" Josh whispered.

Tokiko gave a wry smile. "In this city you don't call the police if you want something done. *Yakuza* are far more effective – watch."

They towered over the hunched noisemaker who at first was oblivious to their presence, but sobriety took hold instinctively as soon as he realised who these men were. The pathetic figure reminded Josh of the lump of jellied noodles: spineless, quivering, and with a green tinge. As the two unofficial enforcers scooped him up under their arms, his belligerence rose again. He roared some incomprehensible gibberish and, charged with alcohol-fuelled bravado, took a swing at one of the *yakuza*.

Tokiko shook her head.

The powerless attack was easily dodged and then met with a disproportionate counter-attack. In one powerful action, the taller of the *yakuza* lifted the man by his throat and slammed him onto plates of food on the bar. He drew a machine pistol from inside his coat and pressed the muzzle so far into the man's flabby double chin that his jaw bone was fully visible. The *yakuza* squeezed the trigger on his pistol and, just before it engaged, he shouted a phrase of English. "Bang, bang!" and once more, "Bang, bang!"

If it wasn't for the palpable fear throughout the entire restaurant, Josh could have burst into laughter at the comic scene that played out in front of him – something he would expect from children in a playground, not the criminal underworld.

For the locals though, the ones who knew and understood the *yakuza* menace, that childish threat was very real. Excruciated horror crumpled the face of their victim, folded backwards over the bar. Shortly it became unbearable and he could no longer look. He turned his face aside and started to wail. Customers cowered uncomfortably into their meals. Harker could not deny the hold these crime lords had on their people, and even admired it a little. This was the strange world that had given rise to Haruto Shimura. This was where Haruto learned to live with respect and dispense fear ... from an early age. He was beginning to realize the gruesome extents to which that lust for control had grown. It seemed to have grown as far as controlling DNA – of his own adopted son. But why? For what reason? Josh needed more answers.

The *yakuza* took the drunkard by the arms and dragged him off the premises. With the hubbub in the restaurant thundering back louder than before, raucous frenzied laughter broke the tension among the diners.

The scene had distracted Tokiko. Josh was pleased to see her return fleetingly to her normal self. Giggling, she said: "If he had embarrassing problems with his wife before, just wait until he arrives home with the *yakuza* taxi service!"

Tokiko tried to lighten the mood further. "So, CIA? Are you spies always so jumpy?"

"I'm still studying for my full spy licence."

She giggled.

"Look Tokiko, this evidence – it won't convince a court of law. No one is going to prosecute Kazuki over this, but we need answers. We need to know what it is about."

"We? You mean American Intelligence."

Josh took a step back in his mind. "Yes. I need your help. I know I'm asking you to betray your family, even your country –"

"Well, I need to know too, for Kazuki's sake. Until I find that out, nothing's for certain." After a considerate pause, she added, "I'll take you to Andrei. If anyone will know what this is about, he will. He was head of research in the biotech division, up until a few months back. He made no secret that he was unhappy there. I wouldn't be surprised if he knows something about these genetic alterations."

A switch flicked in Harker's mind.

"Dr. Andrei Sorokin?" he asked.

"Yes – you know him?"

"Only by name. It came up when I was researching a report on the corporation. Sorokin was one of the scientists head-hunted by Shimura Biotech from an American firm years ago. Where is he?"

"He lives quietly now, in the countryside near Nagoya," Tokiko said.

"The commotion outside will be a perfect distraction. Let's slip away."

Josh took the evidence with him, but left the scanner behind. It would only slow them down. The CIA would have to foot the bill. They ducked out under the curtain at the exit and would make for a capsule hotel to catch up on sleep. Tomorrow, they would have to buy a change of clothes and head for Nagoya.

On the street, Tokiko said, "I understand now why you were slow to tell me who you worked for. I guess you must really trust me, to tell me something like that."

Josh didn't have a good answer for her.

Paranoia is healthy.

TWENTY

Gotunda, Tokyo
16th October – 9:06am

"You asked to see me," said Kazuki on the move, entering Dr. Kinugasa's clinic.

"Yes, please take a seat."

"Could we make this brief? I'm very busy." Kazuki stood with crossed arms. Statuesque stoicism perfected. Tokiko hadn't returned home the previous night, and Haruto was getting anxious. Kazuki now needed to find her.

"Well, I'm not sure that's wise Kazuki. We have important matters to discuss. Critical matters, in fact."

Kazuki sensed the doctor laying a mat to soften a fall.

"The test results have come back, haven't they?" Kazuki asked.

"They have," the Doctor replied, his solemnity foretelling what was to follow.

"I see," Kazuki said flatly, concealing any emotion from his observer. Like a reed swaying under life's gusts, he resolved to remain tough and resilient. He could do it, because he knew this day was coming. It was Kazuki who first asked to see the Shimura family doctor, though he'd never needed him before.

Balance began it, or rather the loss of balance. It was subtle at first, undetectable to all but those like Kazuki who relied on precise balance for their martial ways. A momentary lapse in balance had alerted his target that night. A loose creaking stair step – on any normal day avoidable – let Senator Olsen know he was there. It was one of many slip-ups that grew in frequency. That particular one had cemented his resolve. To be inconvenienced by some minor illness was something he could bear alone in dignified silence, but affecting his ability to perform his duty it became something that had to be shared, diagnosed, and cured. His duty demanded it.

Haruto had never encouraged Kazuki to attend doctors. "Eat well, train hard," Haruto had decreed, "and let the life harmony instilled by your physical discipline govern your health inside too. That way, avoid necessity for any doctor to trouble you."

To Kazuki, entering this clinic felt like one more small failure. His physical discipline wasn't good enough; he'd become weak. If a progressing illness jeopardised his ability to protect Haruto and his family, then that would be the end of Haruto's respect. That would be truly intolerable to the young man. So he'd come. To the doctor. To be diagnosed, and cured. Kazuki had no choice. It seemed a life of no choices. A pre-programmed existence subject to the designs of others. Where, he wondered, had he ever made a choice that was truly his own. Perhaps it was starting now.

Kinugasa had ordered tests and tests. Results arrived on this inconvenient day. Recent days made the need for a solution greater than any inconvenience. He noticed his energy evade him after smaller and smaller periods of high exertion. In his play fight with Harker, that exhaustion had given the American a chance to strike. In hindsight, Kazuki guessed at the purpose of the strike. Proof. It could endanger them all, exposing the link to Olsen's death and implicate the Shimura Corporation. The shame of it would be too much to bear. The man Kazuki called father would never (Haruto had made known) have sanctioned such an extreme measure as Olsen's assassination.

Anyone who would expose Kazuki had to be found and neutralised. Tokiko must be separated from the American first. If his abilities for this task were in any doubt, he needed to know now.

So the indifference he displayed toward the diagnosis was not as it appeared.

"I'm very sorry to have to tell you this Kazuki ... won't you please sit?"

Kazuki shook his head, shuffling from one foot to the other.

Get on with it.

"Unfortunately I have to tell you that you have lymphoblastic leukaemia."

Kazuki felt a pillar holding up his life crack and shatter, leaving his foundations' stability in doubt. His composure was disrupted, only briefly, for as long as it took him to realise he was still standing and hadn't yet fallen.

"But, I've never been ill before."

He appreciated Kinugasa's restraint from saying what he suspected must be on his mind: *well, you are now!*

"Leukaemias quite often occur in children. The symptoms mostly show in very early or very late in life. Cases like yours, while rare, are not unheard of."

Kazuki breathed as his training had taught him, to maintain a steady heart rate. A incensed heart, he knew, would not easily make sense of this predicament. Breathe. Slow. Calm.

"Does anyone else know?" he asked in time.

"Not yet. We should inform Haruto though."

"No," Kazuki said adamantly.

"He is your legal guardian, Kazuki."

"Thank you Doctor, but I'm 20 – an adult now. It is my decision who to tell."

"Your family! Surely you must tell them."

If I knew who my real family were, perhaps I would tell them.

"I will tell them, but in my own way and at a time of my choosing."

"I don't think you understand the seriousness of this situation Kazuki. You'll need their support. If there is a chance that a bone marrow transplant could help, it must be from a relative, perhaps a sibling, with compatible DNA."

"If I have any siblings."

"And only Haruto knows that. Only he knows where you were adopted from. You must inform him of your condition, if only for that reason. And ... your father's contacts, and the facilities of Shimura Biotech, could provide a treatment better than any you could receive in the world, if ... conventional treatment was not an option."

"Not an option? What do you mean by that."

"We need to take you in immediately for additional tests to confirm this for sure, but your balance problems could be a sign it has reached your brain. Don't you understand what that means?"

"That I am dying."

"Well, I wouldn't put it quite like that Kazuki. It can be terminal, yes, but this is why you must act now. Acute lymphoblastic leukaemia, if left untreated, is fatal within weeks. This too is why you must let Haruto know – now"

The young man wasn't entirely present anymore. He now knew the diagnosis and cure, but liked the cure even less than the diagnosis. It would present Kazuki as weak in the eyes of the man who trained him to be strong. Haruto Shimura. The man who Kazuki called *sensei* – mentor, and sometimes even father. Haruto adopted a stranger, gave him a life. Could he now ask more, having taken so much from Haruto and given so little back?

It was all too soon. Time too little.

"I need time, to think," said Kazuki. In his mind, Kazuki was already backing up to the door.

"You don't have that time," Dr. Kinugasa was on the verge of shouting in despair at the departing Kazuki. It was unbecoming of the old gent, Kazuki thought, but volume was his only remaining way to persuade the fleeing youth.

"Don't tell anyone until I instruct you to," Kazuki said just before closing the door behind him.

He stood outside the door, still holding the cold steel handle, head back, eyes closed.

The man in him, the man who had been trained how to dispense death, had duty and obligation to fall back on. He would protect his family. He would find Harker and bring a stop to his run.

The boy still within him, the boy who never had the emotional training necessary to deal with his own death sentence, that boy wanted to bawl, to cry out for the mother he never knew.

Right then he was overcome with a feeling that all his life had somehow been a sham. He wasn't the strong leader of the *yonkuichi* he pretended to be. All his life had been lived as a little boy playing at being a man.

And right now, more than anything in the world, though he didn't understand why, he yearned for Tokiko.

He had to find them.

TWENTY-ONE

Otemachi, Tokyo
16th October – 10:46am

Kazuki had been called to Taro's office. The metropolitan mêlée of Tokyo life played-out for Taro beyond the glass curtain of his office wall. Taro sat back, peering over his glasses like an anxious shrew, and proposed that Kazuki sat, but the guardian of the clan stood ever ready for reaction, sword draped over his shoulder.

"I just had a visit from my father," said Taro. The exclusive 'my' did not escape the notice of an adopted Kazuki. "Tokiko didn't return home last night. He is becoming extremely concerned."

"Interesting that he should approach you, almost as if he expects you to know where she is. Isn't that odd?"

Taro flashed a visceral glare.

"It is you Kazuki, who is supposedly the protector of this family. If there is blame to be taken for her disappearance, it will be yours."

"Her disappearance? You mean you don't know where she is?" Kazuki tut-tutted. The head of the *yonkuichi* tried hard not to gloat at his brother's misfortune, but failed.

"Have you lost her, brother? Or should I say, have your *yakuza* lackeys lost her?"

Now he thought of it, Kazuki felt relief, not satisfaction, that they were still at large.

"Don't play games, " said Taro. "You know what is at stake. Haruto will blame you, his family's supposed protector, if anything happens to his wife again. And if Harker manages to link you to Olsen's murder, then your illustrious position will be in jeopardy."

Kazuki flinched. He saw what his brother was doing, and despised it.

"You would try to manipulate me again, would you? Use my regard for Haruto against me."

"What do you mean?"

"You think I fear to lose his respect, and so use that fear to try and motivate me to do your will. I see you now Taro, I see you for what you are. What you have been all these years."

"Don't be ridiculous." Taro stood up and – deep in thought – paced around to Kazuki's side of the desk. "You're not yourself. What's wrong with you today?"

Kazuki's shoulders stiffened.

"Relax. Haruto doesn't know you killed Olsen," insisted Taro.

"He knows his friend Olsen is dead under suspicious circumstances. He knows I was away at the same time. He puts two and two together Taro!"

"And arrives at nothing. Listen Kazuki: don't let this worry you. I covered this possibility too – the genetic camouflage I made you take, the prototype tools Shimura Electronics provided for an untraceable kill. Haruto, no-one, will ever have real proof."

"Except perhaps Harker. He was at the crime scene, and he took a sample of my DNA. Can you take the chance? Because I sure can't."

"That's exactly why we need to find and kill him!"

We? You are a piece of work brother!

He saw Taro's manipulative verve, how he could take the motivations of Kazuki, his younger brother, and toy with them, enjoying it. How long had he been doing this? Taro had always had the lead in age; how long had he used his little brother as a play-thing this way? Kazuki was beginning to see his brother in a new light. The recent news of his health had unsettled Kazuki. It called many things into question. But the revision of history would have to wait until another day. Kazuki knew he didn't have time for it now. In one thing his brother was right: the pair needed to be found immediately.

A *yonkuichi* guard sidled in and whispered into Kazuki's ear.

"Some news?" asked a curious Taro.

Kazuki had taken a different strategy than his brother's crude pursuit of the couple. *Yonkuichi* spotters were placed strategically around the city, at places where they might next show up: Shimura facilities; routes out of the city; all the usual possibilities. They'd been spotted boarding the *Tōkaidō Shinkansen* train. Kazuki decided he would follow them alone, without telling anyone, especially Taro. He dare not risk more in case Taro sent in *yakuza* who had no interest in Tokiko's safety. The loyalty of Taro's *yakuza* allies was only on offer as long as Taro's arm of the corporation provided technical assistance for their amphetamine production. Kazuki had to keep them out of this.

"If you'll excuse me brother, " said Kazuki, "I have a more pressing appointment," and left his brother alone in his office.

* * *

Taro dialled.

"Doshida-san," he barked down the phone.

"Yes?"

"I think Kazuki's men know where Harker is. Follow him."

"Yes."

"And we have a potentially bigger problem – she never warned us that he was coming. This man was under her direct supervision ... and now he's here. It could possibly mean she's turned. She's gone double on us, or perhaps always was."

"But to send him here, she must know we'd make the connection. Would she be that stupid?"

"Perhaps not, and that raises an even more worrying possibility."

"Which is?" asked the *yakuza* gang boss.

"Someone else is running Harker ... someone higher up."

Doshida went silent on the other end. Eventually, he could think of nothing better to say: "That is reason for concern."

"It gets worse than that," said Taro. "If our contact didn't tell us Harker was coming, then she doesn't know he's been assigned here. She's been kept out of the loop. That could mean someone suspects her."

The line went quiet again. The *yakuza* had run out of responses.

"Either way," said Taro, "she's become a liability. We've taken so many precautions to prevent any links back to the corporation – I won't risk exposing it now. Shut off the liability."

"I understand," Doshida said. "I'll have our allies deal with it."

"No. They aren't to do it directly. If it's discovered the *Yakuza* in America are involved, it'll only direct suspicion toward Japan. I want total isolation. Use the asset recruited for the main operation; this kind of thing is his expertise anyway, isn't it?"

"Won't that jeopardise the main operation?"

"Not if he's as good as we hope. At the amount we pay him, he'd better be that good."

"I'll make the arrangements," he said in parting.

Taro heaved the stress out of his chest once the call was ended. One death following another. It was getting messy. Events were accelerating, hopefully not accelerating out of his control. He told himself the deaths were necessary; he had to secure what was to come. He had the future of the Shimura empire – his empire – to think of.

TWENTY-TWO

Gotunda, Tokyo
16th October – 11:33am

The *shinkansen* bullet train pealed past the slumbering presence of Mount Ibuki. The mid-morning sun cast a sallow tinge on its perfectly snow-dusted peak. It sat there on a platter of Japan like some inviting confectionery with an iced fondant cap. Even though it wasn't consumable, Tokiko thought, it certainly was consuming.

She drank in the vista like a fine imbibing wine that warmed her soul.

Inside the carriage the train hummed. The busiest line in Japan, but at this in-between time it was mostly empty. Her travelling companion melted into the lush padded seat opposite her. Joshua looked lost too in the rotascope scenery constantly refreshing itself for passenger amusement. Now, in the leisurely pace they adopted, Tokiko allowed herself to believe they appeared like any anonymous couple, taking a relaxing day trip to the countryside somewhere. She grasped at that fiction and held it tight like a shield.

Josh appeared in full light today, not hidden by the darkness, nor mood lighting, not blurred by last night's dizzying fugue of events. She looked upon his fully exposed features and saw all she'd missed the night before; the subtle little wrinkles of his skin like the paint cracks on some great masterpiece hanging in a gallery. And yet a fully relaxed Joshua Harker was in another way a blank canvas, revealing nothing, waiting for the application of new colors that would create a new masterpiece in the remainder of his life.

The ebullient eruption of laughter as two children ran down the aisle split the stream of her thoughts into a new tributary, taking her in a very different direction. Her eyes followed the boy and the girl all the way to the end of the carriage before she restarted the conversation.

"Did you have any children, you and your wife? What was her name – Megan?"

"Yes and no," said Josh to a confused Tokiko. "I mean, yes her name was Megan, but no, we had no children."

"Well, that's something I suppose. I mean ... it's harder on children, isn't it, a divorce?"

She fished; Josh bit.

With a heavy soul-disgorging heave of breath he said, "we didn't divorce, Tokiko. Megan died."

Tokiko held a hand to her mouth. "Oh, I'm so sorry. I didn't mean to –"

"It's okay," Josh consoled, "you couldn't have known."

It was good of him, she thought. Good of him to do that, to console her, when his injury must surely have outweighed Tokiko's shock.

"Was she ill?"

Josh held the nail of his thumb to his lower teeth and looked away, across Japan, to a land far away in a world unreachable.

"No," he said.

Tokiko noticed the tensing of his jaw muscles and eyes that glistened more lustrous than before. After a moment of composure, Josh looked around – all the nearby seats were empty – and he sat forward. Only Tokiko was to hear.

"I, eh ... I haven't talked about this in a long time, so bear with me."

"I'm not going anywhere else," she said, giving a supportive smile. Tokiko listened, with tears in her heart, while Joshua excised his own heart.

"I worked in forensic pathology for a time, after you knew me. It seemed like the way to go after medicine, helping to solve crimes and bringing criminals to justice – you remember what I was like then, always wanting to change the world."

Tokiko smiled at his remark.

"Anyway," Josh continued, "in time the gloss wore off the job. When you spend day after day dissecting the bodies of the dead, or analysing clothing for signs of a murderer – clothes that once belonged to someone's child – then the whole thing just becomes one long reminder of the evil that works out there. It became depressing, dragging me down. She was the one bright light in it all – Megan. To this day, I still don't know why someone as perky and optimistic as her could end up working in a forensics lab and stay untainted by it. She saw me growing unhappy there, and always cheered me up. We fell in love and married. Simple as that. She convinced me – not that I needed much convincing – that I should find other work, somewhere I could be closer to making the difference. So I joined the police force itself.

"Those were hard times too. There was some death most weeks, but it was outweighed by the satisfaction of being the one to track down and arrest criminals, to be the one to look them in the eye after I'd put on the cuffs and know that no other victims would look into those eyes again. Doing it personally made all the difference, you see. Megan had known that about me. She was right." Josh's face beamed as he laughed a little. "Feisty though she was, she was always right."

Tokiko popped a question, hesitantly: "what happened to her?"

Josh's voice solemnified.

"I'd just been promoted to Detective. There was this one guy I had managed to put away, a real psycho. We're not supposed to call them psychos anymore, I know. They're sociopaths now, aren't they? But that word didn't do this guy justice; he was a real psycho. You just don't know people like that exist until you come up against them. He didn't have an ounce of emotion in his body other than hate. This guy was a serial killer, but not like any other. He didn't just kill people – he specialized in families. And he didn't just kill, he destroyed; he wanted to crush their spirit before their bodies. But Jesus, Tokiko ... the way he would do it!"

His face scrunched.

"He'd kill the children in front of their parents, then the husband in front of his wife; I couldn't even begin to tell you how bad. It was such intrinsic evil that nobody could ever understand it, not without becoming that insane themselves. No man should have to see what he did to those people."

His voice broke. Unable to continue, he paused in his story.

Tokiko rubbed the warm silken skin of her palm against his forearm. It worked – gave him the strength to continue.

"We caught him: tracked him down just in time to stop him from killing his next victims. I made the arrest, and like all my other arrests I looked him in the eye. Only this time I wished I hadn't. His eyes, Tokiko! I will never forget those eyes: they were black barren pools, like something had gouged them out. I was raised to believe that everyone deserves a second chance, that no one is beyond redemption, but what a strange feeling it was to look at that man and know without doubt he wasn't human, just an animated corpse that kills. No one could give him a second chance, because he was just a shell. The man who was once inside had gone. Even though I couldn't purge from my mind the things he had done, I still managed to join in the celebrations when we finally put him away. At last I was making a difference. Things settled down and eventually myself and Megan even talked about starting a family, and then, a few months later ..."

A lump caught in his throat.

"Joshua ... ?" Tokiko held firm.

"Then it all fell apart, Tokiko. The same psycho I put away was being transferred to a prison with execution facilities. He escaped enroute. Never did find out how. I reckon he made a deal with someone on the inside. Anyway, my Captain followed the advice of the profilers, thinking that he would return to finish the job on his last victims. Myself and Sheridan – my partner in the force at the time – were part of the stakeout."

"Did you catch him?"

He shook his head. "We tend to think psychopaths are stupid," Josh continued, his voice raised now, "after all, only someone stupid would kill for pleasure, right? They're bound to get caught. Well, that would be stupid – to get caught, I mean. To go back to a victim where you know the police would be waiting for you. No, the powers-that-be underestimated his intelligence and his sheer malevolence. He didn't go after that family – he went after mine. He wanted revenge on the man whose forensic testimony put him away."

"Was there no police protection around your wife?" Tokiko asked.

"Oh, of course there was, but it was minimal. Like I said, it was decided it wouldn't be his choice of action, and I was ordered to protect the primary target – they said it would be too dangerous to have me involved in protecting my wife anyway. Too much personal involvement, that I couldn't be detached and professional. So two other officers were given that assignment. Well, when word came over the police band of an attack at my house, Sheridan and me tore over there as fast as we could.

"The two officers on duty had their throats slit while still in the car. They didn't stand a chance. Sheridan ran and was first to make it into the house. He was shot with a pistol the perp had stolen from the cops outside, but managed to take the psycho down in the shoot-out, before the bullet took him. I never even got the chance to let off a shot – it was all over that quick. They were both dead by the time I got through the door."

"Megan – ?" Tokiko asked, with suspended breath.

"I was too late."

Tokiko heard Josh struggle to keep his voice.

"He had killed the baby first," Josh blurted.

"Baby? But didn't you say you'd only discussed having a baby a few months before –" Tokiko gasped. The implication of what she just said hit her. She held her hand to her mouth, as if to contain the horror of what had just entered her mind. Her eyes welled up.

"Yes, I did. Megan was four months pregnant."

"Oh Josh! I'm so sorry."

The words, she knew, were inadequate. Any words would be.

Tokiko stroked the side of his neck compassionately, as Josh stared far into the distance.

"I was the only one who survived. That night I lost my wife, my child, and my colleague and best friend. That was the night I gave up on dreams."

After taking a few moments to compose herself, Tokiko eventually said, "I knew you had changed: I saw it in your eyes last night, but I never imagined what you were carrying."

"It got worse soon after. I couldn't work in the place anymore; couldn't work with a boss who said my wife was in no danger. So I left – another job down the pan. And I had nothing to replace it with, just sitting in an empty home all day."

Josh concluded with a sigh: "Anyway, eventually I forced myself to pick up the pieces and start again, joined the CIA, still hoping ... somehow ... to end the nightmares people cause."

A single clear tear rolled a lonely path away from Tokiko's cherishing eye, broadcasting the heartbreak she felt. As Josh cleared it away from her cheek with a rough callused thumb, she caught his hand and rubbed. Pushing away all her own concerns, she presented to Josh a soft, beautiful gaze of compassion, understanding, and total love, all the while thinking that any expression would be inadequate for its task. Only one thing could express how she felt. She leaned in and kissed his lips. Bristles pressed hard into the soft skin of her chin. Any glimpsing passenger feeling embarrassment at the display of affection would have to deal with it, and she did not care. This was for Joshua Harker alone.

She lost herself in the oceanic depths of his sea-green eyes for a time, unsure for how long, but Josh seemed to join her on that vacation from time and space. She could see him looking honestly at her now, properly. All secrets out. Except one.

"And there wasn't anyone else after her, was there?" Tokiko asked.

He shook his head. "No. There were women, sure, but nothing serious. Flings, that's all. It's just..." he struggled to catch those right words, eluding him like birds in flight.

"... they never seemed the same," Tokiko completed.

"No. There's been no one like her."

"Or else you're ... afraid?"

"Afraid? Of what?"

"Losing someone again."

"You think I've been avoiding loving someone ... is that it?'

"You said it, not me," replied Tokiko, surprised he sensed what she thought. This man, she now realised, had grown a depth greater than the Josh she had known. He was searching for answers. He'd been searching for years. "Poor Josh," she said rubbing his hand more, as if charging it up with solace. "You don't see it, do you?"

"What?"

"You've lost trust."

Josh withdrew his hand and sank back in the seat.

"Listen Tokiko, there's nothing you could tell me that hasn't been through my mind, over and over. You think you understand that pain, but you don't. I've been down all those roads that don't bring any answers. The only truth I've learned is that ... I miss her. It's as bloody simple and as bloody awful as that. And I can't replace her."

"No one's asking you to. But you haven't moved on, Josh. You said *can't.*"

"What?" Josh asked.

"You said you *can't* replace her." Tokiko looked through his soul. "Josh. This *is* about trust, but not you trusting others. You don't see it, do you?"

"See what? Tokiko, what the hell are you talking about?" he demanded, becoming more agitated.

"You believe you can't trust *yourself.* You've never trusted yourself for letting her down, have you? Never forgiven yourself. That's it, and that's why you can't bring yourself to replace her. How can you ... if you can't forgive yourself ... if you can't *trust* yourself with a woman?"

Josh slumped back. His mouthed gaped open. He seemed unsure what to say to next. His eyes moved to-and-fro as he absorbed a new epiphany.

Clearly, it had never occurred to him; Tokiko saw that now. Josh never knew he'd lost faith in himself.

Had he come to her looking for that answer? Were all the stratagems of the CIA, assassinations, and genetic alterations just the background excuse to connect with a person who had known him before the change, someone who could remind him of himself and objectively show him what he lost. Had the terms just been fulfilled of some invisible contract he'd signed with himself as an agreement to take on this mission? And in the elation of revelation, perhaps now all concerns of assassins, and duty, and danger, and valour, and pride, and fear, would all vanish – just for a little while. The old Joshua could appear again for a time, if he wished. Tokiko hoped.

Outside, Japan melted along. With the mountain gone, it was like any rural vista on the planet, except it was disappearing faster than any of them could. Time was running out. Tokiko's own fears returned. What might Sorokin tell her? She'd always steered away from asking him about the darker aspects of the Shimura empire – the domain of Taro Shimura. Now, because Harker had requested it, she could avoid it no longer. The true legacy of her husband and his progeny would become plain.

How alike Joshua and Haruto were, she thought. Both had lost wives at the hands of others, and both worked through the pain as best they could. There was, however, a difference. Josh was still young, and had no offspring to project through. He was perhaps not beyond healing ... that's what Tokiko told herself.

It made the nascent infidelity growing in her heart easier to bear.

It seemed unfair that she should have revealed Harker's heart to himself and yet not reveal her own. When the mood had eased, and Josh appeared calmed, she spoke again.

"You said I don't know that pain of loss. Well, I do know something of it. I'm married to a man who has also been running from the memory of a dead wife for years. I know his fears of true emotional intimacy with a woman better than he knows them himself – that's why I could spot it in you. And I know also about the masks that injured people can wear, not just yours, and not just Haruto's, but because I wear one myself everyday. If I'm honest with myself, then I'd say you were right in what you said back in the *sushi* bar; I did leap at the chance to accompany you again."

She waited, hoping for him to return a revelatory favor.

Josh replied, "I remember what you said in the bar, about how I'd changed. I guess you must be right; I can't really tell. But you certainly haven't changed."

"Oh?" Tokiko was intrigued.

"You still bring out in others what they can't see in themselves. That's your idea of love isn't it? Always doing right by others."

Tokiko looked down.

"Perhaps I do it too much. When I was younger, I tried to please everyone, but now I know I can't. Look at what it cost me – cost us. If only I stood up to my father back then when he refused me permission to continue my relationship with you, the American *gaijin*."

Josh asked her a question no one had ever asked her before. "And what is it that *you* want Tokiko? What do you want just for yourself, not anyone else?"

Now it was her turn to be shocked. The honest instant brought the answer: she wanted a family, a real family, of her own, instead of keeping together the fragments of someone else's. Not a wealthy husband. Not position in society. Not the admiration of her peers. She'd trade it all in for a child of her own. Her own blood and flesh.

She fought back another tear.

"It's my fault," said Josh. "If I'd stood up to your father, stayed in Japan and built a life here, he couldn't have stopped us."

With her eyes, she tried to tell him not to blame himself. If only they'd had this conversation fifteen years ago, they wouldn't have parted and neither would have had to endure the pain in-between. But without the pain, Tokiko knew, this conversation would never have been uttered. It was just one of those awful things life only deals in hindsight, like a hand of cards where the flip of the last one reveals what you've been playing all along.

In the silent comfort of each others' presence, the couple sat, in a train, ever-slipping towards a horizon they could never reach.

TWENTY-THREE

Lincoln Memorial, Washington DC
16th October – 6:03am

Cain tracked the arrival of his contact long before any appearance. Steel tipped heels echoed like the lashes of a whip in the cavernous colonnades outside the Lincoln Memorial. There were precious few sounds to distract from the approaching beat; the hour was too early for even birdsong to come lilting to old Abe. He looked like he could do with it too, so solemn was the chiselled face on the immense statue – the President destined for a stone cold eternity to shoulder the adulation of a nation.

Footsteps punctuating the silence. Those man-made lesions disfiguring the serene pre-dawn air were too solid, too low in register, to be the heels of his usual contact. A man's shoes were approaching. Cain stoked his vigilance.

In the halogen half-light, Cain could just decipher Asian features in the approaching man. He was dressed in a fine dark navy coat and wore black gloves.

Cain noticed him stop just far enough away to avoid any lunging offensive manoeuvres. Wise. Now he was closer, Cain took the proportions of his features to be Japanese.

"You're not the usual contact," Cain said.

"Change of plan. We have an additional service we would like you to perform for us," replied the stranger with an American accent.

He went to reach inside his coat.

Cain dropped his own hand to his side and flipped back the edge of his jacket just enough to reveal the bulge of a holstered weapon.

The Japanese contact raised and exposed the palm of his other hand while slowly continuing inside his coat lapel. He delicately removed a white envelope and took a step closer to Cain who took it from him, all the while maintaining eye contact.

"What is it?" Cain asked before opening.

"A ... deletion. You can do that for us, can't you?"

The mercenary raised an eyebrow. He'd never heard it called a deletion before. Those Japs had funny translations.

"I don't know you," said Cain without opening the envelope. "You expect me to trust you?" He looked out around the reflecting pool, for any sign of unusual movement among the trees – a sting in progress. The FBI lurking perhaps.

"I texted on the usual number your contact uses, did I not? And the advance for this task will be deposited from the usual bank account. That is all the proof you need."

Cain squinted; the logic he could not refute, though he dearly wished to. Instinct told him this stank. With a sigh he ripped open the paper flap, speaking as he removed the piece of paper inside.

"I don't like changes in the middle of planning an operation. If this messes it up, I won't accept responsibility. I expect double payment too, for this."

"Do not concern yourself. Do this too without trace, and you will be paid well," said the Japanese man.

"When do you want it done?'

"Immediately. This task is more urgent than the main operation; in fact, I'm told it will help to safeguard the success of it."

Cain unfolded the single leaf inside the envelope and experienced something rare for him; he was caught off-guard. On the page in front of him was a full bio. On top: the name Rita Silberman. Next to it was a photo of that target. His target. A woman he recognised instantly. It was his previous contact. Now he had orders to assassinate her.

For an instant, he thought about objecting, but arrested it. This was the awkward truth of his trade: fortunes reverse quickly. And the forces that now wanted Rita dead could so easily be directed at him. This wasn't the time to grow principles.

He pocketed the death warrant.

"Consider it done," Cain said.

With a curt bow, the Japanese man left as swiftly as he'd arrived.

Cain took a moment before leaving to dwell on old Abe. The assassinated president scornfully looked down upon Cain, but the retired Green Beret cared not a jot. If Abe's successors had kept up that President's principles, Cain would never have found himself involved in the debacle. The Iraq war. It was the acid that had dissolved his patriotism. Now, he was in it for himself alone. Not even the rebuke of a long dead – assassinated – President could make him think twice about assassinating an agent of the Union, one as un-patriotic and treasonous as Cain himself. One who must have slipped-up.

Bloody amateurs.

TWENTY-FOUR

Gokayama, North of Nagoya
16th October – 1:53pm

A stout old man opened the door to the couple. His fulsome grey beard and hair were as a thick as his knitted cardigan. He exclaimed first in his native Russian language, before coming back to her language. "Tokiko!"

"Sorokin-san," she replied with a smile that would melt the hearts of a charging army.

She bowed several times and he did likewise.

"Well, come in, come in. What brings you here?"

"Andrei, I'd like you to meet Joshua Harker. He has some questions that he hopes ... we both hope ... you can help answer."

He shook Harker's hand with a crushingly welcoming grip. Harker never felt the like in Japan.

"American?" Andrei asked Tokiko.

"Yes." She touched Dr. Sorokin's forearm, stepped close and confided in whispering tones. "Andrei, he is a very good friend of mine."

"You trust him?" Andrei asked, while avoiding the embarrassment of eye-contact with Harker as he did so.

"With my life," she replied.

On hearing those words, Harker's heart palpitated between delight and alarm.

"Very well, then we shall talk. Please, come in!" he said to Harker, who moved off the threshold.

They removed their shoes and stepped into the living area. The space in this plush converted farmhouse was generous, but appeared smaller due to the clutter sitting around on shelves and erupting from the roll-top writing desk by the window.

"Please make yourselves comfortable. Can I get you some tea, or something to eat?"

Josh was indifferent to the notion of tea, or any hospitality. He was just hungry for answers.

"Tea would be lovely, thank you Andrei," Tokiko said.

While Sorokin made tea, Harker lowered himself to sit on the *futon* couch next to the bookshelves. They were jammed with untidy stacks of well-thumbed books. Several markers peeped out from each one, identifying fragments of wisdom. All the seminal works of biotechnology were there, but Sorokin's library ranged through to philosophy, sociology, and the literary greats. Tolstoy and Dostoevsky stood proudly to attention as the intellectual stalwarts in the heart of his collection.

Tokiko walked around, dancing her fingers on all the accumulated paraphernalia of Sorokin's nomadic life: *Katoushka* dolls on a shelf; a signed Red Sox baseball cap hanging on the wall; the Mont Blanc writing set she and Haruto had given him on his retirement, sitting next to a *bonsai* ash tree on top of his writing desk. These were little pieces of the world, of all the places Andrei had called home, and now together they made an oddly unique, eclectic nest that Andrei Sorokin now called home. Harker watched her study something on the desk. The rattling of the ceramic cups told of Sorokin's return. Tokiko eased them all into more important matters with some small talk.

"I see you are to attend this year's UNESCO Bioethics Conference."

"Ah – you've spotted my pass. Yes indeed. I almost didn't get it in time. They sent it to my old office instead of my home address, but fortunately it was forwarded to me. I may actually be able to attend this year, for once, now that my workload is so much the lighter. One of the benefits of being retired. And you – will you be attending?"

"Unfortunately, no."

"Too busy, no doubt," said Sorokin.

"Certainly busy, but I wouldn't mind attending. No, actually there was a memo sent around about it – any Shimura Corporation employees invited are to boycott in protest at the anti-commercial, anti-competitive bias of the committee in recent years. They want a united stand."

Sorokin huffed while pouring tea. "And by so doing gathering a means to influence the agenda of the conference for next year, in line with Shimura Corporation goals. Churlish really. I'm glad I retired before getting that memo; it wouldn't help my heart any. That's exactly the kind of unilateral management heavy-handedness that made up my mind to retire early. I'm glad to be rid of all of them. But not you, Tokiko. I miss your bright face around the corridors!"

She glowed back at him.

Harker remembered a snippet of information he'd gleaned from Stanford back in Langley.

"Didn't Mark Olsen have a seat on UNESCO's Bioethics Committee?" Josh asked.

Sorokin poured the third cup and wearily landed the tea jar, apparently as heavy as his own heart at hearing the name Olsen.

"You knew Mark, didn't you Andrei?" Tokiko asked.

"Yes. Another soul that I will miss seeing. I have read about his death in the newspaper. Very, very sad. Oh, we had our ups and down, but I had known Mark for many, many years and in the end, for my part, I liked to call him a good friend. I hope he felt the same of me. We had spoken just weeks ago, when he was last in Japan."

Tokiko reached out and touched Andrei tenderly on the shoulder. He patted her hand, like a doting father responding to a loving daughter.

"Thank you. But please – drink up while it is hot."

He handed them each a cup before groaning back into position, supported by his ample armchair.

"Ah, I will miss Mark," Andrei said. "The conference will certainly not be the same this year without his rampant idealism. Still, he always stood up for what he believed in; I will give him that. Such fight – he had a soul that was almost Russian, you know." Andrei held up his cup as if toasting the deceased. "We shared a passion for life, for the mechanisms of life. Do you know much about biotechnology Mr. Harker?"

"I specialized in Forensic Genetics for my Doctorate, here in Japan, with Tokiko."

"Ahh!" he replied, long and slow. "Then you know. You know how amazing a thing DNA is. Human biology always fascinated me – a combination of the atoms of just four elements, glued together, climbing a spiral staircase that couples adenine to thymine and cytosine to guanine, supported by a backbone built of a pinch of sugar and a dash of phosphate, twisted up in the middle of little sacks of water laced with ATP and RNA, the food for DNA to replicate itself, once every eight hours, day after day, with only slight mutating imperfections that would ultimately, after decades, bring about the destruction of the person that it had built from its own unique molecular pattern in the first place."

Sorokin chuckled at some private joke.

"The more I have learned from the science of this physical world and its revelations, elegant and simple, the more I see the magic in it, and hope that one day, when my time is over, that I would meet the designer of this universe, if for no other reason than to shake his hand profusely, as if meeting an artist long admired, and say: 'Job well done, sir!'"

He drifted off into his own lofty thoughts, leaving the couple in silence. Tokiko prompted Josh with a long look, encouraging him to ask Andrei questions. He cleared his throat and said, "Dr. Sorokin –"

"Please – Andrei."

"Andrei, I'm sorry to have to tell you this, but it's why we are here and I'm hoping you have information that might explain it. You see," Josh glanced at Tokiko for some moral support, "we think the Shimura Corporation might be responsible for Mark Olsen's death. Specifically –," he paused, thinking it ridiculous now he had to say it out loud "– we think they had him assassinated."

"Ah. And you thought that *I* might know something about this, did you?"

Harker shifted uncomfortably in his seat, sensing Sorokin's rising offence, and looked back at Tokiko. She carried the burden on.

"Josh has evidence that leads us to believe Kazuki murdered Senator Olsen." She went on to explain to him all about the DNA and evidence of genetic manipulation. "The comparison isn't an exact match, but the differences are small, characteristic and homozygous. I wondered could it be the nanosphere gene-therapeutic technology."

"It sounds plausible. We had been working on a prototype of it for just such genetic camouflage applications. Although Kazuki's DNA has so many peculiarities of its own, who can tell for sure?"

Harker's brow scrunched. He wondered what the old Russian meant by that, but before he could ask Sorokin proffered a question of his own.

"Is that what you want me to tell you, that Kazuki was the assassin? Who are you: police?"

"No," Josh said quickly. "I'm not here to take him away, if that's your concern. I need to understand why Shimura Corporation would go to the lengths of killing Senator Olsen. It could be important."

"It does seem extraordinarily risky," said Sorokin. "Yes, yes, I'd say it is important – the most important issue to face mankind in its history."

Joshua's confusion grew.

"Andrei, please," Tokiko interjected, "if you know why he was killed, tell us!"

He squinted, shuffled forward in his chair, and scrutinized the American.

"If you are not police, then who are you?"

"Someone you can trust Andrei," said Tokiko. "I vouch for him. Josh and I go back a long way,"

"Maybe so. But do you still know him so well? Or who he really works for?"

"What do you mean?" asked Tokiko.

"In my position I was privy to much information and some rumors that others would pay dearly to know. If the Shimura Corporation is behind Mark's assassination, then there is one architect of it. Taro. He has his father's ambition and acumen for business, but his moral compass is even more broken than his father's. There are no lengths to which Taro will not go to protect his organization. And the roots of Taro's network run deep and wide, built of connections not entirely ... legitimate. When he permitted me to retire it was on the condition that I not leave Japan and tell no one of my work. And knowing what I know about Taro's ways, I wonder if this man here – a man I have never met before – is some sort of test of that promise I made, and what would be the cost if I fail."

"I don't work for Taro Shimura," Harker insisted.

"So you say. But there were rumors that Taro had agents hidden in the American business and intelligence communities to help protect his interests."

"That's preposterous!" Josh rebutted.

"Is it? Then I can only conclude, Mr. Harker, that you are either a very deceptive or a very naive American."

Harker swallowed. Josh already suspected a double agent – someone must have betrayed his identity to the Shimura's before the party, setting the *yakuza* dogs on him. His attempt to conceal that suspicion must have come across to Sorokin as fake. What kind of agent was he, if he couldn't tell a convincing white lie? Now it threatened Sorokin's trust in him. Sorokin suspected him as a mole. Joshua's faith in himself to convincingly do this job was crumbling, and his mind raced. Suddenly and unexpectedly he felt very, very vulnerable.

TWENTY-FIVE

Massachusetts Avenue NW, Washington DC
16th October – 1:23pm

Cain looked down through a telescopic sight. He lay prone on the granite slabs of the building's roof, blending in perfectly under the camouflage of his grey ghillie suit. If any police drones wandered by overhead, he would not stand out. It was a precaution only; he didn't intend anyone to notice him taking the shot from over half a mile away.

He'd lain there for thirty minutes. The sight of his target approaching the phone booth meant he wouldn't be there much longer. Cain scanned around through the sight. There, pulled up on the far side of the junction, was an anonymous sedan. Two men sat up front. Dressed almost identically, could they have looked any more like CIA Office of Security if they tried?

So Silberman's been rumbled. Now I know why someone wants her dead.

He attached the sight to the rifle and slid it up from underneath his arm, resting the rifle's bipod near the building's edge and he looked again. Silberman paced anxiously in his sights, by the open phone booth, hugging herself. Cain looked at the digital readout on the wind gauge he had perched in front of him. He made one last precise rotation of an adjustment dial on the sight. On his cell, he typed the number of the payphone memorized an hour earlier and left it down beside him. He lined up the crosshairs.

Doing this would protect him too. Time to seal off the leak.

"Hello?" he heard the small voice answer in his ear, and could see her, back to him, holding the receiver. The crosshairs were now aligned with the nape of her neck. He moved the line of fire just a fraction to the right, adjusting to allow for the curved trajectory in the gentle autumn breeze.

It was a delicate affair, delivering death from a distance. Only the hours of practice at Uncle Sam's expense in the Marine Corp test firing range at Quantico had qualified him to be death's messenger today. The bullet had to travel, not a straight line, but an arc trajectory, to land in a one-inch square target which marked her cerebellum's location. Destroy the cerebellum – all nervous functions – and instant death was assured. A slight change in wind, a momentary shift in stance of the target, or a tremor in his arm could botch it; he skipped his usual cup of coffee that morning.

Cain exhaled evenly to release muscular tension and exerted gentle pressure on the trigger. A high-pressured ballistic spit emerged from the muzzle and microseconds later Cain saw Silberman crumple to the sidewalk. One last look through the sight confirmed she was lifeless; he'd hit the spot.

He moved quickly now. The best thing about such a difficult shot was it could be done far enough away to ensure a safe getaway. Still, he allowed himself one last indulgence. He looked through the sight at the CIA staff pool car and smiled at the amazement on the faces of the CIA internal cops. Their Jane had turned into a Jane Doe, crumpling onto the sidewalk, and they would have to answer for their failure before this day was out.

Cain had to move fast, before they came looking for the shooter. He looked along the roof ledge for the high-tensile plastic sheath that had surrounded the bullet. It was a special provision for professional sniper's bullets to have such a casing. The bullet recovered from her cadaver would have no tell-tale barrel marks that could trace it back to his rifle. He located and pocketed the protective casing that had been expelled by the shot, quickly disassembled the rifle and packed it along with his ghillie suit into a backpack, then moved very sprightly toward the fire exit.

The job had been done – the ballistic reward for treachery delivered. With these distractions over, he could now get back to his primary task.

TWENTY-SIX

Gokayama, North of Nagoya, Japan
16th October – 2:23pm

"There is nothing I can say that will convince you I'm on your side," Joshua stated, still caught in the squinted stare of an old Russian bear. "You have only my word, and the trust Tokiko has in me, if that means anything to you."

Sorokin shifted his eyes toward Tokiko.

"It does, unfortunately" he replied. Sorokin thought it over and said to Harker, "the last time I divulged what I am about to say, it cost a man his life. I'm afraid that doing so again will have the same effect. Whether it will be your life, or mine, I do not know. So, I am prepared to take my risk – are you prepared to take yours?"

"Of course. I've come this far," said Josh.

Sorokin sighed and stared into space for a moment.

"I will explain what I know, but first I see you are empty. Please take some more tea," said Andrei.

Josh declined, but Tokiko settled back with another cupful as Sorokin settled into his tale.

"Firstly, let me make clear: I can't say for certain if Olsen was killed at Taro's wishes, or even fully why he would order such a kill. It seems a big risk ... and if Kazuki was cajoled to murder him ... poor Kazuki ... just one of the burdens he will have to bear ... just one of many he isn't even aware of ..."

Sorokin drifted off into his own reverie again until Tokiko steered him back on course.

"What is it that Kazuki is not aware of Andrei?" she asked.

"Perhaps I should begin at the beginning. Before joining Shimura Biotech, I had been head of research at Genesys, a biotech company in Bethesda. Mark Olsen was the major shareholder and chairman on the board. This was back after I had emigrated to America. My experience working for Biopreparat during Soviet times guaranteed me a good, fresh start in America. I joined Genesys and quickly rose to head of research. During my time there, we worked on a number of DARPA funded projects."

Tokiko looked quizzical, so Josh explained to her. "DARPA is the American body that funds research into technology for military applications. Most of their research is done internally, but sometimes they outsource to academic and commercial research groups."

"I don't see what all this has to do with his death," Tokiko said.

"You will, in time ... just a little patience. One of the programmes required a level of expertise that Genesys alone didn't possess. To secure the funding, we needed to take on a research partner. That partner, was Shimura Biotech, in the days before Taro governed it. The Japanese had no qualms about taking American dollars. What became of the alliance – what ultimately led to Mark's death – was one particular project."

A light flicked on somewhere in Harker's mind as he made the connection.

"Project GENAFORM," he blurted.

"Why yes, that's right!" said Andrei. "Although it's pronounced 'jen-a-form'", he said, correcting the pronunciation of the new word in Joshua's vocabulary. "How did you know about it?" demanded Andrei.

"Olsen was documenting it when he was killed. I collected the file from the scene."

"Then you know something of Project GENAFORM?" asked Andrei.

Harker wobbled his head. "The file was empty, probably stolen by Kazuki."

"Ah! That would make sense. Let me explain. You see, Project GENAFORM was an offshoot of DARPA's future soldier initiative."

"I have heard of that one," Josh said. "The aim was to equip soldiers with new technologies for the battlefield of tomorrow – light nano-fibre strike-proof armour, drugs to counteract weaponized bioagents, drugs to boost stamina and mental acuity, that sort of thing."

"You're correct. It was very broad in scope. The Japanese had no scruples either about artificially enhancing soldiers – after all, it was they who gave amphetamines to soldiers and *kamikaze* pilots during the war to combat fatigue. But Project GENAFORM was one branch that took the future soldier notion back to the basic principle – the soldier itself. Instead of spending all that money making drugs that would counteract bio-warfare agents, why not build resistance into the DNA?"

"Gene therapy? Surely that would have been more expensive and risky to perform on a soldier-by-soldier basis than delivering drugs?" Tokiko asked.

"Indeed it is," replied Andrei. "Gene therapy is expensive and risky, even more so back then. It would be easier, would it not, to have the desired gene sequences in the soldier's DNA in the first place – from birth?"

"Are you talking about engineering an embryo specifically to be an ideal soldier?" Tokiko asked. "That's horrific."

"But perfectly feasible, and the ... what they say ... 'bean counters' ... loved the idea. Think of it this way: over the lifetime of a soldier, it costs half a million dollars in training, and even then it might not get spent on the very best candidate. Then there's the cost of identifying and recruiting suitable candidates for the military in the first place. What if all that expense could be short-circuited simply by designing people with all the desirable attributes? Did you know that in World War II, only the top two percent of air pilots were responsible for forty percent of all kills? Now what if the common characteristics of that two percent of combat aces could be identified, along with the genetic and environmental basis for those abilities?"

"You are talking about breeding people just to be militia. It's monstrous. What mother would sanction that for their child?"

"That would be irrelevant. If the child were the property of the military from before birth – ordered, so to speak – then a surrogate mother would be used to birth the child. And all the better from the military's point of view – a soldier with no parents back home to cry foul at the validity of a war that took the life of their son or daughter, then so much the better for the politicians."

Tokiko gasped and held her hand to her mouth. "But that's horrible."

"Don't get me wrong – I'm not sanctioning the ethics or morality of it," said Sorokin. "I'm just explaining the logic that drove it. I don't agree with it, Tokiko, not at all."

"Not now," said Josh, "but what about back then?"

Sorokin displayed an emotion caught between embarrassment and anger.

"As we live, so we learn, Mr. Harker. What matters is, in the end, I disagree with the idea, as did Mark Olsen. In the beginning, this was all just theoretical nonsense anyway. Genesys was glad to take the money for some feasibility work, without any real expectation of results. The technology was still far too young, but to justify the costs, we undertook some simple proof-of-concept experiments."

"What experiments?" Harker asked, with thinly disguised disgust.

"The whole idea was predicated on being able to alter a DNA strand, inject it into an embryo, and incubate it. So we used some base human DNA, and a retro-viral delivery vector to change some of the

145

gene sequences, the ones we understood back then, bit by bit. All we had to produce was a viable altered DNA strand."

"Whose DNA was the basis?" asked Josh.

"We never knew, and quite frankly, it didn't matter. We changed the alleles for hair color, eye color, facial shape, enough that the resultant DNA would not be comparable with the donor DNA. It's an interesting philosophical question, isn't it: how many genetic alterations does it take before an offspring is no longer related to either of its parents?"

"Oh, I'm glad you were enjoying some interesting philosophical questions," Harker spat sarcastically. "That kind of research breaks every fundamental principle of bioethics. It's germ-line therapy; it risks passing faulty DNA to subsequent generations. Any scientist with a conscience is against it."

"True, but biotechnology regulation was light back then. As I said, we were working in a theoretical space," said a stern Sorokin.

"But if any child had come from that process, it would be universally reviled," said Josh.

"Exactly," he replied.

Harker stopped in his tracks, not expecting that answer. It made him ponder, and a dark, horrible thought crept into the shadows of his mind.

"Did they?" Josh asked. "Did they produce any children from the experiments?"

"After we had shown we could synthesize new DNA strands from constituent molecules, the argument was made that the next logical step was to try and incubate; after all, how would we know if the encoding was successful unless we tried the DNA, so to speak? The principles of incubating were well known. It was possible, but very time consuming back then, to synthesise the DNA. Nowadays, machines exist in any genetics lab to synthesise sections of DNA to order. From that altered DNA, we constructed a cell nucleus by replacing a donor egg cell nucleus. IVF has used – that part of the process was known for decades now. The tricky part was that the mitochondrial DNA had to be sequenced too, to replace the DNA in the mitochondria. This ensured developmental compatibility and stability in the growing organism. Then our scientists took an ovum – an egg cell – from the woman who was to carry the embryo, to incorporate portions of her DNA and RNA in the newly constructed genetic material. This last step ensured a minimum chance of rejection of the embryo by antibodies during gestation. Finally, when all was in place, cytokinesis was induced to start cell division by passing an electric current through the zygote cell, and it would begin to divide. Several egg cells never got past the fourth cell division. Two actually did produce embryos, but their physical development failed and mutated early on; the embryos were aborted. Some of the team said it was God's way of telling us not to interfere with human life, that it would not work."

"It was best that it failed," said Tokiko.

Andrei looked at her, with an apologetic gleam in his eye.

"Andrei, what is it?" she asked, animated with concern.

"There was one final embryo. It survived. It thrived, and its surrogate mother gave birth to a child."

"Oh my God," Josh exclaimed.

"There were those who wanted to abandon it, to terminate the experiment, but Mark would have none of it. He said it was a life, and that it would be murderous to terminate it now. He even posited that this one child survived for a reason. Just as much as God may have been warning us in the death of the other embryos, so now he was warning us with the survival of this one. We had a duty of care to it, and God wanted it alive for a reason, for a very special purpose. He thought that way, you know. Mark thought that way about things. Mark saved that child's life, and immediately called a halt to Project GENAFORM when he found out what had been done."

When Harker was able to muster words again, he asked, "what became of it ... the child, I mean?"

"You were right, what you said before, about breaching the principles of bioethics, and Mark knew if it came to light the legal authorities in the States would make it very uncomfortable for the child and for him. He knew too that the child would be hated if it became known what it was, so Mark sought to protect him by keeping his existence secret and moving the child out of the country. He found a willing adoptive family, connected to the project, who knew the secret but would keep it safe and monitor the child's development and well-being."

"Kazuki!" Harker blurted.

"Yes, Kazuki Shimura – the first, and the only 'Genaform', as they dubbed him. Not 'human'. A proof of concept. So you see the philosophy is only beginning, Mr. Harker. Some might consider a Genaform sub-human. And to some others, it may be the inevitable next evolutionary step, our future. It depends on your point of view, doesn't it?"

An eerie silence hung in the room as they all tried to make sense of what had been told. None knew what should be said next, but Tokiko asked what pressed her most.

"Who was his mother, who carried him?"

"His surrogate mother's identity was never recorded. She was just some hard luck case, no doubt, that needed a few bucks in exchange for just nine months of her life. She wasn't Kazuki's real mother anyhow; he had no mother, just as he had no real father. He exists outside the chain of human inheritance. He is ... an anomaly."

Tokiko looked into nothing and shook her head. "Kazuki!"

"Hold that sympathy Tokiko," Josh said. "He killed the man who saved his life."

"We don't know what Kazuki has been told of those matters," she urged, "or what his motivation might have been."

* * *

Outside the house, attached to one of the windows, was a microphone sensor with a small antenna. Close by, within its transmission range, a black clad figure lay on the flat extension roof overhanging the window. A coil from the receiver on his waist linked into an earpiece that was inserted into the ear of the listening Kazuki Shimura.

He took in information about himself that he had never known, indigestible information about the very nature of his existence.

His world dissolved ... for the second time that day.

TWENTY-SEVEN

Gokayama, North of Nagoya
16th October – 2:51pm

Sorokin released more information through his muffling moustache. "I suspect, even if Kazuki did kill the Senator, then the reason for the assassination came from Taro, not from Kazuki himself."

"What reason would Taro have for assassinating Olsen?" asked Harker.

"More reason than Kazuki," he replied, "that much is certain. I can propose possibilities to you. It could be one, or many. You see, Taro's malady is multi-faceted"

Harker grinned, unsure why.

"Even as a young boy, Kazuki worked hard," Andrei continued. "He wanted to please his adoptive father. He wanted to fit in, in a land where he would forever be *gaijin*. Haruto identified with that about the boy, perhaps because of his own childhood as a half-Korean outsider in a foreign land. So the two struck a close bond. But Kazuki would never be given a place in the corporation. He worked hard instead at his training and became *yonkuichi*.

"Haruto always kept Taro as his own true son, the one who was to inherit his estate, the corporation, and carry it forward. However, Taro was kept on a tight leash initially. Their relationship has always been strained, and Haruto is no fool – he knows Taro's weaknesses.

"Haruto is – how you say? – 'old school' *yakuza*. The *Yakuza* always looked after the ordinary people, and the poor. There was honor to be found in *yakuza* in his days. They changed: a new breed of white collar criminal, ruthless, greedy, focussed only on power and self-interest. When he saw the outcome of that new breed of ruthlessness in the death of his wife, he vowed to have no more to do with them.

"He sees Taro and it reminds him of that new breed. His real son has no true morality. It is a constant painful reminder to Haruto. Seeing his failures with Taro, Haruto always tried to instil the old honorable ways in Kazuki, which the boy took to willingly, much to Haruto's delight. So Haruto has the stronger bond with his adopted son, much to Taro's annoyance.

"At first, Haruto gave Taro management control of Shimura's chemical subsidiary, to prove his capability, or lack of it. He wanted Taro to confront his own shortcomings and encourage him to learn from them in a part of the business where he could do least damage. After a time, he entrusted Taro with the greater test of the biotech division. If he could finally prove reliable in that area, he would then be a man who could be entrusted with the entire organization.

"And that ... is where the problems started.

"When Taro took the helm of Shimura Biotech, he uncovered one of the older, forgotten, confidential projects – Project GENAFORM. I think perhaps Haruto forgot the old evidence was there."

"So Taro knows about Kazuki's origins?" Tokiko asked.

"Oh yes, he knows his father's dark secret. And whatever sibling rivalry was already rooted in Taro's heart, it grew stronger. But it gets worse. Taro knew how the technologies to inceive Kazuki had improved since Kazuki's time, and from a purely commercial perspective, saw the profit potential of Project GENAFORM.

"It is rumored that Taro has links, either directly or indirectly, to the *Seishi-kai* – a politicized *yakuza* alliance that wants to repeal article nine of Japan's post-war constitution, which limits Japan's military spending. He wants to open up military funding, with Shimura Biotech positioned to make – excuse my pun, please – a killing, in profit. So, recently, as part of that drive, one of the projects he made steps to revive ... is Project GENAFORM."

"But he can't!" Tokiko exclaimed.

"He is. In conjunction with Shimura Electronics he has developed a new generation of DNA sequencers that can create the DNA and RNA strands with millions of base-pairs. Already he has teams working on software that will allow DNA sequences to be encoded to specification. Ordering up a person as if you were ordering up a pizza."

Andrei spoke sarcastically as if reading from a sales brochure: "Nation states could order their peak combat soldiers today for tomorrow's wars. Want to win the Olympics in a couple of decades? Then don't spend all that money finding and training athletes or bother with enhancement drugs that can be detected, just order up a prime athletic specimen today." His voice sank further into despair. "It is the most insidious and odious attack on humanity yet – to weaponize it, to productize it."

"It'll never work," Tokiko said.

"Oh yes it can. I know – I was made to do the feasibility report again this time around. We know more now about individual genes and their operation in human development than at any time in the past. Shimura labs have been amassing that knowledge on an unprecedented scale. Unfortunately, Tokiko, we can do it, reliably and repeatedly. Not just one-time curiosities like Kazuki."

Harker thought of his shelved analyst's report back in Langley, on Shimura's trawling of the internet's genetic databases. Scientists had known for years of this possibility, but considered it too far down the road. Too much information still needed, and the knowledge barriers to building DNA from scratch were legion: what does every gene in human DNA do; how do the genes encode and hence create proteins; how and when are genes switched on or off in the lifecycle of a person, so that certain proteins are not created at certain stages of life; what do all the proteins do away, and how do they work together; what chemicals in the body do those proteins create? What was needed was nothing short of the entire picture of how a human organism develops from womb to tomb. Shimura Biotech was assembling that picture. Taro's DNA sequencing software would, no doubt, have a few shortcuts in it, perhaps splicing in template sections of DNA here and there. Software would be necessary to track and manage all that information. In Taro Shimura's Genaform software development project, in genetic programming, Josh got a taste of the future direction for genetic engineering, and reviled it.

"Well, it was the last straw for me," Sorokin continued. "I decided to take early retirement instead of overseeing such a fiasco for a second time. So when you say Taro can't do it, remember he does not share your ethical sensibilities."

"But no bioethics body will let him away with it," suggested Harker.

"He will keep it hidden at first, a black source of revenue, under some vague entry in the company's ledger. He has the Japanese Bioethics Panel in his palm; like most national bioethics authorities, it is populated by academics with loyalties to commercial enterprises. Taro will gradually pave the way for the acceptance of Genaform technology. But he does not yet hold such control in the international sphere, and there was one big fly in his ointment – Mark Olsen. Since the cancellation of Project GENAFORM, Mark's re-invigorated sense of bioethics, combined with his international connections, took him to a seat on the international UNESCO bioethics committee. Since then, through his continuing contacts in Japan, he discovered what Taro was up to."

"How?" asked Josh.

"Through me of course. It's one of the reasons he was okay with losing his head of research to the Shimura Corporation at all. When I emigrated to Japan all those years ago, he asked me to monitor Shimura's research programmes for him. When Mark was last in Japan, I told him all I am telling you now. I suppose Mark had some other sources of information too."

Is this what Olsen was going to reveal to the CIA?

Harker expressed his next thought out loud. "If Olsen planned to release this information to the international bioethics community – that would make it very sticky for Taro."

"Taro may be ambitious, even ruthless, but he wouldn't kill capriciously just for that, would he?" asked Tokiko. "It would place the Shimura Corporation's reputation at risk."

"Indeed," Andrei confirmed. "Olsen wasn't just going to make things uncomfortable for the likes of Taro – he was going to make it illegal. Rumor was he would propose a motion at the next conference that would see the current UNESCO bioethical guidelines enshrined in international law. To protect the human genome, the human race, Olsen wanted to see certain lines of biotechnology research regulated more tightly, or even banned. Well, that was like a red rag to a bull for Taro. Not only would that jeopardise the profit stream of the Genaform product, but could put many of his secret lines of potentially lucrative research in jeopardy."

"And you think that is why Taro had him killed," asked Harker, "to stop the criminalization of illegal genetic research?"

"It's just one reason of many possible reasons. The process of legalization was already started, and Olsen had swayed several on the committee to his way of thinking. Taking Mark out like that does seem a bit obtrusive as a course of action – uncharacteristically Taro, I'd say. Unless –"

"Unless what?"

"Perhaps Mark found out something more on that last trip, more than even I know. Oh, but that is speculation."

"There's something else I don't understand," said Josh. "Why use Kazuki? If he did need to eliminate the Senator, why not use an intermediary, a cut-out, that would prevent exposing the connection to the Shimura Corporation?"

Why not use the mole to get rid of Olsen, instead of involving Kazuki directly?

Andrei replied: "I suppose the genetic camouflage evidence you uncovered would handle the problem of identity, isolating a provable link to Shimura. And it worked – you have nothing you can prove, do you Mr. Harker? But I don't suppose Taro ever expected that you, a friend of Tokiko's, would end up investigating all this. He can't see all ends. But his choice of Kazuki was ultimately a perverse one, and one that may mark Taro's downfall."

"Why do you say it was a perverse choice?" asked Tokiko.

"I have worked closely with Taro over the last few years, enough to know the true depths of his devious, twisted nature – flaws that even Haruto will not see in his son. Taro knew about Project GENAFORM and so must have guessed Kazuki's origins. With Olsen having become a liability to be dispatched, I believe Taro took the opportunity to send Kazuki, hoping it would set his father against Kazuki, and so too it was a means of striking at Kazuki himself, because if he ever found out his real connection with Olsen, that Olsen had saved Kazuki's life, then the Genaform man would have to live for the rest of his life with the knowledge of what he had done."

"But that's *evil*" said Tokiko. "I can't believe it."

"Can't you? Taro's hatred for Kazuki runs deep." Sorokin looked at Harker and smirked. "It seems that hatred might have finally brought about Taro's demise this time." He refocussed his attention on Tokiko again. "Well let me tell you something more about Taro's true regard for Kazuki. The genetic camouflage technique is still experimental. It wasn't cleared for use on humans; it was suspected of causing cancers. For Kazuki to use it, it must have been authorized by Taro. He knows Kazuki began as an experiment, and still treats him as an experiment today. To Taro, Kazuki is something less than human. That is how much regard he has for his adopted brother. The genetic camouflage might kill him, even if Kazuki's own flawed genetic constitution doesn't take his life early anyway. And that ... is Taro's true nature. Remember that Tokiko, and Joshua – always be alert to what Taro Shimura is capable of."

"And Taro leaves you here unguarded -" said Harker, "with all of these secrets that you know? Why didn't you tell all this to anyone?"

"I did – Olsen. And look where that got him. Oh, Taro understands me well. He knows there's no more fight left in this old bear. You see Mr. Harker there comes a time in a man's life – it will come to you too – when he has learned enough about the way the world works to realise that it doesn't work. The great and tragic irony of life is that by the time one usually reaches that epiphany, one is too old and has too little energy left to do anything but accept it. Mark Olsen was one of those rare breed, a man I admired, an old man who had passed into seniority without learning – or accepting – that idealism was the province of youth." Sorkin's face turned limp and he stared into space. "God's speed to you Mark. Forgive me."

* * *

Outside, the eavesdropping Kazuki's heart raced, in anger or in fear, he knew not which. He considered the disease, set to consume him within weeks, the vile gift from his adoptive sibling. Taro must have known Kazuki had no relatives, no compatible DNA. There would be no life-saving bone marrow transplant for him after all this. Kazuki was a dead man walking, but knew he could still save her. He could still get Tokiko to safety ... he could get her free ... of all of this.

A rustle from the trees alongside the farmhouse alerted him to a new presence. He saw a handful of men, dressed in *ninja* garb similar to his own, surround the house.

Taro's Yakuza! How could I have been so stupid?

Taro must have had Kazuki followed, to pursue and locate the couple, to ensure they found out nothing more. There was nothing the Genaform could do – he was outnumbered. He froze motionless where he was, not alerting them to his presence. As they broke through the borders of the house, he could hear shouts, a shot, a scream, and the sound he knew of a lifeless body hitting the floor. From his vantage point atop the house he saw two captives being marched out. They were frisked, a mobile phone removed from one of them, which was then crushed underfoot by the *yakuza*.

A van slid to an abrupt halt on the gravel pathway and the prisoners and *yakuza* scurried inside. As the van drove off into the distance, the silence it left enveloped a stunned, motionless Kazuki and left him alone with just the uneasy companionship of his own rampant thoughts.

His world crumbled into hell.

TWENTY-EIGHT

CIA Headquarters, Washington DC
16th October – 3:17pm

"Damn it!" The DD/NCS slapped his paw down hard on the nearest desk. "Get out! Get out of my sight!"

The two Office of Security goons scuttled out of the room.

"Two!" Stanford said to Kressler, the only one left in his office. "That's all I've got to give the Senate Committee. Two dead Americans because of this – one of them their own Senator. A double exposure, and we still don't even know who or why. They'll have a field day. All I can report to them is the ingenious machinations of the Shimura Corporation, and highlight the ineptitude of my own division! A mole in the CIA, undetected! And when finally she was revealed, she was assassinated by her Japanese handlers. Brilliant! And what the hell were the Office of Security playing at? Didn't they think to surveil *around* their target too?"

Mike was brave enough to defend them. "It was a professional hit."

"Oh really," said Stanford, unimpressed.

He stopped and calmed himself. They'd been trailing Silberman for days, ever since he asked Mike to fish out Harker's shelved report. It wasn't the kind of report that protected Shimura, but quashing it did. That's when he'd looked into Silberman, and found some very suspicious activities in her bank accounts. Money that shouldn't be there. You can hide treachery, but never the money. It was enough to raise suspicion, and have her followed to see who she contacted, before reeling her in for questioning. Bad move. Now she'd been shut off. Someone rumbled they were on to her. Perhaps Harker had warned the Japs? Was he a traitor too, after all?

I sent Harker in; prodded the belly of the beast, to see what would happen. Now I know.

"Did you talk to the Ops Center Mike? Have they located Harker?"

"That's the other bad news we have for you I'm afraid. We've lost contact. The tracking transmitters in the phone we gave him – not transmitting any more. Last tracker fix places him eight klicks north of Nagoya."

"Marvellous," said Stanford. "Just bloody marvellous. Did we get any information at all from Tokyo since Harker arrived?"

"No Sir."

Stanford stabbed out some instructions with his finger. "Dispatch a CRITIC to Tokyo station immediately. Ask them for all information on Joshua Harker and his whereabouts ASAP. If they can't find him, pull out all the stops. Monitor every facility with connections to the Shimura Corporation. I want him found. Then I want you to pull everything on Silberman's activities for the last few years. Everything. Pull every file she's touched. Trace every call she's made. I want a pattern analysis, anomalous behaviour, anything. I want to know what she's been up to."

"That could take weeks."

"No Mike, it'll take 24 hours," Stanford commanded.

Kressler left the office with head weighed down like a depressed beagle. He'd be working late, with no sleep this night. Stanford had just given Mike another lesson in the real world of operations. It was a world, he thought, in which men's lives would cost Mike more during his career than just one night's sleep.

Was Harker dead too? On their side or not, Stanford wanted him found. He wouldn't lose a third life to this infuriating corporation. His anger at the Shimuras began to outweigh his concern for his agent. Stanford resolved to find Harker and determine the truth of all this, once and for all. It was his professional pride at stake. Something had to be done.

TWENTY-NINE

South-East of Sapporo, Hokkaido
18th October – 3:16am

Reality came in snapshots as Josh drifted in and out of a consciousness. When it did present itself, it was in a haze, as if viewed through gauze. A piece of trivia popped into his head. He remembered a name, what they called his surroundings – a "birdcage". It was a small cell with walls of bright light, cramped, with space only to sit on haunches. Anywhere he directed his head, he could not escape the light. He could not sleep.

Periodically the encompassing white blur became a black blur. Four arms ripped him out of the cell and tied him to a chair in the dim antechamber beyond. A black-veiled interrogative figure would blur in, bark questions, and blur out again.

"Who in the CIA sent you? Who knows you are here?"

Josh remembered the voice changing each time the questions came. Different men, taking shifts.

"I know nothing 'bout it," Harker rasped with a voice that frightened him, one he didn't recognise. "I'm a columnist for New Genetics Journal. I want to see an American Consul."

A tray rattled, clattering when dropped on the wooden bench in front of him; there was a syringe and some metal-capped bottles containing clear liquids. The labels were indistinct, but Harker made out one: Oxytocin. The trust drug. He assumed one of the others would be sodium thiopental, or one of the newer, more effective, veridical drugs courtesy of Shimura Pharmaceutical.

It became routine. A routine of coercion, breakdown, annihilation of the self.

Except when it wasn't.

Just as one pattern of beatings, interrupted sleep, and interrogation became routine, it would be broken again and replaced with a new pattern. How long had he tried to sleep in the light this time? He didn't know. When were his interrogators last here? Five hours ago, or five minutes? He didn't know.

Lucidity broke in sometimes, in refreshing waves, and the interrogation antechamber (what little of it he could see) was revealed. There was a single light, a bright lamp hanging from the ceiling which hurt his eyes when he looked up too far. The dark walls seemed rough and undecorated, like bare concrete, with metal conduits. And it smelled damp, giving Harker the impression he was underground, in a place difficult to find, and difficult to escape from.

How long had he been chained to this chair? He did not know. Perhaps the headache shooting up from his over-stretched shoulders, tied to the back of the chair, fogged his mind. No daylight, no timepiece, nor rhythm of any kind to anchor him to the real. How long had he been here; hours, days, weeks? Josh shook his head vigorously trying to bring himself around.

Time.

Everyone breaks under interrogation. Everyone. Don't think you'll be any different. It is just a matter of time.

He remembered the sage words of his CIA trainer at The Farm, a lifetime ago.

Time is your greatest enemy, but also your only hope. Bide it.

This was advice from the same agency who issued hidden cyanide pills for those agents who couldn't bide time, in case time revealed secrets.

The *yakuza* had stripped him. Any cavity that might conceal something was searched. They drilled into the fillings in his teeth. They cut off the buttons on his jacket, ran a knife to open every seam in his clothing, took his belt, and replaced his shoes with a cheap pair. In his shredded apparel, he looked like a vagrant scarecrow.

Time.

What had he to do with his latest brief lucidity but think, until the next dark blur arrived?

He thought of the things Sorokin had told him and Tokiko. Tokiko – where was she? What had become of her? Josh drove the worrying thought out of his mind quickly, distracted himself, thinking instead of the ersatz man – Kazuki – the most improbable pinnacle of genetic research. The scientist in Josh felt a pang of admiration at the technological achievement. He could hardly believe that it existed: walking, breathing, thinking, in short – functioning. The principles involved in creating such a form were known to him, and that knowledge made the feat all the more prodigious in Joshua's view.

Though he had never developed the worship of a deity that his father tried to instil in him (Josh had always considered a righteous God to be an absentee landlord of this world), he had found that his scientific studies had cultivated in him a sense of an intelligent designer behind this ballet of matter and energy. DNA was just one of its amazing facets. If human engineers even attempted to build such a complex yet elegant system – he used to ponder – it would fail. Yet one such human did exist.

He had seen it, and fought with it.

A real human. There were no bolts in his neck, no stitches around the brainpan. Physically, Kazuki was perfect. From a purely biological point of view he was a marvel. What maladies this particular monster harbored in its character were not the fault of his genes but perhaps, as with Frankenstein's monster, in the arrogance of its creator. And like Frankenstein's monster, it had killed his own creator – Olsen.

Such hatred must Kazuki harbor to kill that man! A hatred that might, Harker thought, extend to all mankind from which Kazuki had been ostracized from birth. What must it do to a mind, he wondered, when it discovered it was not the product of its parent's love, but rather a prototype? At what age could you reveal such a thing to a boy, and avoid psychological damage, if such a consequence were avoidable at all?

Josh thought back to the look of calm severity in the eyes of the Genaform, full of accusation, when he had fought it. Harker had seen that stare before, in a courtroom, in the eyes of a serial killer, hating every ounce of Harker's DNA. It was the stare of the man who would eventually kill his wife, his family.

Kazuki's stare that day was not one Harker felt specially reserved for him, but one that Kazuki directed at all people: the kind of look that said he could not forgive us for being who we are. A pre-emptive, defensive attitude perhaps; for surely, once people found out about Kazuki, he would not be forgiven for what he was.

So many questions: perhaps that's all Kazuki was ever destined to be – a living question mark. An icon to man's hubris.

And what of Taro? His willingness to productize Genaform told Josh a lot about his attitude to his brother. Both men were playing out the resolution to that sibling rivalry right now. Harker had landed in the middle of Japan's most dysfunctional family.

The straps around Joshua's wrists chaffed as he tried to find comfort. Throwing back his head, he heaved a deep sigh. Josh looked up at the light. It hurt his eyes, but it could never hurt in the same way sunlight could. Would he ever see it again? Or the sky above him: the sky above in which was suspended the KH-12 spy satellite constellation, the eyes in the sky, which could not see in here, underground. The sky. The sky through which microwaves travelled, to a dead cell phone, last traceable to Nagoya, probably far from his current location. He didn't know himself where he was, so how could anyone else find him, if anyone was even looking? If anyone even knew he was in dire trouble.

Tokiko knew. Had she been released? She might warn Haruto of his son's actions. Would Taro let her go? Would he risk the wrath of his father? Josh wondered was Taro so maladjusted, so far gone, that he would not care.

Time is your only hope.

A man can be broken in a matter of minutes by brute physical pain, Harker's instructor had said, but the veracity of the information can be unreliable – a victim would say anything to make it stop. It was the best route if information was needed quickly, but these *yakuza* could afford a slower grinding approach to reliable information. Attrition of awareness through drugs and sensory deprivation. They had all the time they needed.

Harker feared what he knew in his heart.

Nobody was coming to his rescue.

THIRTY

Roppongi, Tokyo
16th October – 9:34pm

Kazuki arrived late at night at Taro's home, flanked by two *yonkuichi* colleagues. Taro sent his wife and children into a back room for safety.

"What's the meaning of this Kazuki? You come here to my house with armed guards!"

"Only as my protection to counter your own."

"What are you talking about? The *yonkuichi* is my protection too."

"Aren't you forgetting your *yakuza* support? Oh, Haruto will be displeased when he hears who you've been in bed with."

"You know nothing, brother."

Kazuki stepped to within a breath of Taro and drilled a crazed stare into him. "I know enough," he said through gritted teeth.

Taro's graven face leaked worry at his adopted brother's unhinged condition.

"Where is Tokiko?" Kazuki commanded.

"How should I know where she is? You were the one sent to find her. Have you now lost her? Then perhaps you should have shared what you knew about their whereabouts sooner, and I could have helped."

"*Helped!*" Kuzuki said with venom. "Oh, I have been blind Taro. What help do you offer! I'm dying, no thanks to you."

Taro looked surprised but unconcerned.

"You look fine to me."

"I disguise it well, my brother. Those experimental camouflage measures of yours cause leukaemias, did you know?"

"Of course not," Taro lied – badly. "If I'd known, I'd never have sanctioned it."

"Oh but I think you did. You thought you'd take out any possibility of a rival for inheritance of the Shimura Empire, and at the same time strike out at your restrictive father by murdering one of his oldest friends and sending his own beloved Genaform to do it."

Taro took a step back at the sound of the word *Genaform*.

"So, you know what you are?" Taro asked.

"Yes, I know what I am. Can you say the same of yourself? You poisoned your father's adopted son; you ordered the death of his oldest friend, and you captured his wife, his only love."

"Don't claim superior morality with me Kazuki. You are the assassin, not I. You are a genetic lab rat, nothing more, and I will accept no lessons in morality from you. What are lab rats for but experimentation? That is what you are for."

Taro saw an insane flicker in his once brother's eye. Kazuki signalled his *yonkuichi* to leave.

"You haven't yet seen what I'm *for* Taro, what I'm capable of – the Genaform unleashed. Now: where is Tokiko?"

Taro kept silent.

"I see," Kazuki said. "You will hold her for as long as it takes to get information from Harker, because if she alerts Haruto, this whole scheme will surely be at an end. And when it is done, you will release her and tell Haruto it was you who found her. The incompetent Kazuki, master of the *yonkuichi*, failed to protect his family, and a new trustworthy master is required to lead them – you. You see, I know your ways Taro. I have listened from the side over the years, brother. I am *yonkuichi*. I know your plans. What madness I have kept from Haruto, just to protect his foolish hope for his one true son! What a fool I have been to do that."

Kazuki made to leave too; Taro lost his composure and shouted after him.

"Kazuki! What will you do?"

"Where is Tokiko?" the Genaform asked one last time.

Taro refused his only chance to answer the question before Kazuki disappeared from his sight forever.

"Kazuki!" Taro shouted after him. "You're just a proof-of-concept. You are property of the Shimura Corporation! Come back here!"

But the Genaform refused to hear it.

* * *

It was late when Kazuki got to the place he called home. Haruto would be asleep upstairs, if he could sleep, alone in his bed. Kazuki called it home, but the word had become meaningless. He realized now that it was only ever Tokiko that made it home for him.

He knelt in the dark, his face lit by the candle of the small shrine. Immersed in all things Japanese as the young boy had been, Shinto beliefs had fascinated him. Deity spirits gave rise to, and pervaded, everything: all that could be seen in the world just an expression of those spirits, even the solitary flame keeping him company now. People are all children of those spirits, and human nature sacred. Kazuki had been so certain of it all, like many childhood simplicities, so easy to believe, so few hours ago.

Now matters of belief weighed heavily on young shoulders.

Was he still a child of those same spirits? Had he ever been? Could a child not born of love, but built by man, lay claim to Shinto spiritually? Does a man born outside the evolutionary line of human heredity reflect those spirits at all? Olsen must have believed Kazuki could. Remorse finally beat upon the young man's heart when he realised he'd killed a man who'd championed Kazuki's life from the outset. From Sorokin's conversation it was clear that Olsen had believed Kazuki's existence was destined and special. An existence sprung forth, not from human love, but perhaps through a divine volition, for a purpose.

What purpose?

Kazuki recalled a lesson of Haruto's wisdom: in the instant, a man discovers himself. Time was the enemy of self-revelation.

I must be fortunate then, Kazuki thought, *to have so little time left now.*

It was time to choose; time to nominate purpose. He knew Shinto belief that it was the purity of a person's soul that determines whether their path leads to good or evil. There must be nothing pure about his brother's malevolence. The contortions of intent with which Taro played out his own insecurities, even his hatred, was anything but pure. A malign, twisted spirit, that would corrupt his father's empire and ultimately bring Haruto shame. Taro – an evil spirit, whose expression on this world's stage, would ensure the name Genaform would be hated forever, if remembered at all.

Kazuki sighed. He felt showered by cancerous weakness again.

He was tired of it, tired of being defined by relationships with people he had no relation to, tired of his brokerage of those broken relationships.

No more.

It was a lot to think about in a short time, more than any boy or man ever should. But the decision fell to him, and him alone. Perhaps that made him special after all. He chose to believe it was so.

He was determined the time left to him should count. If he was a new breed, the first of a new race, then he would make that count too. He would be a new thing, above and beyond. The rest could burn in the fire of their own prideful ambition. It was time to set aside the boy, and become the man. To become Genaform. He knew what that meant now.

The Genaform cleared its mind, slowed its breath, and in the instant ... discovered what it wanted to be.

He knew what he had to do.

Kazuki unslung the sword from his back. It was his companion since Haruto had presented the gift at Kazuki's coming of age ceremony. Now it would need a new purpose. He crushed the scabbard into the blue velvet ruffles in its rosewood presentation box, closed the lid and sealed the clasps. His sword, he knew, would be given the opportunity to perform one last duty for him, but not at Kazuki's own hands.

The Genaform set to work, pausing only to snuff out the flame.

THIRTY-ONE

South-East of Sapporo, Hokkaido
18th October – 4:34pm

The door to Harker's birdcage cell eked open, breaking the wall of light with a welcome crack of darkness. He waited for black arms to invade his cell again and extract him once more. They didn't. He waited longer, but still nothing came. He heard the outer door to his interrogation chamber groan on lumbering hinges.

Harker pushed open the cell door. There was nobody beyond it, and the antechamber door too was ajar.

The drugs, interrogative words, deprivation of sleep and senses, had all left his mind plastic and malleable. Josh wondered was he now hallucinating. He stood out on hips and knees that screamed pain after confinement. His leaden body, cumbersome to move, had gone out of his control, like everything else in his life. He had to take a moment to cope with the pain, even if it meant losing the chance to escape.

Shuffling up to the door, like a crab through molasses, he squinted into the gloom beyond. The clunk of another door's bolt being hefted back echoed through the dark stone tunnel beyond. Then silence came again. Harker eased open the protesting chamber door, opening out onto a corridor of jagged shards of clammy slate. No sentries were posted. For a second, he thought he saw a shadow slide across other shadows, a black on lesser black in this dimly lit labyrinth.

Josh stepped out and followed it. He came to another identical door inset into the wall, similarly left ajar. Peeping through the crack, he saw a parcel of woman lying coiled with eyes closed on a steel cot. His heart skipped a beat. It was Tokiko.

He tip-toed towards her, all the time looking for moving shadows. It was possible, Harker thought, this play was just another tactic to break him. Josh hunched close to her, stopping himself from crying out with the stabs of pain in his compressed knees, and planted his hand softly on her shoulder.

"Tokiko," he whispered. A silent response caused his heart to skip again. He shook her shoulder this time. "Tokiko."

To his everlasting relief, she stirred. Lids rolled back to reveal warm, friendly eyes again. She sat up and, without words, hugged him tightly. The warmth of her body and strength of her bones brought warmth and strength back to him.

"Are you alright?" he asked.

"Yes, yes I'm fine," she said while rubbing his cheek and examining his face. "Are you? You look terrible."

From the way she said it, it must be true, Josh thought. Fortunately for her, she looked to have been subjected to no such treatment.

"Come on, let's get out of here."

They linked each other out the door. Josh needed more walking support from Tokiko than she needed from him.

A shaft of light lit up the menacing recesses of stone as they reached the end of the corridor. As he looked back, Josh saw that the facility had been adapted out of a natural cave. They reached what must have been the mouth of the cave, blocked off, and sealed with another metal door that also rested ajar.

They crept out, cautiously at first, later gathering speed when it was apparent there were no watchmen around. The high clouds blanketing the day gave a light that was dirty grey, but so much softer and deliciously affirming than the harsh light of his little cell back in the cave. Light massaged his soul.

"I know this place," Tokiko said, pointing to the apex of a roof jutting above the trees. "That's Taro's country getaway. He's brought us to Hokkaido."

Towering above the trees of the arboretum, stood the imposing chunky wooden gables of a lodge. It reminded Josh of a Canadian ski lodge, with only the occasional flash of a *shoji* screen through the dancing leaves conceding to stereotypical Japanese decor. It was what he'd expect of Taro – in the style of Hokkaido country houses, but much grander, more ostentatious.

"He and his family use it some weekends."

"And during the week too, it appears, for a little sport with his enemies," said Josh while straightening his back with a wince. "We'd better get the hell out of here. I don't know where those men are – *yakuza, yonkuichi*, whatever – but they'll be back, if they're not already coming."

"I know a back way off the estate. We shouldn't be seen that way."

A new pace was needed now. His heart raced as the adrenalin kicked in. They had to move fast and with purpose. Tokiko clasped his hand and led him.

As they pattered their erratic escape route through crooked gravel pathways, the views of Shimura's gardens robbed Harker of his morning-chilled breath. The landscape through which they escaped fell away inland from the dusky pink *Akan-dake* peaks down to the marshland patrolled by white cranes, and out towards the infinite horizon of a sea beyond. The grounds had been landscaped with ambling babbling streams interrupted by the occasional whispering waterfall. A cultivated arboretum of mimosa, jasmine and cherry trees looked down over beds of cosmos and lavender. It was a patch of heaven, dragged down to earth, and possessed by Taro Shimura.

When they reached the far side of the compound, Josh cried out. "Wait!"

He pulled Tokiko around a corner where he'd spotted a caged lock-up nestled at the back of the arboretum. The door hung unlocked again. A row of half a dozen motorbikes lay inside. Must be *yonkuichi* security patrol bikes, he thought.

This is too easy.

No *yonkuichi* guards either. The same person who opened the doors must have distracted their attention from this side of the estate. A helper, who remained anonymous. Who? Why? Josh didn't have the time to think about, just seized the opportunity.

He headed not for the first, not the second, but the third bike in the row – a red Kawasaki ZX-10. It was an older model, but it was fast enough for a quick getaway. The keys were in it. The tank was full. A short *wakizashi* sword was strapped to the chassis; in the under-seat compartment were some old spark plugs, a pliers, and ... a handgun. If it was good enough transport for the *yakuza*, or *yonkuichi*, it was good enough for him.

"Give me a hand to push this," he said to Tokiko. He wouldn't risk firing up the metal beast yet, in case the noise alerted anyone who might be in the lodge.

After a few minutes creating noises only of scrunching gravel and heavy breath, they unlatched a wooden gate onto what looked to Josh like an empty public road at last.

He started it up without risk of being heard at this distance. The machine purred majestically into life, the gentle thrum beneath him belying its potential power.

He looked at Tokiko through his open visor, smiling to dissipate her concerns.

"That's quite a family you landed yourself there. Real prize catch," Josh said.

She tried to share the joke. "Tell me something I don't know Josh."

"Come on." He invited her as delicately as he could over the sound of the engine. "It's been a while since we had a ride in the countryside."

She laughed a little. In the midst of all the tension. It was nice. His last piece of innuendo, back in Otemachi, had not received such a pleasant response. How different she seemed now to that woman who chased after him in Tokyo. She was the same person, no doubt, but there seemed to be an added determination to her, an extra confidence in what she was doing now. Perhaps her incarceration at the hands of a member of Haruto's family had finally unshackled her loyalty to that family. Or perhaps that was only his hope. Whatever Harker's hopes, whatever the truth of it, it didn't matter now. He didn't know who freed them, but when it was discovered, they'd be followed again. All that mattered was getting out, and getting Tokiko to safety.

She fastened her helmet, straddled the bike behind him, and gripped his waist firmly. On the public road, Josh opened it up, and the engine snarled underneath him like an angry beehive.

As darkening clouds rolled in, night would soon follow. The couple shot southwards on exhilarating mechanical ferocity.

THIRTY-TWO

Northern Honshu, Japan
19th October – 7:41pm

The motorbike lolled like a drunken man staggering down back roads of Northern Honshu. Harker was struggling more and more to shift the weight of the machine with his uncooperative body. Whether it was from the remnants of the drug cocktail still sloshing about his system, or from the lack of sleep and food, he couldn't say. Aside from some cold Suntory green tea and dried fish snacks on the ferry from Hokkaido, he didn't know when his last meal had been.

This weariness was slowing them down, endangering them, and all the time he could feel a malevolent presence shadowing them, just beyond sight but not beyond suspicion.

The rain began to spatter on their inadequate clothing. The spatter turned into a downpour. Roads became greasy under wheel. It had been a gamble coming this way, but on the main highways they'd be spotted and attacked too easily. At least if the roads were difficult for Josh, any pursuers were slowed too. In some places the surface waters formed torrents of mud across already eroded patches of old asphalt. It forced Josh to slow down more and more, ploughing through gravelly sludge. This rough country paste was hardest of all to ride through, and several times his weak arms nearly lost control of the front, avoiding a tumble into a ditch.

Josh felt a tap on his shoulder from his pillion passenger. He slowed the bike and raised his visor to hear Tokiko.

"Josh, please! We need to find shelter."

He shook his head. "No time," he shouted slowly, trying to be heard through a helmet and over a storm. "We're nearly there – two hours at most."

"Longer in this weather. Stop and hide until it clears. You need rest Josh. There's nobody following."

He shook his head – more insistently this time.

"They'll catch up," he said, firmly snapping shut his visor.

Thunder echoed in the distance and flecks of sinewy lightning coursed across the sky. Josh felt his stubbornness soften; nature itself was telling him to take a break. With another tap on his shoulder, Tokiko implored again.

"Please, Josh!"

He could just about hear through the enveloping storm; she must have been screaming to be heard.

Josh pulled up at an old farmhouse. From the battered exterior and the uncultivated lands, he assumed it was long since abandoned. It sat there like a cracked eggshell, fractured down the middle by an old earthquake.

The inside appearance was not much better than the outside. The wind whipped through flaps it had made in the canvas screen doors. Wind was a frequent and welcomed visitor in this house – a house less hospitable for people – but it was still mostly dry, and there was a futon to rest on.

"This is folly," Josh said. "We should keep moving."

"The storm will pass soon enough, and I don't see anyone following us. Those back roads on a night like this are more danger to us than any of Taro's men – they're back in Hokkaido by now. If they were following us, you've lost them."

The CIA agent wasn't so sure. But he had nearly fallen off the bike several times. Tokiko was right. Josh took off his sodden sweater, draping it over a wobbling table to dry. He placed the handgun on the table too.

Tokiko immediately dumped the rat-chewed mattress out into the storm. Some *tatami* mats would have to be comfort enough.

The sword Josh had brought from the bike, strung across his back, clattered onto the floor. He soon followed, collapsing down onto the hard futon. The boards moaned and crunched as Josh's exhausted body hit them with full weight. It was only now when he'd let it all catch up with him that he realised how drained he was. Constant tension and physical demand took their toll on muscles no longer to be called young. He was hungry too. The fish snacks on the ferry were brief and inadequate replenishment.

The physical weakness began to infect his spirit. He found himself wondering what the hell he was doing out here in an old shack in the back quarter of Japan in the middle of a storm pursued by Japan's elite killers. Was this it, he thought? Was this the purpose and excitement he sought in life? It was certainly the hallmark lifestyle that outsiders expected for a CIA agent. But, as always, the reality was very different: he was hungry, tired to the point of weakness, he shivered uncontrollably, and he was afraid.

What kind of a fool lives this life?

Outside, rain burst down. Inside was clammy. He looked over to see Tokiko slide back the screen door and let the invigorating wind inside, lapping across her warm, moist neck.

Josh gazed upon her. She craned back, spilling hair like liquid obsidian down her back. The white silk top clung in wet ripples all the way down to the base of her spine. Lightning flashed, revealing a little more of her profile. Delicate streams of perspiration sprinkled with rain sinewed down her neck, passing out of sight beyond the swell of her breast.

The glimpse of her offered by each pulse of lightning enflamed his desire. In this place, far from anywhere he knew, past all concern of responsibility, and fearful of how short the future could be, Josh felt the melting away of the barriers he'd kept up with Tokiko these last days.

As fear left, so did marital dominion. Any respect Harker held for Haruto had vanished. Haruto had totally failed to protect her from the clutches of his own family. There in front of him stood the wife of Japan's sixth wealthiest man, staring overland like a siren waiting for him upon the rocks. A shivering electric silhouette in lightning.

Josh rose. He walked up behind her and touched a drop on her bare shoulder. His finger stayed there, tracing out curliques. The smoothness, the texture, the suppleness – as if fixating on a tiny part of her was not desiring the all. As if this wasn't really infidelity. That would require a co-conspirator. For now, Josh was just a man, comforting a friend. It was convincing enough for him.

Tokiko turned and looked deep into his eyes with calm abandon, as if resolved to accept whatever happened next. Josh clasped her arm, and turned her body into his. He touched his lips to hers; they pressed back harder. The torrent of his desire was unleashed; lightning struck once again.

As he tasted her, a delicate aroma took hold. A faint trace of perspiration mixed with the faded memory of musky sandalwood perfume applied some days before. Unique. Essentially Tokiko. He knew it took nine hundred genes to develop the body's smell receptors; a task tuned to this very moment, to detect the unique smell that identified this woman as the object of his desire. A primal, natural mechanism.

They embraced and entwined, their barriers collapsing. Without realising it, they stepped towards the futon. His fingers tingled on skin beneath her blouse. Her homely aroma of damp hair intoxicated him.

They lay each other down on tatty mats. She pressed her body hard against his, as an offering. Josh wrapped his arm tightly around her, his fingers clinging into the folds of skin they impressed in her back, kissing her passionately. His hand spread out over the contours of her hips and thighs, visiting all her landmarks familiar to him, and some that had changed over the years.

His head told him this was not the time or the place. It was too risky. What he feared when he started this mission was coming true – she had become the mission, distracting him from his goal. Right now, that goal was to get out alive. So close now. Perhaps he could take Tokiko away with him. To a new life. If she wanted to.

He dreamed of an ecstasy when their bodies could merge into one, so that the boundary between them would no longer exist and Josh could lose the distinction between his flesh and Tokiko's. One flesh. That was the way it was meant to be, he thought. That's what nature ordained for mankind: sweet harmonious union, not the cold, unfeeling commercial splicing together of genes in a phial in some Tokyo laboratory.

He stroked the line of her jaw, slowly and repeatedly. The erstwhile lovers entered into a landscape together, one familiar yet new, one far from Japan, where they were the only two inhabitants. They lay there for a time, in an ecstatic reprieve from their troubles. They became the arbour for each other's soul, and lying next to each other, their hearts negotiated a unison rhythm.

Her fingertips dragged through the hairs of his chest. With every stroke she melted away a pressure from his heart. She was the salve, the ointment that it needed. Quietly and unexpectedly, in one instant everything in Joshua's life had eased. Like all perfect moments it was tainted because it would have to end. Soon they would arrive at Misawa, and Josh would be on his way back to Langley to report. Truthfully, he knew Tokiko would be on her way back to Haruto.

Josh sighed.

"You look so sad," Tokiko said. "I thought I had the monopoly on sadness."

Josh looked at her queerly; he thought it a strange thing to say. Certainly, she seemed bothered lately, and a little distracted. With all that had been going on who could blame her? It was hard to believe the woman he met, so comfortable and in control in the upper echelons of Japanese corporate society, could conceal sadness underneath it all. Either she had been very good at disguising it, or Josh – in some selfish preoccupation – had been blind not to see it.

"I should never have left you Tokiko," he said. "You ... we ... could have avoided all this mess and all that wasted time."

She replied, tenderly. "No regrets Josh. We can't see all outcomes. The best we can do is act as we feel right at the time; if we do that, we can never truly regret."

He'd forgotten the comforting wisdom of which she was capable. Josh missed it. His heart leaped to know fate was giving them another chance to get it right.

The angry turbulence outside whipped the rustling bushes into a frenzy. The house creaked and cracked; was it the wind, Josh wondered, or something else outside? It was too hard to tell in this wild weather.

Flesh was luring others too. Mosquitoes began circling. Time to move. Getting to his feet was like dragging steel from a magnet. Tokiko's tiny pursed mouth curved into a neat smile. Did she regret the past too, Josh wondered? More importantly: would she take a chance now to change it? Whatever psychological magic Haruto used to beguile, enchant, and seduce her to be his wife might have worn off. Her expression of affection tonight gave him hope, but it would wait. They had lingered here long enough, been lucky so far, but it was time to get moving. All he had to do was keep ahead of their pursuers, just a little longer.

She laughed, like a love-struck little girl.

"What's funny?" Josh asked, chuckling too.

Tokiko continued to give a wry, enigmatic smile that said: "tell me what I'm thinking," she teased. No answer was required. Like the lover's game they used to play. Like the look she gave him that last time they parted fifteen years ago. A memory flooded into Josh's mind of the last kiss he shared at the terminal of Narita airport.

All his life since that moment had just been erased.

Harker put on his damp sweater; the sounds outside continued, and in one lightning flash, he thought he saw shapes emblazoned on the canvas screens, shapes of men. Josh scrambled to the table for his gun. Just then, an abrupt clap sounded.

Josh was suspended in time, as was Tokiko. Both frozen.

He checked: "Tokiko?"

No reply came. Her face had drained of expression, replaced by shock. She remained still for an infinity in his eyes, as paralysed as an ex-inhabitant of Pompeii, unable to fathom the situation in which she found herself. Tokiko toppled forward and crumpled onto the bedsheets. In one horrific moment, Harker looked down to check his own gun, half-wondering if his treacherously shaking hand had pulled the trigger. But no salty smoke was rising from his pistol.

Instinct took command.

Josh found himself shoulder-rolling as two more shots spat towards him through the canvas.

THIRTY-THREE

Northern Honshu, Japan
20th October – 2:11am

A bullet whipped past Harker's ear. Coming out of a roll on one knee, facing the direction of the shots, he let loose a rapid volley. Bullet holes of the unseen attacker peppered the screen wall and Josh added a few of his own to it, hoping to take out the assailant.

No more shots rang, but Harker kept moving, never assuming he'd made a killing shot. He wouldn't want to die through complacency born of stupidity; there were still sounds coming from outside, like a scuffle in progress. Sounded like at least two people behind that flimsy wall now. Backup had arrived. He was outnumbered again.

Harker would have to go out, take the fight into the open where he could see the enemy. Stopping, crouching, just inside the door, he paused just long enough to look back at the slumped shape of Tokiko on the futon. She wasn't moving. Josh's heart beat out of his chest. He shoved back all emotions and tried to direct them into actions that would keep him alive. He burst out onto the veranda to meet the man who shot his lover. Holding the gun in the Weaver stance, he crept around the outside corner, his breath sounding to him louder than the storm.

Peering around the corner post, Josh saw a figure kneeling over a dead *ninja*, the unmistakable silhouette of a *katana* hilt visible behind its shoulder. His head scarf was askew after the tussle with the dead man. Underneath, Harker could make out a shock of blonde hair, and cool eyes that showed zero emotion. The last time he had seen them, Harker had plunged a sword into their owner: it was Kazuki Shimura. The assassin held a gun, and a crimson-tarnished knife recently pulled out of the *ninja* who had already been dressed in funereal black. The fool must have tried to stop Kazuki's volley of shots, and paid the price.

Harker's anger exploded.

"Kazuki!" He pointed the barrel of his weapon, ready to fire, but the *ninjutsu* trained boy was already moving. Josh cursed his jaded middle-aged reflexes as he planted two slugs in the ground where Kazuki had just been. A shot singled Harker out, but clipped by him, chewing into the wooden support post. He rolled back off the veranda, out into a mud bath, while firing off sideway slugs with as much precision as he could manage in the frenzy.

That shot couldn't have come from Kazuki. It came from higher; a cover shot from the bushes. Kazuki had backup too. Josh figured his *yonkuichi* mini-militia were in tow.

To confuse the aim of his attackers, he made sure to keep his movements erratic; that wasn't too difficult that night. He stumbled back under cover. It worked: two more projectiles narrowly missed. How close they came, he didn't know, and didn't want to know.

Steadying his nerves, Josh cursed under his breath, reprimanding himself for being so generous with his rounds. He checked the clip – two left. If Kazuki's *yonkuichi* were out there, then it was a good bet the same model gun was being used against him. Glock 19 clips carried up to twenty rounds, so the shadow gunman must be running low on ammunition too. Of course he might have a spare, and there could be more than one *yonkuichi* out there. If that was true, then Josh was finished.

A broken screen on the far side let him re-enter the house without crossing the line of fire. He approached the bed, crouched low with his gun attentively pointed straight ahead. He tried not to get distracted from staying alive, but it was difficult to ignore the dark crimson stain blooming across the mat under Tokiko.

Harker was the next target, vulnerable while he couldn't see his opponent. For all he knew, Kazuki could be lining up on him now through another rip in the weather torn shell of the house. All it would take was one bullet, perfectly placed. The rain hammered on the galvanised roof. Josh knelt, still, and patient, in the gloomy centre of the house with the hilt of his gun pressed to his chest, waiting, for any sign. Tokiko's motionless body loomed behind him.

The pattern of sound changed. A muffled structure came to the noise beyond the clashing torrents of rainfall. Voices. Josh was sure he could hear voices, and they were getting louder. Optimistically, he let himself believe someone had come to his rescue, until pessimism took over, and he wondered if they were Kazuki's *yonkuichi* reinforcements. If so, he was a dead man – with nothing to lose. He rose to his feet and tip-toed toward the open veranda screen. Resting his back on the inside wall, he peeped out.

The glistening undergrowth was tousled by more than the gale – people were creeping through it. A head popped up through the bushes and shouted down to the house in a regional dialect which made it hard to apply Harker's already limited knowledge of the language. Could they be co-ordinating, shouting orders down to the *yonkuichi* already nearby?

Some bullets pealed through the air. Josh flinched, reflexively ducking his head, until he realised they were not aimed at him.

Chaos broke loose.

The air erupted like Chinese new-year. Gunshots pulsed around the outside of the archaic dwelling like belts of firecrackers. Man-made atmospherics to rival anything the storm could produce. Bullet tracers spat into the mud and Josh saw a gunman fall back as though punched in the shoulder.

Whatever was going on, Josh knew this wasn't his fight. He scampered far back into the house for cover, to ride out the battle.

Gradually, the number of gunshots decreased, as the gunmen available to fire deceased. Eventually just a few shots could be heard, and they were moving away. Motorbike roars started up and pursued away until they became just a murmur in the night, drowned out by rumbling thunder.

Harker was left alone with only the sound of the rain and his adrenaline-pumping heart. What the hell had just happened, he wondered? It took him a few moments to shake off the shock and summon courage enough to examine the aftermath. His finger, pressed to Tokiko's neck, told him there was still life. Just. Her pulse was weak. A low groan from the limp body kindled his hope.

Tokiko lost blood, fast. Harker knew blood. It had always been cold by the time he arrived. Not like this. With blood oozing, enveloping his hands, it was the heat that astounded him, so much warmer than the body it seeped from. It was another moment of macabre intimacy for Josh, not felt since arriving too late after Megan's murder. The ingredients of the crimson cream were slowly exhausting themselves, cooling in his hands. Like before, he felt an urge, a desperate irrational urge, to scoop up the blood and pour it back into the wound, as if it would prevent death, as if life could be poured. It was not so easy.

Not again. I won't lose her again.

Harker set to work with obstinate determination. A makeshift compress, fashioned from a sheet, would limit the loss until he could do what was needed. The bullet pierced just beside her kidney. From the size of the entry wound he guessed it was a hard nosed twenty-two caliber bullet – a forty-five or a soft nose would have ripped her guts apart. From the amount of blood, he guessed the bullet had nicked the mesenteric artery. If he didn't do something now, she would die of exsanguination. Even at that, she'd need medical treatment in a hurry. They were still miles from anywhere. She'd have to be moved. The bullet hadn't come out the other side, so it was still lodged in her somewhere.

No way he could move her with a bullet inside. It had to be done. Med school had given him the knowledge for this, but hadn't prepared him for it ... not like this.

Josh tore the farmhouse apart looking for anything he could use. He returned with a half-empty bottle of *sake* and an emergency stove with a dribble of oil left in its burner. It would have to do. Instruments. He needed something to operate with. He would have to go outside. Looking around for any sign of remaining *yonkuichi* didn't disappoint him – there were none. All battle had desisted. The survivors had taken it elsewhere, pursuing each other on open road. There were none to be seen alive, but that didn't mean one wasn't taking aim at him from the bushes right now. Josh found he didn't care. He stood out into the open. No bullets pierced him.

The body he'd seen fall was just a few steps away. Josh frisked it. In a side cargo pocket he found a small throwing dagger. There was nothing else of use to him. Ripping off the headscarf revealed a face Josh didn't recognise. Peeking out over the rim of the polo neck, was an intricate pigment-hammered tattoo popular with *yakuza*. Josh searched another cadaver's clothing. The half-dozen others he checked later all had *yakuza* brandings, all but two. Those two had a simple three character tattoo on their upper arm – they were *yonkuichi*.

There was no body of Kazuki to be found. Josh presumed he escaped. If he survived the hunt on the road, he would be back to finish the job he started. To finish off Harker.

Josh yanked open the under-seat compartment of his bike and took the pliers before scurrying back inside. The stove he'd set alight was bringing to the boil *sake* poured into a rusty food can. He submerged the dagger's blade and pliers' teeth into the effervescing alcohol. There would be many sources of infection threatening that open wound, but Josh would do all he could to minimise the risk to Tokiko. Even at that, the more he looked at his ramshackle field infirmary, the more hopeless it seemed.

He considered for a moment giving her some *sake* to ease the pain that would follow, but didn't know what effect it would have on her recovery. The dilatory effects of the alcohol might increase the blood loss. He cooled the heat-disinfected *sake* with some rain water before turning her belly towards the illumination of the stove light and poured the alcoholic disinfectant into the puncture. Tokiko yelped. Josh held the blade and the pliers steady above the open wound.

"Keep very still Tokiko."

He would need to heat the blade on the flame and cauterize the artery to staunch the bleeding. Then, he would have to delicately pinch out a rounded, slippery bullet, hidden somewhere within a pool of blood on a flinching cushion of flesh. All without damaging any organs or blood vessels.

It would be excruciating for her. He had to do it, he told himself, or she would surely die.

Harker's hand began to shake, not because of any weakness of his body, but because of strain of the heart. Had it come to this? His entire journey, parting from Tokiko that first time, meeting Megan, then losing her too, only to come back to this again. If he botched it, he would be the one taking the life of the woman he loved. He would become that killer, the thing he hated most.

With a slow, smooth out-breath, Joshua pushed in some cloth dipped in *sake* to soak up excess blood, and then he began.

I'm sorry, Tokiko.

* * *

When it was done, Josh staggered out into the night. He lifted his head, letting blobs of rainwater drive into his face and wash blood from his hands. The drained muscles of his legs could no longer bear the weight of his heart; his knees punched into the mud with a wet slap. Bodies of the dead littered the land around him. Head low, back slumped, and soaked through to his skin, he lived at the mercy of the storm. Beaten, deceived, exhausted, abandoned, how could he go on? Tokiko's anguished roars before she passed out from the pain had finally crushed him, and he wondered if he would ever rise again. There was only one feeling left in him; an overriding one that had driven out all others – pain. Only once had he felt it like this before, after Megan's murder. This time it seemed dimmer, and duller somehow. Had he taken too many emotional blows? Was pain becoming such a frequent companion on his journey, that he was becoming inured to it?

How long, he wondered, how long more would he have to court disaster while craving hope, never allowing the former to eclipse the latter?

The CIA agent looked up into the streaming rain. Above it sat a veil of darkness, occasionally broken by a pulse of lightning raging around the cloud crucible, screaming down at him, taunting his rage with its own. Josh yelled back at it, from the depths of his soul, trying to out-scream the storm. But all the screaming could not purge him of the great despair he felt; an existential crisis so deep that no man should have to feel it more than once in life, but he'd had to shoulder this twice.

"Why me?" he screamed.

He lifted a sword fallen near his side straight into the sky, a tempting lure for lightning to strike him asunder.

"Take it!" he shouted. "Take my life! Take it instead of her's. It's all I have left. You've taken everything else, so you might as well finish the job!"

He didn't know who he shouted at, but they weren't listening anyway. A God? A state-funded guardian angel satellite on the lookout for him? Man's efforts would be stymied by God's atmospheric temper that night. No help would come. If he were to get out of this at all, it would have to be through his own resources.

Seconds had passed, feeling like a lifetime, but no lightning struck. Nature failed him too. The sword fell into the mud when his fatigued, lumpen arm could hold it no longer. Even his body was abandoning him.

He was still alive. Once again, he was left alive in the aftermath, and once again he had to make some purpose out of that inconvenient fact, if only because ... he had no other choice. There was still hope for Tokiko, if not for his lost soul. She was his purpose now. Maybe he was still alive because only he could save her now. Josh dragged himself upright and sloshed back into the house. Kazuki would be back soon. Death was all Kazuki deserved after this, and if they ever crossed swords again, Harker would gladly be the one to take the Genaform's life, or die trying.

Josh kneeled down beside Tokiko, held her hand, and pressed a thumb to her neck. A pulse still reigned in her veins, diminished though it was.

"I only ever wished the best for you, Tokiko," he said to an unconscious interlocutrix.

On the floor beside the futon, something glinted at him in the darkness. It was the DNA pendant he had given her – a customary gift for a friend not seen in a while. Those social customs mocked him; it was also customary to take a personal belonging after the death of a friend. Josh put the pendant into his pocket, determined it would not be such a gesture. He would give the gift to her again, he vowed.

"I'm not going to fail you, not this time," he said to her.

Josh got ready to leave and lifted her onto the saddle before heaving on his own reluctant body. Bands of cloth, tied around them both would keep her from slipping off in transit.

"Hold on, Tokiko. Please, hold on."

Josh fired up the bike one last time and headed again for Misawa, hoping Tokiko would accompany him all the way.

THIRTY-FOUR

Near Misawa, Northern Honshu, Japan
20th October – 5:04am

The motorbike became Harker's means of directing his rage out into the world. It pierced the wall of subsiding rain, slipping down the black slick of asphalt at two hundred klicks per hour. He'd returned to the main road, trading safety for speed now time was so critical. Tokiko's time. In the small hours of the morning the road was empty. Misawa was so close he saw its neon haze burning the rainfall on the horizon, beyond the twilight abyss of lake Ogawara.

Joshua's mind raced as fast as the piston cylinders beneath him. Fuelled by adrenalin, he recycled Tokiko's injury over and over. Why did he hole up in that shack? Stupid. It was for Tokiko. Now she could pay the ultimate price for him giving in to that temptation.

He thought of Kazuki, with the gun that shot Tokiko. The boy's corruption of identity, the desire to protect his secret, and the loyalty to protect his Genaform heritage, seemed strong enough to kill even Tokiko. Harker didn't doubt it. Kazuki had murdered Olsen, one of the men responsible for his existence. The boy had gone mad. The *yakuza* he found proved it. Haruto must have kept his old links in reserve, using them now to hunt down the Genaform gone mad. The explanation fitted the evidence. It gave Josh some satisfaction to think of Kazuki in the same position as himself – hunted.

The distant wink of an approaching headlight in the wing mirror caught Harker's attention.

His eyes remained as much on the headlight behind as on the road in front. The orphan glow in the blackness swung pendulously along the banking horizon, frequently disappearing behind some undulation, but always reappearing again. After a few minutes, Harker knew it was matching his own route and frenzied pace, only one klick further behind: a lone biker was pursuing him. That bike wasn't as weighted down as Josh's, so it quickly caught up. Now it was in firing range.

What's he waiting for? He could gun me down right now!

An unknown motorcyclist twisted the throttle and surged forward, lining up alongside Harker.

The lone rider, in a faceless helmet, pointed at Harker with, not a gun, but a leather finger. It was pointing back up the road behind them. Harker looked in the mirror as three more lights appeared in the rear view. Three more motorcycles. The new companion beside him pointed at Harker, and then gestured to the road ahead, before dropping back. Whoever it was, it offered Harker cover.

The throttle was already maxed-out. The extra weight of his unconscious pillion passenger gave the new pursuers speed advantage. Shots rang out. He could see in the mirror his new saviour taking reverse pot-shots at the bikes behind. One fell, flourishing metal sparks abrading asphalt. Two remained. The lone biker took a hit to the forearm. Harker feared this would not end well. His protector was outnumbered, at a disadvantage, shooting backwards. Even odds were the very best Harker could hope for. Until ... his control of the bike gradually faded. Every sway and lurch of the bike took all of his will to control. It wasn't muscle fatigue this time. With his concentration saturated, Josh had failed to notice something: the low fuel pilot warning light lit up.

Damn it!

The bike sputtered and choked, bathed in the dim aura of illumination from the city outskirts – still too far away. His transport rolled to a halt by the side of the road. The fight continued to race past him. His anonymous defender kept point between Harker and harm, taking a shot and bringing a second enemy off their bike, head-flipping into a ditch. This action gave the last of the enemy, stopped further up the road, the chance to take aim and catch Harker's helper squarely in the chest. The bike flipped sideways, and Harker's last hope slapped down lifeless on the road like a flounder washed up on shore.

One leather-suited rider prevailed. Josh saw him kick down the parking stand. Josh unhitched Tokiko and quickly laid her down behind the protection of a boulder jutting out of the roadside ditch, removed his helmet and threw it in a field, then unsheathed his sword from the bike's chassis. He'd exhausted his pistol's ammunition back at the shack and wouldn't get to his guardian angel's gun in time to take the first shot. All he could do was appeal to whatever honor this last assassin had. He stood, sword in hand, like a bullfighter ready to topple a charging beast.

The rider dismounted, and with helmet still in place, stood motionless on the roadside looking down in Josh's direction. Searchlights were switched on within the airbase to examine the commotion so close to its perimeter. Above him, standing in front of the blinding lights, Josh only saw an imposing silhouette with rain streaming down its black leathers.

The silhouette looked over at the searchlights, then back to a nearly-exhausted Josh, who collapsed back into a ditch. Harker pressed against the rock, next to Tokiko.

The rider, seeing the pathetic dwindling form of Josh Harker with no firearm, rested his own pistol on the seat of his bike and unclipped a *wakizashi* sword instead. The moving leather mannequin stepped down from the high ground into the ditch, addressing Josh with his sword in a two-handed stance.

A fair fight – is that what you want?

Preparing for the attack, Josh thought back to his previous sword fight with Kazuki, and reminded himself of the lesson he needed to learn from that experience; that fast agile movements would serve him better than any aggressive brute force motions would – he couldn't muster force in his current state anyway.

Josh summoned up what energy he could, stood, and ignored what his enfeebled body was saying. He let the enemy make the first move, which gave rise to more surprises. The attack was slower, clumsier, and more labored than Harker had come to expect from Kazuki. It amazed him to find he'd inflicted a wound: an incision across his opponent's left tricep. Blood oozed from leather and mingled with rain. The next attack, however, left Harker in no doubt about this man's equal and opposing sincerity in wanting Harker dead. The tip of the sword pierced into CIA flesh where Josh had left his guard down. It stung like hell; surges of pain throbbed into his hip bone. His minuscule energies leaked out in blood down his right leg.

Both men were injured. Josh knew the next to inflict a blow would be the victor; even if it wasn't a killing blow, it would weaken the other enough to enable a kill. He straightened himself, focussed and studied every shift in weight of the man about to lurch. The attack would most likely come from the rider's left side: the wound Josh had inflicted there meant that it would be hard – and painful – for his opponent to move the left side of his upper torso. As the final attack came, Josh lowered the sword on his left side, and took that fateful gamble. He shifted his weight forward, and flicked the sword up and across under the arc of the descending attack. With a turn of both wrists, he ended the manoeuvre with a side step out of the line of his opponent's charge.

Josh heard a slash, a gurgle, and a spurt, before losing his balance on the edge of the ditch and falling into the marshy field behind it.

Harker froze, lying on his back, panting in the dark. He waited for movement from his quarry, any sign. To his relief, it never came. It was just as well; Harker took a long time to rise to his feet again, and couldn't have done it in time to stop another attack.

Steadying himself in the boggy soil, Josh looked down on the defeated. Could it really have been that easy to take Kazuki down? He deferred his growing sense of victory; something wasn't right.

Free from the confusion of battle and in full illumination of the searchlights, the body that Harker now studied did not have the lean agile frame of Kazuki Shimura. He heaved the bulky corpse onto its back and removed the helmet of the would-be executioner. He was disappointed to see it wasn't Kazuki. It was just another unknown Japanese face, another of many that had paid the price for involvement in the affairs of the Shimura family. Josh peeled back sticky blood-soaked leather cotton around the gouged wound running from the corpse's belly to its neck. A *yakuza* tattoo covered the torso. A criminal this man may be, Harker thought, but would a wife cry for him somewhere tonight? How many more would cry because of the Shimuras?

One thing he had to know, before carrying Tokiko those last few hundred meters: who had been his help? He walked back to turn over the body on the road and lifted the helmet.

Josh heard himself let free an anguished groan.

This time the face was of a man known to him, a man he'd only met once, and would now never meet again. The lifeless expression of the man he'd only ever known by his codename Ronin – his fellow CIA field agent from Tokyo. Josh concluded that Ronin sought him out when he'd gone out of contact, perhaps he even shadowed Josh all this time – his guardian angel. It must have been Ronin who released them from their cells in Hokkaido. Now he'd never get to thank him. He looked with sadness upon the man he thought of as his friend, his companion in danger, and felt sorry for him.

Josh was either too sad or too exhausted (he couldn't tell which) to notice an unmarked sedan with flashing beacons pull up. Two men in combat fatigues got out. In time, Harker noticed them approach. His mind swam; the exhaustion and bleeding was taking him. He saw automatic machine guns marching toward him. In his blurred vision, they could have been anyone; more *yakuza*, more *yonkuichi*, sent to finish the job.

Josh raised his sword defiantly. It wavered around in the air, erratically and unintentionally. The two men lowered their weapons and held out their palms in a pacifying gesture. Josh figured he must have looked so pathetic that he couldn't present any kind of threat to them.

"Hey, take it easy," one of them said.

American!

The words were in English, with an American accent. A Tennessee twang, if he was not mistaken. The language sounded almost alien now.

"Are you Joshua Harker?" he asked.

"Yeah," Josh replied. The guttural, exhausted rasp of a reply came.

"I'm Lieutenant Johansson, out of Misawa airbase. We've been looking for you. We were dispatched to find you, Mr. Harker, to take you back home, to safety."

Josh pointed to the curled, rain soaked Tokiko by the rock. "I've got to get her to a hospital."

"We'll take care of it now. You look like you need some attention too."

Josh's ribcage convulsed involuntarily. Pulses of air relieved themselves raucously from his chest. He couldn't tell whether he laughed or cried. It didn't matter: he'd no more energy left. A sword fell from his limp hand, clattering onto asphalt. He looked over toward the airbase perimeter; a lurid dawn broke under a retreating storm.

The land of the rising sun.

The land of promise ... and he couldn't wait to get out of the damned country.

Shuffling toward the troopers, Josh's feet gave out. His mind finally gave permission for his body to do what it needed. All the weight of recent events came crashing down like mighty fists of Thor. Four arms sprang out, ready to stop him from hitting the ground.

The last things Josh saw before passing out were four highly polished toecaps. And the last person he thought of was surprisingly not Tokiko, but the Genaform. Harker had been denied his chance for revenge.

So, he wondered, what was to become of Kazuki Shimura now?

THIRTY-FIVE

Gotanda, Tokyo
20th October – 12:08am

Haruto took his *onsen* bath as usual. It didn't relax him. He wrapped himself in a robe and kicked his feet into house slippers before shuffling off into the loft to hunt for sleep. This would be his fifth night under covers without Tokiko. Five nights since she absconded with the American. Joshua Harker may have been twenty five years younger than Haruto, but right then the aging tycoon could have torn him apart with his bare hands.

A lone *yonkuichi* stood guard on the inner balcony, in the place usually occupied by Kazuki. His head bobbed in respect to the passing magnate who, adrift on the currents of his thoughts, didn't notice. Kazuki also was missing for two days. Kazuki promised he'd find Tokiko and bring her home, as if he knew where to find her. That was three days ago. Haruto tried to call the young man several times, but failed. It was unlike Kazuki. Something was wrong. First Tokiko, now Kazuki. He even tried Taro, but his calls weren't answered. Communication with his father was shunned.

What was happening? His family was unravelling. Most of his life Haruto took control, but on days like today, when caprice took control, he felt powerless, and hated it. Today he was once again the little boy standing by a market stall over the bullet-chewed body of his Korean father.

The past resurged.

Twenty years ago, Haruto stood on the same spot, with Mark Olsen at his side, watching and listening to the nursemaid's singing lullabies to the new arrival in the cot. The haunting delicate simplicity of that traditional lullaby echoed still in the rafters of Haruto's mind. It was his favourite as a child, and became Kazuki's too. The infant's breathing grew gradually faster and deeper as she had caressed his forehead in rhythm with the lyrics. The boy soon fell asleep.

"You see Olsen-san," Haruto had said, "he will get the best care here."

"Haruto, I have no doubt he will receive the best mothering money can buy," Mark had said.

"Your words strike me deeply, friend. Do you think I would simply buy the boy's future?"

"He needs a mother, a real mother. All boys need their mother." Olsen's tone was peppered with regret.

"Then you strike me even deeper, for that is the one thing you know I can not provide."

Olsen backtracked. "I'm sorry. I forget how close you still are to Hiromi's death. Forgive me."

"Forgiveness is not necessary between friends. I know you did not mean to hurt. Your concern for Kazuki's welfare is admirable and one – I assure you – I share."

"It was good of you to take him in," said Olsen. He laughed at a private joke before making it known to his colleague. "The Japanese were always eager early adopters of new technologies, but this is taking it a bit literally, isn't it?"

Haruto just smiled, not so enthusiastic about the joke.

Olsen tried candour again. "I fear what future he would have in the US if word leaked out, from those who know his secret. A worker at Genesys labs might tell the American press someday and they would come looking for the boy. Kazuki would become a freak show. It is better that he simply disappear from there. And here, no one will know. No one will know what he is."

Haruto sighed. "Maybe one day, they should."

Olsen looked taken aback.

Haruto continued: "At the very least, Kazuki must learn of it."

"Is that wise?"

"When the time is right, and he is mentally prepared for it, I think it is essential that the man should know. I intend to tell him someday. This is not a dark, shameful thing we should hide Olsen-san."

Haruto ushered Olsen downstairs where a *geisha* served them a pre-dinner drink – *maszake* for Shimura, gin and tonic for Olsen. Shimura loosened his tie, plonked into a sofa, and was first to speak. The conversation turned from the specific to the abstract.

Mark swirled his drink. "Do you know what Oppenheimer said after his atom bomb test succeeded?"

Haruto nodded. "I am become Death, the destroyer of worlds."

"My fear is that history will judge us just as harshly, responsible for breaking human evolution, and more."

"Breaking it?" Haruto shook his head "Homo Sapiens has reached its natural end. Evolution no longer applies to us. We have no natural enemies, except ourselves. To grow, mankind must adapt, and evolve into something new and better. The next step is for us to guide our own evolution. With our knowledge of DNA and genetics, we have been handed the keys to creation. The Genaform is that next step. It must be encouraged."

Olsen looked up towards the Genaform Kazuki's nursery.

"And with such a ground-breaking paradigm shift, our society will be called on to evolve with it," he replied.

Haruto smiled at Mark.

Olsen drank deep and long before continuing.

"Fascinating as this may be for us – just intellectual candy – it is Kazuki who has to live with the consequences," Olsen said. "What will that knowledge do to a boy?"

"Do not worry, Olsen-san."

"But I am worried," said Olsen. "You posit the future, a grand and distant thing, a new form of evolution, but what we have done is unethical. My fear is for the present – that none of us will out-live the consequences of this."

They were words that echoed from the past to haunt Haruto's present. He missed Mark's sagacity and the rigours of those conversations; he missed his friend. Dead, at the hands of the infant who had lain sleeping in the cot above them, in a room now empty. A house empty, but for the anonymous *yonkuichi* guards.

A phone warbled around the corner. He overheard the *yonkuichi* talking into it.

"*Moshi moshi ... hai!*"

The guard marched around the corner to convey the news to Shimura. Before he could speak, Haruto interrogated: "Kazuki?"

The guard nodded. "The company's pilot filed a flight plan out of Sapporo airport. We believe Kazuki requested the flight."

"A Flight? To where?"

"The filed destination is Paris."

Before Haruto could comprehend the perplexing jolt of information, he was hit with more.

"One other thing: your wife has been located."

Haruto felt a sharp intake of breath.

THIRTY-SIX

Misawa AFB, Japan
20th October – 6:12pm

Joshua gazed through the observation window. On the other side lay Tokiko petrified under white sheets. Despite all the tubes and sensors attached to her, she still painted a portrait of serene glory, at peace. An angel in paralysis, caught midway between earth and heaven. Fluids in and out of tubes kept her alive; machines ensured it was so, sounding regular optimistic chirps to confirm it.

Someone had offered him a comfortable chair, but he chose to sit on a table-top to see over the half-partition. Cups of coffee appeared, which he remembered to sip sometimes, mostly when they were cold. A faulty fluorescent tube buzzed and winked at him down the hall. Medical officers popped in and out of the isolation bay frequently. It played like one of those time-lapsed movies. They moved around Tokiko in a blurred cloud while Josh remained fixated only on her face, keeping it in constant focus, as if letting go would put her out of focus forever and she would be subsumed by the cloud.

Someone had changed the tempo of Joshua's life; he didn't like dancing to this new slower beat any better than the previous beat. The frenzy of the last days was over, replaced by this hell of living. Now, he had too much time to think about what he'd done to the life of Tokiko.

Right beside him, in the periphery of his awareness, a shape pulled up along side. It was the Mike Kressler, Stanford's aide. His jetlagged eyes were bloodshot, and he looked about as happy to be in Japan as Harker did.

"You should get some rest too," Kressler said. "That wound of yours –"

"Will be alright."

The sutures holding his side together under the dressings tugged when he leaned sideways, but the pain was less than the greater wound he pondered ... through glass.

"The CMO tells me you saved her life. If it wasn't for what you did, she'd have been DOA."

What I did?

"Look at what I've done to her! Her condition is still critical," Harker said. "They've stabilized her vital functions, but there's some kidney impairment, and she lost a lot of blood. They're pumping her full of antibiotics and won't know for a while if there's any infection ... or other follow-on effects, like brain damage, until ... if ... she revives from the coma."

"Stanford would like a word with you."

"He's here too?"

Harker stood up, wincing under the painful restriction of those little plastic dictators gripping his flesh.

"Well, not quite." Kressler ushered Josh to a room down the hallway. It was a makeshift operations sub-center, no windows, and bare but for a table with a couple of laptops and a TACSET field satellite communicator. Mike flipped open a laptop and punched in the decryption codes.

"Ok, you're live," he said to an image of Stanford on the screen.

"Ah, agent Harker. How are you? How's Tokiko?"

"Not great. Her chances aren't certain."

"From what Mike tells me, it's a better chance than she would have had if you weren't there," Stanford assured.

"Her best chance was for me not to have come at all!" Josh insisted.

"I'm not going to brow-beat you, agent. This is the reality sometimes. But we keep it professional. Make this mean something," Stanford said. "We need to know what all this carnage is about. You must have found out something here – someone wanted both of you dead."

Josh nodded. "Kazuki Shimura, probably under Taro Shimura's direction."

"Her *family*?"

"Well, I'm not sure that Kazuki would see it that way. Let me explain."

Harker told the DD/NCS all the tales of assassinations, genetic subterfuge, commercial ambition, criminal organizations, and familial power struggles.

"So you see, it seems the whole Shimura dynasty – including the adopted experiments – are a bit unhinged."

"Unhinged they may be," said Stanford, "but capable. Through the *Yakuza*, they're probably responsible for recruiting and running the mole that protected their corporation."

"What mole?"

Harker saw the DD/NCS hesitate, something he'd never seen him do.

"You haven't been briefed on it, have you?" Josh knew that was rhetorical. "I was reluctant to tell you yet, you know, on top of everything else you've had to deal with."

"What mole?" Harker demanded with a louder voice.

"Rita Silberman," Stanford replied, not making eye contact with his screen.

Harker's shock wouldn't have enabled him to make eye contact with the DD/NCS either. His failure was now total. All this time, under his nose. The quashed Shimura report, the appropriated evidence – suddenly it all made sense.

"Has she owned-up to it?" Harker asked.

"She never got the chance. Someone got to her before we did. She's dead."

Harker sat back onto the table, head held in hands for a moment. "How did you find out about her?" he asked eventually.

"Actually, it was you who found her out. I just made the connections."

"I don't get it."

"That report you told me about – the one you wrote about Shimura's biotech research activities – I had Mike dig it out. When I read it I realised this wasn't written by someone trying to protect Shimura – but it certainly could have been silenced by someone trying to protect them. It was enough to raise a suspicion about her. Well, when we dug a little further into her activities it showed some worrying signs."

"Such as?"

"The crime is always easy to disguise, but the money can never be disguised. She was living way beyond her apparent means, above GS-15 paygrade easy. Her husband was a hedge fund manager who took the wrap for a collapsed fund and couldn't get a job ever since. She was funding his rehab since he took to the sauce after that, and still keeping her kids in the most expensive schools. It stank. So we checked her accounts through our friends at the FBI. Seems there were regular payments from a numbered Swiss account. The Swiss still won't play ball with us revealing the owners of those accounts, but we didn't need it this time. We knew. The FBI already knew the account as one associated with amphetamine trafficking in the States. It's a *Yakuza* account."

"Why'd she do it?"

"Why is always the hardest, and the last thing to discover," Stanford replied. "I guess, she did it for her family. To keep her kids in the best school, and to give her husband a chance to make it back."

Now who'll take care of them Rita? How stupid!

"What a mess," Harker puffed. "At least the leak is closed now, I suppose, the damage over."

The way Stanford shifted slightly told Harker that is was not over, a prelude to what came next.

"Silberman was a cut-out too. We traced a list of all her contacts. She'd been assembling a list of mercs, from CIA files. People she had no business knowing anything about in her line of duty. We suspect she recruited and was running a mercenary named Cain. He may even have killed her. He's still at large, last traced to Paris; he's live and under the suspected pay of the Shimura Corporation, or at the very least, the *Yakuza*. We don't know his mission or intent. I was hoping that you might have learned something about it."

Josh shook his head despondently. "I've never heard of him. If he is on a mission, and the *yakuza* were the channel, then it's most likely because of Taro Shimura. What his plans might be – I don't know."

Dismayed silence enveloped the two CIA men.

"I'm sorry we didn't find you sooner Joshua," said Stanford. "When we found out who the mole was, so close to you, we knew you could be in more severe danger than we'd suspected. She might have told them you were coming. And when your handler had heard nothing from you, couldn't contact you, and we'd lost all trace of your mobile signal ... we did all we could to find you in time. We monitored every site with known connections to the Shimura empire. It was only when a UAV out of Misawa caught you on infra-red driving out of their Hokkaido residence, with a swarm of *yakuza* riders in tow, well, then we knew it must be you. We sent out support. I'm sorry we couldn't get there sooner. So you see, I'm just as much responsible for what happened to Tokiko as you are."

A woman in uniform knocked and entered. From her livery, Harker saw she was a Colonel – the base Vice-Commander. She said, "we've got one Haruto Shimura just pulled up at the main gate. He insists on being let in to see his wife."

Josh hung his head. Word of Tokiko's injury must have reached Haruto from the *yonkuichi*. He looked over at the DD/NCS, whose face told Josh ... it's your call.

"Let him in," said Josh. "I'll meet him outside."

Josh left the DD/NCS to his anonymity and stood by Tokiko's window to greet her husband. When the security officer brought Haruto to the observation zone, he left the two men standing in silence.

Haruto didn't look at Josh, but made straight for the view of his unconscious wife. A vein on Haruto's temple throbbed.

"It is well that you hide out here, Harker-san, for if you set foot on Japanese soil again I will have you hunted down and killed for this."

"Your sons have already tried to do that. Tokiko's injury was the outcome."

"Lies! You expect me to believe they are responsible for this."

"Partly, yes. But we must all take our share of responsibility for it, including you. This legacy of yours. I saw it with my own eyes: Kazuki, the Genaform, with the smoking gun."

"So you know." Surprise seemed to rob Haruto of his charging anger. "It is impossible. Not Kazuki – he is not capable of –"

"Murder? The same way he wasn't capable of murdering Mark Olsen?"

Josh could see the old man's gaze deflect for just a moment. Haruto said nothing.

He suspects. Haruto knows that Kazuki was the Senator's assassin.

"Perhaps Kazuki was aiming for me and it went astray," said Harker. "Or perhaps –"

"Yes?"

"Who knows what goes through his mind? Who knows what measures a Genaform would take to protect itself once Tokiko and I discovered his origins."

Haruto – at last – turned to look at Harker properly.

"How do you know about the Genaform?"

"Sorokin."

Haruto nodded an understanding. "And Tokiko – she heard too?"

"Yes. She knows the secret now, just like Olsen knew. Who's next to die for that secret Haruto – you?"

He shook his head violently. "I won't believe it of Kazuki. I won't. He is our family protector. It is not in his nature to do this."

"Nature? His nature is what you made it, set down in DNA, and how you nurtured it. This is your part in this Haruto, your responsibility."

"You know nothing of my family. You should hold your tongue on matters where your ignorance outweighs your insight."

"Well, don't take my word for it – ask Kazuki why he did it. Why not ask him? Perhaps you're afraid what you might hear?"

Shimura gave the American a sheepish look. "I can not ask him because I can not speak to him. He has left the country."

"Left the c … to where?" asked Josh.

"Why should I tell you?"

"Listen: if he's on another assassination rampage ... you have to tell me where he's gone. I can stop this – you can't. It's outside your territory now."

Haruto seemed to think dispassionately for a moment, gazing upon his wife. The silence endured for what seemed like a lifetime.

Come on! Come on!

"The last I heard," said Haruto, "Kazuki was reported to have taken the corporate jet out of Sapporo Airport to Paris."

Paris!

"Stay here, I'll be right back," Josh said.

He burst into the ops sub-center, interrupting Kressler's conversation with Stanford's head.

Josh proclaimed: "Kazuki's fled to Paris. Isn't that where you said Cain was?"

Stanford looked pleased with the new connection made. It was a delight Harker shared.

"It can't be a coincidence," Josh said.

"No: I don't suppose it can. I'll alert Paris station straight away."

In a heartbeat, Josh heard himself saying, "I should go up there."

"No," said Stanford, not pausing for thought.

"Look, I'm no use here. Paris doesn't even know what Kazuki looks like, and they don't know how he operates. I can help."

Stanford sighed. "I have to admit the thoughts of these two loose elements co-operating scares me. It occurs to me this is what Olsen was going to warn me about, what he was killed for. We need every source to assist in isolating this danger, including your experience of the people and the situation, *but* ... I'd rather you do that from here."

"Why? Don't you trust me? You asked me to prove myself. Haven't I done it twice over now? Look at what it's cost me already –" Josh gestured back toward the infirmary. His voice broke off as he wrestled to keep it from breaking down entirely.

"That's exactly it, Agent Harker. I don't want you taking personal issues into the field. If you're emotionally compromised, you're not going."

Not again! I won't have another boss keep me from preventing a disaster because of his stupid notions about my emotional state.

"Personal issues?" Josh scoffed. "You were happy to use my personal connections to recruit me for this cause in the first place. And now that I've come this far, come this close to finding out what these people were killed for–" He stopped and paused before he went too far.

With a calmer voice he continued, "I'm not making this personal," while wondering to himself: *am I?* "You know I'd be more effective on-site than here. I'll take a passenger flight out there myself if I have to. You can't stop me."

Stanford did not look at all pleased with the decision his mind had already made.

"I'll talk to the Colonel, get you on an Air Force flight out of here."

Josh nodded satisfactorily and left to get ready, only stopping by the observation window for one last glimpse.

The CMO had just finished a chat with Shimura and departed, leaving Josh and Haruto side by side again, gazing upon the woman they both loved.

"I've asked to have her moved to Tokyo Medical in the morning," Haruto said in low voice. "She will get better treatment there. It's all I could think of to do." He sighed, a deep guttural thing that seemed to bring with it the leashed strains of many years. "The medical officer tells me, were it not for your actions, she would have been dead. I thank you for that."

Josh gave a disarming smile to show some solidarity with what Haruto was going through. Haruto continued with a candour that took Josh by surprise. The grand edifice of the global tycoon cracked a fraction, revealing the human beneath. It was something Harker never expected from this man for whom saving face was so important, and Harker couldn't help but feel honored that he should choose to do so with him.

"I've never been so powerless," Haruto said. "There's nothing I can do. What do I do?"

Josh turned to him and spoke in a raised, determined register. "You are her husband, Shimura-san – the man she chose as her husband. You stay here with her, by her side, and –" through gritted-teeth, Josh said, "– you don't let her go."

Harker turned on his heels and was half-way out the door when Haruto arrested him with one parting question: "and you, Harker-san – what are you going to do?"

"Me? I'm going to clean up this mess of yours, once and for all."

THIRTY-SEVEN

Place de la Concorde, Paris
21st October – 2:23pm

Harker looked at the paved expanse of Place de la Concorde. This was his first time in France. It wasn't the way he'd hoped to experience its grandeur, through tiny blast-proof windowpanes in the top floor office of the American embassy.

"Here you go."

A puppy-faced CIA case officer in his mid twenties put a cup of coffee in Harker's hand. Milbank was his name, Martin. He'd said it like he was in a movie. A pen peeped out the pocket of his white shirt, a shirt ironed so flat its creases could injure.

The stimulant Harker poured down kept jetlag at bay and him on his feet. The quest, and all it had taken so far, was starting to wear him down. He felt a worrying desperation come over him for real results, before his capacity to care for them eroded altogether.

One thing kept him focussed: Kazuki.

Josh picked up the conversation again. "So, Shimura's corporate jet landed before you could get a tail out to it."

"We're starved of resources here. Langley thinking we can track two targets is bad enough, but telling us only *after they land* ... come on!"

The disillusionment with the job, Harker could see, was already beginning to infect this young man. Paris could do that to you, according to the Langley rumor mill. It was easy to assign to Paris young, enthusiastic, French-speaking case officers with dreams of European espionage, turning French skirt. It was only the young who'd accept the placement; the old didn't want it. They knew better. The French were indifferent at best to Americans operating within their borders, and social interaction – the bones of any case officer's job – proved difficult. The French wouldn't mingle with the clean-pressed, loafer-wearing types like Martin Milbank. A year of too few nights of amorous conquest, outnumbered by nights of ostracism from French café society, watching DVDs alone in his apartment, then Milbank would be out too, looking for something less real and more exciting.

Excitement – the kind Harker went in search of the day he left the Langley cubicle. This was reality. Far too real for his liking. Perhaps such reality, such operational excitement, was best left in the lap of CIA new blood like Milbank, who didn't yet know what waited for them.

Josh burdened the window ledge with his weight. He noticed Milbank look away, seeming uncomfortable with the frailty of this man running the Shimura case.

Do I really look so decrepit?

"Anyway," Milbank said, looking back up, "we did find him eventually."

"Kazuki?"

"No – Cain. Thing of it is, we weren't even looking for him. He popped up on the grid while we were surveilling someone else."

Milbank led Josh to his desk and punched up a surveillance video.

"This guy: Kamal Mugniyah," he said pointing to a grainy swarthy face entering a frozen frame. "His *résumé* is broad. We suspect him of organizing gun-running routes during the Iraqi insurgency, and running an Al-Qaeda cell out of Algiers; he's prominent on our watchlist, and we've been tracking him since he crossed into the Schengen zone. Mugniyah pops in and out every few months, does meet-and-greets with members of the French Algerian community here. We like to keep a close eye on him – two, when possible. And that's when your friend Cain showed up."

Milbank played the video. The CCTV playback showed Josh a row of lockers. The people entering and leaving the bottom of the frame told him it was somewhere public, perhaps a train station. Mugniyah took a key and opened one of the lockers, taking out a white letter-sized envelope. He unslung a satchel from his shoulder and placed it in the locker before locking up and leaving the frame.

"It's a dead drop Mugniyah uses," Milbank said, advancing the playback until a new player in the drama came into scene. He opened the locker.

"Is that Cain?" asked Josh.

"Sure is."

He was shorter and older than Harker imagined, stocky, balding and sporting a salt and pepper moustache. Cain used his own key, removed the satchel and walked away with it. The satchel sagged in one corner, where its mysterious load had collected; from the way he lifted it, Harker guessed it weighed about five or six kilos.

"Do we have any idea what was handed over?" Harker asked.

"Not what was passed to Cain, no. We … uh … we lost him again after the pick-up."

Josh remembered Stanford saying Cain was expert at keeping in the shadows.

"What about that envelope?" asked Harker.

Milbank rolled back the recording to before Mugniyah showed up. There, again, Cain appeared and dropped off the envelope in the locker.

"A straight swap," Josh said. "What was in the envelope?"

"We don't know for sure, but we kept tracking Mugniyah. This morning he rented a small truck and turned up at *Port de Bonneuil*, presented a freight ticket, and collected a crate from the Sumisho Shipping warehouse."

Milbank clicked around and brought up more surveillance material – still photos this time, better quality. A large wooden crate, with few markings that Josh could see, was loaded on a forklift into the back of the white truck.

"Sumisho Shipping," Harker stated, "is the trading arm of the Sumitoro kieretsu."

"You think it's from your friends in Japan?"

"I'm not sure I'd call them friends exactly, but, yeah ... Shimura Corporation is known to use Sumisho Shipping for all their commercial freight. Any way of finding out what's in that crate?"

Milbank shook his head. "We passed the IMINT to a crateologist in Langley, but she wasn't able to come up with any unique tell on the crate. The only give-aways are the size and weight, and they mean it could be anything from a nuclear device to a fridge freezer."

"I don't imagine Shimura Corp is trading in nuclear weapons yet," said Harker.

A wearied attempt at a joke belayed his concern for what really lay in that crate. Kazuki's whereabouts unknown. Cain gone to ground. A shipment from Shimura Corporation in the hands of a known terrorist. The crate, and that envelope, were Harker's only tenuous hope for unravelling this Shimura conundrum. He had to grab the opportunity.

"I want to know what's inside that crate. Can we intercept?" he asked.

"The photos gave us the reg of the truck, and we've been able to track some of its route by toll plaza traffic logs. The last trace was just north of Lyon."

"Where's he headed?"

"Out of France I'd guess, but if he is, he'll take one of the quieter money launderer's exits out of the country. We might lose him soon."

"Then we'd better get down there with some hardware."

Milbank whistled. "Whoa there! Any operation like that will need the assistance and support of the DST."

"DST?" Josh asked.

"*Direction de la Surveillance du Territoire.* It's the French FBI. They've always stipulated in respect to Mugniyah, we can look but not touch, anything more might risk reprisals from the large Algerian population here in France. Any intercept action would need their say-so, and I don't have that kind of influence with them. I doubt even the Station Chief here could pull it."

Harker strummed his fingers on the desk for a second then picked up the handset of the green STU-III secured telephone on Milbank's desk.

"Well, I think I know a man who can," said Harker, dialing up a line that would eventually get him through to CIA's Deputy Director of the National Clandestine Service.

THIRTY-EIGHT

Near Mauves, South of Lyon
21st October – 6:42pm

Shadow fingers from a sinking sun stretched far across the patchwork fields. Josh rested his head against the helicopter's airframe stanchion as he contemplated the rolling arable carpet unfurling beneath his portal window. It reminded him of the speeding countryside he'd mulled with Tokiko on the bullet train. Though his body had left her country, his mind, his heart, and his soul, were still there.

This time for contemplation was the enemy of resolve. He wondered what the hell he was doing here anyway, sitting next to his CIA colleague in the back of a French helicopter sauntering over *Provence*, while Tokiko lay – dying, or dead, for all he knew – on the other side of the planet.

What was he doing on this wild goose chase? Josh rebuked himself for jumping at the first chance to beat his path away from Tokiko. The dying ember of sun illuminated for him the naked truth that he had run willingly from Tokiko's bedside because he was afraid to stand by and watch again the death of a woman he had loved. Josh had abandoned her, failed her, like Megan before, and more than anything right now he longed to be by her side, to be where Haruto was standing. What Stanford said needled him: was he making this personal? Had anger launched him on some vendetta across France, seeking an opportunity to revenge himself on Tokiko's assassin? It was selfish; that was the worst of it. Josh never had the chance to bring Megan's killer to justice. His partner Sheridan did that, and paid for it with his life. Josh knew he needed to keep a close watch on his emotions, or he might end up like Sheridan.

The *gendarme* sitting in the co-pilot's position spoke in French to the backseat Americans through headsets. Milbank tapped Harker on the arm and pointed down. At the edge of an approaching village, there was a parking area with a half-dozen trucks slotted in. In the middle was a mid-sized white truck like Milbank had shown him earlier. The license plate was visible enough for the *Gendarmerie* to identify it with the chopper's surveillance camera.

"*Les Routiers*," Milbank said, in stereo, in Harker's muffled ears. "It's a truck stop."

"Even terrorists need to eat and sleep," Harker said. "Tell the pilot to put us down away from it, out of earshot. I don't want to be rumbled before we can get to the truck."

"Right." Martin translated instructions, which prompted what Josh thought was an unnecessarily large amount of words from the pilot. After some backchat, followed by some ameliorating French words from Milbank, the helicopter circled down two fields away from the restaurant near the village outskirts.

The departing twilight fulfilled its final duty of the day, brightening the churning lake of grass that became their impromptu helipad. Harker took Milbank's lead and was standing, ready to hop out. They balanced on the listing, jolting metal floor plates, surfing the static wave of instability. The pilot feathered the collective control, keeping perfect balance between uplift and ground-effect, to bring them to a cushioned placement on the field.

The first to alight was the *gendarme*, slinging a bullpup rifle high under his shoulder. His assault gear was black – the global color of extraordinary means, as it now seemed to Harker. Stanford's persuasion via the consulate had secured approval of the operation with French authorities, but conditional on the presence of the *Gendarmerie* special ops forces. When clear of the rotors, the *gendarme* unfolded and placed on his head his official *bonnet de police* garrison cap and looked back for his escortees. Josh took up a canvas tool bag and leaped out of the Eurocopter, racing after Milbank.

The three man squad pushed through a hedgerow, scuttled over a field and bunny-hopped the low perimeter wall of the truck stop car park. The stone-clad lodgings looked like any rural bar-restaurant. The ruckus inside from inebriated truckers pleased Harker; no one inside could have heard the metallic rattle of the tool bag dropped on granite cobblestones.

With the *gendarme* circling the environs, his back to them, Harker set to work with Milbank. With the leveraged bolt cutters Harker bit through the shackle of the padlock, enabling Milbank to ratchet over the clasp and release the doors' locking mechanism. The plate steel door moaned and scraped on its unlubricated hinges. Harker winced at the thought of being heard.

He took a flashlight from the bag and waved it around the hollow interior. The truck was much larger than its solitary cargo, the crate, strapped to the cab-end of the space. The two CIA men hopped in, leaving the boots of the *gendarme* sounding their parade outside. Harker prised open the front of the wooden crate with a protesting squeal from six-inch nails. It took the efforts of both men to coax all the nails out and pull off the crate's side. In their eagerness to get to the contents, they had underestimated the weight of the wood and their ability to arrest its fall; the section landed with a crash. Josh shuddered; so too did the flexible walls of the truck that projected the noise like a loudspeaker out the back of the truck.

Harker rolled his eyes at Milbank; Milbank just shrugged. It was too late to do anything about the noise now.

Strips of polystyrene came adrift in Harker's frantic hands. He tore off the protective packaging to reveal a device wrapped in transparent plastic, which he scrutinized with the flashlight. It was about the size of two filing cabinets, stacked on their sides. Most of the front was taken up by two enamelled metal doors. At the top was an alcove with a smoked plastic door, and beside it an inlaid LCD screen panel, and a keyboard with other ancillary controls. Harker opened the left panel door through the plastic sheeting and peeped inside. Tubes fed down to an array of empty glass demijohn jars. He recognized its function immediately.

"It's a DNA synthesizer," Josh told his colleague.

"What's it for?"

"Its basic function is to create large quantities of DNA sections to order. Normally, you'd only find it in a laboratory. DNA synthesizers are used to create simple artificial bacterial life forms, or the gene sequences that can be inserted into retro-viruses, to create vaccines, or for basic gene therapy."

"So what's a terrorist want with one?"

"He could just be the courier, but that seems unlikely. It could be –"

Harker stopped so long that Milbank had to prompt him: "Could be?"

Harker was looking at the brand name stamped on the top left corner of the device: Sumitoro Electronics. It was the same manufacturer as the DNA analyser that Tokiko had designed. He wondered: did she assist in the design of this instrument too? If only he could ask her.

"It's more advanced," said Harker, mostly to himself.

"What?" said Milbank.

"This synthesizer is more advanced than any I've seen. Most biotech labs have one; hell you can even pick them up on eBay. So why would Mugniyah go to all this effort to get one, and why would Taro take such contrived methods to get it to him? I think this is a new model, the most sophisticated on the market. It might not even be on the market yet. Could be a prototype. Older DNA synthesizers can generate strands of just a few thousand base-pairs in length, but this one must be capable of millions. Enough to create some very sophisticated and intelligent viruses."

Or a complex lifeform, like a Genaform.

"So Mugniyah couldn't get it from anyone else?" Milbank suggested.

"Not this one. He must need this synthesizer's unique abilities for some purpose. We're missing something. This machine on its own is no use, and no threat, until a DNA sequence is fed into it. All he'd need is a trained biotechnician to package the DNA strands in whatever delivery vector is required. The important question is: what sequence was Mugniyah, or his allies, going to feed into it?"

Their pondering was interrupted by the sound of a thump and clatter outside. Harker bolted upright, unclipped the sidearm from his hip holster, and tiptoed to the open door, signalling to his new CIA buddy to keep back and out of sight.

Through the opening he saw *Gendarmerie* boots fallen sideways on the ground. From the sound, and their position, Harker guessed he'd been struck on the back of the head. Josh clicked off the safety catch. He eased down to a seated position on the edge of the truck's chassis, a position that would make it easy to step off while holding his gun pointed ahead. That way, he could get off a shot without wasting time aiming. The greatest risk would be getting down, so he did it quickly. It was while looking down in the direction of the unconscious *gendarme* that Harker realised the fatality of his mistake – he hopped off the truck facing the wrong way.

From behind, a belligerent forearm clamped his neck so hard the blood flow through his carotid artery nearly stopped. Simultaneously, a consuming pain ripped his side. At first, Harker feared he was stabbed, but as the pain pulsed away he realised the Algerian prodded the barrel of his gun into Harker's sutured wound.

Josh let out a shout of agonized surprise.

It must have surprised his attacker to hear it, who eased his grip, releasing him slightly, but prodded again to signal Harker to shut up. Josh had to bite his lip with the second painful prod.

"*Baisse il,*" Mugniyah said.

Harker guessed, correctly, the order to drop his gun. The clatter of the ceramic sidearm on stone was as loud, and the rattle as awkward, as he could make it; Milbank must hear all this commotion.

His foe backed up; Harker supposed it was to look inside the truck. There was nothing to be seen there but a busted crate. Milbank must have concealed himself behind the closed half door.

Clever Martin.

Mugniyah let go and shoved Harker, who tripped over outstretched *gendarme* legs. Flipping himself around on granite, Harker found himself looking down the barrel of a pistol. A shot cracked the air, amplified, perpetuated by its echo on harsh cobblestones.

The gunman, who had been looking at Harker, gazed past him, as if the CIA man lying on the ground had vanished, as if his existence had ended. Mugniyah crumpled at the knees, and fell into a foetal curl, adding to the heap of three bodies: the conscious; the unconscious; and now the dead.

Josh breathed again, taking pleasure in the exhalation, and the sight of Milbank standing in the open door holding a recently used Glock.

"The frogs are gonna give me hell for this," Milbank exclaimed.

Any inconvenience Milbank might experience, Harker thought, would be considerably less than Mugniyah's inconvenience at being dead. Josh flipped over the lifeless lump on top of him to make sure he was dead. A bullet hole in the back of his head; no recourse from a deadly shot like that. In the Algerian's open jacket, he spotted a white envelope tucked into an inside pocket. It must have been the one passed from Cain. Harker extracted it, unfurled it.

Milbank jumped from the truck. "What's that?"

"I think we just stumbled on the synthesizer's input."

Wrapped around a credit-card sized optical disc were several sheets of A4 paper. Printed on them was what Harker presumed to be the contents of the disc. The disc could be fed into the DNA synthesizer and produce this exact oligonucleotide sequence that he read – a cryptic code of a hundred thousand base-pairs, represented as a stream of letters A,C,T,and G.

"Any idea what it might be for?" asked Milbank.

"I'd need to do an analysis, but if I had to guess ... it's a virus, and from the size of the sequence, it looks to have a very specific purpose, and it would be particularly difficult to develop an antidote for it. Now we know why Shimura wanted Cain as middle man. If word got out that Shimura Biotech had developed bioagents for terrorists ... if Haruto found out what his son had been up to with his enterprise –" Harker felt his chest erupt into a relieved laugh. "Well, let's just say it'd be worse than sending Taro to bed without dinner."

Milbank smiled. "Then you did it! For a while there, I gotta tell ya, I thought you had us chasing our tails, but you did it – you stopped a virus getting into the hands of terrorists. Well done Joshua," Milbank said. He sounded earnestly pleased for Josh.

Josh held out his hand, looking for help up. "*We* did it Martin."

In a flash, Harker was back on his feet again, wondering how many more times he could tempt that condition and get away with it.

"Come on, give me a hand with this lazy lump," Josh said, lifting the unconscious representative of French protection by one arm.

THIRTY-NINE

Voie Georges Pompidou, Paris
22nd October – 8:17am

Parisian traffic stymied the Mercedes, eking its way along *Voie Georges Pompidou*. It was perverse diplomacy of the motor pool manager to select a German car for an embassy in France. The helicopter pilot had generously dropped them off close to the city center, at *Issy-les-Moulineaux* heliport, but that still left the challenge of rush-hour streets.

"What's with the traffic today?" Josh asked.

"Oh, you haven't had the Paris traffic experience, have you?" said Milbank. "Come to Paris, see the sights, stay for the traffic ... stay *in* the traffic!"

Josh wasn't smiling at Milbank's humor, but the young case officer, obviously buoyed-up by the taste of some real action, wasn't giving in.

"Hey, if you don't mind me saying, you seem a little down. You've just foiled a terrorist plot, but you look like you ran over your dog or something. What's with the attitude?" Martin asked.

Harker spoke without looking at him, gazing at the churning flow of the Seine, moving faster than the car.

"I don't think that's the end of it, Martin. There are still loose ends bothering me, and I'm damned if I can figure it out."

"What loose ends?"

"Kazuki, Shimura's son, is still unaccounted for. We know he's here somewhere, but what's he planning? And then there's Cain."

"He was the courier," stated Martin.

"That doesn't make sense. To select someone like Cain, and pay him as much as they must have, to deliver an envelope? Anyone can do that."

"Mugniyah was probably a contact of his, someone he used for shipping goods in and out of the middle east. He'd only trust dealing with Cain directly."

"Perhaps, but I still say anyone could have passed that envelope to Mugniyah. It didn't need to be Cain." Josh clicked his fingers. "Remember the handover, that satchel we saw Cain remove from the locker?"

"Sure. Cash presumably, to pay for the device?"

"Maybe, but unlikely," said an unconvinced Harker. "Stanford said they traced payments into his account. What would they be exchanging additional cash for?" He threw his hand in the air. "Ah, I dunno! Maybe its just that simple. I've been so goddamned suspicious of this crazy Shimura tribe for so long I'm starting to see things that aren't there."

I'm becoming paranoid about them.

Then he remembered his mantra.

Paranoia is healthy.

Two blue blurs of motorcycle police flashed past on the Doppler accompaniment of warbling sirens.

Milbank filled the lull in conversation. "I haven't seen the traffic this bad in a while; I think there's some conference in town today. They aren't too happy with me, you know, for killing that Algerian. It might stir up another Algerian community riot, and that's the last thing they want today. If a riot kicks off with people here from all over the world, it's sure to get global press coverage, make the French look bad. Heck, I would bet the Algerians would take the opportunity for that kind of coverage anyway. It'd highlight their plight. Nope, they're not too happy with me at all."

Harker began to tune out, oblivious to Milbank's problems, but Milbank kept talking anyway.

"That's probably the cause of all this traffic. The cops are out – intimidating force to warn them not to try anything. And so the cops keep the traffic not moving, as only they can."

Josh smiled. Being stuck like this didn't matter anyway; he had nowhere to be. The last dying amber leaves tumbled in a gust from a riverside tree. They made him think of all those souls who had fallen because of Haruto's legacy, Taro's ambition, and Kazuki's malcontent. As each leaf fell, he read out a name in his mind – an international litany of the dead. Mark Olsen. Andrei Sorokin. Ronin. Kamal Mugniyah. How many had died whose names he didn't even know. How many more would the Shimura crusade claim? Harker had avoided that list, but wondered had Tokiko been added to it in his absence?

Sorokin!

The synapses were not easily quenched. They fired still, making life-saving connections. Could it be that the tiny electrical impulses in one man's brain could save so many lives? He had to check, to confirm, his hypothesis.

"Martin, tell me quickly: this conference, what's it about?"

"Eh, it's in *Place de Fontenoy*, that's the UNESCO headquarters. I think they said something about ... biology ... or biotechnology?"

Harker walloped the back of the driver's seat in front of him, nearly sending his co-passenger and driver out of their skins.

"DAMN IT!" he roared.

Josh stubbed the palm of his hand into his forehead. "Stupid, stupid! How could I have missed it?" The paranoia had been confirmed.

"What's wrong?" asked Milbank.

"We need to get to *Place de Fontenoy*, fast!"

The car crept forward another two feet. The driver with an American accent butted in. "We're not going anywhere fast in this."

Josh twitched and grasped like a drowning man looking for a life preserver. "Then we'll have to hoof it. How far is it?"

Milbank replied: "Maybe a twenty minute walk from here."

"Half that if we run, come on!" One of his feet was out the door before he turned back to Milbank. "No wait: call your man in the DST. You have to get them to evacuate the conference center."

"What? Are you nuts? I have zero, read it – zero – influence with the DST after the outcome of last night's operation. You think they're going to evacuate an international event on my say so? I need a reason."

Harker was trapped between the need to explain and the need to get moving. He couldn't explain on the run, but delaying would lose them valuable seconds. Yet Milbank was right – the French authorities would need a reason. He'd have to sacrifice the time, if only to double their chance of saving lives.

Josh began a breathless download.

"Sorokin – Shimura's head of research in Japan – told us that he was invited to an International Bioethics Committee conference. Olsen was due to attend also. I didn't ask where it was being hosted, but I'll bet you it's the one going on this very day in Paris. He also said that Olsen had influenced the committee to begin moves to criminalize unethical genetic and biotech research, such as that virus we just intercepted, and Project GENAFORM."

"What's Project GENAFORM?" Martin asked.

Josh waved his hand. "Long story. Let's just say that the committee would be a serious impediment to Taro's chosen lines of research and the profitability of his arm of the Shimura empire. He'd lose face if the IBC had the power to shut him down, or – worse – if his father's corporation found itself in front of the International Criminal Court because of Taro's actions. That would be the end of Taro's stewardship of the business empire for good. It would also be the end for Kazuki, or rather the end of Genaform kind."

"How far do you think they'd go to stop the committee?" asked Milbank. Josh could see in his eyes fear of the answer.

"Sorokin said that Taro had issued a memo banning any Shimura employee from attending the conference, supposedly in protest. What if he did it because he knew there was going to be danger there? There are two assassins here in Paris, both linked to the Shimura Corporation. I think they are the source of the danger. Cain's delivery to Mugniyah wasn't his main mission, it was the payoff, for something in that satchel. I think that's why Cain was chosen. Everything we have seen to date has been to insulate and protect the Shimura Corporation. Because of Cain's contacts in terrorist circles, he could source materials to deflect any suspicion anyway from Kazuki, Taro, the Shimura Corporation, or even Japan itself. Cain is the cut-out – his expertise could make a mass assassination look like a terrorist act."

Milbank shook his head. "But you said to me that Kazuki was behind Senator Olsen's assassination. If Olsen was due to be here anyway, and what you say is true, why assassinate him first?"

"Stanford told me weeks ago that Olsen had some suspicions about what Shimura was up to, suspicions Olsen hoped to share when he gathered more information. If he heard about this, knew of a planned attack on the conference, and Taro found out, then Taro would have to take him out immediately, before he could warn anyone."

"Okay. And Kazuki Shimura? If they want to insulate the corporation, why is he here?"

"If I'm right, then that's the worst part of it all. You'd need to know him, how different he is to us, and how twisted it has made him. I think Kazuki is here in person to strike a blow for his kind, for the Genaform. To secure a future for any Genaform that succeed him. To send a message to humanity, that Genaform will exist, and will prevail, that mankind will not legislate against their emergence, their evolution."

"I don't know what that means, but the rest of it makes sense. You could be right about an assassination, or even a mass assassination."

"So you'll make the call?" asked Josh.

"I will. Better safe than sorry I say! I just hope they agree with me, but I wouldn't bank on it."

"I'm not – let's move," said Josh, jumping onto the pavement, which he began pounding as fast as his legs could. Even with a head start, Milbank caught up with him in two minutes. Depressingly for Josh, Milbank's speech wasn't interrupted by the exertion.

"No surprises with the answer –" Milbank huffed, snapping shut his phone. " '– get out of my face'. Looks like it's up to us."

They backtracked and climbed up *Pont de Grenelle*, to cross over the left bank of the Seine. Barges punted off the port moorings below and drifted away like oversized twigs caught in the current. For half a breath, Josh envied their leisure.

FORTY

Place de Fontenoy, Paris
22nd October – 08.19am

Cain sat on his haunches on the concrete, admiring his work. Strapped to either side of the building's gas main was a charge of hexogen. It was KGB legacy explosive, part of a consignment the Russian army overlooked in their claw-back of incriminating arms from Iraq prior to the American invasion. This was part of a consignment that had found its way into insurgent hands, and from there to Mugniyah, and on to Cain. It would fit his client's requirement. In the aftermath, the chemical traces would identify the explosive and make it appear as if the explosion was an Al Queda attack on Western institutions. It might even point the finger at the Russians. The client didn't care which, so long as there was no suspicion of Japanese involvement. This deadly delivery of hexogen from Kamal, in exchange for the envelope from Silberman, fitted the brief nicely.

The double package layout on either side of the pipe was a common incriminating pattern used by middle-eastern terrorists too. It was called a muffler charge, popular in their car bombs. The layout would increase the brisance – the shattering power of the explosive – in the immediate vicinity. It would ensure complete annihilation of the gas pipe, ignition of its contents, and the rupture of the huge twin heating system boilers which were located below one of the primary load bearing columns for the conference hall. The culminated effect would quite literally bring the roof down. It was the architect who should be shot, Cain thought. This building was designed decades ago, in a safer world, far from terrifying, modern realities.

Cain crimped the blasting caps he'd posted into a Paris post office box days earlier. They'd been disguised from customs' X-ray detectors in a graphite and epoxy package. He stuck them into the explosive and connected the trailing yellow and blue wires into a timer device. It would have been more authentic to the requirements to use a mobile phone to set off the explosive, but in this basement, so far below ground under inches of concrete, Cain couldn't rely on the signal. A timer would have to do.

He punched in the countdown duration: thirty minutes. One last look around to make sure his exit would be unimpeded, and he clicked over the toggle that started the countdown.

Cain made his way out of the heating service control, quickly and calmly. He took off his gloves and pocketed them, ready to cast them into a public waste bin when far from here.

His part was over, the climax of his explosive performance would have to play out without him.

FORTY-ONE

Roppongi, Tokyo
22nd October – 07.53pm

Haruto sat at the bedside of his absent wife, holding her soft, warm, tender fingers in the thickened, callused skin of his old palm. If only her angelic extremities would move. Some sign, any sign. He looked out the window of her private room in hospital at the evening illuminations of Shinjuku's skyscrapers, and wondered would she ever come back to him?

Night fell. Another day passed. Time lost all meaning. Aides came by now and then, troubling him with the daily minutiae of the Shimura Corporation, pressing him for responses, or signatures. They thought it was important; before, he did too. Now, he wondered would anything coax him away from this seat again, except a woken Tokiko.

The door was silent to old ears, but it had opened, Haruto knew; he sensed an intruder in the room. By the end of the bed stood a characteristically alert *yonkuichi* in shark-skin suit.

Bowing, he presented to Haruto an envelope. "I was instructed to give this to you at this time." With the missive delivered, he bowed twice more and was gone.

The paper felt rough. It was quality roughness of handmade paper. The hand-written *kanji* name on it – Shimura Haruto – was of the finest quality also. The deep black ink strokes were firm and purposeful, tailing off with deft refinement and control of the pen. They were characters written as if with a sword. That was no surprise, for a master swordsman wrote them. Haruto recognised the writing of his adopted son immediately.

He lifted the flap of the envelope with reverence and took out two pages of words from Kazuki. Reverence for the written word was something he'd always instilled in Kazuki. A man's written words have permanence, he would say, and invite the author to consider their meaning carefullybefore committing to paper. Words written abhor the mundane.

Haruto started to read. It began with one word: *Father–*

* * *

That night, Taro was also to receive a missive from Kazuki, but in a form more cryptic.

214

The heir to the Shimura empire slouched in a sofa in front of the TV, obsessed instead with the pictures in his head, rather than dancing pixels of the screen. It was the two *yakuza* minders seated around him that made use of this animated portal to the outside world, chewing the bland mental cud it served up hour after hour.

Taro had been holed-up in this *yakuza* safe house for days: his eyes ached, craving to see anything but the blush pink crane wallpaper; his lips longed to taste home-made food; his mind longed for any information that would cancel out the fears running cartwheels around his head. What would Kazuki do? What might he already have done? The day he called to Taro's door, his anger seemed total, his taste for vengeance insatiable. It made Taro fear for his life until Kazuki was located, and so was compelled to call on his *yakuza* brethren for sanctuary.

Kazuki came knocking on his door one last time, in spirit. The sharp rapping knock pricked up *yakuza* ears. They signalled to Taro to get into the back room. One hefty gangster took point behind the door, hand on hilt in the holster. The second *yakuza* looked through the peephole, stood aside from the door, unlatched it, and counted a beat before opening it wide.

The apartment door peeled back. Taro couldn't resist peeping out of his inner sanctum. A lone *yonkuichi* stood outside carrying a long rosewood box flat in both hands.

"Shimura Taro," he said. It was part information, part command.

The *yakuza* directed him inside the threshold, far enough to close the door behind him, but not let an unknown delivery near Taro.

Spotting Taro's round bespectacled eyes peeping around a doorjamb, the *yonkuichi* stated: "I was instructed to give you this at this time."

Nobody moved to accept it, so he placed it carefully on the sofa, bowed to all present one by one and left.

Taro looked apprehensively at the box. He feared it, as if Kazuki's very own retribution was locked up behind its clasps. Yet his curiosity won out.

"You!" He pointed to the nearest *yakuza*. "Open it."

With Taro stepping back, the *yakuza* trousered his gun while casting the Shimura heir a disgusted, pitying glance. When the two clasps were unbuckled, the message was revealed. From its velvet lined bed, Kazuki's *katana* in its opal-coated scabbard glinted back at Taro.

This was Kazuki's metallic missive to him. This was the message. It would require – Taro thought – some interpretation.

215

FORTY-TWO

Place de Fontenoy, Paris
22nd October – 08.45am

CIA shoes squelched a frenetic rhythm on the damp sidewalk as they raced under the skeletal branches of *Avenue de Suffren*. The chill morning air of winter's prelude stung Harker's lungs with every syrupy breath he sucked in. Tugging sutures stabbed pain into his sword-sliced side with every step. Legs like lead struggled for the power to keep up with his youthful colleague. It felt like sprinting on sponge. Exhaustion, pure and simple. The demands of these days had sapped the adrenalin he now needed to prevail: the constant running; the lack of food; the erratic sleep; the travel; the jetlag.

The battery was flat in this – the last – push.

His heart beat in his chest louder and faster than it had in years. It thumped as hard and fast as the day he raced to his house to find a dead wife. Beating and beating with the rhythm of his run, as if every beat were a hammer blow to excoriate the amassed pain of years. Beating and beating that memory of a bloodied wife and a bloodied Tokiko in a Misawa shack. It beat mercilessly. Beating out a path to the culmination of it all. One way or the other, he would see it brought to an end this day and this time. Harker would see the insane global rampage of the Shimuras brought to an end – he was resolute.

Milbank reached the security cordon around the UNESCO Headquarters complex before Josh. The CIA officer's State Department ID was enough to grant him entry to the grounds. Much to Harker's relief, Milbank was able to usher him under the barrier so he didn't have to break his running stride. If his stride were broken, he couldn't fix it again now.

They ran up the driveway leading to the stark angular concrete and glass buildings, veering off to the right and pushing through the glass entry doors. On the outside, the conference hall itself was a ribbed concrete wedge of a building that Harker thought ugly. He didn't have much time for consideration of landmarks today, but on his unplanned morning jog it seemed to him that Parisian architecture inspired either love or hate – like so much in Paris – but seldom indifference, which would be the only sin in this city.

His two hands brought him to an abrupt thundering stop at the temporary reception desk laid out along the entrance hall, startling the attractive young woman stationed behind it.

Milbank arrived and started a conversation. It quickly escalated to the woman calling over a short man with a badge and hand-radio clipped to his strained belt. From the way he waved his hand at Milbank, Josh could tell it was not going well.

"*Pas accès sans permis,*" the official said.

Milbank interspersed his continuing conversation with translations for Harker. "He's saying he won't allow us in without an official pass."

Harker's impatience rose. If this stalwart wouldn't even let them into the conference, the chances of staging an evacuation were grim. He took matters into his own hands. With the official and the receptionist distracted by Milbank, Josh flipped through the admissions binder on the desk. There was a list of pass holders, with ticks next to the names already admitted to the conference.

Once the reception lady saw what he was up to she shouted her objection.

"*Non, non! Vous n'êtes pas autorisé*"

Harker lifted the binder, preventing her from snatching it. Turning it over and lifting it so all there assembled could see, he pointed out a name on the page starting with S.

"No entry without a pass, eh? Then perhaps you can ask them, Martin, why they just admitted a dead man to this conference."

Harker's finger pointed at the ticked name Dr. Andrei Sorokin.

The bewildered obstructer did not understand.

"I saw Andrei Sorokin shot and killed in Japan just days ago," explained Josh. "Whoever you let into this conference using his badge – it's not the real Andrei Sorokin. Martin, ask her if she remembers his face."

The young woman shook her head despondently to Milbank's question.

"No, she says there are over two hundred people gone through. She can't remember them all, but she did check that the faces matched the ID on every one."

"The ID has been doctored," said Harker. "It might not even be the original, but a duplicate. Sorokin told us the pass had come through his office in Shimura's labs and been forwarded; Taro could have held it long enough to duplicate it for Kazuki."

"Or Cain," said Milbank.

"Whichever does the final deed, there's an assassin running around here on a false pass. Tell them that, and for God's sake get them to order a security evacuation."

Milbank's French entreaties led to more, but subdued, head shaking and sentences salted with *non*. He was about to interpret again for Josh, who said: "Yeah, I got the gist."

Obstinacy – a universal language.

Josh said, "Look, whoever is in there, we know what they look like. We can spot them. At the very least, he has to let us in."

Milbank nodded and pulled out his most coercive French. The bulldog official waved them through, and they pounced at the chance, running through the double doors to the main auditorium.

The collected audience was only just settling down, and it was hard to check every face in the bobbing field of heads. Starting with blonde heads was easiest, but there was no sign of the blonde-haired assassin. Harker had his suspicion that this was the last place the assassin would be. The fake pass had secured entry, but the dirty deed would not be done in full view of the assembly. Kazuki, as always, would operate in the shadows.

"I don't see Kazuki," he said to Milbank. "I'm going to look somewhere else. If we split up, we'll maximize our chances."

Milbank nodded his assent and continued a visual search of the attendees for a man he could recognise as Donald Cain.

At the far side of the auditorium, a door opened onto a service corridor. The learned babblings of the assembled biotechnology elite drifted away into the background until Harker was left with only the crunching echoes of his shoes on the bare concrete floor and the odd moans and groans of hidden machinery, like the belly of some great ocean liner. Somewhere, off to the right, a clanging boom caught his ear. He turned the corner and saw a plated metal door easing closed on its dampened buffer hinge. Stencil-painted letters on it read:

System de chauffage
Pas de laces non autorisé

Josh pulled back the steel handle to reveal the top of a stairwell leading down. Footsteps tapped up from metal stairs below. He took his gun in hand, and pointed it out in the direction of travel as he took the stairs. On each turn, he popped the gun over the railings, ready to offload, but there was nobody in the target line.

At the bottom of the stairs, Harker stalked through a metal forest of pipes. He guessed it was the building's heating system. The ceiling was low, forcing him to bow under ducts. He clamped his back to the wall and slid along limpet-like, always keeping his weapon out straight in front of him, minimizing the time to kill, guaranteeing precious milliseconds that might save his life from an assassin on the prowl.

At the far end of the room, it opened out, revealing the immense tanks of a double boiler. Some red electronic numerals caught his eye, but he was still too far away to make out the numbers. They were attached to makeshift packets, bound with gaffer tape, that instantly set off a siren in Harker's mind; this thing was totally out of place. It looked like an improvised explosive device.

Just as Harker was studying it from afar, a shape slid out between two pipes, emerging into the firing line between himself and the bomb. It looked preoccupied with the same bomb, not even noticing Harker at first. Then, it turned. Joshua found himself confronting face-to-face the man who shot Tokiko.

It was Kazuki.

Unusually, he appeared unarmed. His surprised expression told Harker the assassin was not expecting him to be here.

Kazuki looked back at the explosive, then back to the CIA agent. He flashed at Harker a strange sort of look, a visual *communique* that Harker could interpret in only a very little time. There was nothing to be said, Kazuki's look told him, nothing that could be said. Then the look was gone, replaced by resigned determination.

Kazuki Shimura turned and ran towards the bomb.

Josh barked an order down the target line of his Glock 23.

"Don't move Kazuki, or I take you down."

His target ignored the command and made a last lunge for the device attached to the building's gas main. Josh couldn't go for the head shot, in case he hit the boiler. He positioned his aim carefully, to avoid hitting any metallic organs belonging to the heating system, preferring instead to select biological organs belonging to the animated genetic system that was Kazuki Shimura.

The CIA agent fulfilled his lethal promise and, in rapid succession, spat three rounds of forty caliber bullets into the young man's back. The bullet casings tinkled on the concrete. It was a payload ensured to take him down before reaching the device. Blood erupting from two of the ragged bullet holes told Harker they had penetrated internal organs, the third embedding in a rib. Kazuki, falling to his knees, made one last lunge at the bomb, before he fell with a wet slap onto the concrete.

Harker ran at the device; kneeling next to the young man's body, he heard a dying whisper.

"Not in my name," Kazuki breathed.

The CIA operative was now close enough in distance to read the digital countdown on the bomb, but he was too close in time to stop it.

Two ... one ... zero.

FORTY-THREE

Roppongi, Tokyo
22nd October – 10.07pm

The neon smear of the *Azabu* district swept past the smoked glass window of Haruto's limousine. In the back seat, he ignored it, reading the letter again.

Father –
I call you father now, because it is my last chance to do so. I know I can never truly own that relationship with you – nor with anyone, as I have recently discovered – but it has always been my sincere hope that my life would earn your love and respect, and that now the manner of my death might make you proud to call me son, if only in name.
I regret now that I will never be able to say to your face the things I write here, for I doubt we will meet again. I will explain why, but first there are things I wish you to know.

Haruto scanned past two pages of handwriting to the sign-off, to convince himself of the author's identity, to make it real:

Shimura Kazuki

The letter told a story that Haruto did not want to believe, but had to. The fantastic tales seemed to belong to another life, not his own. It told of some things Haruto knew, some things he had suspected, and horrors of which he would never have thought Taro capable. He read Kazuki's admission that he had assassinated Mark Olsen, that he had done it at Taro's behest, in the belief that it would please Haruto, sealing off a leak to American intelligence and ensuring the profitability of the corporation.

He read of Taro's new relationship with the same *yakuza* clan who had once been responsible for the death of Haruto's wife decades ago, his infiltration of the CIA, his recruitment of an independent mercenary, his ambition to profit from the antidote to a racial virus in the hands of terrorists, and of a plan to assassinate the elite of the world's biotechnology regulation community.

And of his designs to profit from a revived Project Genaform.

Yes father, I know what that is now, Kazuki's letter said. *I know what I am.*

Haruto clutched the letter in his fist. How had he discovered his Genaform nature? It was to be his adoptive father's job, to explain it to him, to share his vision for what Kazuki could be, when he was mature enough to accept it. Fate had just decided when that was to be.

Haruto continued reading, without even looking at the parchment; every word of the letter was engraved on his heart.

It would be tempting to say that what I am is what you made me, or what your family has made me, but neither would be true. In the end, what I am, is what I make of myself, what I choose to be. That is all any man, any Genaform, can hope to say. I learned that from you: thank you.

I beseech you not to think too harshly of Taro. Your adoption of me, while altruistic and to my eternal benefit, must surely have sat ill with Taro. I was his constant rival for your affections, and perhaps a threat to his inheritance. The extent to which he ultimately went to secure his position I have not the heart to tell you, but the effects of which are evident to you now, or soon will be. Dr. Kinugasa will enlighten you.

Taro must decide for himself where his path will now take him.

My run has ended, father. As I step aside, I hope it will not be in vain – it is time for you to focus all your attentions on your true son, on healing his malignancy of heart, by using the same pride, hope, and wise counsel that you gave to this proxy son, this project, this experiment.

Goodbye Father,
Shimura Kazuki

* * *

Taro sat cross-legged on the futon in the bedroom of his bolt-hole apartment, staring at the sword across from him. It was an extra presence in the room. The sword was Kazuki's message. It was a treasured gift from Haruto, which he never went without in private. Giving it to Taro meant, at the very least, that Kazuki would not be wearing it again.

Symbols – they mean so much in our lives. This sword was a symbol, but a symbol for what? Did it symbolize a gift to Taro, the gift that was Haruto's affection? Had Kazuki handed that affection over to Taro? Was it the symbol of the leader of the *yonkuichi*, signifying that Taro would now be protector of the Shimura clan with all the responsibility it required.

Or was it simply whatever Taro chose it to be?

That was Kazuki's message, Taro knew – the sword was choice. The burden of expectation had passed from the adopted son Kazuki back to the natural son Taro, and the burden of choice fell upon Taro also – he would have to choose what the sword symbolized for him.

A determined knock rattled the front door. The heavy-set footing of *yakuza* beat like drums to the door. Some hushed words were exchanged in the front room. Taro guessed from the sounds that three men had entered the apartment. One of them stepped closer. Looking up, Taro saw his father's imposing figure standing in the doorframe. Haruto closed the bedroom door behind him and started to prowl around the room, like a lion asserting his territory.

"How did you find me?" Taro asked, quietly.

"Kazuki wrote to me; he told me where I might find you. He told me you are responsible for a Shimura rapprochement with the *yakuza*. I see for myself that it is true. This makes me worry that everything else I read in his letter is true."

His father spoke in a calm, soothing voice that frightened Taro more than any shouting could, because he knew what it meant. The benign serenity of that ragged, seasoned voice belied the true significance of it – Haruto had moved beyond rage and into the realm of retribution.

"Where are your family?" Haruto asked.

"At home," Taro replied.

"While you cower in here, concerned only with your own safety, hiding yourself from the repercussions of your actions. What sort of a man are you, Taro?"

"If I stayed at home, it would endanger them."

"Whatever excuses you can live with – it matters not to me," said Haruto. Silence hung in the air for a few more paces. Taro felt his father search for the appropriate entry point into a difficult conversation he already knew the conclusion of.

"Is it true that you recruited a mole in the CIA bioweapons division?"

"Yes," replied Taro.

Taro wondered if beneath his father's graven demeanour there was a struggle in progress to hide admiration of his son's resourcefulness. He hoped it was so.

"We have a right to use a CIA mole," Taro said. "Was it not the Japanese responsible for the existence of the CIA? Were it not for Pearl Harbor, its predecessor – the OSS – would never have been created. The yanks have been looking for uses for their over-bloated, inefficient intelligence service ever since. Why shouldn't we, its progenitors, offer a use for it?"

"So you are responsible for bringing Joshua Harker into our lives too?"

"Indirectly, perhaps."

"*Indirectly!*" Haruto spat the word. The shackles restraining his rage had finally been shed. "You have infiltrated the CIA, exposing my corporation to the possibility of all kinds of covert activities from foreign governments. You have embroiled us again with the *Yakuza* – a tie I worked for years to break – and you have endangered, perhaps even killed, my wife. To lose Tokiko, my second wife, in a *yakuza* skirmish would be bad enough, but for my own son to be the cause of it! It is unforgivable. You have brought great shame to me, Taro."

"That was not my intention, father. I did all this to safeguard the company's future, to show you that I could be trusted, to make you proud of me. I will even revive Project Genaform, to your design. I thought you would be pleased."

Taro fell forward onto his hands in the Japanese gesture of supplication.

"Not to my design, Taro. You are doing it for profit. It is reprehensible."

"So it is acceptable for my father to dabble in biotech weapons technology with the Americans, but it is not for me? You even took the product of that research into your home – did you hope he would be a more fitting son for you than I?"

"That's enough Taro! Yes, I have known your faults; all you do is for your own aggrandisement, to further yourself, and now I see that no means are beyond your use. I gave you an opportunity, albeit limited, to show that you were worthy of the Shimura mantle, that I could pass the corporation into your hands. You have shown me that I can not. I am firing you, Taro, from the management of Shimura Biotech and from the board of Shimura Corporation. My will of inheritance shall be amended so that in it you are expressly forbidden from taking ownership and control of any of my businesses when I die."

Taro bolted up from the floor. "You can't do that!"

Haruto looked his son in the eye and said, "I can." Haruto started towards the door, pausing only to say, "you are my only remaining son Taro. It is for us now to decide where we take it from here."

Taro's eyes looked at Kazuki's *katana* within arms reach, feeling its temptation, to run it through his father. It would secure his inheritance of the corporation by right of primogeniture, before Haruto could cancel it.

His mind froze, stunned by what he had just considered.

This sword. The symbol of his father's affection for his other son – Taro would consider eviscerating his father with.

Confronted with the darkest depths of his own depravity, Taro felt sick. This was Kazuki's message to him. The Genaform – the synthetic, lesser man – had shown Taro his own true degenerate nature. In that instant, he understood and agreed with his father, that Taro Shimura was not fit to reign. If Haruto had been any less of a man he would have taken up the sword and run it through his son himself.

The sword was the message. The sword was choice. Haruto walked out. Taro made a choice. He took out a linen hand towel from the *en-suite* bathroom.

* * *

Haruto stopped to talk with the *yakuza* outside.

"*Doshida-gumi?*" he asked.

"*Hai.*"

Haruto sighed. It was the family of *yakuza* he had belonged to a long time ago. His one time family. But the new generation was different. The old fawning obedience had died away as the old generation died out. The *yakuza* become younger, more ambitious, more violent, and more international. The new young bosses of the Doshida gang would, Haruto believed, have felt that Shimura built his empire on the backs of *yakuza* labors all those years ago. The gang would seek to use Taro Shimura's resources as a springboard for their own international network of criminality. It was a claw-back, revenge, through Haruto's naive, weak son. These new *yakuza* knew no honor. It was time to put a stop to this too.

"You tell Doshida-san, if any of his *yakuza* family have any contact again with a member of my family, or any employee of my corporation, I will slaughter his entire gang."

The two *yakuza* looked long and hard into the old man's eyes. What they saw there, Haruto made sure, would decide for them it was not a statement to be challenged or tested.

A groan and a thump from the bedroom attracted everyone's attention. The *yakuza*, *yonkuichi*, and Haruto went to see what the noise was about. Slumped on his knees, arms limp on the floor, was the body of Taro Shimura. His torso was pierced by the sword with hilt rested on the *tatami* flooring. The cloth wrapped around the blade, in Samurai fashion, lessened the blood spill.

It was a neat Japanese death – the only attempt at honor in Taro's entire life.

FORTY-FOUR

Place de Fontenoy, Paris
22nd October – 09.18am

Two ... one ... zero.

The readout on the bomb froze. Time suspended. Harker waited for this explosive seed to germinate into full deadly bloom. And he waited. His universe prevailed, unshattered. Tense lungs that could hold out no longer puffed their depleted air and demanded fresh oxygen.

Breathing was first to surprise him. It was the same, he thought, after the near-bifurcation of his head back in Tokyo under the sword of the man now lying in a pool of blood beneath him. There he was, the Genaform Kazuki: first of a new breed; the next step in human evolution; nascent paragon of humanity; lying in a blood-soaked suit with lifeless blue eyes; slain in a concrete basement far from his home.

Blue and yellow wires poking out of the Genaform's clenched grip caught Joshua's eye. He prised the fingers apart and lifted out what he found. Held in his hand were the pencil-shaped blasting caps of the bomb. These little charges would have triggered the main explosive; without them, the bomb would not explode.

With his last lunge, Kazuki must have ripped them out, disabling the device. Kazuki could see the countdown better than Harker, and probably realized he wouldn't have time to explain to the CIA man – he had to lunge at the device to disable it, even though he knew Harker would kill him for it.

Why? Why would he change his mind about the explosion at the last minute?

A horrible thought dawned – what if it wasn't a last-minute decision?

"Not in my name," he had said while dying.

He came here to stop the assassination! Why?

Now he could never ask him. In his open palm, Josh examined the blasting caps, like a child examining the parts of a broken clockwork toy he'd accidentally destroyed. He looked at Kazuki, wondering if these parts might go back into its clockwork heart, and make this new-age Pinocchio, lying with strings cut, walk and talk again. Then he could ask him. If he could only undo what had been done. Joshua Harker sat back, looking for a long time – and pondering – over the body of his broken clockwork savior.

* * *

Cain flipped closed the copy of *Le Monde* newspaper he'd been using to hide his face. It was standard procedure after a bomb threat for the police to study TV crew footage for any possible suspects who hung around to admire their handy work. Cain kept away from such electronic scrutiny.

The anticipated time of carnage had come and gone, but no sound of an explosion, no shock wave to ruffle the paper in his hand, no ringing in his ears. Instead, a flurry of angry sirens swarmed up *Avenue de Suffren*.

Someone discovered the bomb.

This was why he always insisted on fifty percent in advance. It wouldn't sit well with his Japanese paymasters. Scratch one client. It would mean he'd never see them again — he hoped. He'd have to disappear for a while; he did that best. Who would think of his inconvenience though, he wondered; his paycheck had been ripped in half?

Never mind.

He stood up from the *brasserie* table, sucked the last of his coffee down to the grounds, fished out a Euro of blood money from his chinos, and fired the tip into the saucer.

Strolling off down *Avenue de Suffren*, taping his thigh with the paper, he assured himself of plenty of other clients out there who wanted his services. Customers were plentiful in such a competitive world, ruled as it was by ideologues with too much money in their pockets, too much time on their hands, and nothing better to do with either than hire him.

Off he ambled, to plan for his next payday.

FORTY-FIVE

Oak Hill Cemetery, Washington DC
30th October – 10.20am

The pastor delivered his blessing and moved off. Two men remained standing above the memorial plaque inset in the ground. After a respectful silence, Joshua spoke to his fellow mourner.

"It was good of you to arrange this."

DD/NCS Stanford replied: "The State Department took care of most of it. We approached Shimura first of course, but he wouldn't claim the body. Haruto is denying all accusations that Kazuki was ever a member of his family, or an employee of the corporation. He's a dead pariah. Receiving Kazuki's remains would be tantamount to admitting complicity in Mark's assassination, I suppose."

"There's another possibility: if Olsen was hoping for legislation to outlaw Genaform development, then accepting Kazuki's body could open Shimura to nasty legal action if the IBC decided to instigate such legislation and make it retroactive."

Stanford hooked his head in disbelief. "He's a devious one that Haruto."

"Not half as devious as his son. I did the preliminary analysis on the virus he was shipping. It's more complex than any natural virus I've seen. The analysis isn't complete, but I'm pretty sure it's an attempt at a racial virus."

"Racial?"

"Yeah. The virus is only activated in the presence of a specific combination of genes in the mitochondrial DNA. Mitochondrial DNA is only passed from mother to child, so it can be traced back through history to certain geographical locations. Taro's virus targets a very specific genetic profile that still exists today in all members of one cultural community, even though they have spread throughout the world and evolved independently."

Visibly aghast, Stanford pursued the thread of explanation. "Which community?"

"I think the intended target of the virus is the Jewish community. It would aim to attack anyone with ancestral Jewish origins. Taro had developed an anti-Semitic virus."

Stanford wrestled with this new dark revelation. He thought out loud.

"Mugniyah had links with the more extreme elements in Hamas. If this ever got out, it would blow the whole middle-east wide open again. Could a virus really do that? Would it be that precise? I mean, surely it wouldn't just limit itself to Jews – wouldn't other races be affected unintentionally?"

"You're absolutely right. It's still an imperfect technology and there could be some other collateral deaths in the wild, but Taro wouldn't care – it would be to his advantage. Don't you see?"

"No – I don't follow," said Stanford.

"Look at it this way: when the virus gets out and is analysed, it becomes public knowledge that extremists have attempted to develop a viral weapon that targets only Jews. The biggest impact of a weapon like that, as far as any terrorists would be concerned, is in the public relations war. It opens up fear and discrimination world-wide against their enemy. People would irrationally fear and avoid Jews as if they were bubonic plague carriers. Of course, the virus would have no such effect on everyone else, but the prejudice it raises would do the most harm. But ... that's not the only aspect of the whole scheme. It would have been a win-win scenario for Taro Shimura also."

"How?"

"Everything Taro did was about profit. I'll bet you any money that Shimura Biotech would not release that virus sequence until they had developed an antidote. If the virus ever hit the streets, there would be mass panic. No one could say for sure that their DNA couldn't be traced back to ancient Jews, so Taro would have an instantly panicked global market begging for an antidote, which he would have ready to ship. Taro would wait long enough after its release not to arouse suspicion of Shimura Biotech, yet short enough to get a significant head start on his competitors. The speed to market would be the perfect poster boy for the superiority of Shimura Biotech's research capabilities and all that would mean ... the share price would rocket."

"Good God!" exclaimed Stanford.

Harker shared the shock and disgust of the DD/NCS at Taro's reprehensible morality, but couldn't help but admire Taro's ability. The plan was all very neat. Taro found a way to simultaneously profit from the nature of genetic heredity in a virus, and at the same time sought to profit from the break in genetic heredity that the Genaform would represent. Our DNA used against us all. Broken evolution.

Kazuki, ultimately, hadn't shared his brother's vision.

Not in my name.

In death, Kazuki remained, as in birth, alone and outside the human family. He was unwanted, with no one to mourn him. In the time since Kazuki's death, Josh had confronted his own prejudices about the boy.

The image of the Genaform kneeling, over a black-clad cadaver outside the shack, holding the smoking gun. Harker had assumed it was Kazuki who fired the shot at Tokiko. He remembered hearing a scuffle before the shot. Was it Kazuki who had fought the *yakuza* for the gun? Perhaps the intended target was Harker himself and Kazuki had saved his life, only in the tussle unable to prevent Tokiko from harm.

The shadow that released them from captivity in Hokkaido. Harker had thought it was Ronin, but since realised that Ronin couldn't have known his location until Stanford told him about the UAV sighting over Hokkaido, *after* they had been released from captivity. Sapporo! Haruto said that Kazuki flew to France out of Sapporo airport, on Hokkaido. What was he doing on Hokkaido ... unless ... it was Kazuki who freed them from his brother's clutches? Did he follow with his *yonkuichi* to protect Joshua and Tokiko and ensure their escape to Misawa, before backtracking to scupper Taro's final scheme in Paris? Harker's sub-conscious, it seemed, was unwilling to take on those inconvenient facts at the time, and that worried him. He had simply *assumed*. Ronin: the man who had once told him assumptions get people killed. Now here stood Harker, at his leisure, considering the evidence beneath his feet of the truth of Ronin's advice.

Harker had started out on this mission with questions to be answered. He got those answers, but only to open more questions he would ask himself for the rest of his life. He could never ask Kazuki now, never get to know the Genaform, never know the man, and never discover what revelation, what alchemy of the heart, turned assassin into savior.

The worst of it was yet to occur to him, however.

Harker realized he had succumbed to prejudice, blinded by his own opinions of what a Genaform is, not what it could be. In this one regard, the Genaform had proven himself to be the same as any person, in that he could become a target for suspicion and prejudice just like any human. And in the final hurtful analysis Josh had to admit, now that his rage had been so vacuously sated, that he had projected onto Kazuki his own anger. He had snatched it as an opportunity to take revenge for a murder six years in the past, when he had been denied that chance to avenge himself on his wife's killer.

The price of that revenge was made known to Harker now. He had let his emotions cloud his judgement, and the disgusting awful ironic tragedy of it was revealed – a new tragedy that he would have to deal with the rest of his life – Josh had become that killer. Josh had assumed that his enemy was the man now buried under his feet, but his real enemy was the unsated hatred that festered unresolved in his own heart all these years.

"It was good of you to come," Josh said. "To mourn him, I mean."

"Pulling strings is what I do Joshua, and not always with good consequences. But for this –" Stanford pointed to the cremation plot at his feet, "– I was happy to do it. Besides, it was your request to bring him Stateside for interment, so you should take the credit."

"*Credit!*" Joshua gagged on the word. "What do I have to take credit for ... killing a boy?"

Stanford looked over his freshly recruited officer, studying him. "You're kinda hard on yourself, aren't you Joshua?" Stanford sighed. "You're still young. Mistakes are part of that. Hell, they always will be."

Josh couldn't think of anything to say; he just stared at the plaque at his feet. Words had run out.

"You never asked me about Tokiko," Stanford said.

Harker didn't reply.

I'm afraid of the answer.

Stanford replied anyway. "She regained consciousness, and they say she'll make a full recovery."

Smiling, a relieved Josh said, "I'm glad for her."

"There's more: our people in the embassy tell me that Tokiko instigated divorce proceedings –"

A runaway eyebrow jumped up on Joshua's face.

"And she's applied for a visa to enter the States. Knowing the recent situation, they contacted me and asked if I knew of any likely impediment to her immigration."

"And what did you say?" asked Harker.

With a mischievous curled lip, Stanford replied. "I said I'd have to check with the relevant authorities ... to see what he'd say."

Joshua looked directly at his new boss and smiled.

Harker didn't know how to reply. Would Tokiko really leave Haruto ... for him? He dared not believe it. He could not believe it. Josh no longer felt worthy of it. All the while during his conversation with Stanford, he couldn't shift the notion that the better man lay in ashes in the ground beneath him. Harker rebuked himself for only seeing the assassin, the murderer, and the opportunity for retribution. Kazuki had been the one willing to make the ultimate sacrifice to save lives.

Harker thought about Olsen's mooted stand on Genaform development, and found himself in two minds about it. A few days before, he would have agreed that no Genaform should see the light of day. But now? Now he looked upon the memorial of the prototype Genaform who was willing to give up his life to save the lives of others, to save humanity from its own folly. In the end, Kazuki had seen more value in human life than the human hands that had engineered him. If Tokiko knew the truth, knew what he had done, knew who the better man had been, would she be interested in Harker anymore?

Stanford made to leave. "Well, I've got a Senate hearing to get to."

Harker was still deep in thought.

"Listen, Joshua: don't run yourself down over this, okay? You did a good job."

"Did I?" Harker's own words sounded tired, feeble and unimpressive to his own ears.

"Yes, I think you can allow yourself to think that. Let's see – you helped to uncover a mole, keep a virus out of terrorist hands, and prevented the assassination of hundreds of conference delegates." Sarcastically, Stanford added: "did I miss something?"

Josh tried to smile again. "No, you got it right. I just don't think I'm cut out for this work." He chuckled. "I once berated Silberman for her weak instincts for this job. Turns out she was better at it than me, blocking me from pursuing or reporting on the Shimura Corporation. My own instincts ... not noticing what she was up to ... they were weak. I thought I was cut out for this work. I thought I wanted it, but the reality is very different."

"You know what they say – be careful what you wish for, you might get it! For what it's worth, I think you've proven yourself an excellent asset in CIA. We'd hate to lose you. It's been a tough assignment; why don't you take some vacation time, think things over?"

Josh nodded. "Why don't I do that."

Stanford made his way toward the awaiting staff car, stopping long enough to share a thought.

"About that mole ..."

"Rita? What about her?"

"At the beginning, I actually suspected it could be you. Shows how wrong any of us can be, doesn't it?"

"You know, I still could be a mole!"

"I know." Stanford smiled. "This is a fascinating line of work this, isn't it?"

Harker smiled back and declined the offer of a lift, preferring to stay a little longer.

Left alone, Josh looked down at the ground. A simple marble plaque lay there among dozens of others. On the side, a name was carved in gold Japanese Kanji script. The name in English appeared beside it. No family name. The original meaning of the Japanese name was engraved below it, translated into English.

KAZUKI

"The first of a new generation"

FORTY-SIX

Columbus, Ohio
14th November – 3.16pm

Elizabeth Olsen packed shopping into the trunk of her Chrysler. A man dressed in a shabby grey crombie appeared through the diaphanous curtain of wafting snow.

"Mind if I help you with that?" he asked, lifting in the bags for her.

She turned, and scrutinised his face for a painfully long time before saying, "it's Joshua, isn't it?"

"It is," Harker replied with relief. The events of weeks since their last meeting had transformed him into yet another version of himself, but he could still be recognised as Joshua Harker.

"Can we talk for a moment Liz?"

"Oh, of course."

It took her longer to sit into the car than Josh did, and when eventually she was comfortable in the driver's seat she asked, "how are you Josh?"

It was a sweet consideration.

"Oh, I'm just fine, thank you," he said, not wishing to convey to her the full complication of his condition at that moment. "I'm just fine. And you – how have you been managing since your husband's death?"

"Not so good Josh. I miss him something terrible. Lord knows what I would do with myself if I didn't have my children and grandchildren."

Josh couldn't help but think of the Genaform again. Since he came back from Japan, he had been more acutely aware of the importance of family in people's lives, the natural necessity of it. Here was another consolation that Shimura's artificial reality would deny.

"Anyhow," Elizabeth said, "I take some comfort in knowing that these old bones of mine aren't too far from followin' him into the grave." She soothed Josh's surprised reaction. "Oh, I know that probably shocks young folk to hear, but that's how your mind gets to thinking, when you get to my age."

"Actually, it was about your husband's death that I wanted to talk to you. Has anyone approached you about it, since the investigation?" Josh asked.

"No one at all. I wasn't sure who to contact about it, what with so many people buzzing around on the day and all. I did ring the local police, got to talk to a very nice officer, a fellow by the name of Robert Mitchell, I think. Oh, he surely is a pleasant man to talk with. The thing is, he didn't seem to know who to talk to about my husband's case either. I think he even tried contacting you for me, but couldn't."

"No, well he wouldn't be able to. I was away."

Josh proceeded to tell Mrs. Olsen, in terms both compassionate and comprehensible to her, about the Shimura Corporation and its covert operations and her husband's idealism, and how he was killed for it.

"I see," she said, wiping a tear away from her eye with a tissue from her bag. "Thank you for telling me."

"It's classified information, so please don't share it with anyone. Strictly, I shouldn't even have told you."

He took out of his pocket a folded, creased sheet of paper and gave it to her.

"I shouldn't have taken this either, but I wanted you to have it."

Liz opened it. "Why?"

He let a sigh free.

"Because it's the last line your husband ever wrote ... the last thing he ever did. You should have it, more than anyone."

Josh cranked the door release and opened it a crack to get out before a hand on his forearm stopped him.

"Josh –," she said.

"Yes Liz?"

"You're a good man, Joshua Harker."

Unsure how to respond at first, he nodded his approval awkwardly. "Thank you," he said. "Take care of yourself Liz, okay?"

Strolling across the parking lot, back to his car, he was accompanied by his thoughts on the whole assignment.

You're a good man.

A good man – he didn't know what that was anymore. The absence of catastrophe left him with copious space to contemplate the reality his mission had taught him. He wondered if perhaps there were no good men, nor bad men, but just the random conglomeration of consequences arising from our fears and decisions. We are all victims of those consequences. Victims together. Notions of good and bad were colored by assumptions, making the concepts dangerously redundant in this muddy grey world of espionage. They were notions he feared he had lost sight of forever. A good man? No: he wasn't. He was just the lucky one, the one who came out alive this time ... again. Only this time he had brought someone out with him, a fellow victim of consequence, and someone who could remind him what it was to be a good man.

As he stepped up to the car, he smiled at the petite but resilient woman on the passenger side – Tokiko. Around her neck, a small diamond DNA pendant twinkled at him. When Josh sat in, she asked, "all done?"

"Yes. She was glad to get it."

"Of course she was – what wife wouldn't? It was a nice gesture Josh. You're a good man."

Josh tried hard to stifle a laugh, but failed. Something was desperately trying to convince him that he was a good man, something not entirely of his own manufacture, for Josh still had his doubts: the people along the way he failed to protect, or had killed himself.

"I'm sorry," he apologized for his scoffing. "It's just that I ... did they tell you, that it was me who killed Kazuki?"

"Yes, they did."

"And doesn't that bother you? Don't you think any less of me because of that? Don't you even think badly of me for walking out on you in Misawa?"

"Do you think any less of me for walking out on my husband?"

"Of course not."

"There you are then, but there was a time I would have rebuked myself for it. But after my coma ... a part of me didn't come back out of it ... the part that loved Haruto. Oh, he didn't want to let me go. Told me he loved me. Why does everyone close to him have to die to earn their love from Haruto?"

Josh stroked her hand while she continued.

"Haruto's family had placed such emotional demands on me over the years. I say *his* family, not mine – they were never mine. But I stayed, to help. All of this, it was Haruto's own doing. When I went to leave, he finally promised a child ... now he needed one ... his new heir. I told him to go build one without me."

Josh held back a smile.

"In leaving him, I'm responsible for the great irony – the man who could build people to order is left without a family of his own ... alone. So you see, none of us is unblemished Josh."

Tokiko looked out the windshield into the sunlight breaking through the abating snow fog, as if all answers could be found out there beyond that veil. "Before I left Tokyo, the doctors told me something else about Kazuki. Would it make a difference to the way you feel if I told you he was dying anyway?"

"Probably not."

She reached up to stroke the back of his neck. A comforting feeling enveloped Josh. There were no more words necessary between them about the past. It was done. They shared it, both knew it, but no longer needed to visit it again with the crude implements of words.

The couple embraced.

It was the future that called them now ... together.

Josh breathed easy. He looked out past the snow; the sun broke through, and under it the lakelands north of Columbus appeared.

"I should show you the sights," he said. "We should do some sight-seeing. That's what we'll do."

Josh started up the engine while Tokiko melted back into the seat and gazed upon him lovingly.

"Where should we start?" she asked.

"Well, there's the highlights of downtown Columbus that I know. That should take all of 10 minutes."

Tokiko laughed as a child would.

"And now that I think of it," Harker said, "there's a forensic investigator hereabouts that promised me a drink."

The rented Dodge careered out of the mall parking lot. As he steered the car, Harker steered his destiny – for the first time in a very long time.

EPILOGUE

Place de Fontenoy, Paris
24th January – 10.27am

Elizabeth Olsen raised the hem of her full-length sequined dress. A blazer-wearing security guard steadied her by the arm while she took the three steps up the podium. An ovation filled the auditorium at the re-convened IBC Conference on Bioethics, to which she had been invited as guest speaker of honor.

She adjusted the microphone stalk and flattened out two sheets of crinkled paper before taking out her reading glasses. One page was given to her by Harker. The other was received in the post at the American embassy in Tokyo, marked for the attention of Senator Mark Olsen's family. No one knew for sure who mailed it, but the piece of paper belonged to the speech that Mark had worked on the night he died. It was a piece of paper snatched in a hurry with all the other papers that night. It was, Liz suspected, her husband's murderer who returned it. For what reason, she would never know.

After the prolonged applause had died down, she said: "Thank you. The following are my husband's final sentiments, that I feel he would want shared with you all."

She cleared her throat and began.

"My esteemed colleagues –

I stand at a turning point in history, and you stand there with me. You may not see it, or feel it, because it has crept upon us silently.

For the first time in our history, science has enabled us to manipulate the material from which we ourselves are built – DNA. We can alter and eventually define the genetic constitution of a human being. With this ability, we begin to interfere with our own evolution as a species.

Be mindful of where this could lead if unmonitored and unregulated. If nature is no longer responsible for selecting the genes of our future generations, then we must be careful what criteria we use to select those genes ourselves. Should parents be allowed to elect that their child have blue eyes? Or choose its sex? For a fee? Harmless, you may think. However, do we want our future genetic constitution determined by the vagaries of fashion? Or commerce? The possible consequences of such fickle and arbitrary genetic selections on our part are clear: a thinning of our gene pool and a limitation of our genetic ability to adapt to natural shocks. All because it began with a fashion for children to have blue eyes.

We are in danger of creating a product where once a human being existed. Do we want profit to be the motivator of our new "un-natural" selection?

There is also the potential for new viral threats, that attack genetic factors that we ourselves nominate. A malign genetic selection, a new age eugenic threat, subject to our human frailties of prejudice, and fear, and hatred, and greed.

Where this road leads we can not say for sure, but it is prudent, if not critical, that we do all we can to guard against feasible disaster scenarios. I have seen with my own eyes indications of such possible futures, and an even greater evolutionary change threatens us – a forced evolution, not only of the human being, but with it, human society.

How many gene alterations are required before a child is no longer genetically related to its parent? A harmless, philosophical question, you might say. Such a question begins the steady erosion of the concept of family. If a person no longer feels connected to the previous generation, there is a danger such a person will not feel part of the human family. The family – the core of our society. We must avoid the things that drive a wedge into it. When families are no longer united, in identity or in love, the personal consequences can be profound, as can the greater consequences to our society. The challenges to human solidarity will increase. We may one day be called to account for the effects on our society of genetic selections we impose on people before they were even born, before they have any say in the matter. Nature will not blame those products of our selection, but it will blame us for selecting them, and we will have to accept its judgement.

I do not wish mankind to sleepwalk into a calamity.

This organization has, until now, guided the ethics of genetic research. More is needed on this brave new frontier. We have known for some time that national systems of biotechnology regulation are prone to the undue influence from commercial and other vested interests. What is at stake here – and I do not choose these words flippantly – is the future of the human race.

I propose the establishment of a new International Biotechnology Authority, modelled on the International Atomic Energy Authority. It would have the power to police biotechnology research across the globe. It would investigate and isolate rogue practitioners. It would have the authority to propose international legislation to the United Nations, therefore making unauthorized genetic research illegal and enforceable through the International Criminal Court.

I dedicate my life to this goal. I call for your support.

For if we take away from nature, and take upon ourselves, the manipulation of the genetic matter of which we ourselves and all future generations are composed of, then so too we must take responsibility for what then becomes possible: broken evolution."

MORE ...

Want to know more about Broken Evolution?

For extra material about the story (including extra chapters), its subject, and the author, visit:

<u>www.brokenevolution.com</u>

www.ingramcontent.com/pod-product-compliance
Lightning Source LLC
Chambersburg PA
CBHW022202170626
46807CB00005B/2306